SHADOW OF THE MARSH

CASSANDRA MORTIMER

For anyone who watched FernGully
and couldn't choose between Zak and Hexxus.

CHAPTER ONE

When I learned that every high fae in Trasia had lost their magic, their power fizzling into a pale imitation of their monstrous abilities, I was helping my brother in his workshop while simultaneously attempting to grind wheat berries into flour.

Dusk painted the trees outside in faded gold as I hurried to and from his desk, my feet shuffling over the dusty wood floors. In his sweet and tempered voice, Conor called out the names of various liquids and powders we kept on a high shelf by the door. Hyssop, motherwort, quicksilver, and white dead nettle. I plucked the vials between my fingers and gingerly placed them on his workshop table so he could inspect and measure the compounds. He was combining them into a substance he swore would make a gas capable of inflating a waterskin, creating a suitable flotation device. Given his recent inventive successes, I believed him.

I rushed to the other side of the room and rolled the pestle over the wheat grains, my arms trembling with fatigue, and hoped our mother would be late coming home from her kilns. Sweat beaded at the crest of my hair and I rubbed my face against my shoulder. The air was still damp with late summer, and though we had the windows shut tight against the wrought, decaying scent of the marsh outside, I was still breathing in its putrid stench.

We wouldn't have even known about our new freedom if it weren't for the screaming of our neighbor, Ida.

It reached us through the heavy glass—her harsh, trilling voice: "It's Aven! Someone help—he's hurt! Mitah, go get help!"

I stopped my toiling to peer through the window and watched Ida amble from her house, something caught on her frayed skirts that trailed behind her in the dust. She waved her arms as if warding off a swarm of crane flies, and then a boy rushed madly into her arms.

Aven had been missing since early spring, and now that the slow summer rhythm of our town was speeding into autumn, I'd been sure we'd never see him again.

"Stay here," I muttered over my shoulder, and then felt like an ass for saying so. My brother couldn't follow me, even if he wanted to, thanks to the wretched fae.

Brushing my hands over my waist to wipe away some sweat, I hurried into the square where a dozen people already surrounded Aven, pecking at him with questions.

"Where have you been?"

"Do you have any idea how worried your ma was?"

"You look like someone's dragged you through the mangrove and left pieces of you there!"

Aven released a breath that was half-chuckle, just as I got close enough to catch sight of the muck and blood coating his arms. He did look ragged; bone thin and pale under the grime, his limbs spindly as they stuck out from beneath a long linen shirt that was sizes too big.

"Of course I'm a mess, I just escaped from the fae lands!" he cried.

The crowd gasped and then silenced themselves, as if the noise would summon the evil creatures. Ida, who had been patting Aven down for injuries while whimpering through her motherly tears, now sobbed openly.

"They took you, my baby? I hoped you'd run away."

Aven shook his head, his body swaying weakly with the motion. "Something grabbed me in the marsh, and when I woke, I was in their castle. I don't..." he trailed off, his gaze going flat for a moment before he dragged himself back into the presence of his mother's arms. "I don't remember much, but I know they draped me in shells and dressed me like a doll. I didn't eat for days. Nothing but wine and..." he shuddered.

"How did you break free?" the local seamstress asked. Her own daughter, Nerin, had been gone for almost two years. I'd been about to ask the same.

"It was strange. And sudden," he said. "Between one minute and the next I was able to move. It was like I'd been asleep with my eyes open and finally came to. I saw a fae woman lying on the ground, screaming, and I knew I had to get out of there so—"

He stopped as another shriek echoed from the tree line. We turned as one to see the wind scattering leaves along the field and a girl emerging from the woods. It wasn't Nerin, who was lissome and tall, but rather someone I did not recognize.

"Help! I've just escaped the fae, please help me!" she screamed.

"What in the worlds," muttered a man at my side.

Her story was the same, as was another boy who minutes later crawled forth from the swath of coast right beyond the marshland, at the edge of the trees. They'd all simply awoken from whatever trance had captivated them and—free of compulsion—were able to flee the sprawling fae compound beyond the mangroves. They were wet and covered with silt, and some sported shallow wounds. All were skinny, and their hungry mouths devoured bread and periwinkle snails while they were bundled with blankets and lauded as miraculous survivors.

I began to see the connections between their tales, a map forming in the recesses of my mind, digging itself in murky trenches. There were the mudflats and tall reeds we knew marked the boundaries of the fae territory, and then drenched mangrove pools beyond, like a never-ending lake made into a maze by the towering trees. The victims claimed the open waters of the ocean beyond were littered with floating bridges and docks, houses on stilts, and an elegant stone castle that stood within the waves. Aven had been below sea level, trapped in a cavernous structure where the air was thin, and he was played with like a toy. The girl—whose name was Melia—had seen the upper levels, her skin soaking up weak rays of morning light while she was feasted upon, as if the salt on her skin had been a delicacy. There were teeth marks scraped into her flesh.

Goosebumps rose along my arms as I studied her. Given the shift of her tortured eyes, it was clear she'd been consumed in other ways.

"The fae woman who was screaming," I asked Aven, "what was wrong with her?"

"Her magic was gone," he replied with a full mouth.

"How do you know?"

I took another step closer and felt a firm hand grip my shoulder, holding me back.

Aven swallowed, his lips still tinged gray. "She would change into this...fish thing, like a flat toad with fins, and she was half-transformed when she got stuck. Her arms were stumpy, and she couldn't move them. It was the only reason I could get out of that room."

My gut roiled at the image but, despite my disgust, the information was a spark to the fuse in my chest. I felt like one of my brother's inventions.

"What caused it?" I prompted. "Their powers failing?"

"Winnie, leave him be." The hand at my shoulder tugged and I turned my head to see Flint, his tan face drawn into a scowl and his dark hair waving in the breeze. A pang went through my heart as memories flashed through me—his mouth on my collarbone, his voice whispering against my ears—until I buried the sensations under layers of hot, furious ash. I shook off his hand and turned back to Aven, my questions too important to let simmer.

"Was it only for a moment? And did *all* the fae lose their magic, or just high fae? What about lower-level creatures—were they impacted?"

Aven didn't have any more answers for me, only assumptions and the vague notion that he'd left behind a castle in chaos while dozens of humans raced for freedom. We could expect more arrivals in the next few hours, freed slaves who were slower than Aven, since he'd been born with the marsh in his veins. It had still taken him almost a full day to reach us.

Still, it was more information than we'd ever had before. Those taken by the fae, whether they disappeared in the night or trudged into the mangroves to their doom, almost never made it back. I couldn't let this opportunity slip by me. The idea of those high fae reduced to powerless, fleshy mongrels that could fall to a blade had me *elated*, beaming even, like sunlight piercing through dreary clouds. They couldn't shoot flames or ice, control minds, or transform into deadly creatures. They had human-shaped torsos that could easily fit a human-made knife, and a human-like mouth that could reveal the cure for my brother's condition, even if it was in-between screams. But I wasn't sure how long their weakness would last.

Desperate energy coursed through my body, and once I'd gleaned everything I could from the survivors, I sped back toward the house. Flint didn't follow, not that I was surprised. The ass had grown tired of me as soon as he'd flipped my skirts.

My mother was just coming down the hill, minutes away, but I ignored her. Quick as the flip of a coin, I was in Conor's workshop.

"Conor, the fae have lost their ability to glamour!" I shouted as a greeting.

He looked up from the notebook and waterskin on his desk, his movements stiff. The terrible illness of his limbs was encroaching every day, and I could see a sweep of shaded bark at his elbow, as dark as death. The fae's powers may have stopped, but the lingering poison in my brother's body continued its vicious course.

"All of them?" Conor asked. His hair was a rumpled array around his ears, which I'd always teased him for being bigger than average. If I had my way, he'd grow into them, stretching taller and taller over the years until he towered over me. He'd live to old age.

It was my greatest desire.

"It would seem so." I looked around the room as if I might find my supplies packed and ready to go. "Aven said they stopped being able to shift into different forms. They have no magic! This is our opportunity. If I can get past the mangroves, they won't have any way to seduce or abduct me. I can get in—get the cure for you—and get out."

"Win, I don't want you to risk that for me," he said in a high voice, the sound reminding me of night crickets.

"And I don't want you gone."

I couldn't handle a world without him—without his twinkling laugh and genius mind and the soft smell of smoke that lingered on his clothes from lightning fires beneath his glass vials. He was my baby brother. He was the only one who saw me and loved me for who I was. To him, I wasn't useless or a disappointment—I was wonderful.

I would do anything to save him.

Conor loosed a deep exhale, his features so delicate that the frown there completely transformed his soft face. He looked older than his twelve years. So much older.

"Winnie?" my mother called from the front room.

"Coming!" I called. I turned back to Conor. "Gather whatever you think I might need for a couple days out on the water. I'll take care of Ma."

"Win—wait," he said, but I didn't have the time. Already the tangled net of my thoughts was spreading wide, taking me over. We didn't know what fae creature was responsible for Conor's condition. All we had was a drawing of the flower he'd sketched; a white-petaled bud he'd spotted as he dug in the shallow marshlands for fiddler crabs. He had leaned too close. He didn't remember much after that, but I wouldn't forget the shape of the wound on his shoulder, or the way he screamed when he awoke days later to the spread of bark across his skin. It was slowly taking over him in pieces, like a rash, freezing his feet in place, and then his legs. His arms were already affected, and soon we feared his lungs would stop, or his heart, and then he would be a petrified corpse instead of the brother I loved more than anything in this world. The brother who looked up to me with adoring cinnamon-colored eyes as I read him plays, and who would chase after me in the reeds. The brother who was lifting us from poverty with his tinkering and constructions. His brilliance.

Ma was washing her hands in a deep basin of water when I came into the front room.

"Did you finish grinding the flour?" she asked without looking up.

"Just about."

Her pause spoke volumes. I had disappointed. Again.

"Conor needed me," I said, which was only partially a lie. I *had* been helping him with his inventions, but I'd also been interrogating Aven and the others regarding the fae lands, squirreling away the bits of information they dropped at my feet.

"I'm glad you're helping your brother," she said, drying her clay-tinted fingers, "but you should not neglect your chores."

I dipped my head. "I know, I'm sorry."

"He only has so much time left," she added then, on a whisper so as to not be overheard. "It's not as if we can make his contraptions when he is gone, and the sale of a few won't make much difference. Perhaps you should focus on keeping him...comfortable." Her breath shuddered on the last word, and I saw the despair in her age-lined face.

Our mother was once so beautiful she apparently bewitched our father at first glance and secured a proposal from him within one week, but since his death she had been weathered by the marsh and her occupation throwing clay into dishware and vases. Her back was hunched now, her black hair thin and brittle. Still, her wide, dark eyes, so like mine, were alight with emotion. She adored her son. Loved him more than the security of our house, and the feel of her bed beneath her weary body—more even than food in her empty stomach and water in her parched mouth.

More than me.

She would do anything for him, and that's why I knew—regardless of how foolish it might be—she wouldn't deign to stop me in my plans.

"I know," I assured her, "but he told me he feels energized today, and wants to finish the waterskin he's working on." Pausing, I cleared my throat. "Did you hear Aven has returned?"

Ma walked around me, heading into the kitchen to pull together something for dinner. We had shrimp and mussels from the thick of the coastal flats, caught by my own hand only yesterday, but she sniffed at them as if they weren't fresh.

"Is that what has everyone riled?" she replied. "His mother must be relieved. He's a friend of Flint's, isn't he? Maybe he can put in a good word for you."

My body stiffened even as my heart tripped in my chest. I hated her for bringing him up time and time again, as if it was only a matter of reminding him that I existed to get him to change his mind. Like I just needed to *convince* him to keep me.

According to her, Flint was just another failure I'd brought on her and Conor.

"I know you think Flint would make life easier for us," I started, "but that would also mean staying here, and we should be trying to leave—"

Ma shook her head. "It would make all the difference for your brother—with money from his farmland, Flint could send your brother to Clarcton. The doctors there could set him right."

I closed my eyes long enough to soothe my anger, imagining the sensation of running over tall grasses that sprang beneath my naked feet, and the shine of silver gravel rippling in clear water, before I could face her once more. She refused to see the ugly truth in Conor's mystical deterioration—even *if* Flint married me tonight and sent my brother on a boat there was little guarantee we'd find a cure for him there; Clarcton had no fae to craft cures against. Money didn't always solve problems.

But action could.

"Aven says humans are breaking free from the fae lands. Some others came with him—I saw them with my own eyes. They say the glamour holding them broke, that the fae are powerless."

"Powerless?" The word was all skepticism, but the wheels behind her eyes were churning as she picked at the shrimp, pulling out their veins with expert precision.

"If they can't control me, I could walk into their midst and find the antidote for Conor." I inched closer, as if proximity would force her to listen. "I've scoured everything on this side of the water, and there are no books that mention the flower he saw, or the bite marks that appeared. This is our only chance."

"And you think you can do this?" Her face was turned down at her task, so I had no idea if she was pained at the idea of me leaving, or even worried for me.

"I do."

I could *try*, at least. But I wouldn't say that. I refused to show her any hint of fear. I was a ruthless knight wandering into dangerous lands, a heroine braving ruffians and murderers, a cunning witch disguised as a simpering waif. I pulled every plot and character from my repertoire and settled my mouth into a determined mask.

With those impressions raising my chin, I waited for her to look up, ready to combat any concerns and questions she had with bravado.

"Very well," she said, instead. Her hands were still slimy with shrimp entrails, her hunched shoulders turned slightly to the left.

I blinked. "You...mean I can go?"

"It's a wonderful thing, to take care of your brother. This curse that's befallen him...if he weren't so preoccupied with keeping us afloat, it may not have happened." Her voice was soft and lilting, as if she were ready to sing a lullaby, but the words were sharp. It felt like an osprey's talons were slicing into my belly. "Boys that young should never have to breach the marsh—it's for older, wiser souls. And if you can rectify this, I think you should."

Rectify this. Because it was my fault.

Everything seemed to be a product of my failures these days: Conor's illness, Flint's rescinded proposal, and even, on one night where Ma was drunk on rum and exhaustion, our father's heart failure. Somehow, I had a hand in all of it. And while logic told me that it couldn't be true, the more she said so, the more I began to believe her. Conor wouldn't have been scavenging if I had gotten Flint to marry me. My brother would be healthy if I had just been the daughter she needed me to be.

Maybe that's why she didn't offer to go with me.

Gritting my teeth and tapping my fingers along the leg of my linen dress, I swallowed the hurt her words laid into me, nodding. "Great. I'll...leave in the morning then."

Before any tears could squeeze free, I turned and retreated to the bedroom Conor and I shared, trembling from head to toe.

Ma didn't call me back. Tomorrow I would head into a watery grave-yard from which almost no one returned, and she didn't even care—not as long as it could potentially save Conor.

Sniffing, I lit the lantern on our bedside table to fight the churlish sky darkening to pitch outside. I scanned the titles of the books I read to Conor each night, the flowery poetry and melodramatic prose of ancient plays. He would need my help later moving into the kitchen for dinner and then into bed, but for now I could breathe in the scent of my sanctuary—the crumbling pages of my private haven. Tonight, when I spoke their words into his hair, it would be the last night we had together like this. Either I would return with a cure, and we could go anywhere in the world with the money his inventions would someday bring. Or I wouldn't return at all.

CHAPTER TWO

In the dim light of our shared room, I held Conor close and spun an elaborate tale of my plan to infiltrate the compound.

I told him what I knew: there would be guards in the mangrove and then floating docks and slide-like slabs of rock in front of the ocean castle which could be hiding submerged creatures. But then I also pulled some tidbits from thin air: there would be a broken wall I could slip through, and a tunnel I could use to remain unseen. I explained how just the touch of my iron dagger would have the fae's skin shriveling and melting from their bones. This last bit was something I had once read and could only hope would prove true, but I didn't clue him into my unease. Years of play-acting with him—reading scripts and contriving fairy tales to romp to in our fields—had made me an expert at pretend. I'd been a pirate and a queen, a droll mortician and a hungry dairymaid. I put those skills to use, assuring him again and again that I wasn't scared in the least, and I'd return before week's end with a remedy.

"At least take some of my devices from the shop," he murmured, slowly succumbing to the warmth of my arms and the late hour.

I nodded into the night. "Of course. I'll want your net launcher and maybe that flotation rig if it's ready."

"I have a glowing powder…" he started to say, but then his voice trailed off. He was asleep.

I spent too much time watching him breathe then, clocking the small rise and fall of his chest, and smelling the familiar chemical residue in his hair, before I followed him into fitful dreams.

In the morning, with my back aching and sweat already pooling beneath my breasts, I hurried to pull on waders over my clothes and gather supplies while the sun was still low. I had no time to waste.

The bag I took was packed lightly—enough salted redfish for a couple of days, a waterskin, an extra set of comfortable underclothes, a simple tunic and pair of pants, a decent dress, a digging tool for clams and snails if I grew desperate, and my iron knife. But as I went to say goodbye to Conor, he weighed me down with contraptions and tools galore.

"I was able to solder tiny pieces of iron on the net," he explained as I carefully loaded the launcher into my sack. "Just make sure you crank until you hear the chamber click."

"Got it. And this will float?" I asked, hefting the empty-looking waterskin, which had been dyed a muddy red, gauging its weight.

"Be careful with that!" He hissed. He wiggled in his chair until I handed the bag back to him. "Crush the bag and the vials inside will break—the compounds together should release a gas that will inflate the skin and serve as a makeshift float. It's small, but it should hold you."

"That's a lot of shoulds."

Conor's look of annoyance almost made me laugh as he returned the contraption to my now-gentler hold.

He grabbed a wooden box the size of his fist and passed it over next. "This is a powder that glows in the dark. If you put it on a weapon and strike it hard enough, it creates a flash. Good for arrows, though I know you don't shoot arrows. Still, it's not heavy, so it can't hurt to take it with you."

I didn't argue.

"And last, here's my device for clean water. It's hard to find the stomach lining for the seal, so I only have the one. Try not to break it?"

It looked like a jug with a thin cover which had been slanted inward in a "v" shape. A smaller jug sat in the center.

"I just put water in it and heat it up, right?"

He nodded.

"Conor, this is amazing. You need to be selling these. Imagine all the trips to the creek people could save if they could drink the marsh water."

"It only makes a tiny amount," he argued, "and heating it enough to drip down drinkable water takes time. Think of it like an emergency cup."

There was a pause, the span of only a few heartbeats, while I stood in his workshop, watching his stiff hands clench in his lap. He didn't want me to go. I didn't want to leave. But he would be dead within a fortnight if I did nothing. I would lie, steal, and kill to keep that from happening. I *would* find out what creature had poisoned him.

"I'll be back soon, gremlin," I said, with as much confidence as I could muster. I kissed the top of his head, and he wrapped his skinny arms around me, holding me tight. I refused to look down at his face, terrified the sight would break me down into pieces, like shattered pottery.

"You better," he murmured into my stomach. "And..." he sniffled, "if this is about Flint, you know I don't bla—"

"Hush." I held him tighter, fighting back tears. "This isn't about him. This is what older sisters do—go on quests and defeat monsters, remember?"

He pulled away and looked at me, his gaze skeptical and eyes red-rimmed. "I'm old enough to make you weapons and you still think I believe that?"

"Yes. Because it's true." I patted his cheek so he would close his eyes, and then I picked up the bag and fled the room with as steady a gait as I could manage.

Ma watched me go from the doorway, her expression carved from stone. She only muttered a quiet, "Thank you," when I passed her, and then she turned back into the house, most likely to help Conor with whatever he needed for the day. Without me taking care of him, I wondered how she would create enough clay and stoneware to sell; I could only hope there was a surplus in her stores. She rarely talked shop with me, so other than us having enough money for necessities, I had no idea how well her business fared.

"Winnie?" Ida called from her window next door. "Where are you off to?"

"I'll be back in a few days," I replied, mirthful and waving, like I was heading to a friend's house.

Ignoring Ida's questioning stare, I strolled through town with no one the wiser of my plans, the meager population of Harnsey ignoring my progress. They assumed I was walking to the mudflats to collect another batch of mussels. They didn't know I would heft my bag high and step into the muck, lurching into the salty brine.

Hoping to avoid further questions, I focused on my shoes as I headed west toward the waterline, knowing they would soon be ruined. While my waders protected me up to my waist, I didn't know what the waterlogged ground in the mangroves would entail, so another layer of protection seemed wise. I'd tucked the linseed oil-coated linen into my leather shoes and if—*when*—I made it back, I'd have to skin and gut hundreds of fish to earn enough coin to replace them. Still, that was a problem I could only hope to have, for it would mean I'd returned victorious.

I passed the well at the town center and the few still-operating businesses lining the main road, smelling the butter and malt of bread as it baked. There were fewer shops open than usual, the town shrinking every season as people who could afford it escaped further inland. Even now, abandoned houses sitting like empty shells peppered the lanes this close to the water, spreading like a disease.

The wood-thatched roofs nearby rustled in a rare morning breeze from the east, and I took the air into my lungs like the final gasp of a drowning man. Any breath not tainted by the odors of the swampy marsh was a gift.

With my eyes closed to enjoy the moment, I almost missed the pair of women's boots as they halted before me.

Stopping quick, I glanced up to see Maire with a gaggle of children trailing behind her. Her eyes were wide with surprise as she scanned me from head to toe, her arms laden with skins for her husband's tannery.

"Where are you off to?" she asked.

There was no lie I could offer her. She knew I had no friends or relatives beyond Harnsey's town lines, and I was carrying too much for a mere foraging trip to the marsh, so instead I crouched and gestured for her daughter Holly to run into my arms. Though my bag was heavy over my shoulder, I was still able to pick her up and swing her in a circle while she squealed.

"Auntie Win, yay! Come home and play with us," she said, giggling as I put her down. Her dress was long enough to trip her, and she kicked up her feet as she pranced a circle around me.

"Can't right now, little skipper, but I'll be over soon, okay?"

"Win…" Maire said, her tone more serious.

I sighed, knowing she wouldn't let me pass until I answered.

"I'm going past the mangroves," I said, hoping that would explain it all.

Maire's oldest daughter, Sorra, who was nine and only just starting to grow into her big feet, gasped so loudly other heads turned our way.

"You can't be serious," said Maire, her hold on her basket shifting as if she intended to physically stop me. "Why on earth—is this about Aven and his story about the fae?"

"If you heard that then why are you asking me?" I replied. She had to know what this would mean for our chances of curing Conor—we were growing more desperate by the day.

"Because I didn't realize you were so eager to die!" she hissed, leaning close. "This is the most impulsive, foolish idea you've ever had, and I've *seen* your impulsive, foolish decisions. You can't go in there alone! Do you think you'll just walk up to the high fae and ask them kindly for a favor?"

Her voice was rising with every word, and I reached down for Holly once more, hoping that by holding her Maire would ease up a bit; I wasn't above using any tool at my disposal to get out of this conversation as quickly as possible.

"I've thought this out, I swear," I argued.

"Oh, I'm sure. For what, ten minutes?"

Holly squirmed and I held her tighter before placing her back on the ground. "I discussed it with Ma, and Conor has made weapons against the fae. I have information from Aven—good, recent information. If I'm ever to try my hand at finding a cure, it's now. And who would I ask to come with me?" I added. "You, leaving your five guppies behind? My Ma, so Conor is left helpless? Marcel and his clicking knees and bent back?"

"One of the fishermen!" she cried.

"No one would go with me, and you know it."

"Yes, because it is *foolish,*" she replied. "And I know you want to leave, Winnie, but this isn't the way. You think the money from Conor's inventions is your family's only way out, but it won't matter if you're dead." She dropped the basket and took my hands in hers. "Please, please don't go. You won't return."

I lifted my chin, my features settling into a costume of confidence. "I will."

I had to.

Maire liked to imagine I was so reckless I would jump at any chance to escape Harnsey, no matter how dangerous or deadly, but I was not keen to die. If I had the choice, I'd be content to scale and gut fish, waiting for my brother to make enough money to convince our mother we could start over—that it was worth leaving our family home. The rules of this town were meant to keep humans safe—we stayed on our side of the marsh and kept to dry land as much as possible, never putting ourselves in fae territory—but to live near them was to live in fear, and even following those rules hadn't kept Conor safe. If my family was going to survive, we needed to leave Harnsey, and if my brother was going to survive to *earn* us the means to leave, he needed a cure. Maire was right that striding into the fae kingdom was not the best way to ensure a long life, but still, it was worth the risk of being caught in their clutches for the possibility of saving Conor. And if now the fae were nothing more than human, this was my best shot. No one else would risk the trip, so it had to be me. It was as simple as that.

Using our clasped hands, I pulled Maire closer and pressed a kiss to each of her cheeks. "Trust me on this," I said quietly by her ear. "And check on Conor and Ma over the next few days, will you?"

Her shoulders dropped, but once I released her, she slowly nodded. As if unconsciously seeking comfort, she held a hand behind her and pulled one of her sons closer. I remembered the day she birthed him—and Sorra, and Holly, and her other babes. The town had gotten smaller, but her family had continued to grow. I wondered, if I returned to Harnsey with a cure for Conor, would we be able to earn enough to take Maire's household with us when we were finally able to seek a better life in Clarcton?

It was an image that made my chest glow with happiness—I'd keep it close these next few days, as I trudged through foul water to meet my fate.

"I have to go," I said, peering down at Holly and her siblings. "Take care of your Ma while I'm away, you hear?"

"Yes, Auntie Winnie," they said as a chorus, making me smile. I wasn't actually their aunt, but since I put on shows for them, enacting my favorite dramas on nights when there were storms or their parents wanted some time alone, I felt the title was well-deserved.

"Stay sharp, stay dry," said Maire, looking like she wanted to hug me again.

I nodded, and then left them on the road, my bag feeling heavier than before.

CHAPTER THREE

Soon enough, I could see the waterline ahead. I upped my pace, mentally calculating the hours I'd need to wade through the marsh before there would be any mangrove limbs to rest on. I could only hope the muscles I'd developed from hauling nets through the mud would see me through.

The first step in was easy, as was the next.

Bugs skittered over the water at my calves while birds nested in the sod and poa grass. Cattails and saltmarsh hay swayed as a metronome, their smooth stems and feathery flutes like the inverted rod of a pendulum clock.

A harrier cried nearby and startled me, but I kept going, the cold water rising along my waders up to my knees, and then my thighs. I walked into the reeds like a sacrifice, as if I would drown when the water crested my head, but the bog stayed shallow as I walked through the morning until midday.

The air around my shoulders was warm, the sun a constant presence on my chin-length hair as I waded deeper, which was the only reason I didn't shiver as I crept closer to the mangroves. The trees started far off in the distance, like a dark curtain I would need to pull aside. I could only pray nothing would grab me before then.

As lily pads brushed my sides, I shivered, understanding the innocent leaves were hiding all manner of mysteries below. This was where Conor had seen the flower. I kept my eyes peeled but there was nothing but the occasional purple sea spurrey and thrift blossom. I saw no white, pointed buds anywhere.

Wind whistled off the water and bugs and birds chirped, filling my ears with a pleasant buzzing.

The water was up to my chest now, and my arms ached from holding my pack aloft as the shade of the trees crept within my reach. The smell of decay and rotten eggs was thick in my nostrils, even more putrid in the sun, but still I dreaded the dark of the mangroves. Soon I would beg for dappled sunlight.

Something brushed against my leg.

I closed my eyes, hoping it was a dumb fish who didn't know better.

"Please, please, please," I whispered.

I felt that same touch against my leg again, near my calf.

Pulse tripping in my neck, I hurried to grab the iron knife from my bag. The handle was cold and smooth in my fingers as I balanced my pack against my head with one hand and brandished the weapon with the other, glancing into the water around me. It was so murky and algae-coated there was no chance I'd see an enemy coming. Not unless they breached the surface or caused a sufficient ripple.

Just as the thought crossed my mind, my eyes caught on the swell of a gentle current, rippling side to side like a snake.

I'd known fear in my life—my father clutching his chest and dropping to the ground, nightmares of drowning, the time Conor screamed at the marsh's edge when a lacewing fly landed on his hand—but this was different. This was terror.

Something was coming at me, and I had no idea if they were great or small, fast or slow, or if they had pointed teeth or claws or poisoned barbs disguised as flowers. All I could do was wait as it drew closer, preparing for it to brush by me again or do something more sinister.

The ripple was close enough to touch when I shot my fist into the water, dagger clutched tight, and felt the blade skate through something solid. I jerked backward as something thrashed, knocking into me. A scent permeated the air like petrichor and copper. I managed to keep my footing and inch away from the creature in the thick mire, as slow as I could tolerate so as to not create more ripples than necessary. Whatever it was still moved and whipped in the muck where I'd struck it.

A face briefly breached the algae; it was monstrous and elongated like a needlefish, but with human-shaped eyes and scraggly hair. Those eyes were wide with fear, though they were fae-black, and I watched as the creature gasped and gurgled, then dropped beneath the surface once more. It was a half-changed fae, like Aven had described, something caught between human and animal.

I wanted to run, but I was worried of garnering the attention of every creature nearby with the splashing my motion would cause. Better to finish this quietly and keep slinking deeper into the watery forest. I raised my dagger with an aching arm, ready to slash again, feeling oversensitive to every caress of the water against my waders.

The ripples slowed, and then stopped, all the more at odds with the frantic pulse of my heart.

Had I killed it?

If luck was on my side, the tome on fae had been accurate, and the iron incapacitated them like fiery poison. That, or I'd struck a vulnerable spot on the creature's body.

I almost released a laugh into the gloom; I'd proven myself capable. I could do this. But instead of celebrating, I kept silent, the smile tugging at my cheeks the only sign of my relief. I was halfway through the mangroves.

Another minute passed, and another. There was nothing but the faraway calls of a heron and the hum of beetles and winged insects saturating the trees. I gentled my grip on the knife and lowered my shoulders, taking a deep breath.

Plodding away from the scene with nervous energy, I breached the dense tree line ahead. As I passed between the thin valleys of root systems, the water now down to my waist as the tide receded, my heart rate finally began to slow.

That's when I heard a scuffle to the right and turned my head, only to spot a tall, inhuman figure a few yards away, his eyes trained on me.

A gasp caught in my throat as I shifted to hide behind the heft of a massive, water-laden trunk. Saplings grew on either side of it, creating a spotty cover, but it was already too late—he had seen me.

I'd only glimpsed him fast enough to catch the unearthly ice-blue sheen of his skin and the mud-like armor over his chest, but that was enough to mark him as *other*. He was fae, and therefore I was his quarry.

The current of the water shifted as he approached, a warning that sluiced over my body.

My time was short.

Hurrying to untie the strings of my bag once more, I pulled out the net launcher before draping the strap over my shoulder. I began to crank the launcher's small mechanical lever, feeling the springs inside tighten bit by bit.

"Show yourself," called the beast around the bend, his accent strange.

"If you're manyda, show your colors and move along," said another, this one with a grumbling voice so low and stilted I barely understood the words.

Shit, there were two of them. And I had no idea what a manyda was, but I doubted waving my red waterskin like a noble's flag was what they had in mind.

Arms shaking, I heard the click of the crank fall into place, and then I realized it was my entire body that shivered. The water here was colder, closer to the ocean's mouth, and I was used to the mudflats that were warmed by the sun. Soon the cold would make moving nearly impossible. I needed to find a low branch soon where I could escape the water and dry off before dark—if I survived this first.

My only chance was to take one of them by surprise, but for all I knew the creatures were already swimming around the tangle of brush and I was soon to be captured, or worse.

With one deep inhale, my heart speeding in a race it could only hope to win, I darted forward and aimed the device.

"What?" was all he said, and then I pulled the trigger. The web of slick twine and iron filings flung onto his torso and weights at either end smacked together, wrapping him in its embrace.

The creature screamed as if in pain. While he wriggled against the restraints, I smelled something like burning hair and sulfur. He fell back into the water then, his thick torso making a wave that buffeted my collarbones.

There was another splash behind him, and I knew the element of surprise I had so depended on was now extinct. Dropping the launcher into my bag, I hung the strap around my neck so it draped over my chest.

With luck my belongings would stay somewhat dry, and the extra layer would keep me alive.

Just as I thought it, the other guard burst from the water only an arm's length away. I bit back a scream, my instincts rearing to retreat, to flee, to hide. But I couldn't. I had already overpowered two fae—well, maybe one fae and a half—and I could take on another.

But this creature was different. His limbs were stitched together as if someone had tried to draw a human figure and dramatically failed. Each dark joint was bulbous, each feature exaggerated. It was gruesome to behold, especially as he reached forward with spindly fingers, the mauve tips elongated to thin points like a sea urchin's spines, with clear webbing between them.

I plunged outward with my iron dagger, slashing it back and forth in front of me as if it might keep him at bay, but all he did was growl through a mouth ripe with tiny teeth and weave back and forth, waiting for his moment to strike.

I tried to back away, but my feet caught on some root. My gaze left him for one split second.

He pounced.

Those piercing fingertips hooked into my forearm, halting my next swing. The pain stunned me with its ferocity, like lightning shooting through my veins and melting me from the inside. Unbearable agony tightened my muscles into paralysis. I couldn't even scream.

But I didn't release my hold on the weapon.

The fae monster reared back and smashed his fist into my jaw. Though I couldn't feel the hit, not compared to the fiery torture of his claws, my sight still wavered. Spots crowded the edges of my vision.

He hit me again, hissing all the while. And again.

I tasted blood.

Breathing was becoming more difficult, the unwavering pain squeezing my lungs, and my flickering gaze drifted up into the canopy. Streaks of sunlight swept over me, dancing, though the treetops were stagnant with an empty wind. This would be the last image impressed upon my mind, imposed on my dark brown eyes for someone to read later, like tea leaves clumped at the bottom of a mug.

I must have tilted too far, because my foot lifted beneath me, sliding in the silty grime. My body fell backward, tumbling into the water, and the creature's hold on my arm relinquished.

Whether he was afraid of accidentally meeting my blade's edge, or if he simply meant to let me drown, I had no idea, but as the water closed over my head, it was like a jolt of vigorous energy coursed through me.

My clothes and bag were heavy around me, but I needed air. Needed it *now*.

Pushing off from the unstable, silty ground with as much force as I could muster, I leapt upward, dagger held like an offering between us, and felt the blade slice an inch deep into the creature's flesh.

He released a low hiss that I felt against my face and his hands started scrambling at my arm, trying to escape me as the knife slid further. Those deadly nails carved into me, but I charged, shoving the blade forward once more. I could barely see through the murky water flowing down into my eyes, but it was obvious this fae wore no chest armor like his compatriot, despite his wide, vulnerable torso. I could make out the gills at his neck and sides fluttering with fear and pain, his bulging joints twitching as he fought me. His long-fingered hand caught me across the face in a back-handed swing, and I stumbled, trying not to break the connection.

While gasping for air, I ducked low to avoid one final swipe of those agony-laced claws and twisted the knife, hearing some kind of sizzle, like meat on a spit. He stilled.

With a shove of my quaking arms, the creature fell off my blade and splashed into the water, sinking below the surface.

My bag was drenched, my arms leaking watery blood from a dozen punctures, and my head was throbbing where the monster had struck me. Blood dripped over my lips.

But I was alive—actually alive.

The first guard was still underwater somewhere, wrapped in the net, and though I would miss the valuable weapon, I was in no state to dredge the depths to retrieve it. Maybe the fae would drown, or simply be corroded by the iron into flakes of bone. I just hoped he would not rise again.

My chest ached as I drew in deep, slow breaths, trying to fight the urge to gulp down every inhale. The sound was loud in the mangrove, and I knew better than to stay still. There was no time to regroup. I had to keep moving.

Conor's bag was soaked around my neck, and I could only hope the mechanisms inside were intact. There was no inflation of gases or spark of glowing powder when I peeked inside, so I had to assume they were fine. Raising it above my head once more, I kept the iron dagger—now dripping with brown-blue blood—ready in my fist, letting my trembling legs carry me deeper into fae territory.

CHAPTER FOUR

The tide receded further while I trudged through the mangroves and toward the open ocean. Like a scythe, it brushed forward and back, time passing by its swing. Thankfully, that meant the water level had dipped down to my hips and my tender arms could lower. Scanning the area around me, I studied the low, draping branches of each thick-trunked tree, picking one where I might rest and wipe the blood from my face.

To my left I spotted a firm, chest-high bough with clusters of vines on either side and used them as ropes to clamber atop it. Water had seeped into my waders, so I was wrinkled with damp and shivering from the cold, but I relished the chance to stop moving, even if I could only spare a few moments. Sitting had never felt so good.

Nibbling on some redfish from my bag, though the wrapping paper was drenched and dirty, I examined the path ahead of me. I had another two hours to go, I wagered. Clumps of algae and moss-ridden logs were my only company for leagues and by my feet were sparse flowers that appeared to be floating, though they didn't match the image Conor had drawn after his attack, so I left them unmolested.

The hot, humid air around me soon had my shivers subsiding and sweat taking their place. My hair stuck to my forehead. I used my wrist to brush the strands aside, wondering if I should have brought some pins to keep them out of the way. Flint had liked my hair long, so I still wasn't used to this new, shorter length. Every time I had braided it down my back, I would remember the fist he'd held it with while he'd taken me in the barn. The harsh pounding of his body and the exhale of his breath at my neck was a memory I'd looked back on with a twisted sort of fondness, until he'd broken off our engagement. Then, I'd just wanted to forget it had ever happened, so I'd taken shears to my hair. Would he find out I'd left town, I wondered? If Maire told any of the fishermen's wives, the gossip was bound to reach him. Would he worry? Would he regret the way he'd unceremoniously stomped on my heart?

I shook my head, then took a final bite of the redfish, licking the juice off my fingertips before wrapping the rest of the food and placing it back in my bag. Conor would cringe at my lack of hygiene, but there was no pretense of safety in the mangroves, let alone cleanliness. Survival was all that mattered.

With purposeful slowness, I eased myself off the tree limb and back into the murky depths, aware of every splash I made. I kept my steps small and subtle, sweeping side to side like a water snake, hoping to remain unnoticed as the thick water undulated around me.

The only change I detected as I got deeper into the wetlands was the sound. What I thought were the normal croaks of striped grass-frogs slowly became breathy and low. The hum of lacewing flies grew louder and louder until it crowded my senses. I started to lose sight of my destination. Was I heading in the right direction? Or did I get turned around? Was that tree the same one I had passed moments before?

There were no birds here, no predators diving into the water. There was only the buzz and drone of insects, and my body began to vibrate against the resonance of it. I was soon to be driven mad.

Clapping my hands over my ears, I struggled forward, increasing my speed as the light began to dim around me. I had to make it to some kind of land by nightfall, or else try to sleep in the limbs of a tree without falling or being found. There were tales of skinny-legged lizards that walked on water at night, feasting on any living thing their mouths could find, and wyrms that rested in the mud until darkness fell, who would then streak through the mangrove searching for meat. I knew there were lower fae-creatures here too, though the books Conor and I had recovered in Harnsey's market only talked about sirens and mer-folk—humanoid monsters similar to high fae—like the ones who had stood guard. Not that I knew exactly which species those guards fell into.

Aven and the others hadn't mentioned the creatures they'd seen, except for the high fae Aven had served. They looked the most like common people, he'd said, except for their black eyes and stretched torsos, or the points at the ends of their ears. If I could, I would capture one and torture them until they gave up the cure for Conor's transformation, since they seemed to be the most intelligent of the bunch. If not, I would take whatever unlucky being at the compound crossed my path.

With sunset looming dangerously ahead, I passed a grove of willows and spotted my first glance of solid ground. There was a stone shelf ahead of me, angling upward like a ramp. It ended on a flat dock that turned into a pathway about the width of three men shoulder-to-shoulder. It floated on the tide, creaking a bit in the gentle waves. I would have followed it while staying in the water, to make sure it didn't end at a full battalion of guards, but the path twisted past a bend of thick trees, so I had no idea how far it stretched. Was the open ocean ahead of me? But surely I would hear the crashing of larger waves and the roar of the wind if it was.

Instead, all I heard was that insistent buzzing echoing in my ears, though I could have sworn the cacophony had faded.

I needed to rest more than I needed safety at this point, I decided. I was exhausted and thirsty, my mouth dry and my head still throbbing with my pulse. That monster had struck me hard, and if it wasn't for the adrenaline coursing through me at every noise and fishy splash, I might have collapsed long before now. My legs were leaden from taking heavy steps through the water for hours on end.

The solidity of the stone ramp was a blessing.

I didn't hesitate to flop onto its angled shelf as soon as I was beyond the water's reach, every part of my body weary and sore. The idea of changing into dry trousers nearly had me moaning, but I needed to stay in my waders until I was sure I was staying on land.

The marsh began to swallow the sun, the oncoming dark spurring me into action when I would have rather laid on that hard, stone slab for days. I pulled myself to a sitting position, ready to follow the docks to what I hoped was the castle, just as I saw him.

At first, I thought he was a hallucination, dredged up from my fatigued memories of heroes and villains.

The man was waist-deep in the water, his chest bare. The sheer size of him was impressive—wide shoulders with thick, corded muscle along his back. He was tall, but his torso was not so unearthly long that I thought he was fae. In fact, he looked more human than I probably did at this moment, with my bedraggled, soaking hair and blood seeping through so many shallow wounds. I wondered if my face was mottled and swollen, but I dared not reach up a hand to check.

He hadn't seen me yet.

Keeping low, I took a moment to study him, trying to discern what sort of monster he might be, but other than being attractively built he seemed...normal. His hair was a mottled blond, waving in rumpled strands over his ears. As he twisted, I could see a swatch of darker scruff along his jaw and a similar line down his firm abdomen. He carried a tight-meshed net over one shoulder, which showed off the impressive muscles of his tanned arms, and his hands ended in blunt, human fingers. Maybe he was a captive from another nearby town, I mused, like Aven or Melia. If he was still glamoured then it was paramount I determine whether he was the exception or the rule; if he wasn't glamoured...then he was on the side of the fae, and therefore just as much my enemy as that urchin-fingered devil. Not that I had ever heard of a human serving willingly, but there could always be a first.

Still, Aven had made it sound like glamoured people were in a daze, moving in jerky motions, slow and stupid, without their control—almost as if their minds were barren. Meanwhile, over the trickle of the marshy seawater and insect hums, I could hear this man...whistling.

He reached down into the water, waving his arm about to clear the sickly-green algae on the surface, and peered into the gloom. Faster than a crayfish snake, he dove, returning with a fiddler crab in his hand.

The man shook his wet hair out of his eyes and pulled forward his net to drop the crab inside. It had all been so quick, and he was so sure in his movements, he had to be some kind of predator, but as I peered closer, I still couldn't see any trace of fae in him.

If only I could see his eyes.

But no, that would be foolish. My best course was to sneak around him and hurry down the curving dock so I could find a secure hiding place to wait out the night.

Taking a slow, silent breath, I rose into a crouch and began inching away. His back was turned to me now, a perfect chance to escape, but I took my time. If I slipped on the wet stone or dock there was no doubt he would hear the splash, and though I had one more net I could load into the launcher, it would take too long. My only choice would be another close-range fight—one I had little hope of winning against a man that size, unless he was a fae who would suffer from my iron blade.

Just then he turned, searching for his next crab to capture.

He must have seen the reflection of my body in the water, because his head darted up and his gaze met mine.

His eyebrows rose and I could tell his eyes weren't the pitch-black orbs of the fae, but his mouth was a deep scowl. He wasn't happy to see me.

"What are you doing here?" His voice was normal, deep. Like Flint's, but smoother, with his vowels more rounded.

He took a step forward, and another; without hesitation I raised my weapon.

"Don't come closer," I threatened. Human or not, he couldn't be trusted.

Scanning me from head to toe and noting the blood on my arms, his expression tightened in confusion. "Did you fight the guards?" He took another step.

"Stop!" I shouted, and then nearly groaned at my own stupidity. Someone was bound to hear us, and if this man was working for the fae I needed to take him out and do so without needless noise.

His gaze dropped to the knife and his nostrils flared, his eyes darkening to a deep, ocean blue as they sharpened with unease. I thought I caught a pointed ear peeking from his wet hair.

Fae.

He sidled closer and I knew I had no choice. Leaping from my higher position on the stone slab, I tackled him backward into the water, swiping my knife so I might cut into his chest, but somehow he turned, pivoting to throw me into the brine.

The cloying, grimy water closed over my head. I couldn't see anything, but I slashed again and again, trying to hit him. Kicking backward, I put some distance between us and breached the surface, gasping for breath. He was right in front of me.

I struck with my unarmed fist, hoping to catch him by surprise, but my knuckles only grazed over his hair as he ducked. The water was lower here, only reaching to my upper thighs, and I jerked up my knee, catching his chin in a bruising blow before I could back up further. I needed room to predict his movements and to get my knife between us.

The man straightened, and I could see blood dripping from his mouth. He smiled, the red coating his teeth and chin like macabre war paint. It made his bulky form even more intimidating, reminding me of a warrior god. His grin was disturbing and yet somehow also...arresting.

"Ah," he said, wiping a hand over his mouth. "So you *did* fight them. Defeated them, even."

I wasn't sure why he sounded so glad at that. His voice was rougher now, I noticed. Deeper. The glee in his voice must have been his appreciation of a challenging opponent.

But that wasn't me.

I'd gotten lucky so far, with my iron and my brother's implements, but I was tired and growing slower by the second. My weary body couldn't withstand another fight. Still, I would not let him know that.

"It wasn't hard," I replied, trying not to huff out my breaths. My chin-length hair stuck to my face, and I hoped it made me look just as wild as he did. I tightened my grip on the knife.

"What are you doing here?" he asked again.

I lunged, stabbing forward, but he jerked backward out of my reach. The water sloshed against us as he moved, almost faster than I could track, and suddenly he was at my side, pulling my arm behind me.

Struggling against his grip, I wiggled the hand holding the knife and felt it graze against his bare flesh.

He hissed, his hold vanishing for a second, but it returned before I could break free.

Flinging my head backward, I managed to hit what I hoped was his nose, and then I used the opportunity of his surprise to spin out of his reach. My head was now home to a hundred bees stabbing at my eyes and I blinked, praying my spotty vision would clear. Heart pounding, I raised my hand again, looking for a weakness I might be able to exploit before every trace of daylight was gone. *Hurry, hurry, hurry,* my brother's voice whispered inside my head. It was getting so dark.

The man looked down at the thin slash on his belly, right over the hard muscles of his abdomen. The blood there steamed, as if poisoned by the iron. Anger settled over his face like a mask and the stormy blue of his irises vanished behind his expanding pupils. His eyes were now pure black, like the others I'd seen. He clenched his fist, and I watched his arm...change.

The limb seemed to evaporate into smoke, the color like the soot always present on Conor's fingers—so dark a gray it might as well have been a moonless sky. The arm kept close to its original shape, just wafting and swirling where there had once been muscle and bone.

I couldn't breathe.

Aven had said their powers were *gone*. Their glamour, their ability to transform, those were supposed to be failing. Most high fae could shift, whether it was into another living creature or into water or even into trees, but I had never heard of someone becoming smoke. And if this man—*fae*—could do it, then I'd been misinformed. And I was doomed.

His torso darkened into the same controlled, shadowy mass, and then back to flesh. The cut was gone.

My iron hadn't injured him for more than a mere handful of heart-beats.

Swallowing down terror, I began scanning for a way out. I could run back the way I came and try to load the net launcher as I sprinted. If he followed, I could shoot and maybe get away. I needed to get home. This quest was already a long shot, but if the fae had their abilities and the escaped humans had only been a fluke, then there was no hope for me. I couldn't fight beyond the rudimentary moves I'd learned playing swords with boys in town, and I would need more weapons from Conor if I was to go up against such power. If iron didn't affect them all...well, I'd need something more up my sleeve. I edged away, trying to appear calm.

"Are you—" the man started, but then his head whipped to the side. "Someone is coming."

Heart in my throat, I turned to run but he grabbed me, holding my knife out to the side while his other arm circled my waist. His hard chest pressed tight against mine, as cold as the water swirling at my legs. Gasping, I looked up into his eyes, watching the black bleed away, returning to a dark blue.

So human. My scattered mind latched onto that thought with desperation.

"Give me your mouth," he muttered.

I blanched. "What?" The spell broken, I squirmed and fidgeted in his embrace.

"There's blood on your mouth." His voice was just above a whisper. "And mine. Pretend to be glamoured or you'll be killed."

He shoved my knife-wielding hand beneath the water and leaned forward, but I lifted my free arm, ready to push him away.

"Please," he added, "do not fight."

"I don't—"

But then he was kissing me.

His lips were chilled, and the scruff along his jaw was rough and wet from both salt water and the blood I had made him spill. I recoiled against the sensation, imagining his lips were like two slippery eels, hiding fangs beneath. He wasn't human. Was he poisoning me somehow with this kiss? Capturing me?

I attempted to pull back, but his hand drifted up my shoulder, resting at the base of my neck, holding me there. It was gentle, despite the strength he used.

"Please," he whispered again, his words caressing my lips. He turned his head as if to get a better taste of me, and his tongue moved over my jaw...licking the blood. I shivered with repulsion and the shock of his warm mouth on my cold skin. When he returned to my lips, he didn't plunge inside. He didn't grip my face with brutal hands and push into me. He was...tender. Small, touching kisses like words he spoke one by one. It was a shock, so I stood there frozen. But then, almost by accident, my mouth started to move with his.

His body swayed as if we were in the midst of a tryst, his fingers caressing along my throat and down my front. He groaned, the sound startling and loud in my ears. Had that been for whoever was approaching? Was he really trying to help me? Or was I being tricked?

I wanted to shove him away, wanted to turn and run, but my body refused to comply. Instead, I stood limply in his arms, his words echoing in my ears. *Please, do not fight. Please.*

"Reed!" A deep but feminine voice called.

The man broke free of my mouth, his breaths panting. "What now, Norrel?" he whined, the tone so different from how he'd spoken to me I almost couldn't reconcile it with the mouth that had just been pressed to mine. "Can't you see I'm in the middle of something?"

His hand was firm on the back of my neck again, keeping me in place so I wouldn't turn to look at the person who spoke. All I could do was stare at the pulse under his chin, how it was fast but steady.

"What have you got there?" the voice—Norrel—asked.

"Since when do you care who I dabble with?" Reed replied. I could hear a smirk laid over his words like a sprinkle of sugar.

"Don't flatter yourself. I wouldn't dabble with your kind without severe intoxication, scum."

Reed took my empty hand and placed it to his heart as if wounded, tilting his body just enough so he could face the woman in question. From the corner of my eye, I could see a trio of fae on the docks to my right. And it was *obvious* these were fae; they were tall and gangling, with a skin color closer to the sickly white of a mushroom than that of human flesh.

"Answer the question," remarked another of the fae, "or we'll request some time with you *outside* the compound."

Reed wrapped one of his arms over my collarbone and spun me, so his chest pressed into my back. Panicked to be suddenly so visible, I did my best to appear glamoured—a vacant glaze to my eyes, limp arms, my posture slouching beneath his hold as if he was all that kept me aloft.

"I wanted to taste her," Reed said against my temple. "I'll be presenting her to Jassin, but I couldn't help but borrow her a moment."

"You're disgusting."

Now that I could see Norrel without obstruction, I was surprised by her vicious beauty. She was lithe, her toned arms decorated in strands of pearls which stood in contrast to the dark armor over her chest and legs. Her hair was white but tinted green in places as if she'd laid too long in bright lichen and been stained by it. The pointed ears and black eyes were inhuman enough that her loveliness didn't fully enrapture me—but only just.

The two men behind her looked so similar I thought they might be siblings.

"What, never had one of the human nibblets?" he asked. "I failed to resist this one. You really should give it a go." His tone was jovial and sweet, as if he hadn't just been insulted. My brain sequestered each word for later study, as if they were a poem I could memorize by rote. And I was only partially offended by being cast as a "nibblet" in this particular verse.

"Hurry up and get back before full night," said Norrel with the flip of an elongated hand. "He wants all the humans accounted for, and no doubt he'll want you to attend to his needs too, *slave.*"

At first, I thought she was talking to me, but then I realized she meant Reed. But wasn't he fae like them? He wasn't as...*stretched* in appearance, but his form shifted to and from smoke with ease. I was also sure I'd seen a point to his ears, and his eyes had flickered black. If he was considered less than them, I hated to think what kind of awful powers they might lord over him.

"I'll be right along, I swear it."

Norrel turned as if to leave, and then paused. "Why is she bloody?"

Oh, right. My arms.

"She may have been...left to her own devices for a moment. Unsupervised." Reed chuckled and dipped his head as if sheepish, rubbing a hand through his wet, blond hair. He seemed to be stalling for a moment, but then his gaze snapped up. "I think something may have roughed her up a bit in my absence. Maybe a swarm of parachins."

The guard to Norrel's left barked a laugh that was at once sinister and oddly melodic. "Better hope Jassin isn't looking for a reason to throw you underground."

"All I can do is hope," Reed said, cheerful as ever.

The trio seemed to tire of his chipper attitude and turned to continue their way down the docks. My eyes were watering with the need to blink, but I kept up my languid trance-like stare, my pulse hammering beneath Reed's fingers.

"One more moment, little perch," Reed murmured.

We watched the tall fae turn the corner and waited another few heartbeats before he released me. I turned, a question for every moment I'd been in his presence suspended on my tongue, but he held a finger to his lips.

"This way." Taking my hand, he started back the way he'd come, reaching down into the water only once to retrieve the net I'd forgotten he'd dropped. There were a dozen or so small crabs inside, motionless with fear. I felt as trapped as those critters as he led me further back into the mangrove, my hand freezing in the tight grip of this man—*fae*—ahead of me. The dagger to my side was as useless as wishes. Whether I was about to be dinner alongside the crabs, I had no way of knowing, but it was all I could do to keep my stiff legs moving forward, praying to the marsh to spare me when it had not spared them.

CHAPTER FIVE

W e had walked for almost twenty minutes and the water was changing into a clearer, cleaner presence against my legs when Reed seemed to relax. His shoulders dipped and he turned to look at me with a rueful smile, finally letting go of my hand. I immediately raised the dagger, keeping it as a barrier between us.

"I'm sorry for that," he said. "It was the best I could do on short notice. Normally I wouldn't kiss someone without discussing it first. Not very gentlemanly to take it from you like that."

"And you think you're a gentleman?" I replied, then clenched my lips tight together. That wasn't important. The kiss wasn't important. He wasn't a man at all, and what mattered was where this fae-man was taking me. Not that I was sure I was going to *let* him.

"I try," he said with a light shrug before continuing on.

I hesitated to follow. "Where are you going?"

"Inside," he said over his shoulder. "I take it that's where you want to be?"

I couldn't very well head back to those docks if they were being patrolled by so many fae, and he did seem to know where he was going, but...

"Not if you're taking me to some fae named Jassin."

At that, he turned.

"I'm not going to *give* you to him, just present you. But I don't have a lot of time—please, trust me and I'll explain everything when we're inside."

I watched his eyes dart around the water, as if fearful of what might be swimming nearby, and the gesture was eerily familiar. It was how I imagined I'd looked just hours ago, wandering through the mangroves.

"Fine, but if I think for one second that you're handing me over, I'll plunge this dagger into your heart and leave it there."

It was a gamble, hoping that shadowy smoke couldn't save him if the iron stayed in his body, but it must have paid off, because Reed nodded in agreement and waved me onward.

We passed a series of floating paths that branched out into rows of small houses. They stood on stilts, just like I'd heard, and even though they were all rotten wood and broken shingles, they were obviously well-lived in. There were piles of shells and jars of feathers at each door-way, many roofs sporting strings of driftwood and sea glass that made tinkling sounds in the breeze. Beings moved within each hut, candle flames or some green algae-like glow throwing their shadows against the windows and open doorways.

"Don't look," Reed muttered, and I darted my gaze forward. No. Why was I listening to him? He may have saved me from another battle, but I wasn't here to make friends. At any moment he could turn on me. But I supposed he could be a useful source of information.

"I'm here searching for something," I said at his back, testing the waters.

"Then I will help you," he replied, his voice light and easy, as if it was a given.

He couldn't see it, but I scowled and raised an eyebrow in a cold look that would have had my brother shamefacedly confessing whatever naughty act he'd committed. Nothing was a given.

"And why would you do that?"

"I need something from you. Now be quiet until we reach the castle." His tone dipped lower. "Things in the water can hear you as easily as I can."

"Why don't we walk on the paths?" I replied in a near whisper. I was tired from the difficult trek in the silt, my waterlogged body heavier with every step. My bag was drying against my back, but now that the sun was well and truly set, the brisk night air brushed against me, sending shivers over my skin. I wondered how he could stand to be shirtless.

"I'm not permitted," Reed replied, and sounded loath to do so. "Now hush. And keep looking dazed in case anyone sees." Grabbing my hand once more, he kept up our steady pace through the maze of houses, carving a wide arc around them as if we were circling the city. Through my peripheral vision, I caught more than one set of eyes following us from the recesses of their homes.

As if his warning had summoned the danger, a horse's torso began to rise from the water ahead, its fur the color of midnight, its eyes a clear, human blue. I startled, but quickly schooled my features into an uninterested mask, Reed's hold on my hand keeping us moving forward. In the dark, it was hard to see the beast's shape beneath the water. The only features I could discern were a mouth of small, human-like teeth when it smiled, and a mane braided with what looked like the ribcages of fish as it flipped its head to and fro.

Reed nodded to the creature, and it dove again beneath the water, a thick, ridged tail flashing into the air behind it with a flourish.

A kelavee. The first I'd ever seen with my own eyes.

I hadn't thought of them as so animal-like. Couldn't they speak with a human tongue to lure their prey? Didn't their faces resemble an elongated human skull? That's what I'd heard from northern travelers' stories anyway. I opened my mouth to ask but feared how many more might be within listening range. Instead, I darted my eyes to the black water on either side of us, nervous of its hidden depths.

When the water was clear enough, I could spot schools of bioluminescent minnows moving in tandem around our bodies, following us with interest. A bird that was larger than a dog dove into the brine beside us, scaring me half to death, only to fly on with a snapper or some other such fish in its elongated clutches.

"Easy," Reed muttered, and I realized my grip on his hand had become violent. The looming houses were spaced further apart now, and I saw my first glimpse of the fae's stronghold beyond.

The stone building that rose from the dark water ahead of us was every bit as grandiose as a castle, yet looked nothing like the citadels I'd read about in dramas and comedies. Instead of stout and solid, it was tall and leaning and utterly unkempt. Seaweed drooped from each window and holes were carved into the sides just above the water line. In high tide, I imagined they would flood, but for now they served as garish windows in the stone. Even the gate looked worn and crumbling—a bunch of planks overrun with cardinal beetles and wriggling grubs. Only low fires spaced evenly at the walls and pale, glowing jars hanging from windows cast enough light for me to see their squirming bodies.

Reed led us alongside the dock, which ended at the front gate, but we did not use it. Instead, he pulled me further and we rounded the compound, coming to one of the gaping holes on its right wall. A rope ladder had been set up against the opening and he gestured for me to move ahead of him.

"I don't—" I started, actively shivering with cold and anxiety, but he held his finger against his lips once more, his eyes going wide with distress.

Swallowing my protests, I gingerly climbed into the tunnel, finding a sort of entryway at my feet. There were shelves carved high up in the room, each housing snail and turtle shells. A wooden door, which was in much better condition than the front entrance, sat directly ahead.

Reed took my hand and led me to the entrance, opening it a crack to check for anyone coming, then ushering me down a hall that was as damp and quiet as a tomb. His net of crabs bounced against his bare shoulder.

The torches were scarcer inside, the light barely enough for me to see the edges of the stones at my sodden shoes. Combined with the putrid moisture in the air, I feared I was heading into a cellar or crypt from which my body would never be recovered. Was it foolish of me to be led along by this stranger? Yes. Did I have much of a choice? Unfortunately, no. Still, I paid close attention to the directions we took, memorizing my way so I could escape if needed.

We passed a series of tall, skinny doors, and I could hear shrieking from inside. The sound vibrated against the walls and pressed on my eardrums like nails I was afraid might pierce them.

Reed stopped me from pressing my palms to my skull.

"It's the syra," he muttered. "The scream can't hurt you. Not now anyway."

What did he mean *now*? Were the fae without their deadly powers or not? Was I walking into a trap, or a nest of vulnerable targets?

Before I could drum up the courage to ask, we were climbing down a flight of stairs. A chilled hand pushed me into the stone wall and Reed's eyes met mine just before a pink-skinned man passed us on the steps, climbing with hard stomps of booted feet and the clang of heavy armor. With my eyes wide and dazed, my form limp, I waited for a potential attack, but the creature left us unscathed. My heart was pounding in my tight chest, but Reed only waited the span of a few breaths and then took me further down.

The air grew somehow colder, and more stale, as if rarely disturbed. We rounded a corner and then came to a stop in front of what looked like a series of prison cells.

Oh, no. No! This *had* been a trap! Tugging my hand, I attempted to break from his grip, and when that didn't work, I opened my mouth to shout. Reed put his free hand on my cheek, startling me into quiet.

"Please trust me," he said in a hushed but urgent voice. "I'm going to help you. Otherwise, why would I have protected you back there?" His eyes darted back and forth across my own, as if begging me to understand, though I could barely see the motion in the dark.

He didn't let me deliberate further, quickly yanking open one of the metal, jail-like gates and taking me with him inside. There was another door at the end of the cell, shrouded in shadow, and I wondered how many layers and doorways this mammoth construction concealed.

The door was plain and had a locking bar on the outside, which Reed flicked open with practiced ease. This time, he entered first and waved for me to follow. Once I was inside, he closed the door and released a heavy sigh.

"By the moon, that was one of the most stressful scavenging trips I've had in ages."

Reed dropped the crab-filled net on the floor and rolled his shoulders before approaching a fireplace that was growing cold, the flames down to stuttering embers. It was the only light in the room, outlining a bedroom of sorts—there was a pallet on the ground, a rug beneath my feet, and some boxes along the stone walls, like makeshift bureaus.

I noticed Reed was shivering just as much as I was, his hand trembling as he threw sticks and dried leaves into the fire from a pile beside the hearth.

"Is it safe to t-talk now?" I asked, feeling annoyed and cold, hungry and terrified.

"It is," he nodded. "Here." He hurried to one of the shoddy boxes in the corner. There was little inside from what I could see, but he tugged out a ratty blanket and handed it to me. "You can change out of your clothes and use this to warm up—I just realized I don't even know your name."

"It's W-Winnie, not that you n-need to know. Now...why are you helping me? Where are we?" I asked, taking the blanket with apprehension. It smelled like the decay of the marsh, the fabric so thin it would barely help against a draft, let alone this bone-deep chill. The room was gray stone all around and had no windows, reminding me of the cells beyond the door.

"We're in my room. And I told you," he replied, his broad, naked back turned once again, "I need something from you."

"And what is that?"

"I need you to lie." At this, he peeled his soaked breeches from his legs and laid them on a stool by the fire, which was the only seating beyond the pallet to my left. I was momentarily distracted by the bunching muscles at his back and the trim waist that ended at a firm backend only barely covered by thin shorts made of tight netting. So they would dry easier, I supposed—I made a note to mention them to Conor.

Reed's legs were thick and powerful just like his arms and I wondered what kind of labor kept him so strong. Climbing the stone walls, maybe? It couldn't all be from walking through the currents. His body was so strangely...*human*. And it was then I noticed several scars against the backdrop of his skin—little nicks and slashes, some circular in a way that reminded me of the bite on Conor's arm, though they were too small. Had he been poisoned by the same monster once?

He turned his head to see me staring.

"Do you mind?" he asked, grin crooked.

I rolled my eyes to the high ceiling and turned away, ignoring the slight burn at my cheeks. "Apologies. You've been half-naked for so long I forgot you were capable of losing more clothing."

I lowered my bag of supplies and wrapped the ratty blanket around my shoulders, covering up enough to drop my waders to the ground and unlace and remove the shirt that was sticking to my skin. Everything was drenched, and the fire he'd built up in the corner was only doing so much to combat the cold. I glanced at the bed with envy, missing my place beside Conor on our hay-filled cushion.

"You're going to want to be half naked as well," Reed commented, and I turned to see him shrugging on a dry tunic.

"I'm sorry?"

"It's the quickest way to warm up, believe me; I've had enough nights freezing down here, and in more dire straits. Wet clothing does more harm than good."

I didn't want to tell him I had already removed my shirt, the sopping fabric pressed into my hip beneath the blanket.

"Before I do anything, I need you to tell me what's going on. I...I saw you transform—you're fae, aren't you? Why the secrecy walking into the castle? What do you need me to lie about?"

"You ask a lot of questions." He tugged on a pair of pants that were ripped slightly below the knee, then held out a long slip-on garment that looked like it might fit me as a dress. He seemed to no longer care that I'd seen him in nothing but his undergarments, but I was not about to offer him the same opportunity.

Still, as I raised my finger to motion that he turn around, he was already facing away from me, staring adamantly at the crackling fire and warming his hands against it. A tiny twinge of disappointment warred with the annoyance he'd been stoking as surely as the flames. If I hadn't thought he might yell for the guards, I'd have struck his head with the handle of my knife and made a run for it long before entering this strange dungeon, but my choices were made and now I had to deal with the consequences. We were together in this room for good or ill, but that didn't mean I wanted to remain blind to his plans.

"I'll need answers to those questions if you want me to help you," I told him.

"Fair enough." He waited until I was clothed in slightly damp breeches from my bag and what I discovered was his overly large shirt, and then sat on the low bed, patting the space beside him. "I won't force myself on you, or turn you over to the high fae," he said, "so in that, you can trust me."

"I'd be stupid to trust anything you tell me," I replied, but I sat beside him regardless, glad for the chance to fold my legs and cover them with the blanket, stealing any iota of warmth. He shifted closer to me, his arm brushing my own.

"Fae can't lie," he said, his head cocked to the side.

Rubbing my hands over my calves, I huffed a laugh. "That's an old wives' tale."

"It's not. You can ask me anything and—should I choose to answer—nothing I say could be knowingly false."

I paused, thinking it over. "But didn't you tell that fae woman you'd be bringing me to Jassin? And that you'd be right along?"

"Eventually, I *will* bring you to Jassin, so to speak," he replied, lifting one shoulder. "And 'right along' is not a strictly defined timeline, is it?"

"Okay, so you were vague, or misleading, but...there's still no way to prove you can't outright lie."

He grinned. "It's difficult to demonstrate, sure. Unless I was confessing something I really didn't want known. But why else would I ask you to lie for me? Why would I need a human to help me?"

"So, you're definitely not human. And you still haven't told me *how* I need to help you." Aggravation leaked into my tone and his calm expression widened into amusement.

"You really are an impatient little thing, aren't you?"

I stood up from the bed and could have sworn his hand lifted to stop me, but it was back by his thigh before I could be sure.

"Either tell me what you want, or let me go," I threatened. "I don't have time to dawdle."

"Right." He nodded. "You're looking for something. I said I would help you and I meant it. Because I *cannot lie*. As for what I need you to lie about—you'll notice I'm not exactly held in high esteem by my peers here at the castle. It's because..." he took a breath, as if steeling himself for a negative reaction, "I am only half-fae."

The fire was licking at my back as I stood there in his room, waiting for something else.

"Is that...it?" I asked.

His laugh was deep and pure, echoing along the gloomy stone walls. "Humans really are lovely sometimes. You fail to see an issue there?"

"Any amount of fae is more than I'd prefer," I replied honestly.

Reed dipped his head in acceptance. "I'm not surprised you feel that way. But here, being half-fae might as well make me a parasite in the eyes of this court. I was already indentured to a certain degree, and then I was forced to sell myself into a more explicit contract." He lifted one shoulder, looking up at me with an open expression that made his face seem younger. "I need your help to break it."

"And how would I do that?"

Reed stood and began rolling up his sleeves in measured movements. "You could lie to the fae that holds my contract, tell him you're buying me out. Forge a missive from some other royal, maybe. Or you could kill him. It's obviously part of our agreement that I can't cause any direct harm to him, plus there's no violence in the compound without consequences, but as a human you're not subject to any such...restrictions."

My eyes were trained on the inches of toned muscle he revealed as his sleeve tightened beneath his elbow. I had seen him completely shirtless but for some reason this seemed more indecent, as if he was orchestrating some kind of show for my benefit.

"You made your way through the entry guards," he continued, "so I know you can fight, though you were a bit sloppy when we scuffled. Tired, maybe. And it seems like you've never seen any deep water fae, so I doubt you have any idea how to handle them. Regardless, you have more of a chance than I do at wounding my owner. And, in exchange, whatever it is you're looking for, I'll help you find it. So long as it's within my power."

His power. The term could be used so flippantly, so ambiguously. My mind turned over every phrase he used, like a prospector panning for gold in a river.

"Speaking of your power," I said, fighting the urge to pace the small confines of the room, "you say you're half-fae, but you transformed earlier. I saw the smoke you turned into, and it healed you—I thought that was an ability only high fae had? And I'd been told those powers had recently...vanished." It was a risk, mentioning that, but I wanted to see how he reacted. I didn't add that it was the only reason I'd braved the journey, or that my fighting prowess was mostly trickery using my brother's inventions. He needn't know either of those truths.

At this, Reed finally looked uneasy. His lips turned down at the sides and his eyes lowered with displeasure. Turning his back, he bent down to put on a pair of simple, weathered shoes.

His voice was so low I almost missed it when he said, "I don't want to tell you about that."

"Well, that's unfortunate, because if you want my help then you will," I replied, crossing my arms. He'd have to tell me a lot.

"I'm not entirely sure why I have my shifting abilities." He was quiet, as if worried about being overheard, though he'd assured me it was safe to talk here. "The rest of the high fae have lost their powers, that much is true. Glamours on some of the human slaves were broken, syra have been unable to change into their full human regalia, and even the royals can no longer move water and call the wind like they could just days ago. I'd be killed just for telling a human those weaknesses. As for me, I can only assume it's my diluted blood, not yet succumbing to whatever has caused this...interruption. For all I know, the next time I attempt to shift,

I would fail."

"So, you don't know what the interruption is?"

Reed shook his head, then approached a copper bowl of water on the floor I hadn't yet noticed. "An illness of some kind, maybe, or a curse. Regardless, now that we're decently thawed, we need to clean you up so I can present you to Jassin. His guards will be expecting it after that little display with Norrel...that is, unless I come up with some mostly true statement about me being unable to fetch you, which is unlikely—and I need you to keep your mouth shut about my ability. If the high fae find out I have more power than them right now, the attitude you witnessed earlier at the docks will look like a loving embrace."

"They'd hurt you?" I guessed.

"They'd murder me," he replied, and if he was to be believed about his inability to lie, he felt that was absolute fact. "I'm basically refuse."

Surprisingly, he didn't sound remotely bitter. If anything, his whole presence altered, going back to the smiley, jovial attitude he'd presented when faced with Norrel and the others.

"But that's fine, because they will underestimate me. And you—being that you are, as you know, human." His grin was wide and oddly charming, his hair drying to a wheat-like color that looked soft to the touch. His facial hair was just long enough to show a hint of curl, and my gaze focused there as he approached me with a square of fabric he'd dipped in the water.

"What are you—" I started, but then he was dabbing the cloth at my jaw where I was sure I had a cut seeping blood.

"Jassin will expect you to be one of the leftovers who are still glamoured from before this peculiar *anomaly*. They're calling it a break in power, and whether it's temporary or not I still do not know, but they've killed any humans in the court who show awareness or any sort of cognition. Basically, keep acting like you're under their control and you'll be fine."

His touch was gentle as he stroked the damp fabric over the slashes on my face and arms, then he reached for my hair. Instinctively, I jerked backward, his body growing too close for comfort.

"Hey there," he said, tone gentle, "I'm just making you presentable. I wouldn't damage such pretty hair or hurt such a delicate face." He smiled and his fingers reached into the strands of my hair, pulling whatever sorts of weeds and underwater muck had accumulated, and then patted down any strays. I felt like a pet being readied for inspection, or one of the dazzling beauties from my novels who were pampered to within an inch of their life and *hated* the attention. On this end of Reed's ministrations, however, I found it hard to muster any sense of indignity. It simply felt...nice.

His movements were cautious and slow, his fingers finally warmed from the fire. I had stopped shivering, at least.

"Here, let's belt this so they don't think you just stumbled out of someone's bedchamber." He removed the blanket around my shoulders and used a leather belt he secured from the same storage trunk to circle my waist, latching it above my hips. It was then, as my pulse started to quicken and my sight refocused on the strong heft of his hands, that I remembered my purpose here.

"Wait," I said, and his fingers immediately halted against the leather. He looked up at me, his face so close I wanted to study the curve of his lashes and the width of his cheekbones. His eyes were like sapphires I'd seen once in the market, the jewels set in sterling silver. Looking at him, I thought the gems might have been even more beautiful surrounded by pale gold. His dark-blond lashes reminded me of morning rays of sunshine on the water, streaking yellow across the surface. I shook myself from whatever trance he'd induced by treating me like a doll, and from my absurd attempt to form poetry around his features. "You...said you would help me, but you don't even know what I'm looking for. If I don't think you can keep up your end of the bargain, I have no reason to risk myself parading like a mindless fool in front of dangerous fae."

"We're running low on time," he warned. "But fine, tell me, and I swear I will admit if you seek something I cannot find."

"My brother was attacked by something in the marsh," I said, my voice sounding stronger than the moment before. "Near the mudflats to the east. He had a circular bite along his shoulder, the size of my palm—it almost looks like...some of the scars on you, but larger. A day later the mark began to turn brown like mud, and soon a thick, bark-like rash crept over his skin, starting at his toes. It made moving difficult, and then impossible. Like it's turning him into some sort of tree." I cleared my throat, fighting the tightness there as I remembered Conor's face when he could not move his ankle, then his knee. "I can't find any note of it in the books I've found, and no one knows a cure. It had to have been a fae, or one of their kept lower-fae monsters, like the kelavee we passed. He has no memory of what bit him, and no healer in our village has a clue what to do. I need to find a remedy."

Reed had grown still as I spoke, but now he resumed his task of straightening the shirt-dress and tucking back my hair to present my very human ears.

"I cannot be sure what attacked him," he said, "but I agree with you it was most likely a creature from these lands. Not a kelavee—they have no poison to spread and are usually more man than horse. I am friends with a perfumer—they're revered in the castle and have a lot of pull—she will either know how to find the cure for his illness, or know who to talk to." He paused. "I will bring you to her tomorrow, if you get me through tonight, acting glamoured and like you're part of the servant staff."

"You swear it?"

He nodded. "I swear it, just as I swear I cannot lie."

Something in my heart sank. I really had no way of trusting anything that spilled off his tongue. I could be walking into an ambush, trussed up like dinner to be served. I could be a puppet in this man's play, following the tug of his strings only to be cut loose at the end. But I supposed I had no choice but to go along with it—without him I was lost, or at least back at the start, where all fae were villains to defeat and I was no closer to helping Conor break free of his curse. At least now I was inside, within striking distance of someone who might hold a solution.

"Then I guess you'll be thrilled to know that acting just happens to be one of my better skills," I said.

With no other recourse, I let his calm touch skate over my skin and readied myself to face a court of evil, vicious fae.

CHAPTER SIX

Reed wouldn't allow me to take my dagger, since there was no easy way to hide it on my person, but I wasn't about to walk into a room full of fae with no defenses. Before we left, I rummaged through my bag, claiming to crave my last few sips of clean water, and then hurriedly stuffed my second—and now only—iron-tipped net into the breastband beneath my tunic. If bunched, it was the size of my fist, but I managed to spread it evenly across my chest into what I hoped looked like a patterned strap of linen.

Reed didn't seem to notice my now slightly fuller bust, and we left his room with a cobbled-together plan of how I should react to the fae of the court.

Despite the list of "dos and don'ts" he'd imparted before we left the supposed safety of his dungeon-like room, I felt like I was walking in blind. My pulse grew more unsteady with every vulnerable step we took deeper into the castle.

After winding through several hallways, we turned down a series of steps that had flooded, and I watched as Reed removed his shoes and handed them to me, along with the small net full of crabs he'd been dragging behind us.

"What am I supposed to—" I began, but then he picked me up in his arms, startling me into silence, and carried me down the shallow stairs while I clutched his possessions.

"Remember to stay off to the sides of the room if you can," he repeated at my ear. "I'll get back to you as soon as I can, but if someone approaches you, just nod along with any requests and try not to get taken into other wings of the castle. Norrel and the others are bound to check that I've delivered you to Jassin, but I only need to parade you in front of him. I'll keep any interaction to a minimum."

"If I have to agree to everything that happens, how can I avoid being moved?" I retorted.

"You seem clever—I have faith that you'll utilize those skills if it means survival."

I opened my mouth to provide some indignant reply, but we turned a corner that angled like a small hill, and it was then dry enough for him to release me. He set me down on my slippered feet, then took back his shoes and the crabs before giving me one last lingering look. For a moment, there was something like fear in his deep, blue eyes, but then it was gone, replaced by the cheerful, glazed facade of a jolly fool.

Opening a door to some sort of kitchen, which I could only determine by the smoke and steam leaking into the hall, Reed chucked the bag inside.

"Fresh fiddlers for you, Edea!" he called into the room.

"About time, you useless boor," a withered voice returned. "I should have sent someone with half a mind to fetch these."

"I do try for you!" He laughed and closed the door once more, hurrying me onward.

"So, they really all treat you like—" Reed gripped my shoulder in warning, and I shut my mouth just as another one of those pink-skinned men entered the hall ahead of us.

On closer inspection, it seemed less man-like, and more like a hulking lizard with smooth limbs and fingers that ended in rounded bulbs, its pink tint reminding me of specimens Conor had brought home in jars for his experiments. Its head was feathered in all directions with waving finger-length appendages, and its eyes were huge and dark, overshadowing a tiny, slitted mouth and near-absent nostrils. It was taller than me by almost three heads, and if it wasn't for the human-like way it walked and the normal-shaped armor on its body, I would have screamed to see it coming.

Reed nodded to the creature as we passed, and I fought the urge to watch its movement with rapt attention. I was mindless, I had to remind myself. I couldn't gawk or question or show any fear. But knowing that monster was now at my back had my stomach twisting.

"An abyssot," Reed provided once we were far enough away. "You won't have to worry about them; they only eat snails and other shelled creatures."

That didn't make me feel as secure as he probably thought it did.

"Here we go," he murmured, and that was all the warning I had as we crested a set of slimy stairs and were greeted with blinding yellow light.

The smells hit me before any clear sights—decay and waste, sulfur and seafood—then cloying smoke and something like...rosemary. It was such an odd scent among the disgusting bouquet that I honed my senses in on it, focusing on that tiny breath of fresh air so I wouldn't retch.

Only then could I focus on the explosion of color before me. Among the stone walls and floor were all manner of creatures, some bedecked in flamboyant tunics and gowns, or just scraps of glittering fabric. There were pearls and shells and glass woven into their hair or draped over their limbs, their skin tones a motley assortment of greens, grays, pinks, and blues. A few creatures appeared human enough I knew them to be high fae, but with others it was harder to tell. Shimmering scales covered a man at my right from head to toe, while one woman ahead was coated in lichen as if it were a type of fur. A squat, globular creature gyrated over the floor in a slow, mesmeric rhythm, a tender and mournful sound following in its wake. All around was chattering and clicking and words here or there I could only just make out in the din.

Reed pushed me off to the side, placing me in a corner like a decrepit piece of furniture.

"Stay," he commanded, that fake smile firmly painted on his lips, and then he was gone.

I kept my eyes unfocused, my head tilted back as if it was too heavy to hold, doing my best to calm my racing heart. Never in my whole life had I imagined I would be surrounded by so many horrible and stunning monsters—or so many human slaves.

It was easy to pick them out among the crowd; they didn't eat or drink or dance like the members of this garish court, only walked dumbly while holding trays of cups or stood still, swaying in place. It reminded me of seaweed moving with the tide. Their clothing was similar to mine—simple shirts with breeches or dresses and little else—but, other than being thin with hunger, they seemed relatively unharmed. It relaxed me, if only incrementally, that they sported no obvious injuries or marks of abuse.

Reed worked his way through the busy room, his blond hair like a lightning bug against the grays and blues of the mingling fae. He bowed at a few he passed, though I could not tell what separated them from the others. Sure, some of the fae he showed deference to were humanoid and decked in gaudy jewels, but another was scaled and small enough to be a child, draped in nothing but brown seaweed and little green tubers that looked like grapes.

Reed dropped to his knees, and I nearly lost sight of him, but a small bubble of space formed around him in time for me to witness a white-haired fae lounging on an elaborate chaise raise a hand in acknowledgement, giving permission for Reed to stand once more. They spoke, though I couldn't hear a word, and I made sure my gaze was off to the side as Reed gestured my way.

So, this was Jassin.

Now that the high fae had seen me, were we now free from any repercussions from Norrel? Could we leave?

Suddenly, a scuffle started to my right, and I had to fight the instinct to snap my head toward the commotion. Through my peripheral vision I watched one of the more serpentine-looking fae strike with curved fangs. While she had the arms and torso of a slender woman, her waist was a thick, green tail that traveled behind her, weaving her long body through the crowd. She struck with the speed of a crayfish snake, her fangs landing on the fleshy arm of a pink abyssot guard, just missing their armor. The abyssot's feathered head trembled as it shouted, but then, before it could hit back, the snake-woman seized as if with fear, and then crumbled to the ground where she could only twitch and convulse. Her human mouth remained open in a silent scream and her hands froze into claw-like shapes. What was happening? Had the abyssot's flesh poisoned her? Was this the kind of creature Conor had been struck by?

I expected the fae around her to leap to her aid, or the violence to escalate into a full brawl, but instead there was only an uneasy wave of laughter throughout the crowd. Another half-snake fae, this one a barrel-chested man, pushed a glamoured human at the abyssot, and I watched the frail boy, who could only have been a year or two older than my brother, slash out at the abyssot with a broken bottle, his body moving by a will that was not his own.

"Ahh, what a lovely waif," hissed a creature to my side, breaking my attention from the muddled action ahead. I hoped the creature wasn't talking to me, prayed to every spirit and divinity I'd read about that I hadn't been noticed, but a cold, stump-fingered hand moved over my bare forearm.

With purposeful slowness, I allowed my head to fall inches to the side so I could see my assaulter. They were covered in shallow bumps and crags all over their gray-tinted skin, the texture reminding me of a toad. They were refreshingly human in shape, albeit stocky, but their eyes were an unearthly white, and other than a pair of glass-belted breeches, they wore no clothing. I assumed it was male, although I dreaded any discovery that would confirm or refute my guess.

"You smell fresher than these soggy specimens," it said in that wet, hissing voice. "And you are soft. Aren't you?"

Bile rose up into my throat as I gave a gentle nod, not sure what else to do. My mind was racing. Did Reed see this creature as it caressed my skin? Would he save me from this, or was I on my own?

"A bit chilled though," the creature remarked, "and I like my lap to be warm." Suddenly there was a bowl in its hand, held up to my lips. I had no choice but to reluctantly open my mouth and let the liquid pour inside. The stuff was sickly sweet yet bitter all at once and I fought back tears as I gulped it down. I didn't want this, whatever this was. I wanted to pull an iron dagger from my hip and shove it into this creature's throat, slicing from end to end like a soldier in battle.

Warmth settled in my stomach and began drifting outward, heating me from the inside out with every drop of the saccharine concoction. It was pleasant at first, like being settled beneath a nest of blankets, but then it grew more intense. Sweat beaded at my hairline, my heartbeat raced, and the warmth in my stomach drifted lower. Something like lust rocked me and the heat in my face now flamed with embarrassment. *No.* No, I didn't feel this way. I couldn't. My chest grew sensitive, and it reminded me of youthful longing, groping against a tree or kissing a neck—things that made your heart race and your body search for more. For pleasure. *No, no, no.*

"That's better," the creature praised, as my breath came in heavier. I was...panting.

Its rough grip tightened on my arm, and it pulled me toward a table surrounded by oddly curved chairs. As inconspicuously as I dared, I searched the room for Reed again—for his broad shoulders and light hair—but only caught glimpses of gangly fae and eerie beings that slithered and crawled along the dance floor, then the circle of space where the human boy was still facing off against the abyssot guard. The snake-woman lay on the floor with her male companion standing over her and shouting encouragement to the glamoured slave. A proxy fight, maybe?

"Here, my little coal bag," cooed my captor.

Before I could think any more about the fight, the toady fae plopped into a chair and pulled me down into its lap, situating my legs to one side and wrapping its arms around me like a favored toy. Its chin rested on my shoulder, its thighs scraping against my skin when it shifted. The shirt Reed had lent me did little to protect me from the sharp, prickly texture of its body.

With no choice but to let my head fall back against the side of its neck, I closed my eyes, hoping this wine or potion or whatever I'd been drugged with would soon pass out of my system. My chest heaved a little with each breath and the creature seemed to derive great pleasure from the feel of my heated flesh against its chest. My body pulsed and ached, and I bit back a whimper. I had only felt this keyed up once before, when Flint had promised me the world and then forsaken me hours later.

Even being back in that dreaded memory was more tolerable than being on this creature's lap, so I let myself drift back to that hay-laden barn. I could remember the smell of horses and leather warming the cool winter air. There was a lantern hanging on a post to my left casting Flint's face in sharp relief as he looked upon me with dark desire. His mouth was wet and swollen from kissing me, his hands tracing over my neck and down past my breasts. He whispered so many sweet words into my skin—that he would never get enough of me, that I tasted so good, felt so good, so right, so hot, so gods-damned perfect against him. And then he said he loved me. The arousal consumed me, even as he turned me around and his loving caresses turned brutal.

The ring was on my finger, a promise as sure as his body moving against mine, though the metal was loose and a bit tarnished. I was still thrilled to be his. Finally, I would have the means to support my family until Conor could sell his inventions. I would have the freedom to follow the passions that struck me time and again—to act, to write, to weave dyed woolen strands into stories that children could read against their fingertips. We would have the money to escape before Harnsey became too volatile.

I was so full of love and lust I was bursting with it. That is, I had been, until, as we laid spent in the dark, he'd told me I'd misunderstood. He wasn't marrying me. He hadn't said anything of the sort.

The creature beneath me stroked a hand over my legs as if fascinated by them, dragging me back into the inglorious present, and I opened my eyes a fraction.

There, a bit to the side, was Reed, his back bent as he offered some tray to Jassin, the fight behind them apparently of little notice. The bulbous slimy creature I'd noticed before was pushing Reed's leg as if to trip him, but he only laughed and stepped to the side, presenting the tray again.

Please, help me, I wanted to scream. *Can't you see what's happening?*

I must have moved, or gasped, or made some infinitesimal shift, because the creature groaned and proceeded to rub its hand harder against me. If it pressed with any more force, I was sure my skin would break.

"I must show you to my companion," said the creature, his touch growing erratic. "To taunt him with my catch...he would give me passage into the king's room if he could only smell you." And then he was standing, pushing me with his hips, and then circling my waist with his hands to maneuver me. It was torture to take every step, my overheated body warring between terror and arousal. I couldn't even turn my head to see if Reed noticed the exodus.

"Jassin...is expecting me," I said, as emotionless as I could manage.

The fae paused, then pushed me again. "Oh, I'll bring you back at some point." Damn, I had hoped fear of the high fae who seemed to lord over the court would be enough to keep me safe. It became ever more apparent I had no idea the structure or rules of this place, and I feared it was now too late to learn.

My mind fogged, and when I blinked, I found myself standing at a large circular hole in the floor, which seemed to function as a passageway.

The room around us was barren, the walls marked with lines where water would rise and fall, the salt carving layers into the stone. We were alone.

Oh gods, we were alone.

CHAPTER SEVEN

M y heart was thumping painfully in my chest.

Was this thing about to push me down into the black abyss below? Or worse, take me with him? And once he "showed" me to his friend—what then? I shuddered to think of the possibilities.

Before I could think twice, I reached my hand into the collar of my shirt and tugged on the net within. The metal filings were sharp in my fingers as I yanked it up, ready to throw it over his toady head, but he was too quick.

His rough hand clasped my arm. "What are you—"

With a twist of my wrist, I managed to scrape at the back of his hand with the net. He released me, a surprised yelp echoing through the chamber.

I spun around, ready to sprint away, but something clutched at my tunic, holding me back.

"By order of Jassin, let go!" I shouted, but the fae only pulled me harder.

With one quick calculation, I kicked backward and bent low, ready to touch him with the net again, but the kick had been hard enough to have him flailing.

I heard a splash.

Checking behind me, I saw he'd disappeared down the hole, but there was no time to feel relief. I hurried to stuff the net back into my shirt and search the hall. There were a few normal doors and a set of stairs ahead. Which way had we come from? Could that thing jump back up from the water where he fell? Would he know I wasn't glamoured? My thoughts were frantic, but whatever the creature had planned for me was worse than fighting my way to freedom, even as unarmed as I was. I'd just have to pick a door and hope for the best.

A sound at the steps had me spinning, completely forgetting to school my features, and then I nearly sobbed as Reed bounded down the stairs.

"There you are!"

Another splash sounded from the hole beside me and Reed's body stiffened, panic sparking through his eyes. He held out his hand and I grabbed it like a lifeline.

"Come on."

We raced around a corner where I caught a glimpse of some kind of library—a collection of scrolls and moldy tomes in haphazard piles around a series of couches—and then we dashed through another door, this one leading to a small sitting room. Closing it silently behind us, Reed kept his ear to the wood. I tried to count my heartbeats in the time that passed, but it was too erratic. My face was still flushed, my hands and legs trembling, but eventually Reed straightened and turned to me, and I was able to let go of my panic.

Reacting on instinct, and the relief of being away from that manhandling monster, I hit him with a palm to his chest. Then again, harder.

"You left me to that...thing!" I whispered, ashamed to hear my voice break.

He grabbed my hand with his own.

"I'm so sorry. Are you okay?" His concerned expression was startling, as was the tenderness in his hold on my knuckles. I'd expected him to fight back or laugh off my discomfort.

The smooth normalcy of his skin against my sensitive flesh...I wanted to grip his shoulders and hold myself against him.

No. This craving was all from that disgusting drink.

Still, I couldn't help the rush of terror and relief and fury as it swirled through me.

I ripped my hand away. "No, I am not okay! His body was like barnacles, and he was going to give me to his friend..." My breath hitched. It was mortifying, to show so much emotion in front of this man I barely knew—this man who wasn't even fully a *man*—and yet...his grip had felt like a buoy in a storm. I regretted pulling away and...I wanted him. But it was only the poison I'd been fed, I reminded myself.

"I didn't expect..." Reed started, and then his face fell into ruin. "It was foolish of me. I apologize." His gaze moved over me, and I wondered if he saw the flush of my skin, or maybe just the bruises that were surely appearing from this afternoon's battle with the guards. "I hoped after mentioning you to the court I could excuse myself to drop you by the kitchens, but then that fight..."

He cleared his throat. "We'll have to come up with some other way to keep you here undetected. If you will stay." The way his voice lilted at the end, the unadulterated hope and rawness in his tone, had my heart twisting in my chest. What was it about him that made me believe what he said, despite all logic screaming I should run away? It was insane to be here in this room with a fae, even a half-fae. He could transform, meaning he could possibly glamour me as well. He could turn me in at any moment and I'd be killed or kept like some kind of pet by the monstrous beasts beyond this door. All I had against him was the knowledge that he wanted to break whatever indenture imprisoned him, but that didn't seem enough to guarantee my safety. Jassin's name apparently didn't strike fear in the way I'd assumed. And still, I found myself searching those sad blue eyes. They seemed to beg me to stay.

"You really think this perfumer of yours can help me find a cure?" I asked, trying to calm my jumbled thoughts, and then quickly added, "Tell me in a full sentence so I know you supposedly mean every word." *If* his claims about his inability to lie could be believed.

"I truly believe my friend Robin is your best chance at finding a remedy for your brother," he said, each word serious and sharp. "If you agree to help me break my contract, I will bring you to her."

Again, I wrestled with his word choice—my *best chance* could still be close to zero, he didn't specify *when* he would bring me to her, and he didn't promise me safety or protection along the way. I wondered if promises were something fae could even make. A promise was just a future truth, wasn't it? But if a future truth didn't come to pass, did that make it a lie? My head hurt with the tangle of it all.

"Fine," I muttered, and was shocked when he took my shoulders in both hands, pulling me into his chest in a crushing embrace.

"Thank you, Winnie," he said fervently.

I nodded.

"With any luck, Robin will have ideas on how to hide you, or at least your scent."

I pulled back, afraid if I spent too much time against him, I would do something foolish. "That's what that...*thing* said. That I smelled good enough he wanted to share me."

"I should have realized that would trump any other excitements." Reed nodded to himself, then looked around the room as if there might be something pertinent to our escape hiding behind one of the chair cushions. His eyes scanned over the pair of high-backed seats under hanging jars that glowed, an empty hearth, then a table laden with jagged crystals squatting off to the side.

"You smell like fresh air," he explained, rubbing one hand over his mouth to scratch at his facial hair. "When the tide goes out again, the decaying scent of the marsh seeps in and nestles in the walls and fabrics. That is why Robin is so popular among the gentile—she's becoming proficient at masking the rank."

"If it smells bad here and the fae don't like it, why do you stay?" I asked.

"This castle has existed for eons," he replied, moving around the room. I watched him pick up a rose-colored crystal from the table, inspect it, and place it back exactly where he'd plucked it from. His body was restless, his steps short in the small room, but with his wide chest and tall stature it might as well have been a broom closet. "The royals aren't going to abandon it just because the marsh has gone...putrid. They assume it's temporary, though I think we know it might have something to do with the nearby towns." At that, he turned to me with a pointed look.

"Are you...accusing me of something?" I crossed my arms over my chest, thankful that the sensitivity there was beginning to fade.

"Not at all." Reed scuffed his booted foot along the thin carpet, as if scraping off some mud. "Just noting that your people are infants compared to the history of this compound, and it's only in the last decade or so the smell has worsened. It could be waste from your people, or maybe you're hunting some aquatic animal that cleans the water or consumes rotten-smelling plants. Who knows?" he shrugged. "I don't claim to be an expert on the health of the land. But, regardless, you aren't yet tainted by the castle, which is why some might find you…too alluring to ignore."

"I see." I looked away from him, suddenly feeling vulnerable. I could play pretend and act like a mindless fool, but my smell wasn't something I had any control of—not if the hours trekking through the mangroves hadn't altered it enough to matter. That could pose a real problem.

"So, do fights like that usually garner such…uneven attention?" I asked, still trying to wrap my mind around what had happened. "And what was with that snake woman falling unconscious after she bit the guard?"

"Violence in the court is prohibited," Reed answered. "If you strike someone or do anything with the intention to physically harm them, the castle puts you down. It's a sort of magic that's been embedded in the walls, which is a shame because if it was a living fae's magic keeping it running, it may have ended with whatever disruption the court has been dealing with. I could be watching them all tear each other to pieces now and hope someone takes out Jassin for me." He shook his head. "Regardless, the effect only lasts a few hours, but it means you're helpless if you were the one to hit first. Human slaves—" he halted, as if apologetic of the term, "are used in place of fae to settle disputes like that, but given how few remain, I was surprised the lendani were willing to risk their servant. It must have been because she traveled with her mate and thought he'd protect her."

Ah, so lendani must be the name for the snakelike fae with human faces. And apparently even lower fae who weren't royalty could have human *slaves*. I fought a snarl as I remembered the young boy holding the broken glass. Was he dead now? Considered another runaway who disappeared forever?

"I don't mean to make you uncomfortable," said Reed, and I looked up to see him finally settling into one of the chairs.

Reluctantly, I followed, though my attention was always partially on the door behind us. There was no lock, and for all I knew that spiny-skinned creature would come barreling inside. Or something worse. Given his apparently low standing here, Reed likely wouldn't be able to stop any creatures who set their sights on me. Every moment in this compound was a risk.

"I want to believe you about all this. About what you say you can do," I told him, after a moment of silence had strained and stretched between us. "But I'm at a disadvantage here. I don't know much about the fae beyond what I've read, and other than a weakness to iron everything else seems suspect."

"And you have some solution to this?" Reed asked. His leg was jiggling with nerves, or some excess energy, and I found my fingertips tapping against my thigh, as if to mimic him. It was a habit from childhood I'd never outgrown, and I briefly considered asking him to stop just so maybe my own body would settle. But it was a distraction I could not afford.

"I do," I replied. "Tell me truths you don't want me to know. Give me some kind of power here. I know you're strong, and that you can heal. You understand the layout of this castle and the creatures that roam its halls. I have nothing but one dagger, and you wouldn't even permit it on my person." I wasn't about to tell him how I fended off the toady fae, in case I needed to turn that very weapon against him.

"If you had a knife under your skirt, would you have kept your murderous impulses in check while that creature pawed at you?" he asked, instead of answering. I had to admit he had a point, but I would not be diverted.

"Please," I added, since the word had held so much power when he'd uttered it earlier. "Give me something."

The request seemed to pain him, and he leaned his elbows on his knees, even while his one leg continued to quiver and shake. He sighed, rubbing a hand over his hair.

"Fair enough, little perch. You want some truths." His gaze met mine. "I entered into this contract to save my father, a pathetic human my mother seduced and left for dead. He survived her attack but still maintained his affection for her. He stayed by the marsh for years, hoping to catch glimpses of her in the water. And one day, he grew sick." Reed paused and cleared his throat, his sapphire eyes dropping to glare at the ground as if with disgust. "I...I wasn't supposed to spend time with him, but I couldn't help myself. He was nicer than the people here—he didn't kick at me or throw me into the brackish water. Though he was poor from having no job, I thought he was a genius—at least I did when I was young. He taught me how to tie a net, how to catch dragonflies to make wishes on them...foolish things like that. So, when he started to wither and die, I approached Jassin about a way to save him."

"Jassin is the fae you serve?" I asked, making sure I understood. "The one you needed to present me to?"

Reed nodded. "He's a friend of the prince, and always at court, whereas the royals disappear from time to time. I knew it was a mistake to ask him, but I did it anyway. He had magic enough to give my father more years of life, slowing his aging down to that of a syra, like my mother, but the price would be service until it was worth it to let me go."

"That's not...very specific," I commented.

"And yet, I agreed. Because I was blinded with love." He sounded appalled by himself.

I wished there was a fire in the hearth, or a window I could gaze out of, because the pain and disappointment on his face was hard to witness.

"If you loved him, then I don't think it was a mistake," I said at last.

"And that, my dear, is where you are wrong." His lips flattened into a smile that was both wry and self-deprecating. "Jassin slowed my father's aging, but the next week I found his corpse by the bend where we would meet."

"Was it…" I started, but I almost didn't want to know. This story could be my own, so desperate to save my family that I had walked into my doom. If this was a premonition of my own failure, it would perhaps be more pleasant to remain ignorant.

"It wasn't Jassin," said Reed. "He was honorable in that respect. It was my mother who killed him. She heard about my deal with the high fae and took matters into her own webbed hands to free me from my father's 'repulsively human influence'—her words, not my own. She was afraid he was making me soft in a world that already saw me as deficient, and she was right. But it was too late." His jittery leg finally stopped, and the stillness was almost somehow worse. "The court already hated me for what I was, and now they knew I'd been willing to sell my body and my time for the life of one human man—a man who did nothing but pine for the creature that wounded and left him."

I was quiet for a long moment while I digested his story. It was so tragically romantic, and yet awful to hear, not unlike the dramas on my shelves back home. I wanted to comfort him somehow, or get revenge on his behalf, but I supposed my presence here was enough of both. I doubted he'd make up such a tale just to placate me, especially one that painted him as wanting, so I was inclined to believe him.

"Your mother…" I said into the space between us. "Where is she now? And you said she is a syra? I'm not sure I know—"

"What that is?" he finished. "It's what your people call merkind. But there are different breeds—some more deadly than others, some that can be human when they wish. Some with power and some without. My mother…she could transform into the water itself, which is also a common high fae power, becoming a wave or a whirlpool or a simple eddy to tug you back to shore. It's why I have the power to change, though my human father diluted the ability to something more intangible. As for where she is," he tilted his head, his blue gaze piercing against my own, "when she found out my deal would not end when my father died, she left. She was revolted by me."

"What you did was honorable," I said, almost to myself.

"What I did was stupid beyond belief, and it is my greatest regret," he retorted, and then seemed to shake himself out of his misery. That bright, counterfeit smile transformed the mask of his face. "As for other truths—I keep a stash of tradable goods in a dungeon two stories below my room for when I eventually escape this place. My favorite dream is one where I dig underground and find buried treasure made of nothing but golden oysters. I once harbored an infatuation with a kelavee woman who refused me by shaving off all of my hair. And the first time I saw you I fought the desire to kill you and bring your body to Jassin to prove my worth, while also simultaneously wanting to protect you like a helpless hatchling." He paused. "Do those help?"

My hands met in my lap, fingers clenching tight against one another. If I knew where he was keeping supplies, it could be used as a bargaining chip. The rest didn't offer me much leverage, only pieces of his life here.

None of them painted him in a favorable light, which felt purposeful, and I appreciated that sense of integrity. It didn't hurt that while he'd spun his history for my perusal, my body had calmed from the terror and unwanted sensations of my attack.

Maybe, for once, I could trust a man's word as truth. Unlike Flint, unlike my father, this man was sitting in front of me with his vulnerability presented like a buffet.

All I had to do was bite.

"It does help," I answered, lifting my chin. "Take me to Robin and help me get my cure, and I will do my best to break your contract with Jassin. Through lies if I can...through murder if I must."

Reed's smile, for once genuine and not falsely bright, was like lightning breaking through a dark night.

CHAPTER EIGHT

We waited over an hour in that tiny room before Reed felt it was safe enough to return to his bedchamber. To pass the time I asked him a series of questions that came to mind—things like what his favorite foods were, how many exits the castle had, and the first time he learned he could heal himself by transforming into that dark smoke. He gave me each answer like a story, and I learned to stop him and ask for certain sentences to be rephrased, so I could ensure they were truthful. It was almost amusing how he could spin a statement into truth. When I asked if he liked soup, he replied about flavors that were pleasant to fae palates, but that wasn't actually his personal opinion. It wasn't a real answer.

"I'll surely be whipped tomorrow for disappearing," he said with a wry smile, as we cautiously left the room, "but it's nothing I haven't suffered through before. Honestly, at this point, the whole spectacle of Jassin's irascible punishments has grown almost boring."

"How can he whip you if the castle doesn't permit violence?" I asked, keeping my voice low. Though I could see drafts of weak morning sunlight creeping in from hallways we passed, I still worried the raucous partygoers from court were still wandering about. Thankfully, whatever concoction I'd been forced to drink had finally drained from my system, and my skin felt cool to the touch as Reed towed me onward.

"He'll take me outside, or have his human slaves do the dirty work for him."

"Humans have whipped you?"

He nodded, saying nothing, and I swallowed the need to apologize on behalf of my species. It was wrong, but it wasn't their fault if they were forced to hurt him. It was Jassin's fault—this court's fault. Everything here was so monstrous.

"What will you tell Jassin?" I murmured instead. "About where you went?"

"I'll say I closed myself in a room with a young woman to have my way with her."

My feet tripped over the uneven stone floor. "What? But that's not true."

"It is, to a degree." He shrugged, but I could not tell if the movement indicated guilt or humor. "My way was simply not the kind you might assume. I *did* get what I wanted from you."

A hallway opened on the left and my gaze caught on two horse-like kelavees guarding the open door to what appeared to be a laboratory of some kind. I glimpsed smoking vials that reminded me of Conor's set up and thick books stacked haphazardly.

"What is—"

Reed shushed me and pulled harder on my hand. "That hall is dangerous, and so are the creatures there. You don't want to get too close."

I wondered how one hall could be more deadly than another in this hazardous place, but before I could ask anything else, we reached a staircase that was partially flooded. Reed hefted me into his arms to descend the set of stairs, his movements slow as he carefully maneuvered the watery way down. The water passed his hips, almost touching my bottom, but he only inched me higher against his chest as we turned down another narrow passageway, the subtle incline eventually pulling us out of the mire so he could release me. I shook my head, disturbed by the way the levels and shapes of the castle made less sense the further we traveled.

The barred entryway of his room was somehow a relief to behold. However, it was achingly cold inside, and I watched Reed drop to his meager hearth, working to raise the near-extinct flame. After it flared to life, he then chucked off his wet breeches without a thought.

"Honestly!" I gasped, turning away, but not before I caught sight of those scars. And his sculpted backside.

I could hear him chuckle behind me. "It's endearing how proper and prudish you are—is that a trait common to all humans?"

"All humans with a sense of decency," I grumbled, then stole a look over my shoulder to see him pulling on the pants he'd left to dry earlier. "How do you have scars if you can heal by turning into that...smoke?"

Reed flopped onto the low mattress that was situated unerringly close to the fireplace. The shirt he wore rode up an inch as he placed his hands behind his head, dastardly comfortable. That strip of skin seemed to mock me as I glanced around, wondering where I should sleep, or if there were any other blankets I might use to fashion some kind of nest.

"If I transformed and healed, they would simply inflict the injuries again. I learned long ago that one punishment was enough." He cleared his throat. "Now come," he said, gesturing to the other side of his bed with the tilt of his jaw.

"I'd rather not," I confessed.

Reed closed his eyes on a laugh, as if he found me utterly ridiculous. "Well, I'd rather you did," he replied. "It will get cold as the tide comes in through the tunnels. You'll want the body heat, and I know I would appreciate it as well."

The room held so few fixtures I understood there was no other suitable place to rest, but part of me still resisted, postponing the moment I knew was ultimately coming.

"If you're half...syra," I continued, my tongue thick on the unfamiliar word, "then why aren't you immune to things like the cold? If your mother lived in the marsh, I imagine she's accustomed to all sorts of ghastly conditions."

"Another downfall of my breeding." His cheery tone turned sour. "Now, come on. The castle is more asleep than not during daylight hours, but I'll be expected to help in the kitchens, clean horrifying messes, and serve Jassin when he wakes in the late afternoon. I swear I won't force any sexual advances on you. We'll just sleep."

The idea of sharing a bed was at once titillating and also unsavory. He was a gorgeous man, to be sure, with low-tilted eyes that made him seem even-tempered, a broad and built body that I was sure would feel solid against my own, and ears that poked out from his golden hair like dainty shells, giving him an innocent, friendly air. I still wasn't convinced that I could wholly trust him, but for now it seemed we needed each other, and that would have to be enough.

I sighed. "Fine."

For my brother I would do this, and I would pretend it was a hardship.

As soon as I was settled on the pallet, Reed turned toward me and pulled me against his chest.

"What are you doing?" I said with a squeal, fighting to free myself.

"Leave me be!"

"Body heat, remember?" His breath fanned over my neck, and I froze. It brought back images of Flint and that barn—the way his hands caressed my body with adoration until his harsher passion took over, his grip turning brutal. He'd left me cold after using and disposing me. His gaze had been stony. He'd cut me with his words, ruined my heart, and all he cared about was adjusting his clothes.

Reed must have felt my breath hitch or my pulse jump because the calloused hand he used to bracket my body lightened, his thumb stroking over the skin of my arm.

"Forgive me, Winnie," he said. "I didn't mean to scare you."

"It's fine," I said without thinking. It really wasn't.

Forcibly unclenching my muscles, I attempted to relax into his hold, begrudgingly pleased by his heat at my back. And then, as if he had cast some kind of spell, I was pulled into a dreamless sleep.

I couldn't tell how much time had passed when I awoke, but I could tell from the air at my back that Reed was absent from the bed, having untangled himself from me without my notice. I wasn't sure why that had me blushing.

What had woken me was the sound of the door closing and I opened my eyes to see him holding a cloth-wrapped parcel in his hands. He was wearing the same clothing as last night and I wondered if he had anything else to wear beyond the two sets I'd seen him in so far.

"I've come to deliver your breakfast, little perch." He placed the package beside my shoulder with a flourish, and I sat up, suddenly ravenous. There were some hard buns inside, and a tin of red jam that smelled like lotus flowers. Inside a separate cloth, there were warm sausages with an oddly fishy odor. I didn't think I would eat them unless I had no other option.

Using a flat knife made from shale, I smeared jam on the bun and devoured the meal with fierce bites while Reed once again tended to the fire. I wondered if he ever let it burn completely out, or if this was some ritual he could exert his limited control over, similar to the way I used playtime with Conor to release any creative ideas that had been percolating in my mind. It was the one occasion where I was the expert and executive of my own faculties, free to follow any path I could dream into existence. I could be a countess with silk shoes who wove riddles for Conor to solve, to win his place as my bodyguard, or I could made us a new dance—letting my feet carry me over the tall grasses, left and back and left again, spinning—pretending I'd learned it at a foreign court and humming to some imaginary song.

"Are you alright?" Reed asked, and I realized I had been staring off into space, my fingers sticky with traces of berry jam. "Do your bruises hurt you?"

I wiped my hands along the cloth, reaching for another bun. My jaw was a bit sore from being struck yesterday, but he didn't need to know of any weaknesses I might harbor. "I'm fine, just thinking. Did you already do your chores for the day?"

Reed shook his head. "I've helped in the kitchen, but I must leave you for a bit before I can take you to Robin. I have a whole host of duties I'll need to speed through to make up for my absence last night."

"I'm to just...stay here?"

"Unless you'd rather help me clean waste from the dungeons and risk being seen unglamoured," he offered, tone dry.

I didn't answer, instead choosing to focus on my breakfast.

"I took a book from the castle's measly archives on my way back," he said, fetching the bowl of water he'd used on my cuts the night before. "It's at the bottom of the bag, under the meat. It's not some exorbitant listing, but it does reference a few of the fae that commonly reside here. You could study up a bit, so you don't die of boredom."

"Oh," I said around a mouthful, "thank you." It was oddly considerate of him. I dug for the book and started flipping through the moldy pages, hoping I didn't look too impressed.

"I'll be back as soon as I can," he said, opening the door. "Don't leave this room. And try the sausages."

I bristled at the command, but he was gone before I could respond, and the sensation of being left in the quiet, windowless room felt eerily similar to a pet being left chained in a pen. I should have been used to it, constantly home with Conor while our mother tarried at her workshop, sweating over her potter's wheels, but at least then I had my brother for company. His incessant mumbling as he twiddled with formulas and tightened springs on his inventions was like the constant noise of an ocean tide. But now there was only the weak fire beside me.

Shaking off my melancholy, I decided to do as Reed suggested while I finished my breakfast and studied the book in my lap. There were illustrations of the lendani, the sketches colored in with murky water which had stained the page. The snake-woman's elongated fingers were tipped dark with poison and her long tail wrapped around her prey, squeezing it to near bursting. Then there were visceral descriptions of kelavee bodies that bordered on obscene, the garish transition from horse to fish to human a spectrum that seemed open for interpretation. Their bodies were based entirely on phases of the moon and the temperature of the water the creature inhabited.

The monster that had molested me at dinner had been a crogwyn—commonly known to tear limbs off each other in battle for territory—which were built with thick bodies and tapering limbs so they vaguely resembled a humanoid starfish. They were a sexless species that repopulated by stretching themselves like wet dough, spawning from the excess toad-like flesh they shed. I shivered at the image that evoked, wondering why it had been so eager to keep my body close if there had been nothing sexual about the advances. That clean smell, I supposed.

There were manyda, which were essentially sentient eels that flashed colorful lights when they moved, and beautiful depictions of syra, the dainty mermaids sometimes lean like minnows, sometimes wider than sharks. In one depiction, the syra was half-hidden in the depth of dark water, her hair floating toward the surface, her skin scaled with blue and gray, and her fanged mouth bared in preparation to strike at a lone flounder.

This was the being that gave birth to Reed?

I struggled to connect him to the picture at my fingers. He was just so...light. In coloring, in temperament, and in his very presence and body heat.

I could still recall in perfect clarity the strength of his hold on me, the secure weight of him. I could have sworn his nose grazed the back of my hair before I succumbed to sleep, but it might have been the whispers of a dream, or an echo of the past.

When the tome offered me nothing more, I doctored the flame back to full height and then paced around my cage. With my stomach not entirely satisfied, I eventually attempted the sausages Reed had left with the smallest nibble and—despite their smell—I was surprised to find them deliciously seasoned and sweet with something like honey. I dared not ask him what they were made of when he returned, but for now they would keep my strength up for whatever step we undertook next.

With hours gone, my agitation at being told to stay put gradually transformed into suspicion. Yes, it was dangerous for me to wander around the castle, but why had Reed been so adamant about that one hallway? Why couldn't I continue to search for a cure on my own? So long as I appeared glamoured, I would look just like another servant on an errand, right? And he *did* say that during the daytime the fae were less active.

Armed with my new knowledge of the creatures in the castle, I dressed in the same clothes as the night before—this time tying my dagger to my waist under my shirt along with the net tucked into my breastband—and took hold of the empty breakfast basket as I tentatively opened the door.

I peeked around the empty cells, watching the sparse torches along the walls battle the inky darkness, and closed the door behind me, taking one final breath before I slipped on my best mask of detachment.

Keeping my steps woozily drifting from side to side, I meandered back the way we'd come the night before, retracing my steps. A metal door clanged to the right and I flinched before continuing on, the slithering sound of a lendani grating against my ears until it faded down another hall. Was it late afternoon now? According to the book, they only woke near sunset, preferring to hunt during twilight.

A trilling laughter sounded ahead, and I paused, wondering if I should take another route. My feet were silent against the stone floor as I stepped to the side, trying to peer around the corner to determine if it was a high fae laughing ahead, where I might convince them with my acting that I was looking for Jassin, or a low fae, where I might become some stupid beast's meal.

"Yes, apologies for the stain," a voice replied, and I nearly gasped in recognition.

Reed.

Hells.

Turning on my heel, I hurried back the short distance I'd traveled, trying not to panic. I didn't want him to know I'd disobeyed his command, but it wasn't like he'd given me much of a choice after all. He'd left me here with little to do and no way of knowing when he'd return.

As I closed myself back in his room and dove onto the bed, I rustled up my earlier disdain, ready to berate him for abandoning me for hours when I could have been searching for my brother's cure.

He finally barreled through the door, only for my grievances to vanish. There was blood on him, from chest to knee, in streaks and splotches that trickled wetly down to his feet. *Apologies for the stain*, he'd said.

Instinctively, I stood, my gut twisting at the sight of him.

"What happened?" I asked as he closed the door and stumbled to the slumping box that housed his belongings.

"Just what we assumed, little perch," he huffed. "No need to worry."

"Stop calling me that. And I think the blood trailing your steps would beg to differ on the worrying front," I argued, rushing to his side. I wasn't sure if there was anything I could do for him, but sitting on his bed while he bled onto the floor seemed uncouth.

"Mostly shallow," he assured me.

He pulled a jar from the depth of the box and placed it on the floor before gingerly tugging his shirt up over his head. The sight of the slashes beneath had my head spinning. He'd been whipped from shoulder to backside, and if the spots on his clothes were to be believed, he would have some wounds on his chest as well.

"Dab this onto my back at the worst of it, would you?" He asked, tone pleasant.

"Excuse me?"

He pushed the jar toward me, and I looked between it and his shredded skin. Sure, it was "mostly" shallow, in the sense that I could not see bone, but it must have been horrific to experience. The worst discomfort I'd encountered were the vicious monthly bleedings my own body subjected me to, with crunching pains and an aching back, but this...this was a level I could not viscerally imagine.

"Please," he said, and that damned word did me in again, prodding me into action.

I made room for him to sit on the bed, but he insisted on staying on the floor so as to keep the sheets clean. He sat on the cold stones with his side to the fire. I watched him stretch a hand toward the flame, as if relishing any bit of heat he could find.

"I'm sorry. This is because of me," I said, feeling guilty that I had just been sneaking out against his wishes. I could have landed him in even more trouble, and then maybe his wounds *would* have been life threatening, instead of just grisly and terrible.

I began gently dabbing the paste onto the worst of his wounds, the balm smelling of licorice. It felt like wet sand on my fingers.

"This is not worth fretting over, I promise," he replied. "I just need them to stop bleeding before we head back into the water, otherwise I wouldn't bother wasting the mallow."

"Mallow?" I asked.

Reed dipped his head with a hiss as I applied the fixative to a particularly long strike.

"Robin made it for me," he said between uneven breaths. I watched him swallow and wondered if the pain was about to make him sick. "I think you'll like her."

Something like envy tingled at my fingers, which I could only assume was a side effect of the herbs now collecting under my fingernails.

"I'm...sure I will."

The quiet lengthened between us, his uneven breaths slowing. The bloody skin under my fingertips grew warmer.

"Has Robin—have you known her long?" I asked to shoo off the silence.

"Since I was small. She has a horrible habit of taking care of me."

"You sound unhappy about it," I noted.

Reed winced, the movement slight enough to be a shiver. "I just know the scales between us will never be even."

"Is that why you've never asked her to kill Jassin for you?"

At that, his whole body stiffened. "There are rules even free fae cannot break, powers the court holds over inhabitants that have layers of meaning and protections. It would be no easy thing for her to get Jassin out of the castle, let alone overpower him, but even then—" He breathed out a short groan at one of the final slashes I applied the paste to.

"Sorry, I—"

"We can discuss this another time." Shoulders flexing, he stood. Apparently, he deemed himself appropriately covered in the mallow mixture, though I had yet to see what had been done to his front. "Come on, we need to hurry if we're to get there and back before true dark."

After dropping his bloody tunic into his basin of water and pulling on his shirt from the day before—proving my conspiracies about his lacking wardrobe—Reed waited while I dressed in the fresh pants and tunic I'd brought with me. I caught him peering at the fabric, as if wondering what it was made of, but he asked nothing as he took my hand and opened the door.

"Remember," he muttered, "if you see anyone approach or anything watching, keep your sight straight ahead and your body limp."

"Yes, I know how to act like a sleepwalking fool," I retorted.

"Just checking."

This time, when he led me from the castle, I endeavored harder to memorize the turns and stairs we used, forcing them into a tune in my head. *Left and down, before you drown, you take a right, and tiptoe light, pass three doors, another floor, you travel low, and here we go.*

Reed was right that more of the compound was now flooded, and even the dry floors bore remnants of slime. It made sense, given the populace of the court—so many of the beings in that book of fae he'd lent me were water-dwelling, or required some sunless cavern to lurk in.

We used a different exit, this one wider and smoother, the tube-like tunnel leading down into the water. While we were encased in shadows, I could see a green-tinted light beckoning from the end and there were inches of water at our feet, rising until it was up to our knees, and then the ground disappeared.

Reed held onto my hand as we landed in the mangrove, his hold tight as we began wading through a thick layer of floating algae and tiny, yellow flowers that tickled my skin.

Soon enough, it was so deep I couldn't touch the bottom, so I swam behind Reed in slow, steady strokes, wondering how his open cuts would fare against the kind of villainous insects, fish, and muck saturating them as he moved. He still wore a shirt over them, so I couldn't be sure if they leaked, but the strong tick of his shoulder muscles seemed stable. He must have been accustomed to ignoring such pain...

He turned to seize me and a heartbeat later I saw the monster swimming towards us. It was one of the syra, her skin a series of green and brown stripes over tall fins which breached the water like a shark. I knew from Reed's book that beneath my sight she was using her webbed hands to speed through the marsh, whipping into high kelp and snatching young groupers and pinfish in her fanged mouth. Keeping myself still was a test in daring, but I managed to float listlessly at Reed's back while he tugged me along, as if I were no more than a buoyant log.

Once she was truly gone, he released me, and we went back to swimming independently. The only difference was now I couldn't stop imagining all the other creatures that might swim underneath my vulnerable body, unnoticed in the ripple of our movements. I had to trust Reed would sense or see them before it could happen.

"Are we almost there?" I whispered, my voice low enough not to echo against the sporadic cypress trunks.

He grunted in the affirmative just as we approached a wall of rock that emerged from the tree line like a faceless giant peeking through shrubberies. There were all manner of flowers and ferns growing off its surface, and craggy holes that might house the stuff of nightmares, but he pointed at an oval-shaped opening to the right, and we aimed for it with sure strokes of our arms.

The cavern hovered a few hand lengths above the surface and Reed lifted himself with impressive ease before reaching down and pulling me up after him. His grip was rough and strong, and I wondered if his half-fae heritage gave him an advantage there, or if his muscles were purely self-made.

"That wasn't so bad, was it?" Reed asked. And then something smacked into him from behind. He stumbled and turned to see what had hit him.

I held back a scream at the sight of his back; it was covered in a thick splatter of fresh blood.

CHAPTER NINE

"Reed!" I hissed, hands up to my mouth, just as malicious laughter echoed throughout the cavern.

He looked confused, one eyebrow raised at my expression, and then he attempted to peek over his shoulder to see his back. He groaned.

"Robin, did you have to?"

The laughter became high and twinkling, then devolved into distracted humming.

"What..." I started.

Reed reached over his shoulder and wiped his fingers along the mess. "It's just beach berries, little perch," he assured me, licking his hand. "Though it would be nice not to be struck so soon after my *morning whipping*." He raised his voice at the end and the humming stopped.

"Moons, I'm sorry," came the high voice, and Reed finally shifted enough to the side for me to see the magnificent woman behind him. She was standing at a long table littered with vials, vases, and bowls, with candles dotting the surface in clusters of twos and threes. Her long arms were paused over her work.

The roof of the cavern was actually shorter than I imagined, or maybe it just seemed that way from the extensive field of flowers and herbs hanging upside-down from unseen hooks. But even without the low ceiling, Robin would have seemed unreasonably tall. Her dark hair was tied in a loose tail behind her, showing off her pointed ears, and she wore frighteningly little clothes—there was a loose sheath of graying fabric over her breasts that draped down just far enough to cover her hips, which might have reached my chest if we stood side-by-side. She watched Reed with the black eyes of a full fae, then turned that gaze on me. I fought the desire to step backward.

"What have you brought me, Reedling?"

"Reedling?" I echoed, momentarily distracted from the feeling of imminent danger currently flooding my veins from just standing in this cave.

"Ignore that," said Reed. He walked further into the cavern and turned to peer at his back in a tall mirror I hadn't noticed leaning off to the side. "Curse you, did you have to ruin my only other shirt today?"

"You should know better than to drop by unannounced," said Robin with a genteel shrug. "I thought you were Orym."

"I look nothing like Orym," he argued, turning from his reflection.

"Am I to eat the human?" Robin retorted, and at that I *did* retreat with the tiniest shuffle back toward the gaping hole we'd entered through.

Reed waved his arm toward me, as if presenting an actor in a grand play. "Robin, this is Winnie. She's going to help me break my contract."

Robin's face seemed to pinch, and I could tell she had little confidence in my abilities. Not that I felt much better—I had no idea how I was going to lie or murder Reed's way out of Jassin's clutches, but I was taking it one moment at a time, one problem at a time. Hopefully we could come up with that plan together later.

"She's unglamoured?" Robin asked, leaving her table to prowl closer. Her movements were fluid and graceful despite her height, and I briefly entertained the imagery of her dancing in leaps and bounds across a stage, a besotted prince falling to his knees under her haughty observation.

"I am," I said, at Reed's encouraging nod.

"Well...that sure is something," she replied.

"Can you help her?" Reed asked. "I need her to smell less...fresh. And less human, preferably." He leaned his forearms on the table and began plucking various vials from the surface, sniffing each of them in turn. Robin moved so fast she was almost invisible, and then she smacked the vessel from his hand.

"I can make her smell horrid if that's what you want," Robin offered, moving around the table with practiced ease and picking up a mortar and pestle to grind something to powder. "But I don't think changing her scent will make anyone believe she is fae. Maybe a halfling like you, but I doubt that will get you anywhere."

"Please, Robin?"

His grin was charming, his blond hair flopping about his ears. I wondered how often that damned word had gotten Reed everything he wanted and more—it seemed to drown strong wills like a monsoon of charisma.

I couldn't tell if Robin was capable of rolling her eyes—the entire space between her lashes was an onyx slate—but given the way she tilted her head to the ceiling, I thought she must have been.

"You really are a pain. Fine, let me think..." she trailed off and moved to the back of the cave where a multi-drawered bureau tilted precariously on the uneven stone ground. She began rummaging through the wooden drawers one by one. "If only I could make her taller."

It was awkward to stand near the mouth of the cavern with my hands clenched at my thighs, so I inched closer to Reed at the table.

"Don't forget your side of the deal," I mumbled, low enough I hoped only he could hear me.

"Ah. Right." He rapped his knuckles on the wood, the move overly casual. "Also, Robin...Winnie would use your knowledge for her own personal issue. She has an ill brother she'd like to heal."

Robin turned her head to look behind her. "Are you sure? I have seven brothers and I'd be elated to see a few of them drop dead."

"Um, I-I'm sure," I said, hating the stutter.

"Very well." She turned back to the drawers and seemed to find what she was looking for—a small metal flask, like one I would see in town. "Drink this. We'll see if it works."

"This will make me smell like fae?" I asked, as she handed it to me.

"I'm not entirely sure what it will do," Robin replied. "But it can apparently...*brighten* traces of fae. All humans tend to have a little bit of us swimming in their blood. While we wait for it to take hold I'll help you with this brother calamity." She aimed a wry look at Reed. "You just keep running up your tally, don't you?" There was a pause as she smiled, the first true one I'd seen from her, and it was wide and sharp and mildly terrifying.

I hesitated to drink whatever potion swirled in the flask, knowing it was both untested and apparently a mark against Reed in some way, but there really was no other option than to unscrew the metal lid and take a swig.

There was surprisingly little liquid inside, and it reminded me of the cream sauce one would put in a hand pie. I didn't want to think about what it could be made of, so I swallowed it down quickly.

"Now," said Robin, straightening to her full height to look down at me, "tell me about this brother of yours." She took the empty flask and placed it somewhere behind her.

It was easy to describe the bite mark I'd seen on Conor's skin, and the way he had slowly started transforming afterward; I'd been thinking of nothing else for weeks. Robin listened with a thoughtful expression, despite her menacing pose, and then stared off into the space beyond my shoulder. I noticed Reed was back to jiggling his leg even as stood, which was causing tiny droplets of water from his pants to speckle along the puddle we'd made on the floor.

"It sounds like an anglock got him," she said eventually. "They're rare this far north but they've been known to periodically visit court. They each have their own unique flower that grows from their head, like an extra limb, and they lie in wait for prey to come by and either land on it or attempt to take it. Mostly mud creatures, I think, so they tend to go for small critters, but if your brother was bitten, he could have had a strange reaction to their toxins. Typically, it freezes their victims in place so they can pull them into the water and slowly chomp away." She shrugged again, her speech detached and aloof. "Must not have injected enough into him to do so."

Heat flooded my cheeks, and I wondered vaguely if it was some side effect of the potion I'd just drunk, or irritation that she was discussing the fate of my brother with such blatant impartiality.

"So, is there a remedy?" I asked between clenched teeth.

It was then that my vision became spotty, the world tilting beneath my feet.

"Winnie?" I heard Reed call out. His voice was far away and then echoing. Too close, too loud.

I kept to my feet by bracing myself on the table, accidentally scattering a few bottles and candles under my hand.

"Sorry, I just..." I placed a palm to my head, blinking hard against the sensation of being drunkenly dizzy. Robin moved and I tried to follow her with my eyes, but it was like they didn't obey me any longer.

"Perfect," she said, like a whisper in my ear. The feel of her breath against my face had me recoiling, but then Reed's strong arms were around me, his touch unerringly gentle as he kept me steady.

The woozy sensation faded, and I could once again feel my legs under me and the cold of the wet clothes dragging against my skin.

"Was that...the potion?" I asked, turning my face to Reed.

His lips parted in a shallow gasp.

"What?"

He separated from me only to place his fingers under my jaw and tilt my head from side to side. My eyesight finally settled enough so I could see the blue irises of his eyes as they traced my features, moving from my mouth to my eyes to my...ears.

On instinct I reached up to my hair and felt the tip of my ear. It was sharper and longer than before.

"You did it," Reed said in fascination. "She's remarkable." He released me and gestured to the mirror I'd noticed before.

At first, I couldn't discern much of a difference, but as I walked closer to the glass, I could see the black that had flooded my eyes and the points of my ears that were breaking through my wet hair. When I opened my mouth, even my teeth looked slightly different—pointed more on either side. My bruises had also faded. I looked...fae. Except for the unfortunate truth of my height.

"I'm still short, though," I said, and even the grumble of my voice was different, the tone slightly changed to something sweeter and more melodic.

"We can tell people you're a baby," Robin offered.

"A what?" I said, turning from the inspection I'd been giving my teeth.

"That might work," Reed agreed. "So long as no one recognizes her from last night."

"I don't understand..."

"Fae lives are quite long compared to your human years," Robin explained. "Pretend to be only forty or so years old if someone asks, and they should believe you still have time to grow." And then she went back to her table as if bored with the lot of us.

Forty was equivalent to a baby? That would work in my favor if I said or did something wrong, I supposed; apparently forty years wouldn't be long enough to know better. But still...how bizarre.

I looked behind Robin to where the flask stood, innocently leaning against a stack of books, and then at Reed as he crossed his arms and paced the small confines of the cavern. He was muttering to himself various reasons a young fae might wander into another territory, thinking of lies I could spin.

"Reed...why isn't this something you've tried?" This potion could be the solution to the discrimination he faced every day from the fae. Robin was friendly with him, sure, but every other creature I'd come across had either ignored him or been outright hostile.

"It's temporary," Robin offered, before he could respond, "and expensive. Plus, I only got my hands on this dose a few years ago. Jassin would have noticed if one day Reed sprouted fins."

"Still would have been nice to know it existed," Reed griped. His eyebrows pinched together and he stared at his feet for a moment as if deep in thought, the omission clearly upsetting him.

Robin didn't look up from her work. "The effects will probably only last a few days, so use it wisely. I'm just surprised it took so well to you."

"Thanks, I guess," I said, feeling awkward with the whole exchange. "And, about my brother..."

"Right. The anglock toxin. I can make you a remedy if you bring me some neluma lilies. I have everything else I'd need." She looked up, as if suddenly excited to describe the plant to me. "They're a bit pointed and soft pink, growing on the far south of the marsh, where it's warm enough for the anglock to mate. It gets the anglock's toxins in their roots and filters them out. The flowers are quite delectable, too. We sometimes—"

Reed cleared his throat. "I'd heard those flowers can only be picked under a full moon. Haven't you?"

Robin paused, her head tilted, and I again wished I could read the expression in her eyes. Was my face about to become unreadable as well? That would be another advantage I could use in the coming days.

"Yes...I have," said Robin.

I did the mental calculation and clapped my hands together, the sound eerily loud to my ears. It seemed my hearing had become more sensitive with these new, lengthened tips.

"Okay. The full moon is just four days away, so that gives us time to break your contract and for Robin to get everything ready for the cure."

Reed grinned, his eyes alight. "Four days is plenty of time, and now that you look fae I bet we can get Jassin interested in you, either romantically or just in terms of business. He'll flirt with almost anyone, and the more he likes you, the easier it will be for you to pretend to buy me out."

"That is how you're going to do all this?" Robin asked.

We both nodded.

"Well, you better have some nicer clothes than that."

I looked down at my bedraggled outfit as it slowly dried around my legs. "I did bring a decent dress," I offered, but the more I pictured the simple green linen in my head, the more I knew it still wouldn't match the elaborate and gaudy pieces worn at court.

"We'll figure it out," said Reed, his tone sure.

We took our leave then, though not before he had a tight-lipped exchange with Robin as I climbed down into the water. Even with my new ears I couldn't pick up what was said, but I had a feeling it was about the "price" of the potion I'd drunk. The idea that Reed could be in some kind of debt because of me made my stomach twist, but that was why I was helping him, wasn't it? We would soon be even, both with our consciences clear.

"You better close your eyes and keep your mouth closed on the way back," Reed suggested as he jumped into the water beside me, making an unnecessary splash. "It's getting dark and there will be more activity near the castle."

"But I look like a fae now," I argued.

"A fae who shouldn't be in the company of an indentured servant the whole compound knows by sight."

I brushed my wet hair away from my face, rolling my eyes like I would at Conor for being childish.

"Fine. So, you want me to swim blindly?" I countered.

"I'll carry you or pull you behind me. Don't worry—I won't let you drown."

"It's not you I'm worried about," I said.

It was the hungry manyda and malicious syra and the unearthly beauty of the snake-bodied lendani that had me shivering. It was everything I'd read about in that book.

Despite my fear, I let Reed take my hand and did my best to float gently on my back, trusting him to lead me.

CHAPTER TEN

Night had fallen by the time we returned, and I'd somehow managed to keep my eyes and mouth shut the entire journey. Reed
hefted me through the same entrance as before and hurried me into his
room, turning his back while I changed into the one dress I had packed
in my bags. It wasn't very elegant—just a simple frock in a pleasant but
old-fashioned sage-green, with a square neck and cap sleeves—but it was
a vast improvement over the rags that he switched between.

"Here," Reed said, pulling a long strand of sharks' teeth and striped
Cardita shells from one of the boxes along the floor. "Use it as a belt,
maybe it will draw attention away from how plainly you're dressed. I
used to have some pearls here, but..." He shrugged, and though his shirt
from the night before wasn't completely dry, he didn't complain as he
pulled it over the healing slashes on his back.

"I could say I lost some finery on the way," I offered. My hands had
started to sweat as I tied the cord around my waist, draping it to one side
to emphasize my hips. Who would attack a young fae, I wondered? An
older fae? An aggrieved crogwyn? Or did I just think that way because
one had drugged me and felt me up when I presented as human?

Reed hummed in thought. "If you must lie, make yourself seem stupid. Jassin is more likely to think he can manipulate you that way. He likes his bedmates vicious but not smarter than him, and anything new should grab his attention."

He pulled on his shoes, and I took his notes in stride, building them into the character I'd become when we left his room.

"Your smell should help you," he continued. "Since we weren't able to change it, it will fit the story of you being a new visitor to the court. You can tell Jassin you're from a growing family in the south, near...Ospil, maybe."

"Ospil?" I asked with obvious disquiet. That country was so far away I knew practically nothing about it. I could fake my way through some small talk, sure, but if anyone had been there or knew anything about its people or customs, I would be found out immediately.

Reed began his habitual stoking of the fire in the hearth, his stack of wood growing precariously low. He seemed lost in thought as he layered logs into the flames, adjusting them so the heat in the room became almost stifling—or maybe that was my nerves.

"Just spin some stories about being sequestered by a protective parent," he offered eventually, his face still turned to the fire. "What's important is that Jassin thinks you are wealthy...and serious about paying an unreasonable amount for a strapping young slave with the kind of strength and attention to detail a glamoured human could not provide."

"And if he sees through my ruse?"

He straightened and turned to me, his normally jovial expression now grave. "Then I will do my best to get you out of there unharmed. I'll be nearby, either serving him or his guests. You will not be alone. But looking like a fae, as you are, he would not conceive you could lie. Only manipulate your truths."

I nodded absently and looked to my now half-empty bag, wishing I could bring some of Conor's weapons with me into the fray. Would it be too obvious to hide a net launcher under my dress? Although now that I would appear inhuman, there was less of a chance I'd be unwelcomely molested...

"Do you have a small satchel or purse I could wear?" I asked.

Reed's eyebrow rose. "I think so, though it is plain. Why?"

"Well, if I'm a visitor, I should have some amount of money or goods with me. A small bag would help me sell the story."

"Alright." He pointed to the box on his floor. "There should be a leather bag in there you can use. Oh, and some serrated pins I once used for picking locks."

"You expect I'll need to lockpick my way into Jassin's good graces?"

"Use them for your hair. Pin it back to show off your ears."

"Oh. Good idea." I rummaged through the small box and found my heart sinking in my chest at the sight of his meager possessions. If his story was to be believed, he'd been in this castle his entire life, and this was all he had to show for it—some socks and a thin blanket, the leather satchel, a length of twine, and a few vials of clear liquid I thought might be perfumes from Robin, or maybe clean drinking water. There was also a small knife, though it wasn't made of iron like my own, and a bundle of candles that had already been melted down to stubs.

I found the pins and twirled the front pieces of my hair into ropes that I fastened at the back of my head, putting my pointed ears on full display. I then put some of Conor's devices in the borrowed satchel to plump it, as well as the few coins I had brought, leaving them loose so they would jingle. Reed didn't have a mirror in his room, so I presented myself for his approval, the bag slung over my chest, shells and teeth at my waist, and the dagger tied discreetly to my inner thigh where I hoped to never need to reach for it. I was grateful whatever potion Robin had given me didn't make me sensitive to the iron.

"What do you think?" I asked.

"It will do," he said with a nod.

"Wow, your flattery has nearly overwhelmed me. I may faint."

Reed's troubled expression lightened, his smile breaking through the gloom. "Apologies, my dear. You look as beautiful as ever."

I hadn't expected that, especially since a voice in the recess of my mind whispered that he *could not lie.* He truly thought I was beautiful? But no, he'd said 'as ever.' If fae could only tell truths, they would be exceptionally good at doublespeak and lies of omission. 'As ever' could mean he'd never found me beautiful, and this outfit changed nothing. I rebuked myself for being naïve—this was no time to let his faux fawning get to me.

"Good," I replied. I lifted my chin and took a bracing breath. "Let's go."

Reed walked with me through the sprawling castle halls, keeping one step behind me as if he was already my servant, until we were in the main foyer.

"Make your way down this gallery and take a left," he instructed me in a near whisper. "You'll see a pair of crogwyns who are serving as sentries to announce visitors and keep out any undesirable creatures."

Considering the type of monsters I'd witnessed already at last night's dinner party, I shuddered to think of what type of fae might be undesirable.

Reed's hand was warm on my lower back, and the feeling lent me an odd torrent of strength. "Tell them you're here on behalf of your family and you wish to speak to Jassin. They should let you through."

Should. Great.

Still, I nodded. I could do this. This was just like a play I was putting on with Conor. He was a haughty and evil fae, and I was the lovely visitor to his castle, there to barter and scheme my way into a deal. The key would be acting like he and I were of equal standing and that I was not in danger. Hopefully that intention would make it so.

The cold at my back as I left Reed behind nagged at me, but I forced my steps further down the cobblestone floor and into the dark entryway. Already the sounds of cutlery and merrymaking were wafting toward me like smoke. I took my last deep inhale, despite the growing odor ahead, and turned the corner.

I almost screamed at the sight of the crogwyns, despite the warning Reed had given me. They were even more atrocious than the one which had attempted my abduction the night before; their hard, jagged skin was mottled with gray patches that smelled of mold and their eyes were dark, bottomless pits. The small, circular mouths at the center of their faces were cracked and bleeding at the edges. I watched as blue-tinted grime leaked from the lesions.

"State your name and dominion," one of them rasped. He—or they, I should say, since they were sexless despite their masculine appearance—carried a weapon that looked like a rusted field scythe.

"Uh, m-my name is Winona. Elmon. I've come from the Elmon house of Ospil, to talk terms with Jassin. I hear he resides at this court." Keeping my chest high, I did my best to look both creatures in the eye with my new inky stare, daring them to contradict me. I was high fae, the top of the food chain, and they had no right to question me. I could only hope that came through in the set of my mouth and the low pride of my shoulders.

The same crogwyn who'd spoken pivoted on their bare, stunted feet and leaned into the room behind.

"Winona Elmon of Ospil," they proclaimed, though their voice was so low and rough I doubted many could hear them over the ruckus beyond.

I inclined my head to the guards as they let me pass, my heart pounding beneath my breast as I got a clear look at the room I'd been placed in like a sack of flour the night before. It was longer than I'd noticed, with multiple tables stretching in uneven lines over the cold floors. A rectangular pond was built into the ground to my right. Various syra propped themselves up from the depths on flat rocks and smooth coral, tails splashing from side to side, and I caught the dark hair and pointed nose of a kelavee before it dove back into the cloudy depths of the pool. A few merkind, seemingly human except for their coloring, looked on at their watery compatriots with envy. I figured these were the fae who hadn't been fully transformed when the interruption occurred—their strange new malady—and now they were stuck with legs.

Most of the attendees of this elaborate banquet appeared human enough that I knew they were high fae, with a few crogwyns sitting in groups of four or five and the pink-tinted abyssots leaning over some dessert table piled high with snails. A couple of elegant ladies in green rags made of seaweed, their long hair tangled over their blue-tinted skin, had to be some kind of nymph or naiad, but I couldn't be sure—the book Reed leant me hadn't covered the more human-presenting fae.

How was I going to find Jassin in this calamity?

"I hear you're looking for Jassin," said a voice at my left. I startled, then rushed to compose myself, my hands tightening ever so slightly against the strap of my satchel.

"You heard that, did you?" I asked haughtily, turning to face the high fae. He was beautiful and dastardly tall. I had to crane my neck back to take in his face, which was angled and sharp, his hair shorn close to the scalp so that his ears seemed to protrude like wings from his skull.

"You're a young one, aren't you? Regardless, I like to know a little about our visitors to court, babes and all. Welcome to the Windstone Court. My name is Ruven. I'm a page to the prince," he said with a dash of arrogance, "and I report back to him. Nothing too invasive, I assure you. I keep plenty of counsel and deign to be casual with my friends." His smile was slick, and he showed off his pointed teeth like a threat. "Unless a more aggressive study would excite you."

I grinned back, hoping my own fangs looked half as intimidating.

"I...have heard Jassin holds the majority of contracted servants and slaves here in all of Trasia. I'm here on behalf of my family, looking for workers to buy." My tone was cold. Professional. "I'd appreciate some direction finding him."

Ruven sighed, as if pained by my disinterest, but then he snapped his fingers, recalling some exciting tidbit to dangle at my expense.

"Jassin is unfortunately absent tonight," said the page with mock sorrow. "He was called away to some errand in the marsh."

"Finding a new crop of glamoured humans?" I asked, glancing around at the various slack-jawed men and women that stood like empty vessels among the partygoers. There were only a handful.

"One can never be sure where he is."

"And here I thought you knew a little bit of everything," I teased. "Being a page and all."

Ruven's smile grew predatory once more. "What an alluring little creature you are, Winona of Ospil." His nostrils flared and I knew he was scenting that clean aroma on my skin and clothes. "Why don't you sit at my table, so I can tell you that little bit of everything over some wine and baby eel? It's served on crusted cattail-flower bread—quite the delicacy."

My stomach roiled at the thought, but I wasn't sure what else to do, so I took his offered arm, searching surreptitiously for Reed in the crowd. I needed to let him know Jassin was away, and that I'd need to try another night. The longer I stayed here the more likely I was to fumble my assignment and get myself killed, but I wasn't sure if it was acceptable for me to leave just yet.

"What can you tell me about Jassin?" I asked, searching for some topic that would keep Ruven talking and me listening.

We sat at a pair of empty seats halfway down the table, the noise billowing in crescendos around us. The scent of salt and rot itched at my nose, barely masked by the cooked fish littering the wide tabletop. Candle smoke was heavy in the air, but it did more harm than good, so when Ruven poured me a glass of deep red wine, I took a sip just to reset my senses.

The wine was thicker than I expected, reminding me of the bowl the crogwyn had poured down my throat, and I quickly placed the goblet back down. The last thing I needed was for that eerie, lustful heat to overtake me.

"He's a fair type," said the page. "Most of the women find him to be a good catch. A bit old for you, though..." he drifted off and I looked up to his face once more, the height difference staggering.

"Oh, yes." I cleared my throat. "I'm old enough now to leave home but I'm—" I couldn't say uninterested, because according to Reed that might be my best chance of buying his contract, but I also didn't want Ruven to get the idea *he* could pursue me. "I'm interested in other...options."

"Ah, well," he said, as understanding and disappointment dawned. Looking over to the syra with their bare breasts and slim waists, he nodded. "I wouldn't blame you for that. I must explore my *options* tonight as well. But find me if you change your mind."

With a move that was more graceful than any dancer I'd witnessed, Ruven rose from his seat and gave me the barest of bows.

"May the moon grant what you seek," he intoned, and I had a feeling this was something the fae said to each other in lieu of Harnsey's "Stay sharp, stay dry."

I simply dipped my head in acknowledgment and watched as he spun on his heel to continue his perusal about the room.

The urge to jump from my seat and speed away from the banquet rode me hard, but then I caught sight of Reed to my left, his shirt smudged red at the back as if he'd opened the whip marks on his skin. His smile was so vibrant and gleeful as he bent to serve a female high fae a goblet of dark wine, I had a hard time imagining it was false.

He was just as good at pretending as I was.

It was another reminder he couldn't be entirely trusted.

My gaze must have been hot on his neck, for he tilted his head and met my eyes, his eyebrow twitching as if to give me a signal. I stood and headed toward him, but then he gave the slightest shake of his head. I wanted to yell across the crowd how much I already hated this little game of guesswork between us, but then his blue stare darted to the doorway beyond the syra enclosure.

He wanted me to go there?

I took a small, shuffling step toward it and he went back to the attention of the high fae, who was caressing a sharp nail over his cheek only to then pull at the short tresses of his blond hair. A lover? But no, as I peeked over on my way to the door I saw him back away, the fae's wicked grin a promise of future violence. She had legs that were only partially transformed, her feet ending in whisper-thin fins that had no hope of holding her weight. Maybe she was taking out her frustrations on Reed.

A few creatures attempted to talk to me or touch me as I glided through the room, but I kept my gaze forward and my expression neutral as I drifted around them. I was here for Jassin, after all—it wouldn't be absurd to snuff the advances of anyone else.

Still, my heart was thumping painfully against my sternum as I ducked into the dark hallway and waited for Reed to appear. It seemed to lead down to a dungeon, based on the depth of the spiral staircase at my feet and the smell of brine thick in the air. The steps were smooth with wear, and I imagined the syra clambering up each one, their tails flicking behind them, the low-lit torches on the wall providing only enough light to stretch the shadows of their long limbs.

A hand touched my shoulder, and my entire body clenched with fear. Thankfully, when I turned, it was only Reed, looking flushed and out of breath. He held a finger up to his mouth before I could ask a single question, then urged me down the stairs.

I expected to hit water before long, but instead found a landing that doubled back the way we came, directly under the banquet hall.

"Jassin is away from court," Reed said with obvious displeasure. For the first time his voice was dark and rumbling, lacking its usual warmth.

I nodded. "Yes, Ruven said he's away dealing with an errand in the marsh. We'll just have to try tomorrow."

With jerking motions, Reed ran a hand over his hair, then winced. I wondered if he'd pulled at the wounds on his back, but something kept me from asking. It was the air of desperation that seeped from his pores, the anxiety and ruthlessness ticking between his eyes like a clock that was speeding faster and faster.

"We can't trust that the potion will last long enough," Reed muttered, glancing around the hall as if he might find some solution in the empty gallery. I could see dark, molding portraits hanging at odd angles along the wall, and a threadbare carpet under my feet that had torn in some places and seemingly...dissolved in others.

"What if he isn't back tomorrow?" he continued. "What if your eyes shrink back to their human colors? You'll be slain without question."

I swallowed around my dry tongue. "Robin said it would be a few days."

"So she thinks. But if he's away...this could be my only chance." His tone turned encouraging. "*Your* only chance."

"To do what?" I asked.

Reed pulled out one of the vials I had seen amongst his things, the clear liquid inside sloshing against the container.

"To poison him."

"Are you sure that's wise? Do you know your contract will automatically end if he's dead?" I wanted to ask how he expected me to poison a person who wasn't here, but my mind could only handle one matter at a time.

Reed tucked the bottle back into his pocket and took hold of my elbow, gently urging me forward.

"At this point, I think it may be my best bet," he answered. "And I haven't seen the contract since I was young and stupid enough not to read it carefully, so if we make it into his rooms, we can check for that while we add this to his supply of wine. I know the way into his suite, and if he is gone there may be a chance it's—"

He clamped his mouth shut as a high fae rounded a corner ahead, and I made a point to stand up straight and shove Reed to the side. "Get behind me, scum. I won't tell you again."

The high fae was shorter than the rest I'd seen, and I figured this to be one of the children of the court, although he looked nearly twenty in terms of human years. He stopped just ahead of me, and my pulse began jumping erratically once more.

"Can I help you with something, miss?" he asked, his voice cracking. "You're a bit far from the party." His outfit was too simple for him to be a guard, and there were no visible weapons on him. I figured him for a young page or maybe even someone's child, roaming the halls.

"I'm fine, thank you. I'm heading toward someone's personal quarters." I winked, and before he could reply, I bent slightly at the waist. "May the moon grant what you seek," I said, repeating Ruven's salute.

The boy rushed to bend as well, going lower than I dared in this dress. "And you." At that, he allowed me to pass while he continued down the hall toward the banquet.

I didn't let my guard drop as I reached the end of the hall and used Reed's silent gestures to take a staircase on my right up three flights.

"You're brilliant," whispered Reed behind me.

"I'm terrified," I replied.

We came up to a hall that was infinitely more cared for; the torches flamed high, casting yellow light against the lush, maroon carpets underfoot, and the walls were lined with elegant tapestries of mountain streams and deep oceans.

Reed kept close to my side, but even that didn't make me feel any safer as we ambled through the wing, which was obviously meant for the upper class.

"Since Jassin is gone, it's unlikely guards will be minding his suite," said Reed, "and I'm one of the only servants with a key. With any luck, your mission will be over as soon as he returns to his rooms."

I could only hope that was true. I didn't think my heart could take much more.

CHAPTER ELEVEN

Jassin's room was thankfully clear of any sentinels, and Reed had been summoned there enough times to know exactly which door to use and which cabinet stored his carafes of aerating wine.

I knew the high fae was a fixture at court, but the rooms Jassin occupied were elegant and well-furnished, enough so that I thought the prince's rooms could not be much better. His bed was opulent, draped in fine fabrics and furs, and the black floor was polished to a mirror-like shine. An ornate desk sat against grand windows, looking out to the ocean, which I caught a glimpse of for the first time since arriving at court.

Somehow each time we entered or left the castle we were right back in the mangroves, but this entire wing appeared to be buffeted by the gentle tide. The expanse of water beyond was as infinite as the sky—I could only make out distant waves because the waxing moon was glinting a silver path directly toward us. As if I might step onto the runner and stroll directly up to the stars.

"What are you doing?" Reed asked, and I turned away from the window. "I can't do this myself."

He pulled the vial from his pocket and held it out to me. Right. If it was simply a matter of killing Jassin he would have done so long ago, but his contract kept him bound from causing harm.

"Are you sure we shouldn't try something else first?" I offered. "I can draft a letter from someone—a leader of another *actual* court, maybe, someone important—and hand it over, promising it's real. We could give it to Ruven and—"

Reed shook his head. "There are too many ways to have materials forged—high fae have access to human slaves, remember? And though your ability to write is impressive, it's not unheard of. It has to come from a fae's mouth, and we don't know if your mouth will last."

"What if we're found?" I hissed, suddenly overly aware of the un-locked door between us and the rest of the castle occupants. Still, I took the vial into my shaking hand. The idea of being caught red-handed had my lungs constricting; there had been so many close calls already. Just by holding this bottle of innocuous-looking fluid, I was involved in a conspiracy to murder—to kill a man I'd never met. Well, not a man, really. Or was he? Why couldn't Reed have gotten one of the human slaves to do this? Were they under some command to ignore him? But then Robin could give the instruction, right? Unless she was afraid to. Like I was afraid to lift my hand and uncork the bottle...

Suddenly my breathing was ragged, the reality of the moment flood-ing my head, making me woozy with fear. I'd never killed anyone before. Sure, I'd listed it as a possibility I could accomplish, like some scene in a play, but actually going through with it...

Was that who I wanted to be? Would Conor understand?

"We are less likely to be found if you hurry," Reed urged.

And then he did something completely unexpected.

His arm shifted into that dark smoke, the transformation as quiet and unobtrusive as a breeze. My new fae eyes zeroed in on the way his fingers kept their shape, his muscles still defined as the black vapor mimicked every tick of his pulse. He caressed my arm with the shadowy tendrils, and then my shoulder and my neck. I expected them to feel cold, or wet, but the fingers were warm and soft, like a kitten's fur.

The touch seemed to take my fear and bury it. All that remained was the sensation of being stroked and patted, my body leaning into every lingering caress. *Please don't stop*, I ached to say, as if the fae wine I'd sipped was coming back to life beneath my skin. Pleasure raced through my blood.

I met his blue eyes, which were searching mine for something I simultaneously hoped they did and did not betray, and then he backed away.

"Feel better?" he asked, voice rough.

I nodded, my fist closing tighter against the vial of poison. I'd forgotten it was in my grasp.

"Yes. Sorry. I—how did you—"

He shook his head. "Don't worry about it. I can explain later."

With a mild wave, he brought my attention back to the half-open liquor cabinet. It housed several bottles of wine and spirits, glasses of every shape and size lining the bottom shelf. A crystal carafe of dark wine winked under the light.

And then there was a commotion beyond the door.

"Do not tell me what I can and cannot do—" a voice shouted, but then I could hear no more, since Reed had clutched my shoulder in a punishing grip and yanked me toward the ocean window, my feet almost flying out from beneath me.

"Wait—" I started, but he already had his hand on the latch and one foot on the desk's chair.

My dagger dug sharply into the flesh of my thigh as he pulled me up onto the desk, and I couldn't help but look down at the dastardly fall that awaited us beyond the window. We were stories high, the waves crashing on the stone walls beneath us like slaps against a stoic cheek. Surely, we couldn't survive that kind of leap, and that was *if* there weren't pointed rocks hidden beneath the spray.

Reed put himself at my back just as the door behind us burst open. I heard a shout and then the plucked *twang* of some kind of weapon.

And then Reed pushed me.

The dark ocean encompassed my vision even as the wind whipped and pulled at my hair. I had enough time to feel my eyes water and study the sharp squall laid out before me, and then I was crossing my arms over my chest and trying to control the fall. The smack of my body hitting the water was so brutal I gasped at the force of it, the water immediately pouring down my throat until I coughed it up and held my breath tight. I had to believe it was my new fae body that survived the power of the current weighing down on every inch of me, for my human lungs would surely have collapsed and my bones would have shattered.

Once I had my bearings about me, I struggled toward the surface, hacking up the last of the salt water, and then worried whoever had shot at us would be waiting. I spun, my stinging eyes blinking in the dark. I couldn't see Reed.

With every ounce of strength I had, I dove below, kicking and grabbing at the water, pushing my way to the right where I hoped I would catch sight of the mangroves around the castle's corner. I was low on air and even lower on energy, but I let the burn in my chest spur me onward, stroke after stroke, my legs working furiously behind me in the punishing cold.

Eventually, I could hold my breath no longer and I breached the surface, panting. I dragged briny air into my lungs and thrashed my head from side to side, searching for Reed while checking for signs of pursuit. After a moment, my eyes seemed to pull every glimmer of moonlight available, focusing it like a prism.

The window I'd leapt from—*been pushed from*—was so high I could barely make out the face that leaned out, blocking the light at their back, but their coloring wasn't human.

A voice wheezed and stuttered my name behind me, and I spotted Reed, his face pale and twisted with a grimace, swimming toward me with one arm. His other hung limply behind him, an arrowhead sticking out high on his chest and the shaft sprouting like a wing from his back.

"Reed!" I swam toward him and grabbed for his other arm, not sure how I would make it much farther if I had to cart his heavy build plus my own clothes-weighted body.

He hissed as I took his shoulder but did his best to keep moving forward with me as an awkward tangle of limbs. "You're a...good swimmer," he huffed.

"Thanks," I said, not sure how else to respond. Of course I could swim, I had been born in the marsh. Was he trying to keep me calm? There was no chance of that—my pulse was hammering and the hum in my ears was growing with every second. Soon I would pass out or we'd need to stop, risking any pursuers finding us.

"Are we being followed?" I asked.

He shook his head, his skin so pallid in the dark it was as if he glowed. "Not yet. I would...it would be the guards outside. They'd need to be told." He coughed, and I thought something dark spluttered from his lips. "The syra will be called. Keep...going."

"Going where? Robin's?"

"Just keep going." He was panting, though he barely moved, and something about his breathing sounded wet. Still, there was nothing to do but obey his wishes.

Eventually the waves gentled around us and the mangrove emerged from the night, the trees bending and curving in a spindly mess. My sensitive ears picked up the sounds of shouting behind us, still far off. It was only a matter of time before those long-finned merkind were whipping through the water, hunting for us by following Reed's trail of blood.

"What do we do?" I wheezed, growing dizzy from fatigue. The branches ahead seemed to sway. They blurred, and I blinked again and again, trying to clear my vision.

"Hide in the trees," Reed said, his voice barely audible, "or along...the roots." He had started shivering in my hold minutes ago and the shaking was growing worse. It was as if his body was battering itself against the pain of the arrow in his chest. "Once the sun rises, we can..."

I waited for him to finish, my legs still kicking as much as they could, but when I looked over, I found his eyes closed, his face slack.

"Reed?" I called. "Reed!"

He was unconscious. *Shit. Shit, shit, shit.*

I licked my lips, the salt sharp on my tongue, and peered into the gloom between tree trunks, hoping to see a low enough branch to hoist him onto. My feet could barely touch the ground, so I had to keep swimming until I found a suitable place to stow him. Reed's leather satchel was a burdensome weight around my shoulder, but I dared not release it. If it wasn't ruined, I could use Conor's flotation device, but only once we found somewhere to hide—the bag would grow too bulky to easily maneuver through the water. My mind whirled, trying to remember what else I had packed that might help us, but other than the dagger and net under my waterlogged dress I had little to offer.

Some creature brushed over my knee, and I took that as a sign our time was almost up. It was light and quick; no claws or teeth tore at my skin, so with any luck it was a manyda passing along, and not one of the syra sent to look for us. Did the fae know it was Reed who had been in that room? Had the guards or whoever entered Jassin's suite gotten a good look at me? There was so much I wanted to ask the unconscious man in my hold, but I had to find a safe place first.

One of the trees ahead had a massive root structure that rose above the waterline. It was an older specimen, its trunk coated in mushrooms and protruding lichen, and I aimed for it, already calculating how high we'd need to move to be unseen from the water.

The stalks of a leafy plant stretched into the air from beside the tree, a perfect hiding spot for spawning flounder, young grouper, and an injured half-fae. I maneuvered Reed's body into the thick of it before rummaging one-handed in my bag. I felt the leather of Conor's flotation device scrape away under my fingernails and pulled the sack free, immediately smashing it against the tree trunk, breaking whatever vials or bottles resided inside.

It took a couple tries, but in the quiet swish of the tides, I heard the hiss of the chemicals within release. The bag quickly expanded, then stretched further and further until a low pad the size of my torso was floating beside us.

"Reed, come on," I said, struggling to lift him onto the device, "I...need you to help me. Wake up. Please." He was sliding off the pad, his body too difficult to maneuver onto the device that was—regrettably—smaller than his chest.

I shook his shoulder, and his bleary eyes opened. They were unfocused and clouded with pain, and I watched him blink slowly, fighting off sleep.

"Climb onto this," I urged. "I can put your legs on a branch and keep you floating, so they don't see our limbs in the water, but you have to help me."

Using his arms, Reed sluggishly pulled what part of his weight he could onto the pad while I helped him turn over onto his back, grunting with the effort. I was simultaneously excited and terrified to see the arrow had at some point been pulled from his shoulder, though I couldn't fathom how he'd managed it alone.

"Did you take out the arrow?" I asked.

His breathing was erratic and shallow, the wet sounds louder now and ratcheting my anxiety to new heights. He didn't answer.

As soon as I had him mostly settled, I clambered up the tree, using some of the bent roots as footholds. The whole structure was a bit...softer than I expected. There was give to the bark and spring in the branches beneath my feet, as if the water inside kept them malleable. It must have been a newer mangrove tree despite its size, I reasoned, still flexible with frequent growth, and it made the climb easier—a slight bounce hefting me higher into its branches. The net of roots was thick below us and I bent to tug Reed's feet closer. His torso was barely buoyed by the flotation device, but with his legs now draped over the highest branch I could fix him on, he was safe from any underwater tracker. To them, it might just look as if a bag floated next to a tree, some refuse from the humans they hated so much as to make them all slaves and meals. So long as his blood didn't pool heavily beneath us, I reasoned we would be safe for the time being.

Reed coughed weakly, and I could see the crimson stain at the corner of his mouth with startling contrast. Crouching in my spot on a curving branch over the roots, I took one of his arms, his skin so cold in mine it was like holding winter snow in my hands. His other arm was draped over his stomach, so no part of him was in the water, but he was soaked, and the cold breeze off the ocean rippled his blond hair. He shivered, still awake—though barely. It was surprising he hadn't passed out once more.

"Are you...okay?" I asked, and then I felt foolish for voicing it. He was bleeding, shaking, and in obvious pain.

"I'll be fine," he breathed. Just then his hand clenched mine and he gasped in a breath, eyes clenching tight. Agony tightened his features like the pull of purse strings. And then he seemed to relax.

"What's happening?" *Are you dying?* That's what I wanted to ask, but despite what my previous rash actions would declare, I was too much of a coward to do so.

"Poison," Reed whispered, and I could see sweat gathering at his temples. Beyond the sound of my drenched clothes dripping onto the marshy water below and our staggered breathing, a cacophony of nightlife slowly began rising around us. We had disturbed them swimming in, but now they were becoming an asset—the croaking and chirping of red-eyed frogs, the buzzing of flies and beetles rolling against the crickets' song, the warning calls of some unseen bird—it all blended into a refrain that hid us as well as any cloak. While they continued their melody, it seemed we were safe, and if they went silent once more, we would know something approached.

"Poison?" I repeated, keeping my weary voice as quiet as I could. "Is that why you took it out? Will you be okay?"

Reed dipped his head in a shallow nod. "I will live, just...need some time."

"And did they see us? Do they know it was you?"

He shook his head, then winced. "No. I don't think so. Maybe my back, but the voice was a..." he stopped to catch his breath, "crogwyn I did not recognize. I hope they think I was just some foreign fae, trying to steal."

I looked around us, the mangroves dark and menacing in every direction, hiding us but also closing us in. A prison cell floating in the night.

Moving to release him, I found Reed's hold tightening on my fingers.

"Don't leave," he said, voice straining.

"I'm not. Just adjusting," I promised.

He sighed, the sound between relief and exhaustion.

"Try to sleep. I'll keep watch. If something comes...well, I have my knife, but it's been nice knowing you."

"So pessimistic." His chide was weak, as if he was already caving to my demand. And then he asked, "Talk to me first?"

"About what?"

"Anything. Softly. I just..." a slight groan laced his breath, "I like your voice. There's a rhythm to it."

Heat brushed my cold, wet face, as if the night had breathed a lover's sigh onto my skin. Reed's rough hand was trembling beneath mine. I stroked a thumb over the veins and sinews there, trying to calm him.

If I heard any change in the night creatures around us, I'd have to stop, but for now I could give him this one request.

"Okay, then," I said, voice low. "Let's see...Conor was wading in the marsh, his pants rolled up to his knees. His soft, curling hair was drifting into his eyes as he bent to study the silt floor. He kept flicking it to the side, the muddy water making its way onto his face, but he didn't notice. We were digging for mussels to cook in a stew. It was our mother's favorite, and it was her birthday, so we were planning a feast. Conor takes birthdays very seriously. He'd made this creation for her—a rod that would somehow protect her studio from lightning—and since I'd helped pay for the copper and iron that made it by doing chores for nearby farms, he'd say it was from both of us, but I still felt guilty. So, when I found a loose pearl in the muck, pink and nearly perfect, I asked Conor how I should make it into a necklace. We didn't have money left to see a blacksmith, but he thought maybe with some sap and the cord from..." I trailed off, noting the measured rise and fall of Reed's chest. His face was void of pain, his fingers limp in my palm. Finally at rest.

I stayed that way, in my uncomfortable crouch, for hours as the tide continued to mount bit by bit, soaking the tips of my shoes, my ankles, my calves, and then started its gradual descent. The night slowly faded into morning, my sensitive eyes picking up the gray break of dawn.

Beyond a few splashes out of sight, I neither saw nor heard any signs of our pursuers. Even still, despite my cramping legs and aching back, I dared not move.

I told myself it had nothing to do with how I wanted to keep hold of Reed's hand.

CHAPTER TWELVE

When sunlight began streaking through the canopy, peppering Reed's face with a pink glow and making his now-dry hair gleam, he finally roused from his sleep. With a shuddering groan, he opened his ocean-blue eyes and cornered me with a look that reminded me of an injured fox, sad and scared but still willing to snarl.

"Let's get you home," I said, my voice oddly tender.

Our journey was slow, but only because Reed's strength seemed to flag off and on as we walked through the now low tide of the mangroves. Parts of his body flickered with smoke only to reform, like a reflex as his body attempted to push the toxin from his blood. He assured me the search for the perpetrators of the break-in would have ended before daybreak and that, if there weren't guards waiting for him at his room, we were safe for another day. I didn't ask what would happen if they *were* waiting, but I was already planning a host of lies I could tell as part of my exit plan.

So long as he showed for his late-afternoon chores, he said, or at least his night duties with Jassin, he'd avoid suspicion of being the culprit—not that I was sure he'd have the strength for either.

Sweat dotted Reed's face and neck, his breathing still labored, and at one point he started muttering something so low I could not hear, even with my pointed ears. When I asked him what he'd said, he didn't know what I was talking about. Fever was overtaking him. At one point his entire arm vanished into that black shadow and I nearly dropped him.

Getting him into the tunnel at the rear of the castle was a staggering effort, but we managed, and when the dungeon and hallway leading to his room were vacant, I heard him release a thick, coughing sigh of relief.

However, his whole body stiffened when we made our way inside.

"The fire's out," he rasped.

His weight was torture on my shoulder as we stumbled toward the low bed, my heightened senses the only reason I could see in the pitch-black darkness of the room. Once the door was closed it became evident how much of a windowless cell he lived in. The small opening in the ceiling, where the hearth smoke typically drifted, was just as dark, and I realized I did not know where it led. Apparently not directly outside.

"Don't worry," I assured him, "I'll light it." With as much care as I could, I lowered him onto the pallet.

"...so cold," he murmured, and then moved as if to turn or get up.

I urged him back down and tugged off his wet trousers with perfunctory motions before grabbing the threadbare blanket he'd once lent me to tuck around him. His neck craned back, chin pushed into the air as he hissed at the pressure. I whispered an apology and turned to the rest of the room.

There were still a few logs waiting off to the side of the fireplace, and a stack of paper I could tell he'd ripped from a book beside the pile of leaves he'd pulled from earlier. But there was no flint or striker I could find.

"Reed," I called from the fireplace, searching the ground, "how do you light it? What do you use?"

My fingers scraped along the sooty floor, searching for the smallest rocks in case my fae vision was failing me.

"Reed?"

I looked over my shoulder to see him shivering violently on the cot, his eyes shut.

Something clenched in my chest at the sight of him sweating and shaking on the bed, the perspiration darkening his hair. Without thought, I moved to his bedside and brushed aside some strands on his damp forehead. His face turned toward me, as if relishing the touch. *Don't do that*, I almost whispered. *Don't act like you need me. Like you want me.* I couldn't stand it. Not after Flint and not after seeing so much of Reed's vicious, horrible world. As soon as he was freed, he would be gone, and as soon as I had Conor's cure, so would I—back to human lands and my human life. The sharp teeth and black eyes I wore like face paint at a festival would wash away along with this whole experience.

I pushed those thoughts down for later.

"Reed," I said, louder.

His eyes drifted back open, a weak smile softening his lips. "Little perch?"

"How do I start the fire back up?" I pressed.

"Under...the bed."

I dug my fingers between the mattress and the floor, feeling for anything out of the ordinary, and found a box so small that it might have housed a ring. As I pulled it free, I could see it was made of some dull metal, clasping at the center like a locket. Inside was a small pile of powder and a sharp quartz stone that had to be his flint.

Taking a pinch of the powder, I placed it on a wide, crispy leaf and struck the stone against the metal box. It sparked at once, catching on the powder and starting to burn a hole. I rushed to nestle the leaf among the other roughage in the fireplace, nursing it into a tiny flame and then building it with the kindling and logs he had left.

The difference in Reed was almost immediate as he warmed. His breathing evened out and he seemed to regain his wits. Still, when I pushed him to sit up so I could remove his bloody shirt, he gasped with pain. The wound where the arrow had lodged itself was blackened at the edges, the poison snaking its way through him like ink spilling in water.

"What can I do for you?" I asked as he lay back down, his bare chest shining with sweat and seawater.

He shook his head. "Just have to...wait it out," he said in an exhausted voice. Though he had slept hours out in the mangroves, I imagined it was taking all his energy to battle the toxins inside him. His wide torso, built with muscles from hard labor, still filled out the bed, but somehow he appeared smaller—vulnerable. It seemed a struggle to breathe but he kept doing so, and I saw muscles at his abdomen clench on a wave of discomfort.

"I understand," he said on a hiss, "if you leave." I dragged my gaze up, and his eyes pleaded with me to do the opposite.

Not knowing what else to do, I took his torn shirt from that morning's whipping out of the bowl of water beside us, wringing it out before dabbing at his face. The one time I'd been frighteningly ill, my mother had done so for me—albeit with a much cleaner rag—and I remembered the sensation of being cared for, how it had soothed something inside me.

"I'm not going to leave." With the wet cloth, I wiped the sweat from his brow, and the scent of the marsh and his blood began fading against the familiar fumes of the fire. "I keep my word, and our business is not yet done. Now hush, *Reedling*, and rest." If my voice shook at the end, despite my teasing tone, he did not notice.

"Yes, my dear."

"I could...go get you some food?" I offered. "Or I could visit Robin. I remember the way; I could see if she has some medi—"

"No, just...come here," he murmured, voice low. At that, he pushed my hand away from his brow and then tugged me forward. I began to tip toward his chest.

"Reed, I..." but before I could say anything more, I had dropped the rag and found myself pressed against him. It was awkward at first, my feet still touching the floor and half of my pants damp with grimy water, but I shifted, huddling into his side to offer what warmth I could. Being careful to stay clear of his injury, I cradled my head against his neck, his pulse under my chin. His skin was clammy.

We stayed that way for a while, in the quiet of the room. It was as if the crackle of the fire to our side was subdued, listening to me, hunting for signs of surrender.

"I feel like you're manipulating me," I whispered against his skin. He didn't seem to hear me, his breathing shallow and even so I was sure he'd succumbed to sleep. "I just...don't know what to do about it."

Staying up all night in the mangrove finally caught up with me and I began drifting into slumber, warmed by the fire and Reed's body heat.

At one point while we slept, his arm had curled around me, wrapping me in his salty, smoky scent. I hadn't really noticed it before—his smell—and I wondered if my fae senses were finally able to distinguish it among the unsavory odors of Windstone Castle. It was also...sweet. Like freesia, maybe, or jasmine. I inhaled it as I woke, my body stretching against him. If only I could get a few more hours...

"Morning," his voice grumbled under my ear.

I pulled away so quickly I almost fell off the edge of the bed. "Oh, good morning!"

Brushing hair away from my mouth, I quickly scanned him for signs of the poison that had wracked him the night before. His color was back, and the dark marks around his wound had mostly faded. His grin became wry at my inspection.

"You mumble in your sleep, did you know that?" he asked with a playful glint to his bright, blue eyes. The fire behind us was low, but still bright enough for the curve of his mouth to tug mine like a fishhook. I smiled back.

"I've heard that before."

His eyebrows rose. "A lover?"

"A lady never tells."

And then his jaunty tone brought back the dire circumstances of the night before, the fear I'd suffered at watching him writhe and shiver in this bed.

I smacked at his arm. "Don't do that again!" I hissed.

"What, startle you awake? Or let you live?"

At that, my breath stuck in my throat. "Let me...What do you mean?"

"The guards right now are equipped to kill humans, since those who escaped their glamour in the *interruption* are currently the focus of their hunts. The poison on their weapons only slows fae, but you would have died had that arrow struck you, since you're all human under that guise. I'm only half."

I was stunned, my jaw working like an empty forge. Nothing emerged.

Reed laughed, the sound a bit forced. "Don't worry, I'm much improved. See?" He spread out his arms, his skin glowing in the light of the fire, warm and hale. Only a smudge remained where his wound had festered. "Now, I am sure I'm late to launder Jassin's things. Hopefully no one has yet reported me for missing my afternoon errands. It must be past midday by now."

He moved to stand up from the bed, and my heart did a strange flip beneath my ribs, twitching out of rhythm as I caught sight of his muscled legs and lean waist. I barely managed to turn my head as he changed back into his now-dry clothes, his movements only a bit stiff.

"Let me help you," I blurted.

"You want to help me...do laundry?" he asked.

I peeked over my shoulder to make sure he was covered. "I do. I owe you, and I don't like owing anyone. Besides, I still look fae, don't I? What if some opportunity arises to help you out of your agreement?" I tilted my head up and to the side, already knowing from the echo in the room that my ears were still tall and pointed, picking up every little hitch of my own breath like a betrayal. I wanted every opportunity to scope out the castle.

"You do still appear fae." He paused. "Very well. Pretend to be dragging me somewhere or scolding me if someone sees."

The idea turned my stomach, but I nodded.

After he used the twine in his makeshift-bureau to sew the holes in his shirt—barely discernable against the other tears stitched shut—he fed the fire and we left his room.

The route through the castle we took was different from the others he'd subjected me to before—there were small tunnels we squeezed into, and he left me standing in a dark corner while he fetched Jassin's clothing from a cavern billowing with steam.

As soon as we were out of earshot of the chamber I peered into the loaded basket in his arms.

"Was that the washroom you just went into?" I whispered.

He nodded, keeping his eyes downcast and his steps just a smidgen behind my own in case he had to play the dutiful servant. "Jassin prefers me to handle them personally. Though he was missing from the castle last night, he still manages to leave me plenty to clean. Sometimes he hasn't even worn them—he just likes having me wash them again."

It was like a sad fairy tale, the wary and pure slave in bondage he could not escape, honored to be good and true even while he suffered. Was that why I was becoming more aware of his place beside me? Of the body heat that seemed to stretch lazily between us, like a cat in the sun? I had to remind myself I was not his savior, or his muse, or any other romantic notion I'd read in the scripts at home. This was merely an exchange of services.

We passed a few storage rooms of grain and netting where he snatched us both some hard bread to eat, and then we exited the castle through a den that was astoundingly dry. Beyond it was a set of stairs built into the wall facing the sea. I was almost blinded by the sun-blanched stone, but as I placed my hand over my sensitive eyes, I could make out the light glimmering off a vast and steady ocean, the fury of its waves tempered to a gentle tranquility.

"It's beautiful," I said, nearly stunned.

Reed halted ahead of me, the stairs narrow enough I was sure he couldn't turn while holding his basket, but he managed to gaze back at me over his shoulder.

"I've seen things more beautiful."

Before I could study his expression or review the cadence of his tone, he was once again treading down the steps. I knew better than to trust vague flatteries—Reed was a *man* after all, and a fae—but I did feel the tiniest flutter as I followed.

We approached a series of docks not unlike those in the mangroves, but these were more precarious, moving with dips at each step and leading us toward a curving patch of land that made a pale beach. The docks continued onto the sand, and then into a thin swath of forest.

"There's a creek here that Jassin prefers his clothes be washed in," Reed supplied. "It's right by the wooden path, so be careful of what you say if the guards come by."

"If guards pass here," I started, "will it raise suspicion if I'm helping you do the washing?"

"I suppose it might." I could hear the bend of a smile in his voice, though I couldn't see his face.

"And yet you allowed me to come along? Even though all I can do is just...sit here?"

"Maybe I like the company," he said, tone nonchalant. Another answer that was not really an answer. "Or maybe it's unlikely guards will pass at this time."

I was almost sure he wouldn't put me at risk, so I stayed quiet. He needed me, at least for now. That would have to be enough reassurance.

We approached the creek, and I sat on the uneven planks while he worked, some bar of soap from the basket creating perfumed suds between the fabric as he scrubbed a shirt against itself. The water was up to his waist, but he didn't seem to mind; his gaze was focused on his work, fingers gripping the cloth as he searched for any errant stain. When the garment was sufficiently cleaned, he laid it flat on the path beside me to dry. The heat of the day was sweltering, despite the turn of the season, so they would thankfully be done soon.

Sweat had gathered at the center of Reed's back, darkening his shirt, and I watched him lift the hem to wipe his face. The glimpse of his firm stomach and lean waist had the blush at my cheeks growing ever darker. I was pleased to note the slashes on his back were already closed, the edges pale pink with new skin.

"Would you like to play a game while you wait?" Reed asked.

"Huh?" I looked up from his body, flushed with shame.

"You might be bored watching me work. And you're right, it isn't exactly safe for you to be in here with me unless you're seen harassing or injuring me. A game may give you some reason for tolerating my presence. Say you ordered me to entertain you."

He cleared his throat, barreling on. "My father—when he was alive—used to do this with me. We would pick some yellow mulberries further up the creek and throw them into the water, seeing how many fish we could trick into thinking they were insects." He turned his back to me, starting work on a set of pants, and his voice turned soft, as if he was worried of being overheard. "I would always win, though I think he let me. He said the trick was to try and skip them, so the ripples stayed shallow, like a water strider. Those are...some of my happiest memories with him."

I paused, waiting to see if he would say more, but he just concentrated on his task as the afternoon sun sailed slowly above us. In just a couple of hours it would be twilight, and the fae court would come alive, but for now, with only the two of us here, I was...content.

"While that does sound fun, I'm enjoying this moment of peace," I told him, gently. "I'll just start kicking you if someone approaches." And then, because I felt he had exposed himself to me, revealing a vulnerability I knew was probably rarely seen, I gave him a story of my own.

"I used to play something similar with…with this boy I knew—"

"Your lover?" Reed asked, his voice lingering on a teasing edge. I remembered him asking me that before, but I felt more brazen now as he worked before me in the sun, like I had been dared.

"Technically, yes," I replied. "We used to wade into the shallow edge of the marsh away from town, picking cattails and any bare stalks we could find along the coast, then go into my neighbor's farmland to play with the pigs. We would drag the cattails along the ground and watch them scamper after them, only to bite them and spit out the fluff of their seeds." I paused. "It sounds cruel to hear me tell it back, but we gave them scraps from our tables whenever we met in town, so it seemed almost fair. The farm was halfway between our houses…"

I trailed off, my memory back in the barn, the smell of the hay and the prickle of it against my back—the feel of Flint's body pressed against my own.

"You don't play this game anymore?" Reed asked, turning from his work to meet my gaze.

I shook my head. "We don't see each other anymore. He ended it. Right after he proposed to me." I didn't know why I told him—it was a private failure I'd only disclosed to my family, and only so that any rumors that found them could be fought. Maybe because Reed was so far removed from that world, it was like speaking into the wind or writing it down on paper only to hold it over a flame.

"He changed his mind?"

"He got what he wanted from me." I was proud that my voice held no inflection, no despair, but Reed seemed to hear it anyway.

"Ah. Well, I can only assume the man was a fervent imbecile."

A quick bark of a laugh escaped me and then I pulled my legs to my chest, leaning my cheek against my knee so I didn't have to look him in the face. "I appreciate that. But honestly, I was the imbecile for falling for his tricks."

After a breath of time, I found Reed in front of me. I hadn't even heard the splash of him moving, but his rough, warm hand was at my chin, lifting my face toward his. With me sitting on the elevated path and him in the water, we were almost the same height.

"Look at me," he said, tender and slow. His blue eyes were so close I could see the thinnest streaks of silver in his irises. "You have so much to offer. Your drive, your loyalty, your creativity, and your quick mind…I've seen all that and more, only knowing you for a couple of days. If this boy was blind to those qualities, he's as daft as those pigs."

"Th-thank you," I stuttered out, dumbfounded.

He couldn't lie. *He couldn't lie.* He really meant those things he said—he couldn't promise me one thing and then rescind it. If anything, Reed was Flint's opposite. *No.* I shouldn't even be thinking like this. He was beautiful and sweet and charming, but this wasn't why I was here, and I still wasn't entirely sure I could trust him.

I shouldn't be looking at his eyes and breathing into the space between our lips, calculating how much I'd need to lean forward to entice him to kiss me. That quick press of our mouths when we'd met in the mangroves was just a ruse, but I recalled the softness in his lips, despite my initial revulsion.

"You're welcome," he replied, barely above a whisper. Those eyes drifted down to my own mouth, and I wondered if he would make the decision for us.

I slanted the tiniest bit toward him.

"Will you—" he started, and then the sound of boots scuffing against the wooden docks had us both twisting our heads toward the shore. His hand released my face and the sudden movement had me rocking forward. I would have fallen into the water had Reed's chest not been there to break my fall. As it was, his hands clutched my upper arms as he stumbled back, but then his eyes widened with panic.

Without warning, he ducked down into the waist high water, taking me with him.

CHAPTER THIRTEEN

My backside grazed the rocky sand at the bottom of the creek, and before I could orient myself, my body was being drawn backward toward the wooden docks. Reed's hold on me was secure so I tried not to fret as he drew me into the shadows.

We were under the path.

With my knees on the floor, I figured I would be able to breathe in the small amount of space between the planks and the creek water, but my hand found the dock, submerged. There was no inch of air to sip from—the path was floating right on the surface,

Heart pounding, I turned my head and tried to make out Reed in the gloom. My fae eyes seemed to sharpen under the water, now that the silt had settled from the commotion of our movement, and I watched him match my kneeling posture, his blond hair floating in delicate curls around him like shining flames. Shafts of weak sunlight streaked over his face, his shirt rising and shifting with the rush of the water.

He held a finger to his lips, as if I would somehow scream underwater and alert whatever person had been heading toward us. Had I not been so scared, I would have rolled my eyes at him. Already my chest was clenching, begging for air; there had been no time for a deep breath before he pulled me under.

If we had to stay here much longer, I would drown.

Gesturing with a fluttering hand toward my throat, I tried to tell him as best I could about my anxieties, but he only nodded like it was obvious.

I pointed up and watched him shake his head.

His grip was still solid on my arms so I couldn't gesture as vehemently as I needed to. I wanted to strike him and push off from the ground, guards or errant fae be damned. I was not going to die under this wooden path in shallow water. But just as I moved to escape, his hold tightened, and he pulled my face to his.

The kiss was hard and fast and then his jaw shifted, forcing my mouth open. Air poured in, slow and warm, filling my lungs. His lips were firm, moving just enough to be more than curative. His chest brushed mine.

We broke apart and I released some of the air back into the water, bubbles tickling at my nose and cheeks. There was a smirk on Reed's face, as if he had conned me into this second kiss, and maybe he had, but I couldn't find it in myself to be upset. He looked young then, like the boys in town.

Foolish as I was, I wanted to kiss him again—a real one.

It was impudent and immature and I was half-sure I would regret it, but my fingers reached out to clutch the linen of his shirt, tugging him close. Somehow, when our mouths met again, he pushed more air into my lungs, though I'd expected closed lips. I wondered if he had some secret gills inherited from his syra ancestry, but I had seen him nearly naked on more than one occasion now, and I was nearly sure I would have noticed.

His arms wrapped around me, our thighs touching as we stooped in the sand. His lips grazed and moved over mine. Bubbles were everywhere now as I breathed out and he breathed into me, and then my hands were on his face, holding him still so I could lick inside his mouth. I swore I could almost hear his groan, even underwater.

Seconds passed like that, in a strange limbo of time, where we sat buoyant and yet tethered, sharing air and heat and touches like seaweed twining in the tide. It was stupid and wrong to touch a fae this way, but was there really any harm in it? It was just a kiss. We were just two people bound together by strange circumstances, and if his need for me was enough to set my blood on fire, I was just reckless enough to let it.

We only stopped when Reed pulled back and gestured upward. The coast was clear.

He took my hand and tugged me out from under the dock, and we broke the surface as one.

"They're gone," he said in relief, and then shook out his hair like a dog, droplets spraying me in the face. I couldn't help but laugh as I wiped away my own hair and looked around the creek. The water was ripe with ripples, the wooden planks where I'd sat bare as ever.

"Wait..." I started, "where's the laundry?"

The basket was missing, as well as the pieces that had been drying on the path of docks.

"Oh, by the moon," Reed sighed, and then he took a deep, mournful breath, as if bracing himself. "Tonight is not going to be pleasant."

"Maybe someone brought them back to the washroom?" I offered, though even to my own ears, the notion sounded improbable.

"It wouldn't hurt to check, I suppose," he said, and then paused. "Actually...that gives me an idea. Come on, my dear. Back to the dungeons." With a smile and a wave forward, we went back the way we'd come, with

Reed dutifully trailing at my heels and my gut churning with disquiet. I didn't ask about the kisses, and he didn't bring them up, but I could have sworn his steps seemed lighter than before.

The shadows had strained and pulled themselves into dusk, but the castle was coming to life around us as we traversed the halls. Torches were being lit by crogwyn guards and the feathery-plumed abyssot were decked in rags that shimmered with fish scales.

I waited patiently outside the washroom, the steam curling the strands of my hair that lightly brushed my shoulders, only for Reed to return with a bundle of clothing in his arms.

"You found it?" I asked, pleasantly surprised.

He shook his head but didn't answer, only jerking his head for me to lead the way back to his rooms. I had a better understanding of his patterns now, I realized. During the day, when most of the fae had retired to their own caves or underwater abodes, he could wander the castle with little risk of being caught or abused, but as soon as the sun hit the horizon Reed returned to being cowed and humble. Anytime someone made a snide comment or rude gesture his way he took it all with a grin or sociable response, but as soon as he took a corner, his eyes would shutter. My own mother didn't appreciate my worth in contrast to my brother, but that was no comparison to the levels of vitriol Reed experienced every moment in this compound.

The flames were down to smoking embers when we reached his room, and as soon as the door closed behind us he dropped the clothes onto his bed and hurried to build up the fire.

"Can you not see in the dark?" I asked, suddenly curious. His eyes weren't black like my current fae eyes, and I wondered if his half-human side dulled those abilities even as they apparently protected him from the interruption of power his high fae masters suffered.

"I can see better than a human," he replied, his back turned to me. "It's more for the heat than the light."

"It doesn't seem that cold today," I mused, "since it was so warm outside. Like it seeped in a bit." I pulled off my damp trousers and sat on the pallet of his bed. I should have surreptitiously cleaned my own undergarments and spare clothes in the creek while we were there. Although, I guess then we would be missing those now as well.

"I...I like to be warm," he said eventually, and his tone was too simple, too easy. He couldn't lie, but there was something else he didn't want to say to me...a stark reminder I couldn't start seeing him as anything but a stepping stone to jump from on my quest.

Ignoring the pang of disappointment, I began inspecting the clothes at my side. There was a filmy skirt in mossy green and a thin blouse that seemed loose enough to slide off the shoulder. A dress was rumpled beneath them, a blue so subtle I thought it had been soaked in the juice of a single berry, with ribbons down the seams.

"I take it these are for me?" I asked.

Reed nodded, his concentration still on the fire growing beneath his palms. I thought I caught him shiver but couldn't be sure.

"Jassin will be in attendance tonight for sure," he said to the hearth. "The wealthier and prettier you look, the better, so I called in one of my last remaining favors—we only have the gown for the evening. We don't know how long that potion of Robin's will work; this could be our last night."

This could be our last chance, is what he meant.

"I'll do my best to be...appealing." Annoyance colored my tone, but I doubted he noticed, and honestly, I wasn't entirely sure *why* I was annoyed with him. Because I wasn't getting all of his attention? Because he was keeping something from me? Because he reminded me that we had a mission, and that mission had a time limit? Those were all things I should expect, and nothing I could begrudge him for.

Sighing at my own circular thoughts, I stripped out of my wet clothes while his back was turned and hurried into the borrowed layers of my costume. The blouse hung underneath the dress like the tease of a Venus flytrap, the wide neck visible over the shoulder straps which were only as wide as two of my fingers. The green and blue tones against my skin made me feel like some sort of creature born of the marsh, blurring the line between fields and empty sky. The skirt swished around my legs, giving the gown some twirl. I kept my dagger where it was, secured to my thigh, in case I should need it, and the net at my breasts, though it itched. I added back the belt from the night before and finger-combed my hair into what I hoped was a presentable array.

"So, what do you think?" I put my arms out and, when Reed finally stood to look at me, turned in as graceful a circle as I could manage.

He didn't reply and I stopped to search his face. He looked...enthralled. Or maybe impressed was a better word. After all, he hadn't seen me in much more than my farmhand-best since meeting me.

"I, uh..." he pressed his lips together, as if gathering his thoughts. "You look beautiful." He cleared his throat. "Jassin will definitely take an interest in you."

The brief spark of joy in my chest reduced to smoke.

"Especially," he continued, bending to the box of his belongings in the corner and retrieving one of those clear vials I had noticed before, "if you wear this."

"I hope it's not more poison."

I had yet to see the vial from the night before, and assumed it had been lost in our escape, crashed against the ocean waves and castle walls, but for all I knew, he had a hidden supply.

Reed approached me, his body blocking the fire behind him, so he encompassed my vision like an eclipse. "This one is perfume. I bought it from Robin back when she first started her apprenticeship. Her services were...cheaper then." Uncorking the vial, he took my forearm in one hand and placed the pale skin of my inner wrist against the opening, tipping both so the liquid blotted against my pulse. "It's a scent the high fae enjoy—a mix of musk and dainty flowers that manage to cut through the stink of court. Rub it in."

I did as he said, aware that his eyes were watching me so intently he might catch the goosebumps that peppered my flesh. The shadow he cast over me somehow pulled at me. It made me want to reach forward and burrow into his chest, the heat of his body on my cheek, his heartbeat in my ear.

Shaking my head, I backed away a step as if adjusting my stance, the scent on my wrist already invading my senses. That must have been where those cravings began, I reasoned.

"It smells lovely," I told him.

"It does," he said, his nostrils flaring. A muscle in his jaw clenched, drawing my eye to the strong, sharp line of it beneath his light beard, and I watched as he seemingly fought himself against saying more. The sight did something to me, and I swallowed down whatever heady, frivolous sensations were gathering in my body. This was no time for foolish hungers, but I couldn't move away.

Tension built between us, as steady as the fire in the hearth, but Reed was the one who broke it first. He looked down at the vial in his hand

and re-corked it.

Just like that, the strange spell between us was severed, our potential third kiss—the only one which wouldn't have been started to save me from imminent death—had vanished.

"After you, Winnie."

For some reason, the fact that he used my name instead of "little perch" or "my dear" felt like an ill omen my mind could not overlook.

Walking into the banquet hall was starting to become my nightly torment, but with Robin's perfume on my wrists, a borrowed dress hugging my waist, and Reed following diligently at my back, I was able to stride between the grandiose tables with some amount of gravitas. My well-worn shoes were thankfully hidden by my skirts and I straightened my spine, lengthening my neck and tilting up my chin for an air of arrogance. The role I was to play was a beautiful monster, flush with gold and my family's thirst for bodies to serve our every whim. I allowed a malicious glint into my eye, scanning the room as if for prey.

"I'll go to Jassin," Reed muttered as he passed me. "Wait, then follow."

I didn't dare nod or give any indication we were speaking, so instead I busied myself amid some high counters littered with bowls. They all glimmered with shallow pools of wine and spirits, some so poppy-red and slick against the glass I thought it might be blood.

From the corner of my eye, I watched Reed approach a high fae seated near the head of the table furthest to the left. The seat at the center was empty, most likely reserved for the prince, but the surface was laden with elaborately plated meats, and desserts flaked with gold. Given the finery the other tables lacked, that section of the room must be for higher-ranking members of the court, I reasoned, but I was starting to regret not pressing Reed for more background information on the roles and politics at play.

The fae Reed approached had silver hair tied back in a braid to emphasize the long points of his ears, and eyes black as onyx, which narrowed as Reed bowed to him.

Putting a goblet of red wine to my lips and feigning a sip, I watched as Jassin elegantly twisted his hand in the air, his mocking tone reaching me over the chaos of the banquet hall. A lendani at his other side laughed in response, her skin shining like a pearl and her hair like a waterfall of melted sugar that fell to her scaled tail. Their outfits almost matched—though Jassin's black-feathered shirt was cut along his chest, revealing skin dusted with silver hair, while the lendani's top was more reserved, the rich, black plumage flowing to settle against her long body. Every fae near her stared with rapt attention as she swayed in her chair, her admirers mimicking her once or twice before they caught themselves and blinked away her thrall. Despite the fae losing their ability to glamour, her beauty was a close approximation.

My gaze swept back to Jassin just as he slapped Reed across the face, and I almost dropped my haughty posture in shock. I could barely stifle the gasp as his head snapped to the side, the tray in his hand somehow unfaltering. Witnesses close to them went silent, watching the scene unfold with rapt attention.

"Left unattended, they could have been found by anyone," the silver-haired fae scolded, the snide tone grating on my ears, his voice almost a shout. "Taken. Sold. Ruined. Have you no honor in serving me when your very..." but I could not listen any further. Feeling the tips of my sharpened teeth with my tongue, I prowled through the crowd, letting my hips sway, my eyes falling like heavy bedroom curtains, inviting anyone to look.

Jassin must have sensed me, or maybe the quiet hush of the crowd around my steps alerted him, because he glanced away from Reed and focused on me, his sneer becoming a dangerous smirk. His inspection of me went from my bust to my belt, then the length of my legs, unimpressive as they were.

"Hello, little fae," he said with a subtle purr.

I dropped into a gentle approximation of obeisance, my head dipping softly. "I'm looking for Jassin, and was told I might find him here. Your reputation for an appreciation of beauty—" I looked once more over the elegant black of his clothing, the smooth silver braid laying over his shoulder with no strand out of place, "precedes you. Unless I have been misdirected?"

Oozing innocence, I blinked my eyes at him, ignoring everyone else in the room, including Reed and the stunning lendani.

"You have not," said Jassin, obviously pleased I'd heard of him. "Come, sit by me. Tell me what I can do for such a sweet, young thing."

His voice was as oily as a slug trail, but I smiled demurely and took the empty seat on his other side, grateful to put more space between myself and the eerie attraction of the woman to his left. If I looked at her too long, I might fall into her serpent's gaze, trailing her to my death.

I opened my mouth, but Jassin held up one finger. "Wait, one moment." He turned his cold gaze back to Reed, who stood so petrifyingly still it reminded me of a rabbit about to be struck. "You have failed me twice in so short a time. I'm still waiting for that human the guards said you carted back here for me—am I to assume you lost her?"

"Yes, Jassin—she was taken by a foreign crogwyn that night...and I believe the human is no longer. I am sorry to disappoint you." I'd never heard Reed act so timid and...droning, like his voice was as dead as his spirit. Still, his words were clever. After all, he did briefly lose me and I was currently quite *inhuman.*

"So, you have no idea where she is?" Jassin continued.

My pulse jumped at Reed's pause. He couldn't lie, and this was a simple yes or no question.

I leaned forward. "So sorry to interrupt, but is this human your servant?" I asked. "He doesn't appear to be glamoured."

"You are half right, child," Jassin praised, pressing his long, spindly fingers against my arm, as if to test the softness of my skin. "He appears human because the wretch only has one fae parent. A halfling. Isn't that so...vulgar?"

"What a revolting creature," I said, meeting Reed's blank expression. "No wonder you hit him!" I laughed a bit at that, letting my pointed teeth show.

This seemed to please Jassin, who turned his shoulders away from Reed, completely distracted, and moved those same fingers in little strokes along my flesh. I tried not to let the nausea show on my face as he raised his hand to his nose, inhaling my scent there. For a moment, I worried Robin's perfume had failed to mask my human smell, or that he'd felt the rocketing pulse under the thin skin of my wrist. But his smile only curved further.

"That's actually why I've come here," I continued, simpering. "My name is Winona Elmon, and I've been sent to find some servants for my household. I hear you're the man who can make this happen for me."

"I can make many things happen for you, Winona," Jassin rumbled. "Though you seem so young. Not yet sixty?"

I shook my head, scrambling to do the math in case he asked when I was born, but then he stood abruptly.

"Let us talk in my quarters." He held out his hand. "I can review my stock with you. Discussing prices of such things in the company of the court would be a bit ostentatious, don't you agree?"

Swallowing around the fear and disgust of being alone with him—no Reed, no witnesses, no veneer of pleasantry—I took his offered fingers and stood, letting him lead me back into the murky halls of the castle.

CHAPTER FOURTEEN

I pretended to wonder at every doorway and creature we passed, as if impressed for the first time with the lavishness and the sheer breadth of the compound.

"And you live here full time?" I asked as we climbed a set of stairs.

"I do. I am just as much a fixture as the prince—even more so, given I have no responsibilities that take me into other territories." His shoulders moved, as if the way he walked was a subtle dance. Though it was not subtle at all.

He was prideful, which would already be easy to play to, but now I also had the sense he craved a status above his own. With luck, I could spin some sort of tale where favors to me could glean him future admiration.

"Where are you from, little fae? I don't believe you said."

"I come from a city far south, at the edges of Ospil," I replied, smooth and steady.

Jassin turned to look at me with white eyebrows raised. "That is quite a journey. Have you been in this country long?" At that, we reached his door, now bracketed by two guards. One was high fae with coral-tinted hair and impressive muscles and the other was a crogwyn. I did my best to keep my face averted from the latter in case they had been the creature to see me leap from the window within.

"Oh, I was enjoying myself along the way, taking my time, so yes I've been in Trasia for a while now," I said.

The opulence of Jassin's bedroom was expected this time, but I did my best to ooh and ahh at the furs on his bed and the mirror-like floor. I rushed to those same windows I'd leapt from just the night before, admiring the view and studying the fullness of the moon. It was nearly time; I would soon be able to fetch Conor's cure.

"I have one of the best rooms," said Jassin at my shoulder. His hand rested on my arm, taking easy possession of my body. I debated shrugging him away, but I needed him on my side. I needed him to want me.

"I can see that. You are truly appreciated here, it seems." With the subtlest shift, I let my body lean back into his space.

"More than appreciated. I have power here," he replied.

My breaths were becoming shallow at his closeness, though I was sure he assumed it was lust instead of fear. I opened my mouth, searching for some opening line, some way I might broach Reed and servants without being pushy, but he beat me to the punch.

"And yours?" he asked, with a pause that hinted at some...discomfort. "What is the Elmon power? Can you transform at will here, or have you endured the unforeseen...*interruption* plaguing Trasia?" He tugged me backward, the move so slow I almost didn't realize it was happening until my back pressed firmly into his chest, the skin at the opening of his shirt hot like steaming coals. There was a tinge of unease to his voice, and I wondered if he feared being in the arms of a fae who had abilities when he did not.

"I've found my powers have deserted me some days past," I confessed. "Though at home I was able to transform into the water itself, becoming a wave or a whirlpool or a simple eddy—well, I'm sure you know the type. I'd hoped it was just a temporary affliction from traveling into an unfamiliar territory. This is my first time with a bit of freedom from my family and I…I am a bit nervous about it." I spun in his hold and put some distance between us, as if distressed. The curve of my backside hit the edge of the desk. "You're saying every fae in this country is encountering the same?"

"Unfortunately, it does seem that way," he replied. He looked down at me, his height towering over my own. "You are *such* a young thing, aren't you?" With a lick along his teeth, he leaned ever so slightly closer to me. "And yet your divine smell is one of…developed appetites."

I nodded, my gaze going hard as if offended. "I may be young, but I assure you I have been sent with strict goals and a heavy purse. I have little time for dallying. And if Trasia is powerless, I should want to return home as soon as possible. Your contracts for sale—"

"Oh, we are not powerless," Jassin corrected. He backed away from me, his expression so twisted with dark glee I almost grasped for the dagger beneath my dress. But he only turned to pad up to the wine cabinet by the door—the very one I had attempted to poison—and uncorked a bottle. I watched him pour a honey-colored liquid into two short glasses, then present one to me. With a wave of his hand, he gestured for me to sit in one of the overstuffed maroon chairs while he took one on the opposite side of a short table.

"How are you not powerless?" I pressed. "According to talk in the court no one can transform into their natural elements or compel a human to servitude."

"Humans *are* the new power, Winona." He sipped from his drink, and I mimicked him without actually opening my lips, looking to the liquor as if surprised by its flavor.

I tilted my head. "I don't...understand what you mean."

"I have always been in the business of bringing retainers into the castle; Prince Aeden adores me for it. I pick the young, the beautiful, the skilled, and one by one I either glamour them to fulfill mindless tasks, or I buy their service with contracts, as you mentioned. You have seen these humans in the castle?"

I shook my head, the pressure of a trap about to snap closed weighing on my chest. "Only heard rumors. Though you said that half-human mutt is under contract with you?"

"He is a...unique situation. But there are others. Humans I allow to retain their faculties while they fill my glass or stoke my fires. Use their skills to sing or perform stunts. *Whatever* I ask of them." He smiled, his innuendo clear. And if I wanted his favor, I had to act like I was on the same page.

"That's fantastic. I strive for the same." I put down my glass, as if with excitement. "My family is looking for help in the home that can't be met with simple glamours. After all, they are so dull that way, don't you think?"

"Exactly." Jassin downed the rest of his drink and licked his bottom lip in what I'm sure was supposed to be a seductive glide, but just made my ears heat with embarrassment.

"And do you have some of these humans for sale now?" I asked.

He paused. "A few."

He wanted me to beg, I realized. It was in the way he watched me, his expression hungry. Did he expect me to drop to my knees for him? Or lay on my back in the garish bed off to the side?

"I have a hefty amount of gold for the purchase," I assured him, keeping that innocent tone. "And connections with my family's court that could prove useful to you. Why, you would be treated like visiting royalty in Ospil. After telling them what I've witnessed, they would welcome you with open arms and make a myriad of trade deals with you. The more types of power, the better, isn't that so? And we'll pay handsomely for it."

"Those deals would have to be made with the prince," Jassin said, slowly. Carefully. "Isn't that so?" he parroted.

I shook my head. "So far, it seems to me that the prince is a figure out of touch with his people. *You* are the one who is here. *You* are the one who provides." I kept my eyes trained on his, imagining it was Flint across from me or Reed—someone whose skin I'd touched with my own fingertips. I thought of that now as I smiled.

Jassin leaned forward, and I worried I'd played my hand too strong, but with his elbows on his knees and his shirt gaping wide, he stared at me with such an appetite I thought he might very well pounce on me.

"It's validating to hear you think so, sweet little fae," he leaned ever forward, ready to close the distance between us with a kiss, or worse, "because—"

"But a question, if I may?" I interrupted, attempting to stall my thumping heart. "You say this loss of powers is recent, but you've been collecting these contracts for some time. That's genius planning on your part—I would never have thought to...*diversify* my power like that. My family only concentrates on material wealth, but wealth of the flesh—that is truly original thinking. If you were looking for some station beyond this, my father would be in line to give you a permanent seat of power if you could help him with the same."

Jassin paused. "And your father is in a position to grant such seats?

You are from the edges of Ospil. There are no courts there that I know."

For a moment, my mind drew a blank. What would a haughty princess say? Or...a warlord's daughter?

"There is no court...yet," I answered. "But my father is a powerful man, soon to be on his own throne. Which is why we're growing our staff."

"I see." His mouth turned stony.

It was as if the room grew colder around us, the windows shaking ever so slightly from the winds off the ocean. They rattled the glass and shook my confidence. Retracing every step I'd made in this conversation, I wondered if the dance was about to come to an end. Could my disguise be fading? All he needed to do was snap his fingers or call for his guards, and I was done. He could easily overpower me.

As smoothly as I could manage, I tucked my hair behind my ear on one side, glancing up to him with a coquettish bat of my lashes so he wouldn't notice the way my fingers delayed over the tip of my ear. Still pointed, thank the moon.

"So...a powerful man like you can name your price," I said, gaze low. "But, given I've borne my intentions before you, I am hoping for a good deal. How much for an unglamoured human, or for that half-fae mongrel? My seven brothers would love to break him." At this, I twisted my lips into a wicked sneer.

Jassin steepled his fingers together, his expression tighter now, less slack with lust. He suspected something, but knew I could not outright lie. The chance I'd left a hole in my story he could claw his way into had sweat gathering beneath my breasts despite the cool room.

"You are fortunate, for the interruption of power did not lose me too many slaves—I have some hidden away," he said, "but the unglamoured are special. That, along with some weapons we'd recently acquired and melted, means I also do not need much steel. However, the beauty of gold and gilded jewels will always be an asset to the court. I will give you an unglamoured servant for...twenty pounds of gold, or its equivalent in rubies. For the half-fae? Fifty."

Somehow, I managed to keep my mouth closed and my outrage masked in a light visage of contemplation. Inside, however, I was furious. Twenty pounds was an outrageous amount to ask for one person; a single pound could feed a family like mine for a year, it was so rare in the villages. We dealt mostly in copper and trade, and my mind spun, trying to find another avenue to try. I could pretend to have as much, but he might ask to see a portion of my claim now, blowing my chances.

"What about an exchange?" I asked. "A promise from me, on behalf of my family, freely given, for your place in our court guaranteed and double your fee at a later date. I could write it now and vow it to you."

He shook his head, seemingly disappointed. "I'm afraid even with a fae promise, I cannot wait so long for payment. My place for now is here, until my affairs are...settled."

"What could this court, as beautiful as it is, offer you that a new one could not? Beside the ages worn into the stone?" I pretended once more to sip from the glass, my anxiety spiking with every second. My time was running short here. If I didn't make this deal soon, I would have to flee his chamber, or risk being forced to continue the charade of my infatuation.

"I have certain projects in the works," he replied, and the vague answer tugged at me, as blatant as a frog's tongue stuck to my cheek.

"Projects having to do with your contracts? Or to counteract this...interruption?"

"Speaking of that—when exactly did you notice your powers were absent?" he asked.

"Days ago," I replied, scrambling to think of somewhere close enough in case the situation was localized, but far enough to believe I hadn't been lurking in his territory unannounced, "in a town to the south called Sleetgrave, I believe."

"Interesting."

Suddenly, he seemed finished with our conversation. He stood, and his tone turned dismissive. "If you decide you can meet my price within the week, you know where to find me. Until then, I'm afraid I must get back to the banquet." A future transaction was apparently more vital than ravishing me—a blessing, but also a curse.

"I *can* pay," I announced, and then cringed at the hint of desperation in my voice. "I have access to the gold, but obviously I can't carry so much in my bodice." I leaned forward a bit, as if to present my cleavage, reminding him that he wanted me—that I was an object he could have, in exchange for this deal.

A single brow rose in interest, his shimmering braid shifting to fall over his back as he flicked his head to the side. It reminded me of a horse flaunting its mane, prancing in a paddock where it believed it ruled over every speck of dust.

"Bring me the gold and you can have what you desire," he drawled. "I'm never above a good arrangement, and the half-fae can be yours, along with a few others, if you can pay. But beware, the mongrel should be kept underground—you'll want to make sure you have the necessary accommodations for his kind." Walking to the door, he held it open for me, gesturing to leave.

"Oh, why…might I ask?" I knew he kept Reed in that dank, window-less room, but I assumed it was because of his low station. "I'm afraid I know little about keeping half-fae—we usually just kill them."

"He derives his health and abilities from heat, even the sun," he replied. "A trouble, if you want to keep him docile. Not that I've concerned myself with that since the interruption—keeping him starved and beaten haven't been necessary as of late to lessen his strength—but if you were to travel far enough..." he trailed off and then puckered his lips with annoyance. "I really must be getting back." He opened the door and gestured for me to leave. "After you."

I strode down the hall, barely able to feel my legs beneath me, my head buzzing with half-formed thoughts and questions. Each time Reed had pulled me close, shivering. In his bed. His panic when the fire was out or too low. His shirtless chest basking in the sunlight as he caught fiddler crabs.

All this time, the cold had been his weakness, and he hadn't told me. He'd used me instead—my body, my warmth—just like Flint.

No. We were using *each other*, I reminded myself. This was a transaction, same as the one I attempted with Jassin: a business relationship. Reed didn't have any obligation to tell me what might hurt him.

But I was putting my life on the line for him.

If the potion had drifted from my system while I spoke to Jassin, or any time before that while I wandered the halls of this deadly castle, I would be murdered on sight. Surely that level of risk entailed some equal offerings on his part, and so far he'd done nothing for my brother except take me to Robin. We had an aim, but no solid progress. Was he really holding up his part of the bargain?

I nearly groaned aloud as I reached the banquet hall, Jassin only a few steps behind me. I couldn't handle another minute in this place.

"Excuse me," I muttered with a bow to the high fae, and then tacked on, "May the moon grant what you seek."

"You as well," he said, then strutted around me to the lendani he'd abandoned before. She immediately crawled into his lap, licking at the skin on his neck while he downed a goblet of that fae wine.

My feet flying beneath me, I kept my composure as much as possible as I fled.

CHAPTER FIFTEEN

I nstead of heading back to Reed's room directly, I used this precious
time alone to truly investigate the halls and rooms of the castle. For
the most part, doors were closed to me. Opening each was a risk I dared
not take, so I wandered, aimless and confused, peeking into any empty
room that happened to be exposed. Once in a while, if I heard no noise
inside, I'd knock and say, "Palmera, are you here?" before trying the
knob. It was a name I'd read in an old fae tale, and I had a backstory ready
about running into her in the mangroves where she'd saved me from
getting lost. But each time I'd find the door locked or nothing inside but
empty beds.

There was an old dining hall coated in a thin layer of broken snail
shells, and one closet-sized foyer clogged with the shed skin of some type
of iridescent reptile, but nothing that could help me. At some point,
as I neared the dungeons where Reed resided, I found the weapons
Jassin said they had confiscated—swords and pitchforks and a few trow-
els—things the men of a small town would hoard for eventual attacks.
Shame sat heavy in my chest when I calculated how many dead human
hands had held those weapons. As for why fae would suddenly need
steel, their new missing transformative abilities had to be behind the

acquisition. Still, the tools would be of no use to me since they weren't iron—and I barely knew how to wield my dagger—so I carried on.

The fire was low in the hearth when I entered Reed's cell. I was careful to make sure no one had followed me or seen me enter this section of the compound, but still I felt watched as I prodded the logs and made room for the flame to breathe, placing the very few leaves and twigs that remained from his stash on top. Just hours before, I had been at his bedside, holding him close, praying for his recovery. Now, I felt a bit like a fool.

Glancing around at his sparse furnishings, I realized how truly little I knew about the half-fae whose hands I had placed my life into for safe-keeping. He had a human father, a syra mother, and a single friend—if that's what Robin could truly be considered—but beyond that, did I really understand him? It was too simple to say he was biding his time in this castle, serving while waiting for his moment to strike and break free. He was tortured and belittled but showed moments of cheerfulness I thought signaled strength.

Perhaps he was only a good actor, as I was.

Jassin didn't know Reed's powers were still intact—to some degree—but it did seem like he'd known the interruption was coming. Either that, or the handfuls of contracts and indentured servants he'd been collecting were a happy accident. I didn't like the feeling of either thought as they slithered through my brain.

Reclining on Reed's low pallet, the marsh smell of the castle barely held at bay by my fading perfume, I stared at the light flickering over the stone ceiling, trying to pull apart the threads of this tangled mess ahead of me. And that's how Reed found me, over an hour later.

The door banged open, startling me, as he stopped at the sight of me on the bed.

"By the moon, Winnie, I thought Jassin had thrown you to the kelavees or slain you in his room!" He stomped forward, raking a single hand through his blond hair, but despite his concern I saw him glance with some appreciation at the healthy fire at the end of the room. "Where did you go?" he continued. "Jassin returned to the banquet, but you never surfaced. I feared the worst."

I sat up, taking his threadbare blanket with me despite the warm layers of my dress. "I wandered back here after attempting a deal with him—I was trying to think our way out of this."

He sat on the corner of the pallet, his hip by my feet and his expression still tight with anxiety. "What did he say? I take it then you weren't able to lie your way into buying my contract?"

I shook my head. "His price was too high, and he wouldn't accept a delayed payment, no matter how I promised it or what I offered to sweeten the deal."

Reed's eyes widened, the blue reflecting the fire like some chiseled amber. "Sweeten the...Did you offer—did you give him..." His gaze darted down my body.

"What? No! Well, it was implied, but that is not what we should be focusing on." I adjusted on the bed, sitting up straighter. "He wanted *fifty pounds* of gold for you. It's absurd! He obviously doesn't want to part with you, despite his assurances he was flush with servants, both glamoured and not. And..." I hesitated, wondering if I should share everything I'd learned, given I now knew Reed was still keeping such big pieces of himself secret from me.

"What?" He pressed, and then his hand was on top of my own, his rough, blunt fingers cool against my skin, so unlike the heat that had poured off of Jassin while he'd held me, caressed me.

Shivering with something beside a chill as Reed's thumb stroked over the back of my hand, I pulled away.

"He claimed he'd been buying up contracts for some time now, and he was well-stocked for the period of powerlessness the court is plagued with. That it's a form of power he'd cultivated."

Reed was quiet, his mind absorbing the information like a sea sponge.

I watched his face for hints that he was holding something back from me. What that would look like, I had no idea, since this was the face I'd seen since the first moment I met him. But again, why did it matter? Aggravation tore at me, and I found myself reaching for him. As my palm met his jaw, I tilted him to look at me, waiting until he could see the seriousness of my gaze.

"Reed. I need you to tell me. Why do you keep the fire going in the hearth with such fervor? Why is it important?"

It shouldn't have been so important to me that he tell the truth, but I needed it as desperately as my next breath. My heart kept flipping in my chest, prompting me to run and then begging me to lean closer.

"Tell me," I urged at his lingering silence. "Please."

"The heat makes me strong," he said eventually, his eyes wandering back and forth over my own with sorrow and something like shame. "My powers have always depended on it."

I released him. "There. Was that so hard?"

"Jassin told you," he guessed.

I nodded. "Instructed me to have some underground facility to keep you if I could meet his price, so you would be easier to control."

"I'm sorry you found out that way." He seemed genuine, and I knew those words couldn't be a lie, *per se,* but I knew better now than to assume they were the whole story.

"Why didn't you tell me? When you were sick or even the first night we shared a bed. Had I known..."

"What?" he asked, voice surprisingly tender. The light from the fire at his side embraced him with a tangerine glow, smoothing his features, waving over the curve of his lip and the almost-human bow of his ear. "Would you have laid with me more willingly? Stripped your clothes and pressed your bare skin to mine?"

I didn't answer. I wouldn't have, and he knew it, but I still felt betrayed in some way, being kept in the dark.

"If you were like any other creature here," he continued, voice low with dread, "you would have doused me in ocean water and stamped out every fire in my vicinity. You would take my clothes and the one blanket I've managed to steal and force me to curl on the stone while you starved me."

My breath caught.

"You would have taken the ice from the buckets in the kitchen and pelted me with blocks of it until I bled. Until I was scraped raw and my lips turned blue. And then you would have added chains—"

"Stop," I whispered.

"That is what I would have begged," he pressed. "To stop. To have mercy. But this place has none to offer, and neither does Jassin. They knew I could transform into smoke—hated my capacity for it, even though it's not an uncommon power, just because of what I am—and they wanted to make sure I never had the strength to do it."

His voice hardened. "I was expected to serve wine and food to any high fae who demanded it, and handle Jassin's laundry and rooms. I cleaned up after his nights of debauchery, and I served as a whipping post for visiting dignitaries or any creature with a grudge, brought beyond the gates so they wouldn't suffer for hurting me. I had to do that all while freezing and weak."

"Reed."

I couldn't stand hearing more. It was too horrible to imagine him growing up like this, abused and brutalized.

"I can see you're upset with me," he said, and though we were still close on the bed, our knees barely touching, it seemed as if he reached miles to touch his fingers to the pulse at my neck. "But please know...I keep this part of myself a secret for good reason. I don't tell anyone if I can help it. My omission wasn't meant to hurt you. I would never...want to hurt you."

He would never want it, but it would most likely happen anyway. It was unspoken, but so bright a truth I almost closed my eyes against the glare.

I wondered if the pulse at my throat was fluttering as quickly as I feared. He had to feel it, his fingertips lingering as they were. My breath was shallow, but I knew he would see the rise and fall of my chest in the firelight. His eyes darted to my lips and then away, and he started to remove his hand.

Before I could think better of my actions, I grabbed his palm and returned it. His words from the creek drifted through my memory, like the notes of a song I couldn't escape: *Your drive, your loyalty, your creativity, and your quick mind.* He had seen so much of me, appreciated me, and even though our time together had been brief, there was some power in knowing he could not abandon me like Flint. Tomorrow was the full moon, and we would be leaving each other once Robin used the blooming lilies in her antidote, equals in our solitary missions. But not until then.

Like two strangers passing in the street, we were in the same place and time for only the shortest span of a heartbeat, only then to be two ever-shrinking silhouettes.

If he was only mine for the moment, I wanted him mine in full. I wouldn't be ashamed of my attraction to him—this beautiful man who had suffered but still smiled, still tried. Who was desperate and attentive and sweet. Even though he was half-fae. Half a monster. At least for tonight, just physically, I could be the one to initiate. This would be on my terms.

I had little reason to deny myself.

Leaning forward, I pressed my lips to his, knowing there was no other intention behind it but *want*.

Reed's sharp inhale tickled my ears, and then he was kissing me back, rising up more on his knees to get closer to me. His mouth opened against mine and instead of air passing between us, or blood, there was just the press of his soft tongue stroking over mine, causing a spike of heat to shoot through my body.

Despite every play and poem I'd read, the sensation of actually kissing Reed was hard to describe. It was rhythmic and primal and aggressive, his chest pushing me down into the pallet, his knee a solid presence between my legs. But it was also furtive and lingering—an exchange of secrets we spoke in slow whispers with our moans and sighs, all *longing*. His mouth moved and I moved with him. He shifted against me and I gasped a breath against his lips, eager for more. Gods, I wanted to explore him for days.

When it wasn't to cover the blood on my chin or breathe air into my lungs, Reed kissed like the subject was one he'd mastered. The way he was gentle with me, while also stoking the rage and fire of passion in my body with his hands and mouth, erased every rushed and demanding kiss Flint had ever pressed into me. I hated to think of him now, wished I could push him from my thoughts, but comparing Flint to Reed was like at once thinking of clay, and then the kiln that forged it—they were too different. I was so grateful it was different.

When we broke for a respite, Reed kissed down to my collarbone, biting at it only to lick away the sting. I trembled as he pulled down the straps of the dress and stripped me of the shirt beneath.

"We shouldn't do this," he whispered against my flushed skin. My flesh pebbled.

It was another truth, but one I didn't want to hear. I could make any excuse I wanted—that this exchange of heat between us would keep him strong for tomorrow night, when we might need it, or that I owed it to myself to enjoy my body and his while I could, as someone who had no other ties and a desire for *living* I couldn't quite escape—but at this point my need was mindless.

With a strength I didn't know I possessed, I rolled us, so I straddled his waist, both of us panting and rumpled. The sight of his lips, wet and mussed from our kisses, had my hips twitching.

"Do you want me to stop?" I asked, stroking my hands under his shirt to meet the soft skin of his abdomen. I lifted them up to that broad, sturdy chest, my nails pricked him along the way. There was the slightest trail of honey-blond hair wandering to his breeches.

He groaned, closing his eyes and tilting up his head in surrender. "No. I don't want you to stop."

Another truth. A simpler one.

I leaned down once more, relishing his kiss like wine I could savor.

For someone with so much strength, he touched me with tender hands, only being rougher with me when I begged. It was a science we studied one lesson at a time. I learned he liked a slow, torturous grind and soft pulls at his hair. He learned to place his calloused hand at the top of my neck and hold me still for a kiss, to keep my moans quiet. We were rubbing against each other, and then there was a frenzy of motion as he tore off his garments and finished divesting me of my dress, so we were bare against each other. Before he could remove my breast wrap, I managed to turn to the side and slip it off with the length of netting still neatly hidden inside. The last thing I wanted was for him to reach for my skin and be met with burning iron instead.

On my back once more, he didn't hesitate to stroke over my flesh, cherishing the sight of me like a sweet he couldn't wait to devour.

The potion in my veins that coaxed my fae blood to the surface like a blush made me sensitive to his exhalation as it brushed warmly over my skin.

"Tell me what you want." His hands gripped my sides, the length of his fingers holding me secure as he mouthed at my stomach, then the jut of my hips.

What *I* want. Not what he wanted from me, or what he could do to me. I wasn't a pillar to rut against, but rather some creature he was worshipping; it was intoxicating to hear the desperation in his voice, the groaning undercurrent of it, and know it was for me, while he also cared about my place in this bed.

"Your mouth," I whispered. "On my breasts."

He dove to comply, sucking hard at the peaks and kneading them while I writhed. My breath became labored, my hands buried in the short strands of his hair.

"Your fingers," I panted, as my knees fell wide. "Inside me."

He stroked along my center, playing and teasing there so my entire focus narrowed to the glide of his fingertip.

"Reed." The demand was a whine.

He pushed one finger inside me, then two, slowly stretching so I released a sob against the back of my hand. As he pumped them in a steady rhythm, palm grinding at my apex and the friction of his fingers working me into a mess, I let my thighs spread wider. My core clenched and pulsed, and before it was too much, I grabbed at his wrist.

"Stop."

His head tilted up to meet my gaze and I realized he had been staring at his hand as it moved inside me. It would have made me press my knees together but before I could feel self-conscious about the lurid display, his eyes flashed black.

"Your body is begging for me to taste it. I want to taste it."

He cannot lie, he cannot lie, he cannot lie.

But I was too close, too empty and needy for him. I shook my head again.

"I want *you*. Inside me."

Cradled against my thighs, his hard length nudging against my entrance, Reed let me pull his mouth back to mine, closing his eyes so I could no longer see if they were human-blue or fae-black. I kissed him with a brutality that would have surprised me on another occasion, but with all the fear and danger and secrets of the castle around us, the outlet of our bodies was too appealing to ignore. Instead of fighting my desire, I let myself have every touch I craved.

When he pushed inside me, deliciously slow, I dug my fingernails into the skin of his backside, urging him deeper. Harder.

I could practically feel the power in his body growing as we sweat against one another, the hearth a goading presence off to the side, building us into a scorching frenzy. His arms bunched with strength as he held himself just above my chest, using the muscles of his abdomen to pound into my body. When I arched my back, he let loose a dark chuckle. It was like intoxication was taking him over, and then me. It was all encompassing, and in the throes of every thrust I had no problem contemplating how best to kill Jassin, if only I could feel this every day, every night. The pleasure was sweeping, cresting higher, pushing him into me, me into him, like we could never get close enough.

He slowed for just a moment, the low-lidded desire in his once-again azure eyes a mirror of my own, as if taking the time to appreciate the rapture on my face. And then he was taking me over, all hips and heat and teeth biting into my neck. The pressure inside me built as I clutched at his heavy shoulders, lost to everything but the sensations.

I was blind with it, burning and writhing against his body. I called out his name in a voice that would later embarrass me, if only I could muster up the strength. The moan Reed released into my skin was toe-curlingly deep, so different from the breezy and sweet voice he used to get his way.

He pulsed inside me, hot and deep, satiating some hunger within me that had been gnawing at my ribcage without my notice.

I breathed freely against him, our panting slowing into an easy rhythm that felt like relief.

We lay boneless in each other's arms then, Reed warmer than I had ever felt him, like a fever that would have killed another man. Small shocks of pleasure streaked through me as he trailed a lazy palm over my waist, my thighs, my breasts. His rough fingertips nearly had me moaning for another round but—regrettably—the days of stress and exertion, plus an exquisite release, caught up with me. As the light slowly faded around us, I was pulled into a heavy sleep, my cheek sticking to the muscles of his chest, as content as if I was back home in my bed.

When I woke hours later, a crick to my neck and my limbs pleasantly sore, I found the cinders in the fireplace smoking, and Reed missing along with his clothes.

There was no note for where he'd gone, but then again there was no parchment or ink here to write with, so I assumed he was gone again to fetch me breakfast. It was unsettling, but I found myself looking forward to that fishy-smelling, honeyed sausage.

I shifted, my legs a bit sticky, and noticed the room was slightly...muted.

Moving my tongue over my blunted, human teeth, I gasped. My disguise was gone, and there was little chance Robin had another dose. I hadn't been able to buy Reed out of his contract as a high fae, and now—as a human—I was even more useless. I had failed. We'd have to return to our back-up plan: kill Jassin. I would need to *actually* kill him. Just last night I'd been fine with the idea, as I lost myself in Reed and his body, but now I wasn't sure how it would ever work.

Dressing in my outfit from home, the bland trousers and tunic more tattered than I remembered, I tried to filter what I knew about this compound and its inhabitants into useful scenarios. As a would-be glamoured human, I could again try to slip poison into Jassin's drink, just more directly than before. Or I could find out his schedule from Reed and fall into his path, an unconscious human for him to take advantage of, only to stab him through the heart with my iron dagger—though he would most likely recognize me before I could strike.

If I hid in the mangroves as he was leaving the castle for an errand, I could load my net launcher and trap him—if he didn't have many guards with him. I played each situation to its conclusion, but it was hard to imagine an outcome where I lived and also escaped back to Harnsey. Not to mention, there was still the issue of collecting lilies for Robin's proposed antidote for Conor. I didn't know how long it would take to brew, but if I was a wanted criminal in the court, having just murdered one of their highest-ranking members, I had no hope of lingering to retrieve it.

Groaning with frustration, I prodded the fire, but there were no pieces of wood left with which to build it. The remaining few book pages caught and then died within seconds. The flames needed something heartier to consume.

Inspecting the sparse room, I wondered what to pass my time with, but the only thoughts circling the drain of my mind were about violence and espionage. Eventually, after waiting in vain for Reed to return, I grew anxious and placed last night's dress, neatly folded, on the bed—to let Reed know I had left without any duress—and cautiously exited his room. With my dagger back in its rightful place along my thigh and the net in my breast wrap, I was as armed and prepared as an unglamoured human could be. There had to be *something* I could do, I reasoned. Sitting still had never solved my problems before.

If I took the stairs to the right, which led toward the washroom, I would pass by storage that might have burnable materials for Reed's fire, like the crab nets I'd spotted. Or, if I went straight, I could take weapons from the collection Jassin had curated, in case I needed to fight my way out of here. I could also travel to one of the libraries in the hopes of coming across some magical solution to my homicidal needs, but I didn't want to think more about the murder I'd need to commit.

So, I went right.

Making sure to keep my steps slow and halting, with my face vacant, I was ready for any creature to approach. I wouldn't use my weapon unless my life was in imminent danger, but given the muted daylight seeping through the cracks of the castle walls, I hoped the hallways would be mostly deserted.

What I didn't expect was to hear a slow, squelching sound, like mud scraped off a boot, from the turn ahead of me. Right where the storage room was located.

I halted and leaned against the wall as if resting. With my eyes flat and my mouth agape, anyone would believe that I was a puppet without a master, slack without purpose.

The sound happened again, closer, and then a monster lumbered around the corner, heading right towards me. It was like a mound of muck had been given life. Around a pair of barely-there eyes, there was only wrinkled, brown skin, slick with some kind of mucus, and an amorphous body that rippled and heaved inches down the hall. It came up to my chest, and I would have called it a slug if it weren't for the short arms hanging limply at its side and the circular, toothy mouth nestled in the folds beneath its eyes. A mouth that tugged at my consciousness.

I'd seen that shape before.

There were thick, hair-like appendages laying smooth against its head, like hair it had tidied, but upon seeing me those strands straightened and then tipped forward. At the end of one limb, which stretched longer than my arm, was a flower—wide, with white, triangular petals that seemed to shimmer. The flower dipped close to my face and my heart hammered against my chest, but I kept my breathing steady, my eyes unfocused and aimed somewhat to the left.

It wiggled the blossom, as if to tempt me, but I did not move.

This creature was the thing that bit my brother. An...*anglock*, Robin had called it. Whether it was the exact same monster or just a member of its species, I could not be sure, but either way I had to fight the urge to clench my hand into a fist. I had to remain motionless, empty, but inside I was roiling.

Robin had said they sometimes visited the court, but how much of a coincidence was it that I'd spotted one?

The thing lingered, swaying the flower until it almost brushed the tip of my nose, but it must have grown tired of my inaction, for it eventually backed away to continue down the hall. It took forever to leave, and I counted my breaths to keep centered, waiting until the coast was clear to move along. I would kill the monster right now if I thought it would save Conor, but with luck the thing would bite me and I'd be in even worse shape than him. Rare or not, with Reed or not, I'd hunt for the lilies in the southern tip of the marsh as soon as the moon rose tonight. It was all I could do. Then I could bring them to Robin—

I had turned down the wrong hallway, I realized. The storage room I'd imagined was instead the hall Reed had warned me against. Maybe I'd taken a right instead of a left, but I couldn't be sure. Still, there were no kelavee guards present, and the open room ahead wasn't the laboratory he'd said was dangerous, so I peeked inside. It seemed to be a pantry of some kind. Barrels of wine were stacked in towering piles right near the door, a row of crates clean with new polish and sharp corners nestled beside them. One was full of wrinkled yellow berries, and the next...a shallow container of soft pink flowers, their six petals like long, dainty curls—pointed. Exactly how Robin had described.

Neluma lilies, which supposedly only grew in the marsh under a full moon. And yet here they sat in droves, daylight dragging through the sky outside. My heart staggered and then sank down to my gut.

This was Conor's cure. There was a mountain of it, readily available for the court, as if freshly delivered by the monster itself.

And Reed had lied to me.

Again.

CHAPTER SIXTEEN

Holding open the bottom of my shirt like a basket, I gathered as many of the blooms as I could fit, all while blinking back heinous tears. Behind this container was an older one, nearly hidden from view until I stood on my toes, which held a few decaying lilies browning with age. Last month's supply, then. They had been here all along.

How foolish I was to think Reed's abilities and the source of them were the only secrets he kept, the only omissions he let fester between us. And that's exactly how this wound felt, like something had been carved out of me and only putrid, rotting flesh remained. He told me to avoid this area, as if the kelavee guards protected something nefarious, but that room was further down. This was just storage, there was no way he wasn't aware of these flowers in easy reach. And if Reed knew this...did Robin as well?

I'd never seen her within the walls of the castle, but she was supposedly Reed's closest friend. I tried to remember the conversation where she told me about the lilies, but it was all a blur of drinking that potion and hatching our plans. Had she said something about hearing where they were? Or wondering?

Sniffing down my disgusting despair, I hurried from the hall back toward Reed's dungeon, ready to fetch my bag and flee.

Only, there was a lendani blocking my path.

I just managed to halt before running headfirst into her, my breath coming in panicked gasps as she looked me up and down. Her body was covered in wispy rags, so she appeared to be hovering in a thick mist, her dark hair the only color shining against her pale skin. Even her eyes were so light a blue they were nearly white—there was no pupil or iris I could discern.

I was obviously unglamoured, and it was too late to pretend otherwise, but I hesitated to drop my treasure and reach for my dagger. Maybe she wasn't as dangerous as the books had painted her; after all, she was a beauty meant for luring innocents to their death and—beyond her elegant features—I did not seem to be immediately affected by her. So long as she kept her tail behind her, I hoped I had nothing to fear.

But then she smiled. A hum echoed around her, like a swarm of bees, and her skin began to glow. Her hair thickened into soft waves and her mouth widened, lips pink and thin like my mother's. Then her maw grew wider still, until she might swallow my skull in one bite.

She held out a hand to me and I backed up one step, and then another. The hum intensified, and I found it harder to move my legs. They were heavy, like my arms and my eyes. I blinked but it was slow.

The lilies tumbled to the stone floor at my feet, and I stumbled at the weakness in my limbs. My hands barely cushioned me as I fell onto my backside.

"No…" I managed to whisper, ready to beg. But the lendani only flicked her tongue, a soft, lulling note merging with the hum like its own song. My arms trembled and my heart slowed.

She bent, the move so graceful and fluid I wondered if she was made of the ocean itself, like how Reed was made of smoke.

Reed.

Anger suffused me, keeping the exhaustion in my body at bay for just a second longer, which was all I needed. Letting myself fall onto my back, I weakly reached into the loose band of my pants, grabbing the handle of the dagger tied there.

The lendani's torso bent over mine, her hands hovering. I watched her fingernails grow sharp and long, becoming talons.

My back was pressed into the cold stone as the vibration intensified, pulsing inside my mind and my lungs, as if my entire being was being shaken apart. I managed to pull the knife free, my movements agonizingly slow.

With almost tender affection, the creature raked her claws down my stomach, digging deeper as she went. White, hot pain blinded my vision, and my breath froze in my lungs as I bucked up from the ground in agony. I held back a scream, some part of me still demanding I play a part. If she thought I'd succumbed fully to her charms, she would get closer. The thought was broken and slow, but I knew it was my best chance. Using the movement of my arch, I shifted my hand higher, managing to turn the handle upward. But I couldn't thrust it. I needed her closer.

Turning my head to the left, as if passing out from pain, I tried to soften my breaths.

I could only watch as she sighed with pleasure and sucked on her fingers, her long tongue eerily blue. She thought she had won. And then she dipped her head—to lick at my wounds or tear at my throat, I couldn't guess—but this was *not* how I was going to perish. Rage and love and terror had my arm twitching with as much force as I could muster, and it was just enough. The tip of the blade struck the creature in the chest, below where my own heart would have rested. The knife was only an inch or so deep, but I could not push it further.

The hum went dead as she peered down at the wound, mouth floppy with surprise. The sizzle of cooking meat reached my ears. Iron burned through her and she shrieked, the sound so loud it echoed against each wall around us, bombarding my eardrums until I thought they would burst.

Scrambling backward so the dagger slipped free of her flesh, the lendani hurried away from me, crawling on those sickly talons, her tail thrashing behind her. It smacked my foot and then swerved out of sight. As soon as the droning whine of her magic stopped, my mobility returned, and I could finally hold a hand to the open cuts on my stomach. They were not so deep that I thought she had hit something vital, but I was losing blood fast.

I needed to get out of here.

Grabbing bunches of the lilies from the floor with one bloody hand, I held the fabric of my shirt to the wounds with the other and stumbled onward, my heart pumping so hard it was a wonder I could still feel the sharp, twisting ache where her claws had sliced into me. If that was a lendani during this interruption of power, I could scarcely imagine how strong her control would have been only a week before. It was hard to think of myself as *lucky* in this moment, but I knew that's how Conor would have seen it.

Thankfully, Reed was still absent from his room. I rummaged through his belongings for another shirt to press against my wounds, uncaring of the streaks of blood I left on his meager possessions. His spare dirty tunic would have to do for now, and I used some twine to tie it in place. Dropping the flowers into my bag and hoisting it over my back, I left his room, ready to never see it—or him—ever again.

I kept myself small, checking every corner and passageway before I entered, sneaking my way back to the closest exit. This route, at least, I felt confident I knew well enough to traverse on my own. *Left and down, before you drown, you take a right...*

Shallow water crashed against my ankles, louder than thunder in my ears. I was approaching the exit tunnel, but every second felt wrought with inevitable peril.

I didn't know why I assumed I'd feel relief once I fled the castle walls for the deep expanse of the mangroves. Probably because I was a fool.

The jump into the mire was beyond painful, and even more arduous. Every splash of algae-coated brine against my stomach was like a slap, the salt grains burrowing into the slashes there like maggots chewing on me from the inside out. I couldn't tell if the tide was coming or going, but my fury kept me pushing onward. It didn't matter if I had to swim or crawl through the muck at my feet, I would make it. I shoved through the waist-high water, gasping with the effort. Sweat beaded at my hairline and dripped down my cheek like tears.

The wall housing Robin's cave was vast enough for me to spot from leagues away, now that I knew how to look, and I focused on the looming cliffs, counting my breaths and blinking away the dizziness that teased at my body.

Something brushed my leg, but instead of panicking I continued on. I dared some syra or manyda to pull me under. My knife was still solid in my grip, my other hand pressing the borrowed clothing to my injuries, and I was ready to slash and strike anything that touched me. The flowery language constantly lilting through my thoughts had abandoned me, and something feral had been left behind.

Keeping to the left of the cave entrance, I slowed so as to not make ripples that would give me away. Luckily, I had the whistling of a sprinter bird to cover my approach, and just as it flitted into the grove's treetops, I reached the wall. The slick and mossy surface brushed against my back as I strained my human hearing, but I could make out only the quiet shuffling of motion inside. There was no way to tell if Robin was alone.

I would just have to risk it.

Heaving myself upward, my gaze found Robin, her tall, pale form stark against the dark interior. She looked at me with wide eyes as I clawed my way into the cave.

"Winnie," she said, tone uneasy. She left her place at her worktable and stepped towards me, her eyes pinned to the crimson blur spreading down my tunic. The thin trails of blood dripping down my waist would be obvious, but I hoped she couldn't tell how weak I was as I unsteadily made it to my feet.

"What's happened? Are you alright?"

"I have the flowers," I bit out. "You'll make the antidote for my brother."

It might have benefited me to *ask* for her help, to pretend like I'd been injured looking for Reed and had no idea the lilies in my bag weren't picked by him. I could have said I found them a few miraculous hours before nightfall. But my ability to pretend had been stripped of me, just like the fae and their capacity to transform. I was nothing but the raw materials of my body, the rage and resolve that kept me moving.

She took another step, and I brandished the dagger.

"Don't," I warned, letting the rucksack drop from my shoulders. I kept her in my sights as I rummaged inside and clutched a handful of flowers, then stumbled forward to drop them on her table. The high fae had her hands raised in surrender, though I was sure she could easily subdue me.

"I will make the remedy," she agreed, moving toward her mortar and pestle. Her hands moved with careful and deliberate ease as she pulled the petals from their stems and added them to the shallow bowl. "But you need to tell me what's happened to you."

"Why do you care?" I asked, wondering if I could sit without risking falling unconscious. "And no half answers, or questions, or statements that evade me."

She nodded, her wrist twisting as she ground the petals into paste. "I care because you are a person, and I dislike harm coming to people. I care because I worry you've been hurt battling Reed, and I want to know if he is alive. I care because you have obviously been through a lot and—from what I can tell—you probably did not deserve it. Then again, deservedness has never really had much bearing on the way things are."

I laughed, but it came out as half a sob.

"If only I had fought him," I murmured. My legs wobbled and I allowed myself to sit, catching my breath but keeping my knife at the ready. "These are from a lendani. I was in the wrong place at the wrong time." My hand tightened around the handle of the dagger. "Did you know the flowers were in the castle this whole time?"

Robin paused in her work, and I knew she was wondering how to spin her response—how to lie without lying.

"Please," I said, wondering if this same trick would work on her as it did on the man I'd slept with just last night. "Please, just tell me."

"I did," she confessed. "Or at least, I assumed they were. The lilies are common in some desserts the prince favors."

"What about the full moon?" I continued.

"Reed said he'd *heard* the blooms could only be collected then. It's a common folk tale about neluma flowers..." she paused, looking at me, and I nodded for her to continue. "How a gorgeous young man found them on the full moon and plucked them for his lover, only to be murdered and eaten by a kelavee. His death cursed that particular grove, where all plants withered until the moon's light brought them back, since that is when his lover wept over the vacant lily pads. I simply agreed with Reed...knowing he had probably heard that tale."

Having it all spelled out had nausea rising up my throat and saliva filling my mouth. I shouldn't have asked. It only made me angrier.

"Hurry up," I said through gritted teeth. My pulse was slowing, though it remained strong, so the blood loss must have steadied. I figured I could most likely make it back to the shallow marsh ahead of my hometown. There would be women hunting for mussels there, or maybe even Conor—with Ma's help—searching for those pink-tipped crab claws he swore could emit electricity. The closer to home I was when I collapsed, the better.

"Done," Robin responded. "This was all I needed. The rest was ready." She took the pink, mottled paste of the flower petals and added it to the very flask I had drank out of days before, using a funnel to pour it in. She capped and shook the container, her pointed ears held close to the metal. "That should do it."

Her towering form drifted closer, and I raised the dagger. "Leave it there." I gestured to the floor.

She placed the flask on the ground, just within my reach, before backing away.

"I am sorry you're going through this," she admitted, and though I knew at least that was true, that didn't mean she would assist me any further. For all I knew, she would turn me in to Jassin or Reed or any other high fae in this compound as soon as I turned my back.

I reached for the flask, hissing at the stretch of my wounds, just as I heard the splash of someone moving beyond the cave entrance. Turning, I managed to stumble off the chair and move to the side, my blade in one hand and the flask in the other, just as Reed pulled himself up into the room.

He was drenched from head to toe, his clothes sticking to him, and I watched him shake out his short hair before raking it back with a hand. His easy grin was in place until he caught sight of the blood staining my torso.

"Winnie...what hap—" he took a step, and I raised the dagger once more, ignoring the shake of my arm. Gods, I was tired.

"Don't come closer." I edged sideways, gesturing for him to keep his distance, but he ignored me.

I blinked, and he was there, face pinched in concern, those blue eyes tracing my features with affection and worry and a whole host of other emotions I couldn't stomach. His hands reached for my arms, as if to hold me.

I struck.

His gasp was like the sharp, tinny sound of a sword on a grindstone. He glanced down at the superficial slice in his side with something like surprise, his fingers touching the injury and coming away dark with red. The slice sizzled and smoked, and he grimaced from the pain of the iron, but he remained standing. He didn't back away.

Guilt dug its claws into my shoulders, but I held firm. "I...I told you not to come closer. I'm leaving. And if you follow me, I won't make so shallow a cut next time."

"She found the flowers, Reed," Robin said behind him, but he didn't look at her. Instead, his gaze was swallowed by my own.

I shifted to the left once more and this time he followed my lead, twisting to keep me at his front as he backed away. His shoulders hit the cave wall and slowly, as if with despair, he slid down the craggy surface, hand still on the wound I'd inflicted. I wondered why he didn't simply shift into his smoke form to heal it. Maybe he wanted to suffer. Or maybe that was just another secret he kept—something he didn't want even Robin to know.

"Please, Winnie," he whispered, "let me explain."

I shook my head, breathing deep as I moved closer to the hollow exit. "I can't. I won't." My voice shuddered and I hated the emotion that leaked there. It was as if my shame was trickling onto the ground along with my blood. "I know you wanted me here to kill Jassin or free you. I couldn't buy you out...that was my failure. But we're both too good at pretending to be someone we're not. I don't—" I took another step, wincing at a pulse of pain along my abdomen. My time was running short. "I don't know how I could have ever trusted you."

Finally, the back of my foot reached the exit, and I readied myself for a painful leap into the water.

"Don't follow me," I warned. Then I turned and jumped.

My vision grew spotty as my feet hit the silty bottom, the water's salt piercing me with every push into the marshy sweep. Sounds grew hushed and it took more and more energy to open my eyes when I blinked, but I carried on. Images of Conor chased me, urging me forward. I could see his hair dipping into his face as he blew on a puff of dandelion seeds, then the toothy grin he'd made behind our mother's back right before she found the worms he'd left under her mug. His scent, like sea poa grass and the sulfuric powders he collected, was strong in my nose, just as the earnest strength of his soft voice played in my ears. He'd promised with pure enthusiasm to sell whatever inventions he made to bring me to Clarcton, to fund the dreams I had of acting on a stage or writing the next great play. He didn't care how long it took to support me, but I was running out of time to save him.

While I marched through the longest section of the mangroves, avoiding the sprawling platforms of the compound, the water continued to rise. I had no choice but to halt and put the flask and knife in my bag so I could use both arms to swim. The labor of it had me tipping, then coughing up water as I righted myself, and I took a breather against one of the wider tree trunks I passed. The forest was growing sparser, so at least I knew I was heading in the right direction, but beyond that I had no idea how much longer I needed to travel—hours, at least, even if I rushed despite the noise it would make.

I nearly cried then, the heat in my eyes threatening to spill. One tree's roots prodded my knees as I passed, and I debated sitting in their mesh, taking a rest, but I didn't trust myself not to fall into the water as I slept. No, I had to keep going.

I pushed myself off the woody network, only to hear something to my left. The sky was darkening, the tide high, so it could be any manner of creature beneath the water. A syra or lendani or kelavee. It could even be an anglock, but I dared the sky to send one to me so I might enact my own type of revenge as I severed its flowered limb and stuck it like a harvest pig with my knife. Maybe I'd wrap it with my iron net and slowly tighten it until its muddy, gelatinous form poured from the spaces between the twine.

Rotating slowly, I scanned my eyes over the water, searching for any ripples beyond my own. There, just a few trees back, was a gentle crest where there should only be steady tide. Something was following me, hiding when I faced it.

Carefully, I leaned back into the tree trunk and pulled my bag forward. At the top was the wooden box of glowing powder. Good, that could work. I was probably too weak to crank the net shooter anyway, even if I had the time to pull and unravel the net from my breast band, but I could throw something, albeit not very far. The only thing that was light enough in my bag was the water filtration device I hadn't needed. I guess now I did.

Opening the box, I dipped one side of the cylindrical device into the powder, then the other, wary of tapping it too forcefully. I tipped my head up, but with the lengthening shadows and my own dizziness, I couldn't be sure if whatever stalked me had gotten closer.

Readying the bottle, I inched toward the source of the ripples. Something flashed beyond the bark like a dark, nebulous stain. Like smoke. Wrath granting me strength, I threw my makeshift weapon.

I shut my eyes tight, blocking my face with my hand, but I could still make out the blinding flare against my eyelids. A familiar voice cried out in shock, confirming what I'd thought I'd seen. Reed was following me. To kidnap me and give me to Jassin in exchange for his freedom? To convince me to try one more time to murder his master? Either way, I would not be caught. I refused. Conor needed me, and I'd already been gone for days. Who knew how far the petrification of his body had progressed?

With any luck, the flash of light had blinded Reed and the damage would last a few minutes while I hurried away. Taking a sharp turn, I rushed through the water in long strokes, ignoring the agony in my gut.

My heartbeat faltered, my chest constricting as I gasped in a wet breath. My arms gave out just long enough for my head to dip under the water.

I pushed myself back up through the surface, coughing and thrashing.

The spots in my vision grew and I put every ounce of concentration and energy in my body to the task of getting myself to another tree. If I could hold onto the roots or climb onto a branch, I would be safe. At least for a little while.

My heart stuttered.

And then there was a wave of peace that crashed over me. My eyes closed and my body went limp, the darkness taking me over in its embrace.

CHAPTER SEVENTEEN

I woke to a woman's scream and the feel of rough hands pulling at me. The agony in my stomach had somehow lessened, but I felt woozy as I opened my eyes, blinking against the sunrise. It was morning already? It hadn't even been night when I...I had been reaching for a tree in the mangrove. And yet here I was in shallow water, being pulled from the reeds. Mud coated most of my body, and somehow my bag was still wrapped around my shoulder.

"Move, girl!" The woman yelled, then turned to shout someone's name over her shoulder. I found myself able to kick at the sludge and help her drag me upright. My throat was sore, and I coughed through a harsh breath, feeling as if I must have swallowed some of the saltwater.

"Where am I?" I asked, voice hoarse. "Is this Harnsey?"

The woman wore a shawl to ward against the early autumn winds, a woven basket tipped over at her feet. Her scowl was impressive, as was her strength as she hauled me to my feet.

"The edge of it, yes," she said as she released me. I wobbled a bit but kept my feet. "Did you fall in? You look a bit rough."

"Oh. Yes." I looked down at my tunic to see the blood was mostly disguised with layers of mud. If I told her I was from the fae lands, there was a chance she would turn her back on me, worried I was a monster masquerading as human. Or she might believe I was one of the blessed escapees like Aven and Melia. But I needed to get home. There wasn't time.

I scanned the swath of coast from left to right, studying the cordgrass and the height of the cattails. An egret lazily glided on its stilt legs closer to the shore, searching for dawdling fish. The landscape was familiar enough, but the marsh was not the same shade of limpid brown as home.

The man my rescuer had called to ran up to us, out of breath. He was elderly, with a stooped back and thin, knobby legs beneath his knee-length trousers. "Lynette? Everything alright?"

"No, it's not alright!" The woman replied, one hand on her hip. "I called you five times to help me get this poor girl out of the mud, and where were you? Playing cards with Conall again?"

She turned and yelled at him some more, but the feeling of being watched caused me to glance back toward the water. The mountain of mangrove trees towered far to the west, and the vast fields of high stalks ahead of me were broken only by narrow, opaque streams of water. I could see no one else. A fog was rising in the distance, clouding my view, but I still felt as if something spied on me from within.

"Girl," Lynette called, "are you from here?"

"What? Yes. I must be going. This is south of Harnsey?" Without delay I lifted my legs through the muck and started toward the shore.

"You look a mess," she said at my back. "Are you sure you wouldn't want a wash first?"

I shook my head. "No, thank you." I hoisted my bag tighter against my back. "Stay sharp, stay dry."

"You as well," she called, and I headed northward, knowing I was only an hour or so away from my brother.

At first, I thought it was my determination and a full night's sleep that had me feeling so improved. However, as the mud started to dry and stick to me like an uncomfortable weight, I peeled my shirt away from my skin, expecting the pull of my wounds, only to see a murky paste beneath the cloth.

Halting, I inspected the injury, but it was coated in a gritty veneer that smelled like licorice.

"Mallow," I said into the empty air.

The same salve Reed had kept for his frequent beatings.

Dropping my shirt back into place, I ignored the pang in my chest and hurried on. He had helped me, maybe saved me if I really had blacked out in the water, but I couldn't think about that now. Couldn't think about his gray-tinged face as he slid down the wall in Robin's cave, fractured and desolate. As if he *needed* my forgiveness, was heartsick without it. My confusing emotions could wait.

I came to the edge of my hometown, the ramshackle houses and wooden fences as familiar as the planes of my own face. A few children chased each other down the dirt-packed streets as I passed the central well. There was a line for the townswomen to fill their buckets, eyebrows low with concern and murmurs of gossip traveling on the breeze. Nothing had changed, and yet it felt remarkably...different. Was it always this cluttered? Was there always so much dust? So much tension?

"Winnie?" A little girl ran up to me, her long hair tangled in the salty air that squatted over our town, and it took me a second to recognize Maire's eldest, Sorra. "You're back! Ma said maybe you were eaten by a marsh monster!"

"I bet I look like it," I said, conscious of the grime covering every inch of me. "Hey, Sorra, do me a favor?"

The girl's dress was a bit short since she continued to grow as fast as her mother could sew, but Sorra tugged at the edges and made a dainty bow. "Of course! At your wish!"

"Go tell your mother I'm starving for some of her seeded bread, and I'd love for her to visit me tonight." Whether or not this cure was successful, I would need the company of my only other friend, to confess my stories—and my sins. If anyone could understand the tangled web of my emotions over Reed, especially after the mess with Flint, it would be her.

"Okay!" She scampered off and I trudged through the town, ignoring questioning stares and more than one hand-covered rumor circle.

My house was a strangely welcome sight, considering how often I'd dreamed of leaving, but where I thought I would feel elated to return home successful, there was a lingering sense of...defeat. I'd gone into the fae lands, tricked more than one monster, killed a guard, and found the antidote to the toxin destroying the person I loved most on this earth. And yet, there was no bubbling elation or triumphant glee as I pushed open the creaking door. Just...exhaustion.

My own mother wasn't even there to greet me. The living room was empty.

"Conor?" I called.

"Win?"

I dropped my bag and pulled out the flask, uncaring if I left muddy footprints or puddles on the wooden floor.

Conor was right where I'd left him, as if he were one of my mother's clay statues collecting dust on a shelf. As soon as I entered his workshop his neck turned, his clear-eyed expression and overly large ears a welcome familiarity, but that was all of him that moved. The rest of him remained stagnant in his chair.

Rushing to his side, I couldn't help but catalogue the way his illness had spread. Though most of his skin was covered by a long-sleeved tunic and pants an inch too long for him, his hands were covered with that same bark-like texture. Even his neck showed signs of its spread.

"Conor," I said through a sniff, running one of my muddy hands through his hair. "Gods, I missed you. I'm sorry I took so long."

"Win, have you been with the fae this whole time? The town—"

"Here," I interrupted. Unscrewing the flask, I held the opening to his mouth. "It's a cure for the bite."

His lips parted and I tilted the liquid down his throat, a wet laugh escaping me at the scowl he made. Apparently, it didn't taste like honeyed mead.

"Ugh, what is that?" he complained.

"Other than some very specific flowers, no idea," I replied, almost laughing as a hot tear tracked down my cheek.

Out of habit, I brushed my thumb under Conor's chin as he swallowed the last of it, catching any spill. It was what I'd done when he was much younger, when I was the only one home to care for him, but being back in this house made me feel as if I had traveled in time. Here was my baby brother—the one I'd held when he cried, danced with when he completed a new project, and laughed with as we splashed in the marsh. He'd needed me, and now I was finally reunited with him. It was like a weight that had been dragging me underwater had finally dropped away and I could see the surface.

The floor was hard on my knees as I knelt at his chair, but I didn't care. I bent my head to his lap and released the tears that had seemingly been collecting for days. For the violence I'd taken part in and witnessed, for the monsters that I'd passed in hallways and seen streak toward me in the water. For the terror and confusion and helplessness of being a human in that evil castle, surrounded by villains.

Conor shushed me, and I felt the tick of his fingertips as he shifted his hand. He petted my hair. With a gasp, I looked up to see the darkening of his wrist's flesh retreating by increments. The cure was already working. And the first thing he did with his new mobility was stroke my head, murmuring quiet and comforting words into the space above me.

"Thank you, Win. I don't know what…I'm just…so grateful. I love you. Just, thank you. Thank you so much."

I wept harder.

By the time I could collect the tatters of myself into something resembling his capable, devoted sister, Conor's arms were already able to bend, and his chest was expanding with deeper breaths. I helped him into the kitchen and made us both a cup of tea. Despite the filth on my clothes and the itching of my healing wounds, I didn't want to set up a bath; I couldn't let him out of my sight.

"The town's been a mess," Conor told me as he cupped his hands around the hot mug. It was one our mother had made especially for him—the divots and curls of the clay making low, easy waves around the surface. She'd even paid for special paints that had tinted the surface blue in her kiln.

"How so?" I asked. The chair groaned beneath my weight, and I understood the feeling. My body *ached*. I rolled my shoulders, looking for relief, but everything hurt, even my face, which still felt raw from crying.

"The day you left…someone found Elmyra dead by the water." He raised the mug slowly, as if reacquainting himself with the movement, and took a grateful sip, smiling a bit as he swallowed. Warmth tingled through me for the first time since I'd found the lilies in the storage room.

"The healer?"

He nodded. "She'd only just stopped by here that afternoon, and then that night she was gone. No one would give me specifics, but I could tell from the way they spoke around it that it must have been...gruesome."

"I can see why that would have everyone worried."

Elmyra hadn't been able to help Conor with his condition, but the townspeople relied on her to help with births, to break fevers, and even to reset bones. She was the main reason we hadn't lost half our number to a sweeping flu we'd endured last winter.

"It's not just that." Conor leaned gingerly over the table, lowering his voice. "The blacksmith was also attacked. Bitten by the same thing that got me. But he wasn't so fortunate..." He cleared his throat, looking guilty. "He was fully petrified within two days. Stopped breathing and just...froze. I can't tell you how scared I was, and how incredible this is. To even raise my mug." He huffed out a laugh that sounded more like a sigh. "Gods, Winnie."

I put my hand over his, nodding in understanding. And then my brows drew low in confusion. "So, the healer and the blacksmith are gone."

Conor hummed in agreement. "Plus...there's been talk in town of selling children to the fae, to stop the violence. Better to control it in some way, they said. Since the deaths might be revenge for people escaping when they did—like Aven. Mother is fighting against the council, though. She tried to keep it from me, but I could tell from her hoarse voice she'd been shouting at the last town meeting."

Inhaling the steam from the tea, I tried to imagine how desperate my town had become, and how quickly, to be considering something so heinous. They must be drowning in fear—and for good reason; our village was small and already struggling. This many deaths, and to such important people...there was something unusual about these attacks, beyond their increasing frequency and the potential retaliation behind it. And though there were sometimes one or two individuals who went to the fae lands on purpose—those who had no one left to turn to or were near starving—the idea that children would be sacrificed into their clutches was unthinkable. It was too easy to imagine them like those mindless bodies swaying at court, collected and groped, malnourished and abused.

"Where is Ma?" I asked, though I was loath to do so.

"At her studio. She's been coming back every hour or so to check on me, so she hasn't been getting much done, but sales are down so...I guess it doesn't really matter. People are becoming afraid to walk the streets alone, let alone visit her store. Too close to the coastline," he explained.

I watched him stretch out his arms, bending and unbending them to loosen the sore muscles. He'd still need help over the next couple of days while he regained his strength, but I knew he'd be back on his feet within hours. He was stubborn.

"Anything else?" I asked, still mulling over the details.

"A couple more women have gone missing, and what's even more worrisome is that one of them resided close to the center of town, near the market. She wasn't even a mussel digger."

"So, there shouldn't have been any occasion for her to be snatched away at the water," I concluded.

"Exactly. Though we don't know if the women left willingly or not. Their families swear not. Still, I've started shifting my experiments on those crab claws from utility to weaponry, just so mother has something to keep her safe if I...in case I was gone."

I remembered him describing those crabs to me—their pink-tipped claws seeming to glow if you got too close. Conor swore they emitted some kind of power, one that could send a wave of pain through you, raising your hair like a nearby strike of lightning. He'd been working on harnessing that energy for weeks, thinking it might burn metal or give off light, and now that I knew how many bizarre creatures lived just beyond the marsh, that sounded more than plausible. I remembered the pain of that urchin-fingered devil and wondered if they did something similar.

I opened my mouth to ask if he'd had any success yet, but at that moment the front door opened and our mother stepped inside, only to halt in her tracks at the sight of me.

"You're back," she said, almost dumbly, and then her gaze went to Conor. To his hands on the mug and the shift of his posture, different from the slumped arch of his back he'd been falling into. She cried out in relief, rushing to him and wrapping her arms around his shoulders so tightly his body jerked. The last of his tea spilled onto the table.

"Oh, how I prayed to the moon and stars you would be well!" She kissed the top of his head, beaming with delight. "I can't believe my prayers have been answered!"

I gripped my own mug more tightly, fighting the urge to roll my eyes. She had been here, caring for him, but *I* had been the one to rescue him—not her prayers.

The scrape of my chair went unnoticed as I stood. "I'm going to run a bath," I said.

My mother turned her head to look at me, her cheek pressed into Conor's hair. He tolerated her squishing with good humor, but I could see the mild exasperation flattening his lips.

"Thank you, Winona," she said, tone somber.

I nodded, surprised she'd acknowledged me at all. It was a small shock to my system—how I should have felt vindicated and appreciated and...whole. But I didn't. I was almost numb as I walked away, leaving her to it.

Drawing my own bath was a pain, and I only heated one pail of water over the fire, leaving the rest cool. It wasn't the most relaxing wash, but I was impatient to inspect the cuts on my body and rest my weary limbs in the water. It was so much warmer than the brine I'd waded through every day for the past week that it didn't bother me nearly as much as it used to.

The gritty salve along the lendani's slashes had kept me from bleeding out, but the marks were still angry and puckered as I cleaned them. It stung like hell, each line a fiery trail that had me hissing. Collapsing against the metal rim of the tub, I released a shaky breath and let my eyes drift shut. For some reason I couldn't stop my mind from turning in circles, like a child lost in the forest. Each thought towered over me like a leaning willow, each feeling like a rustle along the ground. Spinning, I searched for some clear path through the wood, but I only got more lost as I wandered.

Conor's attack had always seemed to me like a gust of unlucky wind; it could have happened to anyone who was too deep in the shallow mud. Anyone who was hunting for crabs would have met the same fate there. And the healer...she could have been in a similar location, rummaging for herbs. But what had the blacksmith been doing so far from his forge?

And why had a woman going missing from the densest spot in Harnsey?

Jassin had spoken of acquiring humans to build power, so if there were more people than usual missing, he might be behind it—but the deaths? Those were unusual, and the fae had no reason to kill off so many, especially if they were looking for extra help now that their powers had failed them. But was Jassin the only one supplying that help? And was it just a coincidence that I'd seen an anglock at the castle, just as the blacksmith was poisoned by one of their bites? Was that what had killed the healer, Elmyra? Conor hadn't said...

I was shivering from the cool water when my thoughts finally stopped orbiting the trouble here at home and drifted to the trouble I may have left behind. Reed would have turned to smoke to heal, so I wasn't concerned about the stab I'd taken at him, but his expression as he slid down the cave wall, hand to his abdomen, was haunting me. Those blue eyes had once looked at me with such...affection, though maybe that wasn't the right word. Not warmth, either. But fondness? Understanding? I'd felt *seen* by him, and yet it had been a lie. I was so desperate to feel appreciated and wanted that I'd swallowed every crumb he placed on the floor at my feet. I'd pecked like a hungry hen. But that expression as he'd fallen, almost like despair...I couldn't stop replaying it. It had to have been because his plan had failed and he'd lost this opportunity for someone to slay his master, I decided.

Climbing from the tub and dressing my wounds took so long that Conor called out from the kitchen to ask if I was alright.

I was pulling on a fresh tunic and about to answer when someone started pounding on our front door.

"Winnie!" The voice was small and sharp. Sorra.

Mother opened the squeaky door, and I heard the girl's frantic steps as she ran inside. I tied my pants in place and went into the kitchen, only to have her sprint into my hip, nearly knocking me over.

"Sorra? What's wrong?" I tried to dislodge her, or at least shift her so her head wasn't pressed into the lower edge of my injuries.

"Ma is missing!" she cried, voice thick with tears. When her head tilted up to me, I could see her wet, reddened face and the terror in her wide eyes. "Ma is gone, she's been taken!" She wailed, her fists clutching at my clothing, and I watched as Conor and my mother shared a look. Concern and resignation had their eyebrows low and their postures tight.

Upset, but not surprised.

"You're probably mistaken," I said, trying to soothe the girl. "I'm sure she's just out fetching something from the market or doing the washing in the stream. Have you checked everywhere? We can help you look."

My mother shook her head, and what started as confusion became a muddled sense of dread weighing down my chest. Why wouldn't we help to find my friend? To search for this girl's mother? And what was the alternative—to ignore her pleas for help? That wasn't who we were.

I hardened my voice, narrowing my gaze at my mother. "We *will* help her look," I demanded, then, "What's going on here? Tell me."

CHAPTER EIGHTEEN

The story Conor and my mother spun for me was one that sounded like a familiar fairy tale encased in glass, only twisted while molten hot so the pictures within distorted beyond recognition. It wasn't just the healer and the blacksmith that had been killed, and it was not just a couple of women that had gone missing. In the past week, while I'd been gone, the constant low-grade fear of being taken by the fae had risen to a pitch the people of Harnsey could no longer stand. It seemed the fae losing their ability to glamour hadn't lessened their propensity for generating terror.

Sorra was ushered away by our neighbor, Ida, to collect her siblings, while the few men in town still willing to search the marsh headed out in their waders. Their torches and farm tools reminded me of the stores of weapons I'd seen in the castle, and I wondered if they were marching to their deaths as they drifted further from town.

"We have to leave," our mother surmised, as Conor pushed himself from the table. He was careful to test his weight on his newly freed legs, wobbling like a foal. "Now that you're well, we can put our plans into motion."

"And we're going to," Conor agreed, "just as soon as I can sell the lightning rods." He turned to me. "Then we'll have enough money to go wherever we want. To Deercross, or Bronzen, even, if Clarcton isn't far enough."

"Just abandon the town? Is it not worth it to fight?" I asked, still trying to wrap my mind around what they'd told me. Dead bodies were washing up on shore—a teacher, a horse breeder—and even more were missing. Some of the details, confessed through my mother's trembling lips, my brother hadn't even known, and Conor was already primed to escape now that he wasn't facing a slow, immobilizing death. I'd wanted to leave Harnsey before, sure, but not at the expense of others. Not when I finally understood what they were up against, and knew I could teach them to defend themselves.

Ma shook her head, thin hairs escaping the twist at the back of her neck. A pile of dry goods was already packed on the kitchen counter, and periodically she would think of something and run from the room to fetch it. It seemed she'd been preparing for days now, just waiting to leave until Conor recovered, or he was gone.

I noticed nothing about her arrangements had hinged on my return, but said nothing.

"Fight for what?" Conor asked. "Now that you are home, there's nothing keeping us here. All that matters is keeping each other safe, right?"

"Of course, but who is to say any other town will be better? Fae aren't *just* at the ocean. They live in the woods, in the mountains, in the streams and creeks we fetch our water from when the well is busy. The array of creatures I saw in their kingdom was baffling, and there were some even visiting from far-off lands. If the fae-folk are taking humans, even killing them, then..." I stopped, my mind returning to Jassin and his saccharine smile. He was building up a supply of slaves, sure, but he had plenty, or so it had seemed. Still, this level of activity was startling, the deaths nonsensical. For the most part, the humans of Harnsey had an understanding with the fae in the marsh—stay away, and you were safe—but now, that deal was obsolete.

"That's why I'm building weapons." Conor beamed with pride. "Soon, I'll have a spear that pains with just a touch. Like a blast from the lightning rod, but without danger to the holder! I have the gloves ready, I just need another day or so to adjust the energy storage so it can hold more than one charge. Then nothing will dare touch us on our way inland."

I looked over my shoulder. "And you agree with this?"

Ma dipped her head, her hands buried in a bag of old clothes she was sifting through for some reason. "Things have changed, and it can't hurt to try someplace new. Your brother is a brilliant inventor; I have every faith he'll keep us safe."

"It's not his job to keep us safe," I retorted. *It's yours*, I wanted to shout.

"Don't be stubborn," she replied. "This place is dying, and we'd be fools to die along with it."

"But this is so sudden," I argued, and then I felt foolish for saying so. I'd *wanted* to leave, and I should be glad Ma was finally on board, but...now something felt wrong.

Frustrated, I left the table, my anxieties mounting as I pictured what a life far from the marsh would be like. The room I shared with my brother was just as I'd left it—dirty, with overstuffed bookshelves and the blanket we constantly tugged back and forth throughout the night. I sighed, overwhelmed. This had been our home for so long, I barely remembered the house we'd shared with our father. There was a yard, and chickens I could chase, and a larger fireplace, but other than that it was all a blur. Would a life inland be bucolic like that? Or worse than this, with crowded streets and the filth of thousands instead of hundreds?

I'd dreamed of going to Clarcton with Conor before, where he could work and I could write or act, but it had all been that—an unrealistic dream I whispered to myself to fall asleep. If we went, would we just be running from one problem to another? Ma wanted to go now, but only because things were at their worst.

I should want that too.

Part of me yearned to stay close to the sea, to the dreadful, dangerous world I knew waited beyond the barrier of mangrove trees, if only for familiarity's sake, but I could see the wisdom in running; I wasn't a fool. We were bound to be in the fae's sights if they were stocking up on human captives. Conor could make whatever armaments or gadgets he dreamed of, but I'd seen the strength and ferocity of the creatures living so close to our watery border. My brother might even be considered a threat.

The word "threat" echoed, bringing to mind Jassin's sharp eye and Robin's towering frame, as well as an anglock's teeth and a lendani's humming. Inventions were Conor's weapons, just as a healer was a weapon against their toxins, and a blacksmith was a weapon, should he ever take his turn at shaping iron. For all I knew, ours already had: Conor had to have sourced the pieces for his net-shooter somewhere locally, and—though it was more rumor that fact—I now had proof that iron *did* work against the fae, at least ones that couldn't transform. Maybe the blacksmith had known that too. A teacher could have known it, maybe...and a horse breeder would have been instrumental in allowing people to flee.

There was a chance that these deaths weren't random occurrences. Or maybe I was grasping for any excuse to stay close; some self-damaging inclination begging me to wait for Reed to come drifting out of the water, chasing after me once more.

My torso twanged with sharp pain, the slashes along my ribs stinging as I sat on the bed. Even if I was right, and the deaths were tied to Windstone Court, there was nothing I could do about it. Beyond my iron dagger and some insider knowledge from my time in the castle, I didn't have much to offer a resistance, if I could even form one. And why would I want to? Sure, there was a chance the next town would be just as troubled, but we could always move on to the next if Conor garnered the funds to keep us going...

I shook my head, annoyed with all my conflicting feelings, and then placed my elbows on my knees, covering my face. This was all just so fast. Was it just yesterday I had been in a half-fae's arms, contemplating murder for his sake?

I lingered there, visions of past and present muddling into a grim future, before deciding to lend a hand with the search party. Maire's children were being cared for, but it was only a temporary fix, and I prayed to the sky we would find their mother alive.

Hours passed as I swept the coast from north to south with a handful of townsmen. My wounds itched, missing the mallow paste that had protected them from the salt of my sweat, but I ignored it, fanning out my steps as if the sand might swallow me whole, my eyes on a constant swivel. We called her name, checked ditches, and inspected every fallen tree or collection of boulders. But there was no body to be found.

The sun was nearly gone when I made my way back to Harnsey's main road, empty-handed and dog-tired. There were fewer stalls open in the market, I noticed, as if some of the townsfolk had already abandoned ship. The wine merchant, however, was still enjoying plump business, and I stopped by his stand to buy a bottle. My heart ached, and it seemed like a decent enough remedy for now.

And that's when someone started screaming my name from far behind me.

It was masculine. Strained.

"Reed?" I whispered to myself, and then I plopped the bottle back onto the seller's table. "Hold onto this for me!" I told the merchant.

Turning, I began racing through the sparse crowd. The voice called again, and this time I saw someone up ahead waving their arm—brunette and slim, their clothes well-fitted.

Not Reed.

As soon as I recognized my ex-fiancé, I almost swiveled to run back the way I'd come, but his face was drawn with fear and his voice cracked as he called for me once more.

"Winnie! Someone in the marsh is demanding to see you! It's a fae!"

My heart stuttered, hope flickering through the muscle like a spasm.

"Hurry!" he said with a wave.

An inner voice warned this might be a trap—Flint could be calling me into the marsh to get me alone, or to simply mock my desperation. Maybe gossip of my adventures in the fae lands was already circulating and he was being painted a cuck for letting me slip through his fingers. No, that was unlikely. He was an ass, and a user, but Flint wasn't violent or cruel.

"I'm coming!" I replied, jogging to reach him.

Flint's hair was windblown, and the pink high in his cheeks reminded me of kissing him there, of the scruff of his face and the smell of hay masking the marsh's ever-present odor.

"Why is a fae asking after you?" His tone was accusing, even though he was panting.

"I've just come back from their court," I answered.

"The truth, Win."

"That is the truth, *Flint.*"

It shouldn't have surprised me that he didn't believe me. I'd barely believe me, except for the fact Aven and the others had returned and Flint had been there to witness it. He'd known Conor was suffering from a fae-borne illness, though it had been weeks since he'd ditched me in the barn and crushed my heart. Gossip is a cup all the townswomen drank from, even his Ma. Had he not even realized I'd been gone these past few days?

I shook my head. It didn't matter if he did or didn't, all that mattered was why Reed had come here to my very *human* town. Or...

"Is the fae a male?" I asked as my shoes kicked up dust. Keeping myself purposefully a few steps ahead of Flint, I strained to see the crowd gathering ahead, and the creature in the water beyond them, but they were still too far.

"A male..." Flint slowed, and I chanced a look back at him. His mouth gaped open. "Did you fuck a fae to cure your brother?"

The words were a slap across my cheek and I almost tripped, but he had no right to sound the least bit indignant. I was pissed that he could somehow tell from my tone there was something going on, or maybe he just assumed I had sex with every man who crossed my path. Either way, I wouldn't bite my tongue like a simpering waif.

"At least fucking him got me *something*," I snapped, and then I raced ahead, leaving him in the road.

Within minutes I reached the local divot in the quagmire where women dug for snails. The soughing of the wind along the marsh grass sounded like the rustling of a snake. And then I saw the fae. *Her.*

Robin was waist-deep in the water, one of her long arms around the torso of a young girl who struggled against her grasp. A group of townsmen stood uneasily on the squelching pasture beyond the tideline to my left, some flourishing weapons, all shouting at the fae to leave their land and release the girl.

"Bring me Winona!" Robin cried, her fingers tight on the girl's throat. It took me a moment to see through her tears and mud-streaked face to recognize the girl as Maylin, the daughter of the teacher who had been found dead just days before. She wore her darkest mourning clothes, soaked with seawater, and clawed with desperation at her captor.

I skidded to a stop on the sand, pushing between the crowd. "Robin? Let her go, I'm here!"

The fae released Maylin, who stumbled forward into the water and half-swam, half-crawled her way into the arms of the waiting townsmen, panic making her movements fitful.

Robin straightened to her full height, as if she'd been crouched to hold Maylin still, and seeing her so close to my home, her pointed ears on full display, her too-long arms ending in fists, made me briefly consider the prospect I was in some sort of waking nightmare.

"You have to come with me," Robin called, her voice carrying over the ripples. I wondered if she was afraid to step onto land, or if the distance she kept was out of some form of respect for the boundaries we'd always minded. "Reed needs you."

"Reed will get out of his contract without me," I shouted back. "I'm sure he can find some blackmail or pay some creature to kill his master eventually."

Robin shook her head. "Jassin has put him in the dungeons to be tortured." She paused. "You must help me break him out."

"I *mustn't* do anything."

The townspeople who hadn't run from our display were watching with rapt attention, their heads shifting from the water to the shore, following our conversation like a sport.

Robin closed her eyes, as if pained, and I almost mirrored her. The idea of Reed in the cold, in discomfort, dug at me. But I would not be persuaded.

"You are right," she said. "You have no obligations—he wasn't exactly honest in his dealings with you. But he told me how you broke into the compound, defeating guards with human weapons. Iron weapons. Without you, I have no hope of rescuing him. They may even kill him. And..."

"And?" I prompted.

"And he was gathering information for you when he was captured."

I raised one eyebrow and crossed my arms over my chest. "What kind of information? Tell me he wasn't snooping for his own benefit."

"He was not snooping for his own benefit, to the best of my knowledge," she repeated back at me, her tone now harder. "He accepted that he would remain Jassin's slave, but when he found out anglocks were in the castle, he looked into their business. He wanted to know why they'd gone after your brother so far from the court, and why they were visiting—if they were related to the...disturbance in court. I'm not sure what he discovered, exactly. I cannot get close enough to him to find out. But you could."

A hand grabbed at my shoulder, pulling me around, and I came face to face with Flint, his brown hair mussed and falling over one eye. "Winnie, why are you talking to that thing? They're not *male* so unless you've gotten more...adventurous, they aren't your lover. And even if they were, it's a monster." He looked around at the crowd. "Someone throw a spear at it!"

I shook off his hand. "She doesn't mean any harm!"

"Tell that to Maylin."

"Is Maylin hurt?" I asked. When he didn't answer I turned to the nearest man beside us. "Is she?"

The silence in response spoke volumes.

"Let me handle this," I told Flint. Turning back to Robin, I watched her long hair, tied low with a leather cord, drift in the wind off the water. Her expression was fierce. I remembered Reed talking about how she was the only fae not to treat him like a leper, and how he loved her dearly. She clearly loved him the same way in return.

I understood that kind of love, like how I felt for my brother, but that didn't mean I was willing to put my life at risk—again—to free him. Reed's life was his own, and his mistakes were as well. But as soon as I thought it, the idea rankled. Reed had been kind to me, had fed and sheltered and helped me, knowing it would put him in danger. It had partially been for selfish reasons, and he'd lied to me more than once, but did that mean he deserved to die? No. He was desperate, and I understood that experience intimately.

Still, that didn't mean I had to be the one to save him.

"I'll give you some of my weapons," I called out. "But arming you is all I can offer."

Robin paused, mouth twisting with a grimace. It looked like she would argue, but after a pregnant pause, she nodded.

I focused on the small group of people watching us, their heated stares uncomfortable against my skin.

"She means you no harm," I announced, hoping they wouldn't attack her as soon as I turned my back. "Leave her be and soon she will be gone." And then I hurried home to plead with Conor to hand over our best defenses to one of the enemy.

CHAPTER NINETEEN

"You must have lost your mind," my mother said over my shoulder.

I ignored her, my gaze steady on my brother as he sat in his workshop, back straight with surprise at my request. His hands were covered with thick gloves as they hovered above a bowl of gray powder.

"Please, Conor," I added. "I know this seems...odd, but the fae who kept me safe in that castle deserves at least a chance to be free."

"And this wom—this fae at the water can wield an iron weapon?" Conor asked. "Won't it eat through her the same as those guards you fought?"

"It would, if she touched the iron directly. But the launcher or some of the flash powder could help." I didn't mention Reed's ability to heal from those wounds, worried of confusing Conor further, and I spared a moment to debate whether—when not interrupted by whatever affliction held the fae court in its thrall—others could heal themselves as well.

My mother pushed her way past me, only to turn and cross her arms. "This is absurd. We'll need protection on the road and means of trade. Your brother's inventions are all we have now that your engagement to Flint was rescinded."

"My engagement to Flint was a farce, Ma! He wasn't going to marry me, it was all just so he could—" I ran a hand through my short hair, feeling tangles snag in the strands. Why did I think returning home with a cure for Conor would garner me *any* goodwill with her? How was I so foolish? So naïve? I swallowed a groan and drowned the disappointment swimming inside of me. If I didn't hurry back to the water's edge, someone was bound to move against Robin or start a fight they could not finish.

"We have your pottery to sell," I said at last, as calmly as I could, "and I'm not suggesting we hand over everything we have. Just enough to give Robin a fighting chance."

Mother scoffed. "The idea that you're using that thing's name at all is laughable."

My teeth were clenched, grinding, but I took a step to the side to meet Conor's gaze once more. "Please. It's what a venerable prince would do."

My brother nodded, slowly, his young face unblemished by the weary hatred that had been beaten into the rest of the people of Harnsey, and gave me a weak smile. The venerable prince was his favorite part to play when we acted out scenes in the fields. Mine was an evil witch, and the sensation of standing on the blade of decision seemed apt—one step toward wickedness, one step toward compassion.

"If you think it's right," he said.

My mother threw up her arms and stormed from the room. Her disdain would have bothered me, if she didn't already consider every move I made to be some form of mistake. I was beginning to realize I'd find no shelter there—in this story of mine, she was only as much of my mother as a booming ghost.

"I do also have one more weapon the fae might consider useful,"

Conor said, pulling my attention to the powder beneath his gloved fingertips. "Let me show you."

I sat beside him at the long wooden table and watched as he grabbed a radish from a burlap sack off to the side. Placing the little red vegetable beside the bowl, he sprinkled some of the powder onto its surface. I leaned closer, waiting for some reaction, but there was none.

"Give me that dropper?" He nodded toward a rack of glass vials, one of which was full of clear liquid.

I handed it to him.

"Lean back and do your best not to breathe this in," he warned, and then he tilted the fluid onto the powder. Immediately it began to smoke and sizzle, the radish dissolving under the compound as if being bitten by invisible insects.

"What the..."

"The powder is dangerous on its own and will slowly erode anything it touches, but with water the reaction is violent and fast," he explained.

"Just water? That's incredible," I said on an uneven breath.

Conor's eyes were crinkling with the appraisal. "If you throw it on a person and then they get wet...I imagine it would kill them almost instantly."

Such vicious and casual words sounded uncouth in my little brother's mouth, but he had been tinkering with machinery and these compounds long enough where I imagined the destructive properties were old hat by now. And to think, he was only about to turn thirteen. It was bizarre to imagine what he could create now that he had more time—years of it.

"You can give some of this to the fae," said Conor. "And I have a few nets and caltrops tipped with iron nails as well. Enough where we can still keep some for our journey south. I was rushing to make whatever I could with the iron I had left."

"Thank you," I said. "I appreciate this, Conor."

He began bundling up the weapons and pouring portions of powder into the vials before sealing them with metal caps. "I don't..." he started, his fingers halting over the bag he was packing, "I don't know exactly what you saw over there. But I hope, when you can talk about it, that you can tell me more about the fae. I want to know *everything*. And not just to help kill them. I just...want to know."

He seemed sheepish to admit it, and I couldn't stop myself from leaning down to wrap my arms around his shoulders in a gentle hug. Conor's curiosity is what constantly kept him inventing and trying new things. It's what made him listen to my plays and poems. With his gentle heart and sharp mind, I knew he would do truly incredible things, now that he was cured.

A cure I owed partially to Reed.

Guilt gnawed at my hollow stomach, and I released him. "I'll tell you everything," I promised. *When it didn't hurt so much.*

The men and women of Harnsey watched me with suspicion as I made my way back to the coast. It was as if—now that they knew I associated with someone who was fae—I might be just as dangerous. Flint still lingered nearby, leaning his shoulder against the wall of a house with his arms crossed and his posture overly casual, his eyes hard as his namesake. I would have found it unbearably attractive just weeks before, but now it only made me clench a fist. He didn't deserve my scowl, or even the roll of my eyes. He had lied to me and betrayed me—*just like Reed*, a voice in my head whispered—but he had done so maliciously. He'd taken from my body as if it was his personal property, feeding me pretty words about marriage and a future and hope—and I wouldn't forgive him.

I wasn't sure I could forgive Reed either, not that I'd be given the opportunity.

Hefting the sack higher over my shoulder, I avoided my ex-lover's damning gaze as I passed the last of the buildings.

Robin's tall form still lingered in thigh-deep water.

Instead of making her come to me, I braved some deep-seated fear and stepped into the murky brine, sloshing up to her.

"Here's what my brother could spare," I said as a greeting, handing over the bag. She took it with ease despite its weight, then peered inside.

"I could use my tunic to hold the spikes, maybe" she said, "but what are the powders?"

Explaining them as best I could without a hazardous demonstration, as well as the net launcher, I tried to ignore a growing sense of restlessness churning in my gut and an agitated jitter spreading down my legs. Shifting from side to side, I wrestled with the urge to run back to my family and also my desire to follow Robin into the mangrove.

The area around us was quiet except for the muted sounds of conversations blocks away; it seemed the townspeople had listened to me. But now I wished one or two had remained—to remind me where my loyalties should lie. Because the longer I stood in Robin's long shadow, the more certain I became that seeing her off with well wishes and a wave was...cowardly.

This close, I could see the bruised circles beneath her eyes and the tight press of her mouth as she nodded, listening intently.

"Thank you for this, Winona," she said, tone solemn. "I will take these weapons, though I am not sure I can use them. Violence in the castle, as you know..."

"Oh. Right." I'd forgotten that fae couldn't harm one another in the compound, at least, not without serious consequences. The image of the lendani as it crashed to the floor, twitching in pain and incapacitated from the court's magic at play, flashed through my mind. "Can you lure the guards away from Windstone to fight them?"

"Either that or make deals. Threaten. Remove them without harm, maybe, if I am careful. Once I am down to the last guard holding him, I can strike. It is worth the danger."

Robin shouldered the pack and turned to go.

"Wait!" I called, hand outstretched, but I immediately withdrew it. "I...that doesn't seem like much of a plan."

"I know where he's being kept, and I know the type of creature in his cell guarding him," she answered. "As for the level of security between the gates and his room...I cannot be sure, but I can do my best. Jassin is aware of our relationship, so I haven't been able to get too close—not without inviting suspicion."

I wanted to ask more about what kind of monster would be used to subdue Reed in that prison, but I had to remind myself that—no matter the answer—it *wasn't my concern*. Robin was strong and fast and knowledgeable in a way I could never be. I may have encountered a few of the more prominent types of fae in the castle, but beyond a mediocre skill with my dagger and a wealth of iron-tipped weapons, my only other talent was acting, and there was no way I could act the high fae once more. My only option to enter the castle would be as a servant of some kind...a servant that could perhaps walk the halls unnoticed, scoping out the way and reporting back to Robin with a more robust strategy.

My silence as I pondered this must have read as concern on my face because Robin placed a long-fingered hand on my shoulder, her touch pleasantly warm.

"I'll tell him you aided me, if you wish. I'm sure he could do with the relief of knowing you absolve him of his misdeeds, at least to some degree."

"I doubt I mean much to him at all," I griped, hating the whine submerged in my voice.

Robin shook her head. "Though I only saw you together briefly, his comfortable way of moving around you, his easy smile…those are not his way. It was almost like the mask he uses with the high fae, but with you it was genuine—at least from my view. A rare thing for someone who spends all his time trying to hide his size and keep his gaze to the ground."

That wasn't the impression of Reed I'd gotten, watching him flit from character to character in the castle, but I really hadn't seen him interact with Jassin or the high fae beyond the meals in the banquet hall. All those times he'd left me in his room to do chores or fetch me food—when he'd been whipped in punishment, or been attending Jassin—was he different from the smiling jokester persona I'd witnessed?

My heart dipped in my chest, and I hated it. This was not my battle; he was nothing more than a dalliance. The means to an end. But I found myself clenching my eyes tight with misery, giving in to the voice yammering in my head and through my blood that to stay back was to fail him, and myself, in some irreparable way.

"Fine, I'll come with you," I said, taking a deep breath. "I can help you get through the castle and get to Reed. But then I'm gone."

Robin's wide grin was glowing and ethereal, her features somehow softer and sharper at the same time. Sunlight grazed her cheekbones like a caress.

"I agree to your terms, and I know Reed would be brimming with affection to hear it."

"Yeah, yeah. Sure." I didn't care, but there was no benefit to saying so. Instead, I stepped back, charting the low glare of the sun. "Do I have time to get weapons of my own?"

She shook her head. "I have to go now. He'll be much weaker at night, and with most of the compound asleep, daylight is our best chance. If I bring you I will be slower, but we will still reach the court by morning. I don't know how well he will fare after another day."

"Shit."

All I had on me was my iron dagger—carrying it now more a habit than anything, though maybe a premonition as I'd strapped it to my waist to take part in Maire's search party. What I'd given Robin from Conor would have to be enough for the two of us, and with any luck we would be at the castle and back before tomorrow night, giving plenty of time to resume my family's preparations to leave Harnsey. I hoped.

There were no townsfolk to see us off, or to take word back to Conor and my mother of my departure, but I had to assume they wouldn't leave without me. Conor, at least, wouldn't allow it.

This time, as Robin and I made our way through the shallow tide, the current felt weaker. Or maybe I was stronger, my muscles growing used to the strain of pushing through the mire. With nothing but peace and a few errant splashes between us, I allowed myself the grace of finally asking every question to Robin that I'd never had the gall to voice to Reed: how fae and human relationships worked, what sorts of tasks the unglamoured servants specialized in, what other monsters visited the castle from time to time, and what purposes they served. It was the only way I could pass the time without the anxiety and terror in my chest bubbling into insurmountable discomfort. I pushed the sensations down as if I was squashing grapes for wine, focusing on each step and each question, rather than our destination.

I soaked up the information about rare camps where exiles who dallied with humans lived, and how each servant at Windstone catered to their fae counterparts. Some chores were normal—cooking, massages, errands like fetching or sewing garments—while others were disgraceful and cruel—acting as a footstool being the kindest. Chores I had little intention of ever describing to Conor if I survived. The fae lived long, but their hierarchy was unstable—violence ruled beyond court boundaries, and betrayal was common—and Robin described to me the court gallantries Prince Aeden expected, as well as what went on behind his back. It was all just fascinating enough to keep my steps sure, even in the growing dark.

When we reached the thick tree line of the mangroves and the buzzing started in my ears, I took the caltrops from my brother's bag and held them at the ready. Robin hefted the loaded net launcher. She kept close to my side, and I wondered if it was to make us a smaller target or because she feared I would be attacked without her fae scent wafting over me. We slowed then, our breathing growing hushed as we wove through the root systems in the rising water. Already my chest was submerged, only my shoulders adorned by the pale moonlight. Now that we had to stay silent, the reservations I had about our surroundings began to constrict my lungs.

A splash to my right had me raising my hands, the iron-tipped metal spikes ready to soar, but it was only a fish jumping to swallow some insect. I released my breath, just as Robin clenched a hand in my hair—a warning to stop.

She made a quiet shushing sound, and I clenched my lips together in a tight line, doing my best to breathe in slow, unobtrusive measures.

A series of curving waves approached, as if there was some great beast swimming off to the side, creating a massive wake behind it. But the waves didn't move in a way that made sense. The line of cresting water was pointed at us, growing closer. Something swimming sideways?

Robin's fingers gripped tighter as she moved herself to stand directly in front of me.

I wanted to ask her what was happening, but I dared not speak. All I could do was stare at the shirt on her back and breathe into the space between her shoulder blades.

And then the waves moved around us, and I registered the glowing creatures passing by us on either side.

They were bright yellow snakes, flat like long pieces of seaweed, and moving in a group not unlike a school of young fish. Their elongated tails slashed the water in tandem, making those strange waves, and I felt a sharp slap against my hip as one of them passed by too closely.

Robin must have felt me stiffen, for she made that shushing sound again, trying to soothe me. It was all I could do not to scream as the snakes surrounded us, brushing our legs and bumping into us in blind haste. Did they have fangs? Poisoned barbs? When they found out I was human would they attack?

The sound of them breaking the surface as they slithered was a long, constant hiss that had the hairs on the back of my neck prickling.

"Another minute," Robin whispered, so soft it may have been the breeze.

Because the snakes were only the entourage.

What followed was a wave so violent and crashing that the mangroves shook, leaves flickering and drifting to the water's surface as it approached.

The force of the water reached us before the creature did, the crest breaking over my chin. My hands trembled around the jagged caltrops. If need be, I would slash my hands into the water, raking the twisted iron tips over the flesh of whatever advanced, but if that didn't immediately kill it, I knew a monster of this size could destroy me with little effort.

Then its head broke the surface. It was the closest thing to a dragon I'd ever seen beyond the pages of a storybook. More snake than lizard, it breached and fell back into the water, all while gliding side-to-side, sprays of water glinting in the air. It had small arms lying flat against its aquamarine body, and sharp fins along its back that ended in wicked, black points.

The tiny glimpse of it beyond Robin's arm was enough to make me retreat into her shadow, clutching tight to her back like a child in their mother's skirts.

Robin hissed and I realized one of the caltrops' iron nails had grazed her skin through her linen shirt.

I jerked my hand away, but it was too late—the area was sizzling as the poison ate through her flesh.

While her body quaked from the pain, Robin turned her head to give me a subtle nod, as if to assure me she was okay.

I knew that was a lie. We just couldn't risk any attention.

The giant water dragon, or whatever it was, slowed its progress, as if to study us as it passed.

Robin rose a shaking hand, a metal vial clutched in her fist. It wasn't one of the glass ones Conor had given us, so I had no idea what would happen as she punctured the thin membrane of the cap with her thumbnail and poured the contents into the water.

The smell of rancid meat clogged my nostrils, and I fought back a gag.

Sound seemed to mute, like the mangrove held its breath as much as I did against the odor, and the dragon paused. I could see its skin glinting under the rippling water, algae and silt foaming up around its gentler movements. I prayed the beast couldn't sense the vibrations of my pounding heart.

And then it turned slightly to its left, traveling by with long strokes of that massive tail, so close it almost thrashed us.

Robin sighed in relief, and I followed suit, the sound shaky and weak.

"Hells, Robin, I'm sorry," I hurried to whisper. Taking a step back, I inspected the light scrape in her shirt and the angry skin beneath. The iron was doing its work, bubbling her skin with its poison, though much slower than the deeper stabs I'd made on my first foray into the fae lands. "What can I do?"

"I will treat it later," she said between gritted teeth.

"With what?"

She started forward again, and I had no choice but to follow, overly conscious of the dip in her arms as she hefted the net launcher once more. Already weakened. I wondered how much longer she could hold out against the pain and the toxin now coursing through her.

"There's a mushroom we grow in one of the towers," she replied. "We call them Luada bites—little green-capped things. Tastes worse than the stink potion I poured in the water to deter the wyrm, if you can believe that, but it will help. Just...have to get to it. I'm sure more than one creature has been visiting our stores, considering your visit." She raised one eyebrow with humor, as if to lighten the mood.

I thought of the guard I'd put down the last time I ventured close to Windstone, and the damage I'd done with my nets and knife. Had either of those fae sought treatment before they drowned? Or, if a scratch was enough to make Robin falter, was a stab wound too harmful to overcome? Maybe Reed had been okay because of his human father, or again, that ability of his to become dark smoke.

"Can all high fae heal iron wounds when they transform?" I asked, keeping my voice low.

She shook her head. "Some. Only those whose forms are elements and who come from the right bloodlines."

"And I take it you are not one of them?"

"Alas, I am not. Even before the interruption, it was not one of my advantages."

I wondered if Reed's bloodline was a reason the court hated him so much, beyond being a halfling. But, more importantly, I wondered how long Robin had before the iron did enough damage to take her down.

"Come on," she urged, echoing my thoughts. "Reed won't last much longer."

"You said he was being tortured. Would they have already—?" I lengthened my stride, doing my best to keep the waves we made low while picking up the pace.

"When I last saw him, it was clear Jassin intended to make an example of him for snooping through his things. I don't know if he'll let Reed die, but we can't risk it."

"And Reed wasn't just looking for his own contract?" I asked. "You're sure?" She had already sworn it had been on my behalf that he'd been caught, but I couldn't figure out what else he'd been hoping to find. I'd gotten the cure for my brother; there wasn't anything else I'd been after.

"It was some agreement with the anglocks, about their increased presence. Reed said he'd been checking it for you, but I'm not sure why—that was all I was able to find out before they pulled me from his cell. I know his state will only have gotten worse since I left, though I got to your town fast."

Images of Reed chained and bleeding flashed through my mind, his wide chest pale and graying, iron marks burning at his skin, his fingers broken or worse, his legs crushed. Who knew what kind of brutal and sickening torment the fae considered fair recompense for treachery?

I pushed forward, my steps growing more frantic as we traveled through the night.

CHAPTER TWENTY

It was early morning, and the only guards we encountered were stationed right where I'd faced them last—defending the gates to the compound but with bored expressions and slouched shoulders. One was an abyssot wearing armor made of thick hide, but the other appeared to be a well-dressed high fae, his humanoid features sharp and elongated as he leaned against a half-submerged tree near the floating docks. It seemed strange that they hadn't upped security, but maybe my fight with the guards as I'd fled was a common occurrence.

Robin and I paused behind a thick trunk, right on the edges of their vision. If the abyssot turned his pink, feathery head he might see something in the water, so I kept my breath still, trying to be invisible.

"Do we fight?" I whispered. "Or pretend I'm glamoured?"

"Neither," she replied, out of breath. The damned iron was killing her right in front of me, wearing her down from the inside, and I could do nothing to stop it. Guilt squatted heavy in my chest as she turned her pale face toward me. Over the hours she had slowed significantly, more than just for my sake, I feared. "You go underwater and make your way there." She jerked her shoulder toward the far side of the castle, where Reed had once snuck me inside. "I'll distract them. You know the way after that, yeah?"

"Well, yeah, but..."

She was leaving me to break Reed out alone? That wasn't the plan.

"He's one level below his room. I would join you but..." she shuddered as if cold or fighting some kind of seizure, "I don't think I'll be much help unless I get to the Luada mushrooms first."

"I'll go with you," I offered. "If he's being guarded, I don't think I can make it past more than one or two—"

"You must," Robin interrupted. "I'll join you when I can, but you need to get to him before the sun is high and the rest of the castle wakes."

"That's still hours away." The sun was rising in tiny specks between the thick canopy to my right, and I knew in any other location it would be a beautiful, bright orange.

"I don't think we can risk the delay if they—" suddenly she stumbled, catching herself against the tree trunk. We both froze at the sound of the splash.

My attention narrowed to the space ahead and the guards who lounged there. I counted my heartbeats against the jarring calls of some osprey trilling on its perch. I dared not peek beyond to see if the guards had noticed.

Thankfully, after some time, it became clear they'd either been deaf to the disruption or taken it for some natural occurrence.

Robin shifted to gently rest against the tree, wincing as her back came into contact with the bark.

"I'll walk toward the guards and tell them I've been injured by humans," she whispered. "They'll run off in pursuit and I can grab the remedy while you start toward the dungeons."

Suddenly the net launcher was thrust into my hands, and Robin had only narrowly avoided scraping herself on the caltrop still clutched in my fist.

"You'll have this, and the weapons in your bag. You know Reed, and you know this place better than you think. I believe in you."

Faith had never done much for me before—only kept me tethered to a family and a life I would have preferred to escape...and almost gotten me killed more than once—but it didn't sound as if I had an option to refuse her.

I shouldered the launcher and moved the two caltrops to one hand, feeling oddly bogged down by the weapons.

"Fine," I muttered, still wrestling with my remorse. If it weren't for me, she'd have been able to help. She probably would have been inside with Reed by now.

Robin nodded, then lurched beyond the tree without warning, making a loud gurgle as she flailed her arms, feigning panic.

"Help! Guards!"

From my hiding place I could only imagine how far she moved toward the guards before they met her, hoping it was far enough. Tucking the launcher into my bag, I took in a long, slow breath just as the guards began interrogating her.

"Quick," I heard her shout. "Humans, that way!"

Lowering myself into the grimy water, I pushed off the silt floor and did my best to stay under as long as I possibly could. I let my lungs burn and my heart stutter, using wide, gentle strokes to swim in the direction she'd told me. If I stood with a gasp and the guards were still too close, I was doomed.

It helped to imagine the scene that might be waiting for me—Reed cold, alone, wounded—and I managed another few seconds, my lungs close to bursting.

When I finally rose, algae-tinted waters sluicing from my face, I whipped my head from side to side while gulping in air, trying to orient myself. There were no guards in sight. One of the raised platforms lay ahead, wet from some previous creature's recent arrival at the compound, but I hurried to climb up regardless. With luck, it was a courtly high fae or some harmless monster, and I wasn't about to run into the path of another murderous syra or lendani.

Arms shaking more from nerves than fatigue, I scrambled onto the elevated dock and rushed to the side entrance Reed had shown me once before. Musk and decay assaulted my senses. I placed a dripping sleeve over my nose, breathing shallowly through the fabric. Had the stench always been this bad and I'd grown used to it in my time here? Or was some dead thing just ahead?

In the wide foyer, its stone floor tinted blue, the receding shadows revealed nothing but half-empty shelves and the scuttling of some crab trying to hide in the far corner.

I trod carefully forward, regaining my hold on the caltrops.

The scuttle sounded again, and I looked over to see another crab, this one with pink-tinged claws, inching toward me.

"Back off," I muttered, stepping backward, and then another crawled from the shadows. And another. A sound like humming echoed off the cavernous space and I felt the hairs on my forearms and the back of my neck stand in warning.

My foot knocked against something, and I looked down to see an empty shell, transparent and as delicate as lace, break against my shoe.

They were molting.

The hum grew more intense, the claw-tips of the nearest crab emitting a soft, rosy glow. With a start, I recognized them. These were the creatures Conor had sworn he could weaponize, the ones who incapacitated with just a touch, powerful as lightning. Another handful appeared, swarming from unseen caverns and corners. If struck, I would face the painful touch of that urchin-fingered guard, times a hundred.

"No, no, no." Spinning on my heel, I rushed toward the empty door frame, jumping over a crab that was still only partially free from its old shell. Another couple wriggled closer to help it, or to attack me. I couldn't be sure.

My chin-length hair splattered in wet strands across my eyes, and I shook them away, nearly running directly into a creature in the hall.

I stumbled, managing to catch myself against the wall on my left. The iron-tipped nails in my hand made an unearthly screech as they scraped against the stone and mortar.

Rough-skinned hands reached for me.

I registered the crogwyn just fast enough to slash out with both hands, catching the creature's arm right below the edge of its shell-like armor. It screamed, the voice deep and so loud it reverberated all around us. In a panic, I lurched again, slamming the caltrops deep into its stomach.

The smell of its breath was rancid as its circular mouth exhaled in my face. I gagged, alarm making my movements jerky as I tried to free my weapons from its gut. I needed to get out of this hallway. There was no telling how many guards or high fae were rushing toward the sound of its screams, despite the early hour, and I couldn't be here when they arrived.

Twisting, I managed to pull the nails free, and I watched as the guard fell backward into the crabs' range. It landed right on top of two of them.

The crogwyn jerked and spasmed, its strange flat mouth pulsing open and closed. Blue blood leaked from its wounds as it seized. The crabs' strange power was coursing painfully through the monster's entire body.

I fled.

The hallways were dark but familiar as I made my way to the right and then down a flight of stairs. They were so slimy I slid, landing on my ass and falling down a few steps, but I righted myself and continued on. Breath scraped its way down my throat as I hurried to remember the way, traveling even deeper into the castle's abyss and darting down a series of corridors as soon as the coast was clear.

A kelavee slunk down the hall ahead of me and I had to pause and wait for what felt like eons for it to turn a corner before continuing on.

I finally made it to the familiar iron bars of the dungeon that served as Reed's room, but the door was open, and he wasn't inside. Right, I needed to go down further, to some even deeper and darker dungeon. Just how many levels of this awful place were there?

I rushed down another flight of steps—albeit with slightly more care this time—and heard a low snuffling sound up ahead.

Peeking my face around the stone staircase, I spotted the murky trail of an anglock. It was thick and uneven, as if the monster had recently passed by more than once.

Sure enough, by my next breath, the dainty flower extending from its head crept into view, followed by the creature itself. Bulbous and slow, it inched along the ground, trailing mucus as it swayed. I watched it move to one end of the hall, then slowly curl in on itself to turn. A lit torch on the wall somewhere to the right threw its shadow in stark relief against the ground, so I could track its slow, cyclical movement.

With my heart nearly bursting from my chest, I shifted my bag as quietly as I could manage, resting it against my chest so I could rummage within. I had to hope the launcher was dry enough to work, or else I would be reduced to stabbing at the thing with my dagger or throwing caltrops into its sticky body. Both options weren't worth the noise they would bring.

Cranking the handle on the net launcher was a test in patience.

I was afraid that moving too fast would either break the mechanism inside, or that—when it notched into place—the sound would betray my location. Thankfully, the quiet *click* went unnoticed by the pacing monster below and I readied my sight, breathing deep as I took aim.

Just as its flower passed me, I fired, the kick of the launcher almost throwing me back against the steps as the net expanded and wrapped around the anglock. The sizzle of the iron against its muddy flesh was music to my ears; I watched as it thrashed and shrank, eaten away by the metal's poison.

I would have felt sorry for it if I didn't know the kind of misery it might inflict on any poor soul who stumbled across its floral bait.

Though the creature shuddered and hissed, the sounds were miniscule compared to the crogwyn's screams. Still, there was no time to dally. Before it had even truly died, I was jumping down the remaining stairs and pushing at the door it had guarded.

Locked.

I sighed, frustration tightening my shoulders, though it was stupid of me to be surprised. Reed was a prisoner being tortured, with a guard stationed at his cell. Of course he was locked in.

Checking behind me, I listened for sounds of pursuit but heard only the general groans of the castle and the crashing of waves against the exterior. The gurgled cries of the anglock were fading, growing indecipherable.

Reaching into my pack once more, I grabbed the vial of erosion powder Conor had prepared for Robin. My hand was dry enough to unscrew the lid, but I still trembled to handle it, tipping the opening toward the knob and keyhole of the door. The powder dotted and congealed on the spot, but nothing else happened.

Shit.

It needed more moisture.

Dropping the empty vial to the ground, I squeezed the fabric of my drenched shirt, letting it drip and puddle into my palm before flicking it at the door a few times. The destruction was quick then, the compound eating at the wood and metal like it was nothing but wet paper, and as soon as the lock was weakened enough, I stood back and *kicked*.

The door slammed open, and I readied my caltrop, but I wasn't prepared for the scene inside.

A syra, glowing a cold white, was draped around Reed's form as they lay together on a high pallet. It seemed like a loving embrace, her arms wrapped around his broad chest, her long tail twining around his legs, and then I realized the glow wasn't actually emitting from the merkind woman—it was the reflection of wide, shining mushrooms nestled close to the ceiling, the light bouncing off her skin.

Skin that was mostly comprised of *ice*.

I briefly thought it was shards of glass coating her scales, but the damp, cold air sweeping over my face and arms didn't lie. And neither did the blue tint to Reed's skin, his shallow breath ghosting from his trembling lips like incense smoke. The room was an ice box, and the syra was somehow the source.

The woman's pale gray hair shifted as she turned her beautiful face toward me, mouth opening in a wide hiss. Her clawed hands gripped Reed tighter and he groaned.

I couldn't see if he was injured, pinned beneath her body as he was, but I had no doubt he was in extraordinary pain. At the sound of the door opening, he'd tried to turn his head toward the sound, but it was like he was stuck—paralyzed except for the minute shaking of his torso.

Shouldering the door closed behind me, I kept to the edge of the room, inching closer to them while keeping the chilled stone at my back.

The syra watched me with black eyes—the only color on her frosty body—and hunched as if ready to pounce.

The easiest thing would be the net launcher, but I was out of net. The powder could hurt her, but there was a chance it would land on Reed as well. My only choices were throwing the caltrops, and praying my aim struck true, or getting close enough to use them or my dagger hand-to-hand.

Edging further to the side, I waited until the syra moved to whip her head around to my new location near the foot of the pallet, and then I attacked.

I missed her by a hair's width when I threw the first caltrop, the iron clanking onto the stone floor, but I pulled the other back and let it fly just as fast as the first, imagining it was a crabapple being used in a game of catch with Conor.

This one smacked into the syra's back, and where I expected the iron to hiss and embed itself in her flesh, instead it bounced off the ice of her skin.

Still, she shrieked, thrashing and wriggling on top of Reed to spin over him. Staying on her belly, and still covering her captive from head to toe, she faced me. Rage narrowed her black eyes, and her jaw opened so wide I could see the vertebrae of her throat as she screamed. The fangs in her mouth had shivers racing up my arms, even more so than the frigid air.

Somehow, the temperature seemed to drop further as she crawled down Reed's legs toward me, making my limbs feel slow and heavy. I was shivering already, the water on my clothes turning to ice.

The only weapons I had left were my dagger and one final caltrop. If they could even pierce some place on her skin.

"Shit," I breathed.

The mushrooms near the ceiling pulsed brighter, as if affected by the power the syra emitted in chilling waves. My wounds, still tight and sore under my wet tunic, began to freeze and stick to the fabric.

Panicking, I plucked the shirt away from me with one hand, pulling my dagger free with the other.

I would have circled the bed had there been room to do so, but it rested along the far wall. This was as close as I could get without placing myself within swiping range.

Shuffling back to the front, I debated my next move, but no matter where I lunged, I had no leverage. Nothing but my blade and the bag on my back. And my acting.

I paused, then—ignoring the sting at my abdomen—pulled back my shoulders. "You're going to want to let him go," I grumbled into the air. Then louder, "I don't want to kill you. But I will."

The syra screamed once more, jerking toward me like a threat. Did she not understand me? Did she not care? So much for that idea.

I stepped back, reassessing just as her long nails slid into Reed's arm.

He jerked, blood trickling onto the bed. A frail wheeze trembled from his lips.

"Reed!"

She gripped tight, digging her claws in further.

Holding the knife in front of me as if it was a sword, I sprang forward, slashing. The attack was weak, and easy to swat aside, but it brought me into close range. I should have taken the time to grab my last caltrop from the bag—should have thrust it upward like a clever warrior from one of my stories—but my only thought had been to stop her from hurting Reed further. To save him any way I could.

As soon as she smacked my arm aside, I used the momentum to spin, thinking I might surprise her with a second jab. But it was too late.

Her other hand, tipped with those wicked claws, was already embedding itself in my gut, right over the slashes left over from the lendani.

The sound that ripped from my chest was a wet gasp, and then I was choking on it as the hot, blinding pain brought me to my knees.

Blood splashed on the cold stone as the syra pulled back, steam rising from the puddle. I wondered if she had pulled part of my body with her; it felt as if my lungs or my entrails or even my spirit was being flung onto the dungeon floor. But no...as I looked down, it was just a slow, hot trail of blood, seeping from four identical punctures.

I clutched the wound with one trembling palm and tried to stand, my legs shaking.

The syra screeched, moving to carve her fingers into me once more, but I let myself drop to the side. Rolling backward, I took a second to catch my breath. At any moment she would be upon me.

Except...I took one agonizing breath, and then another. She still hadn't left her place atop Reed's body. Craning my head, I could see the edge of her long, icy tail slithering over his neck and face.

She couldn't leave him—had either been commanded or glamoured not to do so—and as long as I had her attention, maybe she wouldn't hurt Reed further while I planned a new form of attack.

I groaned louder than I needed to, cutting off the sound in a whimper, and then moved as if to sit up but purposefully failed. Better she think I was weak and near death rather than just biding my time.

"Reed, I'm sorry," I whined as I curled in on myself, writhing so my bag was closer to my dagger-wielding hand. "I tried…"

"W-w-win…" Reed said on a shiver. Darting my eyes to him, I saw there were speckles of my blood on the arm he kept closest to me. And where there was blood, his flesh seemed to…darken. At first, I worried it was rot of some kind, like a poison the syra was infecting him with, but then I realized it was a weakened version of his shadow form, trying to push toward the surface of his skin.

My blood was warm, hot even compared to this icebox of a room. At least, until it cooled. Hells, was I going to have to bleed all over him to set him right?

I'd worry about that later.

Thrashing and squirming on the stone floor was like a sharp, frigid scrape along all of my senses, the pain in my stomach making my heart pound in desperation, but I managed to hug the bag to my upper chest, as if mindlessly clutching it in the throes of my death.

"Arghhhh!" I wailed, then peeked one eye to the syra, her dark eyes ravenous on me. Syra ate the bodies of their victims, I remembered reading. If I died here, she'd have a free meal. That is, if she was permitted to leave her post at any point. But I couldn't take the chance that she'd been commanded to wait until Reed's death.

The monster's bloody claws were still outstretched, as if she'd been in the process of attacking when she'd been instead mesmerized by my performance.

Hitching my breath in pain was easy to emphasize, given the stinging pulse under my hand, but shaking hard enough to open the flap of my rucksack was a masterful—and difficult—maneuver.

Finally, I had the last caltrop under my fingers, and I gripped it tight, pulling my fist against my body as if it was just another attempt to stop the blood from pouring out of me. With obvious effort, I pushed myself to my knees, back turned to them both, and then shifted in tiny increments to turn.

"Reed," I pleaded, my voice breaking once more. "I'm here. I won't leave you." The words felt heavy in my mouth, as if there was an inkling of truth in them, instead of just an act. I hunched low over the floor, curled like a shrimp, before either of them could see the dagger and caltrop in my fists.

"Win, n-no," Reed breathed, voice like a soft wind.

Shuffling forward, my knees grating and bleeding over the rugged floor, I released a labored sob.

"I'm so sorry, Reed. I..." I sniveled, "I had a plan, and if I could just get you warm I would..." A hiccup was their only warning as I got within striking range. Gathering what strength I could—despite the pain of my stomach and the panic rushing through my veins—I peered up to the syra's greedy face just as I shoved both arms forward. Like a mighty push, I punched both iron-tipped weapons at her, knowing with her body still tied to Reed's, she would need one hand for balance. And only have one other to defend herself.

Sure enough, she was able to swat aside my dagger once more, but she didn't have time to dodge the iron nails poking out from my left fist, which I aimed for the stretch of human flesh at her collarbones, the only part of her not fully coated in sparkling ice.

Two of the caltrop's pointed tips embedded themselves into her shoulder, and the hissing and smoking of her skin was the only sound for one heartbeat. Until her shriek became a scream.

She wriggled, widening the holes around the iron nails, trying to get away from me, but I pushed up onto frail legs, following her. When she lashed out, her talons catching and slicing into my arm, I used the movement to pierce her chest with the dagger, and then her pale, wild hair flung wide in a wind of her own making, swiping across my face so my vision went momentarily dark.

I shook my head, spitting it from my mouth.

Reed coughed. "Win!"

The syra scratched at me again, this time dangerously close to my neck, and on instinct I twisted the blade.

Her torso tumbled backward and she fell from the bed. Her body was still coated in icy scales, but they were dropping like bits of shale as she collapsed onto the floor, the frost melting away into ash around the wounds on her chest and shoulder. Wounds that were growing by the second. The iron was eating her alive.

I sat, stunned and leaking, waiting for her to somehow reassemble, or for another monster to barge into the cell, but there was only the quiet hiss of her decay. It echoed in the room like a gale.

And then Reed groaned, drawing my attention. He was attempting to sit up, his body stiff and blue from cold, his lips purple. His chest heaved from the effort and his arms quaked.

Instinct had me hurrying to help him, but the deep claw marks in my stomach throbbed with fresh agony. Dots peppered my vision.

Great. With both of us in such a miserable state, we were unlikely to leave this room, let alone escape the compound entirely.

"Win, I..." Reed started, and then his arm gave way, his torso slamming back onto the slab. "Hells." He shivered there while I bled into a pool on the floor, just feet away. I had no idea what to do. Could I pull him down to me? Cover him in my blood before it cooled? If only I could start a fire...

The door behind us flew open, and I used what energy I had left to lift the caltrop, still frosted with the syra's innards. But it was Robin who came barreling inside.

She looked rough, with gray crescents beneath her eyes and an uneven gate carrying her into the dungeon, but she was still one of the most beautiful things I'd ever seen.

"Oh, th-thank the moon," I whispered as she took in the scene.

The long-limbed fae pulled a bottle from a pouch tied somewhere under her shirt and unstoppered it before throwing it onto the ground to my left. It landed right beneath the altar where Reed still struggled to move.

I watched the slick liquid splatter around the stone, but nothing seemed to happen. The syra was already gone, vanishing into floating dust that thickened the air.

"Um...I don't think you need—" I started, but then she pulled out a flint and a shining stone, cracking them together. A spark drifted to the puddle, and it immediately caught; fire leapt along the liquid in a loud rush.

I inched sideways, away from the blaze, still clutching my side. The warmth that swept my face was harsh compared to the chill on my cheeks, but I was grateful for it. It meant Reed would be healthy soon. He'd be strong.

I'd done it. I'd saved him and he was safe.

The relief had my head tilting backward on my neck, my body swaying with the weight, and then I was falling.

Robin's hands caught me before my skull could bang on the stone.

My last thought before everything went dark was that I was tired of saving the men in my life from evil creatures, and I deserved a nap.

And then I was out.

CHAPTER TWENTY-ONE

I woke up to one of those pink-clawed crabs scuttling over my arm. Before I could scream, a hand swatted the critter away.

"Be gone with you, menace."

Reed.

I turned my head, vision swimming, and there he was—his scruffy cheeks flushed with pink, his eyes blue as the morning waves. He smiled at me like I was the most precious thing he'd ever beheld, his fingers caressing my jaw, my chin, my neck. His fingers were cold.

"There you are, little perch."

Wasn't I supposed to be mad at him? I should be shooing away his affection. But something in my pain-addled mind demanded I smile back at him and lean into the touch. I couldn't help it.

"We have to move before the tide comes in," said a feminine voice to my left. Robin stood at the open doorway, her gaze darting from the crabs click-clacking at her booted feet to the hallway beyond. I dimly recognized the room the little monsters had been molting in before—where I'd left the crogwyn to die.

Reed seemed to recognize the thoughts on my face as he helped me sit up. There was dried blood on my tunic and pants, but I could feel the sticky mass of some kind of salve over the puncture marks the syra had left behind.

"Don't mind the shockstones, Win," he said with a weak smirk. "They only react to sudden moves and intruders on their molting grounds."

"The shocksto..." I looked down to see a host of the crabs moving about unbothered, shaking themselves free of their old skins or climbing over one another like a mass of bugs in the dirt.

"I feed them bristle worms and any seagrass I collect during my chores, so they like me," he explained. "Don't do anything hasty and they'll leave us be."

I had to trust him at his word. After all, he couldn't lie. Not that it stopped him from omitting certain truths, or bending words around his true meaning. *I'd heard those flowers can only be picked under a full moon...*

I stood, feeling both the deep *and* shallow wounds on my body pull with the movement. He'd tricked me, used me. But he'd also saved me. And now we were even.

Freed from his icy prison, Reed could drown for all I cared—I'd done my part.

"Glad to see you're alive," I muttered, holding onto my side while gaining my bearings.

He watched me from the ground as if afraid to stand, or maybe still too weak despite the color in his face. I wondered how long I'd been unconscious. Was it midday already? "Now I'll take my leave, and you can keep on with your—"

Robin held up a hand, shushing me. Her pointed ears were aimed toward the hall. I stiffened, glancing around my feet to see if my pack or my weapons had been carted along, but all that surrounded me was a mass of turquoise crab shells and waving rose-tipped claws. After a handful of tense heartbeats her shoulders lowered, and she nodded to us.

"I don't know how long we have," said Reed, voice strained and gravelly. It was then I noticed the way shadows seemed to ripple over his skin, like a dark glaze setting in my mother's kiln. He looked as if he was fighting the transformation that would shift his flesh into smoke. "But I wanted to tell you what was happening. To the fae. To your people."

His forearm flashed black, going from smoke and then back to skin. I wanted to reach out and drag my fingers through it, wondering if it was warm, if it felt soft like I remembered, but I clenched my fist tighter. I needed to get out of here before it was too late. Conor and my mother were waiting for me. We had our chance to get far from here, to start over...but the puzzle of the fae's dampened powers was like an itch I'd failed to scratch, consuming my attention.

"You have two minutes," I said. For all I knew, we had less, but that was as much as I was willing to lend him.

"Jassin's made a deal with an alchemist." Reed's eyes were troubled, and focused so intently on me I could not look away. "I found a series of recipes in his things, a mix of metals and herbs that could be ignited. Like a burst of energy. It would interrupt fae power, so the demand for humans would increase, and Jassin could get more nobles to enter into contracts with him. Slaves, security, entertainment—he had price lists for different categories, and estimates on his sales from week to week. It was all plotted out so each house of the royal fae would sign contracts with him, to increase his power."

He looked at me as if he'd just delivered some incredible information, but my side was aching, and my patience was waning. This all made sense;

Jassin's price for Reed had been unreasonably high because he'd known how valuable a servant like Reed would become as the interruption continued. And it explained why healers and blacksmiths had been targeted in our village—so no one could discover or combat the amalgamation of minerals and plants that made Jassin's spell. In all the local towns, I was sure those workers had been the first to disappear. But this didn't help me moving forward, it only gave me the *why*.

"Okay, and what does this have to do with me and Conor? Get to your point, Reed."

"The anglock that attacked your brother...Jassin hired them to sow unrest and bring any living victims back to him—Conor must have escaped before the creature could pull him under. It's all to make humans desperate and scared so Jassin can fill his quota of slaves and skilled servants, more to sell off to the fae." He grabbed my hand, a move that seemed to surprise us both. I looked down at it, a series of emotions roiling through me too fast to name. "Without the ability to shift or use heavy magics, the fae aren't able to hunt or take care of their households. And it won't let up. Not anytime soon, until Jassin has his fill. Until he is more powerful than even the prince."

I pulled my hand away, slowly. Conor could have been taken, or killed, all for the greed of one fae? The chaos and fear choking Harnsey was to drive frantic people into Jassin's arms, hoping for salvation in the form of indentured servitude?

I shook my head, struggling to assemble the pieces Reed left between us. There was something he was getting at, some question he wanted to ask me. I'd only known him a short while, but I could hear the way he stepped gingerly toward his purpose. Hand back at my wound from the syra, I waited. A crab crawled over my foot, its legs like prickling branches skating over my toes.

"Things will only get worse for the humans near this realm, until his desire for business is satisfied," Reed said, finally pushing to a stand so he could look into my eyes. "And that time may never come. The only hope you have for your people is to stop him now, by killing him or his alchemist. Otherwise, more and more people will be taken—hundreds, maybe thousands."

"You're saying you want my help to murder him," I stated. "Just like before."

"I'm saying it would benefit you to stop him."

I stepped back. "Spoken like a deceitful schemer."

His face fell, and Robin shifted from her place by the doorway, as if ready to leap between us.

My heart pounded painfully in my chest.

This was the moment the hero would think of their family and their people. A good, *just* person would jump at the chance to right a wrong, to protect those who could not protect themselves. To return the world to order. But all I saw was another hurdle to leap over, another struggle. I wanted the people in Harnsey to be safe, but this was so much bigger than me. Besides, killing Jassin might stop him from taking human slaves, but it might also bring back the fae creatures' powers. And the same was true for going straight to the alchemist. Was it worth it to stop chaos if the power imbalance would always remain? Was the old world order worth saving? With those powers, certain fae could heal from iron injuries, and my people would go back to being at their mercy.

My brother was cured, and Reed was alive. Surely that was enough.

But even if I went home to Conor and my mother now, there would still always be fear snapping at our feet. We could run further from the coast, but fae were everywhere—in the woods and under fields, in rivers and lakes, and even cold places swept blank with snow. If this ploy worked in the marshes, would another selfish and power hungry fae try the same thing elsewhere?

A soft groan drew my attention back to Reed, and I realized his form was growing somehow more unstable. His entire torso was flickering like a flame.

"What's wrong with you?" I asked in a near whisper, and then I regretted even opening my mouth. It didn't matter. I had to *leave.*

"His body is trying to heal itself," said Robin from her place by the door. "I couldn't keep him by the flames long enough—not when there was a chance Jassin or another of his lackeys would check the cell."

"It's fine," he said with a grunt, closing his eyes. "I've had worse." His blond hair, wet with melting ice, slipped over his forehead as he made a low, scoffing laugh. I imagined pushing it back from his face, putting my warm hand on his cheek.

I shook my head, looking down the tunnel to my right that would lead back out into the mangrove. "I'm doomed either way. If Jassin or the alchemist is dead, he stops taking humans—*maybe*—but then we're right back where we started." I backed away another step, angled toward the tunnel. "We're always subject to the whims of the fae. Even breaking all of his contracts would only be a momentary solution."

Robin moved from the door, her body lean and towering, like a bending tree. "What if things could be better for you? For all the humans?"

My foot halted, so close to the edge of the tunnel I could feel the damp breeze at my back. The light was dulled from heavy cloud cover outside, and shadows were creeping closer by the second. Already passed noon then.

"I don't have time for your riddles," I said. "Speak now or I'm gone."

"Jassin is using this disorder as a ploy for power," she mused, her graceful hand gesturing with the words. "We can tell the prince, and he may take care of Jassin *for* us. His powers have been affected as well as ours, he must be looking for an answer. If we tell him how they were taken and who to target, he would most likely offer you a prize for the information."

"I could buy safety for my town," I said aloud as I realized it.

I ignored the brush of inky black that caressed Reed's neck, and the way he tilted toward Robin and then away, still unsteady.

The tall fae nodded.

Well shit…that was something.

"And you would be willing to let *me* share this information, instead of you?" I turned to Reed. "Even though this could potentially buy your freedom?"

"If Prince Aeden kills Jassin, then I am free either way," he said, and something tender took over his eyes. "But I would rather you benefit from his favor than me."

It was said so simply that I couldn't find the lie hidden within. I wanted to ask why, wanted to needle him into spouting something outrageous, like his feelings for me, or some hidden advantage he could secure through me, just so I would have some clue to how I should feel in return. Because right now I had one foot moving towards him, and another moving away, and soon I would split myself in two.

But feelings could wait.

"Fine," I agreed. "Let's go see—"

The door opened behind Robin, and in strode a murderous-looking Jassin.

CHAPTER TWENTY-TWO

All I saw was silver hair and flashing black eyes, and then Jassin was pulling a sword from a scabbard at his hip. That's when Reed stepped in front of me.

"Who told you to leave your cell, filthy mongrel?" The fae's voice was as sharp as steel. I looked to Robin, hoping she would intervene on Reed's behalf, but she stood stock still, seemingly frozen in fear. "*Kneel. And stay there.*"

Reed dropped to his knees with a painful crack that had me wincing. The command in Jassin's tone was laced with something deeper and darker than any cavern, and then the brutal fae's gaze met mine.

"Ah, Winona, wasn't it?" His black eyes traced over my features, my face betraying me with its full cheeks and rounded ears. "Interesting. A human playing dress up." With a flourish, he brandished his sword, an evil smirk twisting his thin lips, raising it as if readying to strike.

I had no weapons, no strength, no defenses. My bag of tricks was gone, my caltrops missing.

"I—I still want to buy Reed out of his contract!" I blurted, scrambling for a bargain I could make or lie I could spin. "I have gold—"

"A human's words are worth less than the worms that feast on your corpses."

I blinked, and with fantastical slowness, I saw the sword coming toward me, a slashing arc intended to split me in half.

It was then that Robin acted. I hadn't seen her reach into a pocket, but she had a small leather pouch in her fingers, and just as Jassin went to strike me, she blew a yellow powder over him.

The dust sprinkled like sugar over his rich emerald-green tunic, landing on his shoulders and the hand holding his sword. He paused in confusion before it started glowing, and he screamed as if doused with fire. It was like the mixture Conor had given me, but instead of eroding, it *burned*. I could smell it, like the hair on my arms when I reached too far into a kiln.

With his sword clattering to the ground—narrowly missing landing on Reed's golden head—Jassin flailed, attempting to shake off the powder. It was chewing him like hungry mouths, red and black flesh peppering his pale skin, now visible through the burnt sleeves of his tunic.

The crabs around us started to flee, some of them touched by the murderous powder as well.

Reed gasped, drawing my attention. "Robin!"

She had slumped against the stone wall, sliding down to flop onto the ground.

"What?" I asked, stunned as my eyes bounced between Robin and Jassin, both on the floor, one quiet and one still shrieking and batting at his clothes while the flesh dripped off his hands. "What's happening?"

"Punishment for violence against a fae," Reed rushed out, still on his knees. "Quick, put her on her side."

"What does—"

"Now!" he shouted, and I hurried to do as he said, just as Robin began to convulse. Her body jerked and spasmed as if she'd been struck by hundreds of shockstones.

Reed leaned forward to hold one of Jassin's arms to the ground, his other pressed to Jassin's mouth, quieting his screams, though there was little hope he'd remained unheard. We were about to have more company, and Reed was still kneeling. Could he not get up until Jassin released him?

Beneath my palms, Robin's body slowed its quaking, but her expression remained stuck in an open-mouthed grimace, her hand still partially extended.

Jassin finally succumbed to the pain and fell unconscious, his panting breaths and screaming subsiding into an echoing silence. Only then did Reed stand, apparently freed from his owner's command.

"We have to move her." His voice was stronger, but his muscles shook as he grabbed Robin under her armpits and attempted to haul her outright. "Hurry. Someone will be coming." He grunted, and I helped him raise Robin to a standing position. Her limbs wouldn't move—frozen in the position she'd been in when she fell, the magic petrifying her just like Conor, only there was no bark to be seen on her skin.

We hobbled over Jassin's body and away from the room—both crippled by the weight strung between us and the injuries plaguing our aching bodies—and attempted to climb a set of stairs to our right. Each step was agony on the slashes in my gut. I knew blood was seeping from beneath the crusty salve; it wouldn't be much further before I collapsed again. My body ached like it had been beaten and scratched on every spare inch.

"Where...are we going?" I asked on a wheeze.

"The prince," he replied. "The plan...hasn't changed." He sounded as rough as I did.

We turned a corner, and I stumbled over my tired feet, almost falling onto my face. Thankfully I caught myself on a wall, but the weight of Robin along my back pulled a muscle in my side and I hissed with the pain of it.

"Winnie?" Reed asked. I couldn't see his face, his form blocked by Robin's body, but I could hear the concern in his voice.

"I'm fine, I just..." but my voice gave out. I needed to concentrate on breathing. On moving one step at a time and following his lead. I wanted to pause and rest but there was no telling how many creatures were heading to the shockstones' cave, and how they would react to find Jassin half-flayed from whatever powdered root or mushroom Robin had spewed over him.

The final set of stairs almost defeated me, but after huffing out harsh breaths, my legs trembling with fatigue, we made it to the wing where the royals apparently met their beds.

Guards lined the entrance of the hall. The two nearest to us—a crogwyn with its starfish-like stature bending forward as if to sniff us, and a humanoid fae leaning away as if repulsed—gripped their weapons tighter, shifting to block our way. Blood and salt were stiffening my clothes into a shell, my face was flushed pink with exertion, and my hair was a wet, tangled mess, but I had a feeling the fae's objection to us was based more on the human shape of my ears than anything else.

"We have important information for Prince Aeden," Reed announced, trying to sound sturdier than he was. I hoped his body wasn't still flashing into bits of smoke, or he was about to get way more attention than he wanted. "He will want to hear it immediately."

The crogwyn's long face drifted toward me, its circular mouth pulsing closer and closer to my skin, breathing in my human stench. It shook its head, even though its gaze flashed with interest at Robin hanging between us.

The human-looking fae, with black hair and bronze skin that glimmered, made a shooing motion. "Get out of here, half-breed waste," he said in a gravelly voice. "And take the human slave with you."

Reed's shoulders rose on a deep inhale. "If the prince turns me away after what we have to tell him...I will allow you to beat me within an inch of my life."

His voice was so casual, like maids gossiping around the well while they collected water. *Did you hear Kali and her sister fighting last night? Yes, after that spot of rain. And Reed being beaten within an inch of his life—how droll.*

"Reed," I hissed, ready to argue, to lie, *anything*. But the fae grinned so widely his pointed teeth seemed to take over his entire face—a vision I knew would filter into my nightmares.

"You have a deal!" The excitement and bloodlust in the fae's eyes were enough to have my weakened stomach churning.

The guard moved aside, gesturing for the crogwyn to do the same, and we continued to shuffle toward the double doors ahead. The carpet here was finer than anything I'd seen in the castle so far, soft and speckled with silver threads in the shapes of fish and waves. I couldn't inspect the walls or ceiling, because if I dared look away from my feet I was sure I would drop Robin and crash onto the floor.

We passed another set of guards, both lendani who flicked their tongues at us, but the fae behind us must have gestured to them to let us pass because they slithered off to either side like the fanged guardians of some cosmic gate.

After an awkward pause, Reed adjusted Robin over his shoulder and knocked on the prince's door. I expected a page or another servant to open it, but the man who greeted us could only have been royalty; his boots were fine leather with dark, embroidered edges and his legs were wrapped in breeches made from the scales of a crimson syra. As my gaze traveled up his form, I noticed the bejeweled sword at his side, and the dark pearls lining the hem of his tunic. Wealth and status practically oozed from the languid pose he made against the doorway, his arms crossed over his chest, and when my eyes finally reached his face, I saw such a horrible and beautiful set of features, I wondered why there weren't countless portraits of him in the castle. His pointed ears were longer than my hand, his lips so dark they were almost purple, and his black eyes were heavy-lidded under porcelain skin dusted with red creams. Fangs shimmered like the inside of oyster shells as he grinned.

"What a...sorry sight," Prince Aeden commented, and then leaned forward to check that his lendani guards were still in place. Since we looked like ruined and messy intruders, I could understand his confusion. He cocked one eyebrow in interest, the red of it matching his ginger hair—a natural shade I hadn't expected—and gestured for us to come inside.

His rooms were similar to Jassin's, though there were fewer gaudy accents. The sofas that were angled around the wooden table to our right looked comfortable and well-used, their purple fabric faded in some spots. There were no gold tassels in sight. I only had a moment to take in the tall ceilings, dark marble floors, and brass drink cart, before I stumbled under Robin's weight, dropping her onto the couch and falling down beside her.

The prince strode to the far end of the room to sit behind an ornate desk made of rough-hewn planks of mismatched wood. I wondered if they were trophies from ships he'd sunk, or if he just had a strange sense of style.

"Tell me what I can do for you..." he waved an elegant hand, gems winking from his wrist.

"Reed," he introduced himself.

"Ah, yes. I've seen you at banquets. And miss?"

I cleared my throat. "Winona."

"A human," he said, as if amused, but I could tell he was close to sneering.

"Yes, your...majesty."

"Royal Highness," he corrected, but his tone was still deceptively jovial as he plucked a few papers off his desk and began rifling through them. "Now, why are you in my rooms?"

"We're here about the disruption of power," Reed offered. "We know who is behind it."

At this, Prince Aeden's bemused expression grew flat. I could see something like flint in his onyx eyes. A spark of rage, or the kindling of fascination.

"Speak in short sentences, half-fae, and if you have information that I find useful, I may offer you a kinder fate than your owner. For daring to taint this wing, you would be owed steep pain by us both."

"My owner is the one behind the disruption," said Reed.

I nodded, as if my confirmation meant anything, but the prince resolutely stared at Reed's face, as if they were the only two people in the room.

"Your blood keeps you honest, or at least that is what we've always thought," said Prince Aeden. He dropped his papers and came around to our side of the desk, his long legs carrying him to the couch. He bent at the waist, his dark eyes peering into Reed's. "How am I to know you haven't simply formed this opinion under the surety of his malicious treatment of you? You believe he is the culprit, but do you have proof?"

Reed's chin went up, as if he was forcing himself to sit straighter. The blood and wet hems of his clothes made him look like a ferocious warrior, his blue eyes blazing. "I found the documents in his belongings. They outline his plans for using the outage to garner more power in court, to be the sole supplier of humans to the fae in need. There were schematics...like a recipe, for a device some alchemist was developing at his behest."

The prince watched Reed's expression the whole time, only now lifting back to his full height. "And you do not have these documents to show me?"

Reed swallowed. "I do not."

"And do you know that these papers were written or signed directly by Jassin's hand?"

"The writing matched what I've seen of his." But now he was looking less than sure.

"Did you tell anyone he would be a good target for this accusation? Maybe someone placed the documents there to be found."

At that, I leaned forward. "We know it was him!" I blurted, but then immediately bowed my head in apology for the outburst. I hated to think we'd gone through all of this just to be turned away by the only person who could help.

Prince Aeden held up his hand, his scowl deepening. "I will not take the word of a human unless it is to tell me how much pain they are in."

My mouth went dry, and I leaned back in my seat, the unconscious form of Robin like a statue beside me. He hadn't asked about her yet, but maybe finding fae petrified was a common-enough occurrence, since any violence within the court led to this state.

"I have been working with Winona to—" Reed started once more, but then he hesitated.

"To get out of your contract?" the prince guessed. "You hate Jassin, and you wish to be free of him. I would assume you'd give anything for such a chance, even lie and use this human girl as fodder."

"I...did use her." Reed took a deep breath, aiming an apologetic glance my way. My hands were starting to sweat from more than fatigue as the seconds ticked by. "I asked her to attempt to buy me out of my deal, but Jassin would not sell me for anything reasonable. He outright told her he was the purveyor of slaves for the castle, and that he was increasing his stock to gain more influence."

"None of what you say is a violation of our laws. And none of that proves he is the one responsible."

"Then *let* us prove it," I said. "We can find the alchemist. Maybe even reverse what Jassin has done."

"You're looking to make a deal?" At this, he laughed, throwing his head back so his red hair swept back and forth across his shoulders. "A deal with a human! And for what? Your word? What a night, to have seen the shadow of a dark moon and hear it call itself full."

"I..." I started, but I wasn't sure how to respond to that. I looked over at Reed and he seemed just as lost. This wasn't going nearly as well as I'd hoped. I wished Robin could speak, since her full fae blood meant he'd believe her words as unequivocal truth.

"The deal will be with me," said Reed, his tone somber. I thought back to the guards in the hall, how he'd offered them the chance to beat him if he was wrong. He had the same expression then as he did now. "You know I am beholden to oaths, or I would have slit Jassin's throat years ago. Give us brief leave to find the alchemist and stop the interruption of power. If we succeed, I'll take a boon from you—my freedom. And if we don't...I'll forfeit my life to the court."

My breath caught in my throat. "Reed, stop. You can't just—"

"If I make this deal," prompted Prince Aeden, his grin sharp as the barbs on smartweed stems, "you will vow it with your blood. And die if you do not return on my mark."

I looked back and forth between Reed on the purple sofa and the prince standing in front of his desk, once more crossing his arms smugly as if he'd won some kind of game. At turns I found him charming, then terrifying, but the casual nature with which they both seemed to treat life...that was the real horror here. Still, I knew I couldn't get Reed to change his mind—knew it from the set of his jaw and the sure breath he took before he nodded in agreement. His sacrificial nature was like the cut of his waist, or the way his golden hair flopped over his forehead; it was a part of his very makeup.

"I vow in blood," Reed intoned, "to either bring you the alchemist responsible for our current interruption of power or force them to reverse it. If I do not return by the date of your choosing, I...I forfeit my life, either to the court or under my own hand."

He held out a palm, streaked with blood, and I wondered if he'd made a fresh wound or simply showed us its red gleam from one of the syra's many claw marks. The cut leaked sluggishly down his fingers.

The prince licked his lips, as if hungry to accept, and then in a blur he raced forward. I only saw the flash of his red hair before his mouth was on Reed's hand, his long nails gripping the palm to splay the skin wider. He slurped at the blood and my stomach dropped, nausea curling in my throat until I looked away.

"You vow it in blood," said Prince Aeden with a satisfied rumble in his voice. "You have two nights and two days. I leave then for a meeting with the queen of the kelavees, and once I am under the water and in her kingdom, your death will be mine."

Reed lowered his hand, and I found myself stunned. I couldn't believe I'd just sat beside him while he gave away his life for a mission we had such little hope of accomplishing. We didn't know where the alchemist lived, or how they communicated with Jassin. We didn't know *anything*. The deals of each fae were like the threads of a web that interlocked and swirled and caught us all in its middle, helpless but to trip over some strand or another. And the best-case scenario here, if all the deals were met, would be for us to just...continue living? With no change? Reed would be free, but my home would still be in tatters—still constantly on the edge of ruin.

"We need more," I said.

"We?" echoed the prince, once more raising his eyebrow. I swore I could see a trickle of blood on his lower lip, like an artificial shine meant to seduce.

"Yes, we." And before Reed could open his mouth to object, I hurried on. "If Reed is hunting this alchemist, he'll need a liaison into the human lands. Despite how you treat him, he *is* a member of your court and won't be able to accomplish this task without my help. I can go where he cannot, and I can lie. I'll go with him, and we'll set your entire kingdom to rights, ensuring the creatures within these walls go back to shifting and glamouring...even hunting *my kind*. That sacrifice deserves a payment, not just the stay of a blade above his head." I gestured to Reed.

"I don't make deals with humans," he said again, this time with an open sneer. His nose wrinkled, as if he found the very idea distasteful.

"And I'm not looking for a deal," I retorted. "I'm looking for your understanding. You take responsibility for the syra and lendanis in your court—the crogwyns and kelavees and abyssot and even the anglocks that nearly destroyed my family. I am willing to take responsibility for the humans along your borders."

"I tire of talking to you."

The prince waved his hand for us to go but I remained still, my fists clenched at my sides. My entire body ached, and my head was woozy with fear and blood loss and exhaustion, but this couldn't be the culmination of all my efforts. Conor was saved, and I was grateful, but my town was a shell of its former self, my people were scared. And we were so *tired* of being scared.

"We all use the same water, the same air," I continued, pleading, "and I know the smell in this castle will only continue to get worse while they both decay. We can work with you to keep the land healthy. We could have an alliance. All I'm asking is that when we return, with a solution to your problem, that you consider the possibility of a union between our peoples, to keep the habitat here as we would both appreciate it."

"Win..." Reed whispered, but I dared not look at him. I couldn't bear for his expression to be discouraging or bleak. I needed to hope things could be better, and that if I just exuded enough confidence, and played my part to perfection, this performance could lead to some positive change, and not just more generations of being picked away like petals ripped from flowers.

The prince raked his long-fingered hand through his fiery hair. I could see my words had actually made him pause with consideration, his head moving side to side as if stretching his pale neck.

He didn't need to accept any offer from me, I realized. He could send us on our way. He could kill us. He could let Reed sway in the wind for two days and then watch as he was forced to kill himself. He held all the power. But I could lie.

"I love this land," I said. *Truth*. "I grew up here and I know the coast and the shoals as well as my own hands." *Truth again*. "If you agree to humor me when we return, I will serve as liaison for the people of Harnsey and all the seaside towns north and south of us. A deal could be struck, so you don't need to take the unwilling—so we don't need to fear the water. In exchange for labor and care for the mangroves, if you would let people return home—"

"You talk beyond your station."

I clenched my teeth so tight my jaw throbbed. "I do not. I am the magistrate's daughter. And what harm could it bring to engage in some form of politics with us? Your borders could be lined with allies and not just victims building iron weapons and contemplating war." *Lie. Lie. Lie.*

A knock sounded on the door, and the prince left us to answer it, all the while Reed was shooting daggers at me with his eyes.

"What are you doing?" he whispered.

"Saving more than just you."

A hushed conversation was happening in the doorway, but I couldn't see who Prince Aeden was speaking to. Was it Jassin? Were we about to be well and truly screwed? But the prince only nodded and closed the door.

"I have a couple of syra waiting to dance for me," he said, a dismissal if ever I'd heard it.

"So, you'll consider my proposal?" I reached for Robin, but her eyes were closed, her form having unclenched into what appeared to be a deep sleep.

"Depending on what you accomplish in the next two days, I'll consider it then." His tone was hard, brokering no arguments. "Until that time, you are nothing but a leech on a fae's ass, better not to be seen. Now leave the perfume woman and get out of my rooms."

"Robin?" I asked. "But—" and then Reed was grabbing my arm and bowing low. The prince's stark eyes followed us with something like hunger as I was pulled from the room.

I stayed quiet as Reed led me down the hall, past the guards with very put-out expressions, and down the stairwells into the cavernous hub of the court. As the stone became wet, and I heard the rhythmic slosh of the tides against the walls, I stopped short, ripping myself from his hold. I may be helping him, but it was for my own benefit as well, and I refused to go back to blindly trusting him with my wellbeing.

"Are you going to tell me where we're going?"

The circles under Reed's eyes had grown darker, his face pale with fear. As it should be. He'd bargained his *life* on proving Jassin's guilt—and stopping the increased hunt for human servants by proxy. He made it seem as if the gamble was partially for me and my people, but I didn't believe it. It was for his freedom, a prize he'd been willing to die for without hesitation.

Fool me once...

"We're going to procure a boat," he said, "and hope we don't get eaten on the way."

He took my hand again, gentler this time, and I resolutely ignored the warmth of his blood between our palms.

"Wonderful," I bit out. "Sounds like a plan."

CHAPTER TWENTY-THREE

I assumed by "procure" Reed meant we would steal the boat in question, but when we reached a half-submerged dock on the north side of the castle, with stairs leading down to a hidden harbor, there were half a dozen vessels tied to posts in the water just waiting to be used. A single guard sat slouching on a chair, lazily picking at his teeth with the points of his claws. He appeared to be syra, just trapped in his human form, his hands webbed around those wicked points, his gray-tinted body lean and sinuous where he lounged. The legs sprawled in front of him were thin and so smooth I couldn't tell exactly where his knees were.

"Peleg," Reed said as a greeting, pushing me a bit behind him.

The syra looked up slowly, as if drugged. "Ah, the golden slime on my scales. Is today the day I use your rib cage as my jewelry cache?"

Were we about to try and flee this syra in one of the vessels at our feet? A few had oars and a couple relied on sails I had no hope of maneuvering without help. Did Reed even know how to sail if we made it out of here alive?

I looked from the slick stones along the wall to the boats floating beside it. The tide was gentle, but it echoed in the chamber, making the space seem smaller than it was. The sound was menacing, pummeling us from all sides.

"Not today, I believe," said Reed. "I have something to trade for your mercy."

"No more heron skulls, I hope." Peleg's tongue lolled from his mouth, unnervingly long; it flickered in my direction. "Though if it's this human girl...I am oddly tempted. She'd be a lovely addition."

"In my room you'll find a vial of perfume from Robin. Worth a barrel of hogfish if you bring it to the kitchens, or...it could buy you an audience with Ruven."

The syra's eyes narrowed. "And why would I want an audience with Ruven?"

Reed shrugged, his voice as airy as a field of saltmarsh hay. "Just something I thought you'd find of interest, given the way his eyes follow you. Or the way you slow when you pass him at banquets. Do with the perfume as you will, but it is yours—for lending us a boat."

The stench of low tide tickled my nose but I dared not lift a hand to scratch. Silence stretched between them as Peleg debated the bargain.

"Or I could kill you and take the perfume anyway," he said, eventually. "You look like one hit could take you out."

Hells, did every single creature here resort to murder for every occasion?

"You could, but then you'll be petrified," I offered, inching to the side. "And I'll steal the perfume for myself."

Peleg leaned somehow even further back in his chair, his thin legs limp on the stone floor. I wondered how he didn't fall off.

"Fine. Perfume for the schooner." He pointed to the smallest boat, a simple thing with a tiny, triangular sail and a set of well-worn oars. There was a flat swath of deck at the rear I imagined was for waterlogged creatures to slide off and on, but other than that it could have been one of my neighbor's personal fishing vessels. Only this one was half-covered in soggy moss and looked as if it hadn't been used in months.

"Many thanks for the stay of execution," Reed said in a sing-song voice, and before the syra could respond we were hurrying down the slippery steps. I watched Reed untie the boat from its mooring with practiced ease—maybe he *did* have some knowledge of sailing after all.

I stepped onto the swaying planks of salt-eaten wood and fell onto one of the two worn benches. It creaked under my weight, and it was a pleasant surprise to find no leaks under my shoes.

"Hold on."

Reed grunted as he pushed off from the stone dock with one leg, his strong arms instantly reaching for the oars. I wondered if he was hurrying in case the syra changed his mind, or if he was already feeling the ticking clock of Prince Aeden's deadline.

The lowering sun blinded me as we exited the cave-like port, a cool wind coming in from the east as we moved toward the horizon. There were splashes and unnatural waves rippling around us, but I refused to look down. If I saw the face of a lendani or the eyes of a kelavee, my racing heart might truly combust.

"So, am I to be a delicate maiden, ferried around while I watch you exert yourself?" I joked, trying to calm myself. I felt so very out of control as I sat passenger in front of him, like I was being carried along on brutal current, my feet unable to scrape at the floor and find purchase. How had I gone from finally being at home to this glorified dinghy captained by a foolish—and *selfish*—half-fae?

The castle loomed over my shoulder, growing smaller like a fading nightmare, and beyond that there was nothing much else to look at beside Reed's face. His color seemed to be slowly returning, but the stiff way he moved betrayed the chill I imagined he couldn't quite shake. How long had he been on that block of ice with that creature weighing him down? And did his torment mean I forgave him? I wasn't so sure.

"I'll let you take a turn, if you like," he offered. "I know you are no delicate maiden, but the sunlight is giving me some strength, so the exertion is not so bad." His smile, though weak, was wry as he squinted into the sun over my shoulder. It raced to kiss the horizon, and I knew full dark was only a couple hours away.

"Where exactly are we headed?" I asked, and then all the questions bubbling to the surface of my mind spilled over. "And do you even have a plan for finding this alchemist, or did we just sign your death warrant? Can I get word to my family from here? They need to know I didn't just disappear. Also, was it wise to leave Robin with the prince?"

"Clarcton—a port town not too far west from here. Yes, I have a plan. And yes, I can call down a harrier if you need to send a message." His tone was bland, though slightly out of breath as he rowed. "And we didn't have much choice, but I trust Prince Aeden won't cause Robin any unnecessary harm—she's too valuable."

He tilted his head, waiting for me to be impressed.

"I know Clarcton," I replied, ignoring the rest. "Why there?"

"The pages I found in Jassin's things had the address of a tavern listed in one corner. I assume that is where he found the alchemist, or where they would meet, and it's in Clarcton."

I crossed my arms, the wind causing bumps to pepper along my skin. "You don't think that would have been information to share?"

"You heard how Aeden questioned everything I'd found. He'd most likely claim it was another misdirection."

"He doesn't trust very well, does he?" I asked, a sneer pulling at my lips. At first, he had seemed so charming, with his easy way of speaking and his calm demeanor. But he had been just as much a monster as any beast in his court.

"So," I started, then paused, trying to rearrange my thoughts into something that wouldn't resemble a naïve and heart-sick girl. "You really were looking through Jassin's things just to learn more about the anglocks? Or were you also looking for a way out of his service?"

"There is no document that could have freed me," he answered, "and I knew that. I felt...remorseful of how I'd used you, of keeping the flowers from you, and I thought if I could figure out the cause for all that you've been through, I could offer it as some sort of apology."

I absorbed his answer, deciding not to prod any further. There may have been ulterior motives, but he was sorry, and he wanted to make it up to me. That was enough for now.

My throat was tight as I licked my dry lips. "Good. Thank you, I mean. Oh, and please...call down a harrier." I hurried to latch onto another topic. "That's something you can do, you said? I don't know why a marsh bird would know to take a message to Harnsey—"

The muscles of Reed's shoulders bunched and relaxed as he released the oars and cupped his hands around his mouth. The sound he made was one no human could match. It was shrill and warbling, echoed with a howl that reminded me of a wolf. I'd never heard a harrier bird make any sound like it.

When he was done, we both looked up expectantly at the lavender clouds, but the bird calls had faded as we drifted farther from the castle. I didn't think any creatures beyond those swimming beneath the boat would hear him.

"What if they don't—" I started, and then a tiny hawk no larger than the palm of my hand swooped low, as if dropped from a star. On instinct I jerked backward, watching it flap its wings to land on the edge of the boat. It was the color of cooked shrimp, oddly pink in a sickening way, and I knew this was no creature I'd seen in the saltmarsh.

"Just tell him what you want to report," Reed said, once more picking up the oars.

"We don't need to write something and tie it to his foot?"

I'd seen osprey and hunting hawks travel from town to town with news, trained and bought with exorbitant funds, but they were merely carriers of small notes or baubles.

"Do you see ink and parchment on the boat?" Reed's eyebrows rose, and his lip lifted in a comforting grin, as if pulled by a bait-laden angle he had every intention of biting.

Instead of dignifying his sardonic response, I faced the pink bird. It looked up at me with moss-green eyes that seemed to have no pupil, and I swallowed down my unease. "My brother Conor will be at the house with the metal poles in the yard, on the south end of the town of Harnsey. Please...tell him to wait for me. That I will return in a few days, and he should not leave until I do." I paused. "Okay?"

The bird waited, as if to make sure I was done, and then cocked its head toward Reed. With measured slowness, Reed held out a hand, and at first, I thought he meant to pet its feathers or shoo it into the air, but the bird pecked at his finger, drawing blood. And then it pecked some more. It drank up the wound, cocking its head back to swallow.

"What in the Hells?" I asked.

"Nothing is for free, little perch," Reed intoned, and then the harrier finally went on its way.

I sat there, stunned, as Reed's wounded hand flashed black, swirling with shadowy smoke, and then reformed back into strong, tan fingers, wholly healed. I noticed he no longer swayed, and his arms no longer shook—the sun had removed any vestiges of his icy torment, even though the sky neared blue-black with twilight.

He went back to rowing, letting me sit in my astonishment.

Soon after, all I could hear was the lulling rhythm of his oar strokes as they swept through the black water. My heart had calmed somewhat, knowing that my message was hopefully on its way to my brother. I took comfort in that we had a destination in mind, one that was only some hours away, thank the moon.

My eyes grew tired a bit later, but I didn't want to sleep while Reed did all the work. It felt...wrong somehow. Not that I owed him a turn at the oars—this was all his fault anyway. I had been *free*. Conor was cured, and I had been so close to being done with the fae and their dangerous world. But instead, Robin had dragged me back. Sure, it had been my choice, but the *guilt* she'd laid into me might as well have been a leash pulling taut. If she hadn't needed my weapons, I wondered if she would have sent one of those creepy harrier birds to tell me of Reed's death.

"I have a question for you now." Reed's voice was soft, even as it stretched toward me in the dark. The moon and a smattering of stars made it so I could trace his form with my eyes and watch his arms move back and forth, slow and steady.

"I can't promise I won't lie," I said.

I could have sworn he smiled.

"What is the real reason you're negotiating with Aeden?" he asked. "Is it really in hopes of peace with the fae? Or is there some other scheme you're concocting?"

"I'm not sure peace is possible." The admission was sour on my tongue, but it was true. "But if my home could be...safer, that's enough. Less people being taken, less fear—it would be enough."

"You love your town that much?"

I lifted one shoulder. "Not the town, really. I have dreams of leaving, once my brother makes enough money from his trade, but who knows if that day will come, or if life in Harnsey is any better or worse than anywhere else. The town doesn't hold me as much as he does. I've always wanted to go exploring, visit other cities and lands, but...we would still have Harnsey to return to."

Reed nodded. "A home base. That's all?" He still sounded skeptical.

"It may be a simple town, but its where all my favorite memories took place: playing in the wheat fields with Conor, swatting at each other with fake swords, fishing for flounder on lazy mornings in the spring...my mom giving me a chance to throw clay at her potter's wheel and laughing at the lopsided bowl we made together. It's where I had my first kiss. Where I saw my friend Maire give birth to her daughters..." I yawned, the day catching up to me.

"I guess I've never felt that sort of love for a place," Reed mused.

"Not surprising, if your home was more like a prison."

My backside was starting to get sore from the bench, and I wriggled in place, trying to get comfortable.

"The winds are shifting," said Reed. "Soon, I'll be able to use the sail and take a break, maybe catch some sleep. You should as well, little perch."

My shoulders stiffened. "*Why* do you call me that? It's just a type of fish, isn't it?"

"A cute one. Yellow with brown stripes that look like finger marks."

"And that's all?" I asked, parroting his earlier words back to him.

He chuckled, the sound warming me like a cloak. "I used to watch schools of them on the edges of the mangroves. One time, I caught one in my net and took it home—kept it in a bowl I'd made from a hollowed-out tree trunk. It was sweet, how it lazily swam from side to side. I fed it bugs and berries for days, and it even ate from my hand, but after a while it grew restless. It seemed to get agitated every time I came near. And then one day it jumped free."

"So, I remind you of a cute but agitated fish who eventually escaped you?" I chuckled, but it turned into another yawn.

"That about sums it up. Now sleep." He jerked his head behind him, to the flat panel at the rear of the boat.

I stood while trying to keep my balance, eyeing the spot with caution. "Won't I just fall off into the ocean?"

Reed looked up at me, his eyes gleaming in the moonlight.

"I would not let you fall."

I refused to acknowledge the swooping sensation in my chest, or the momentary lapse into absurdity that had me itching to lean forward. I could so easily drop into his arms and be seated on his warm lap. It was a contact he would probably crave from me soon regardless, if only to ward off the damaging chill of the ocean air.

"Okay then." Clearing my throat, I did my best to curl into a position on the flat deck that wouldn't hurt my aching ribs or agitate the wounds on my stomach. "And don't think of getting too comfortable with me. I know you could use the heat but...I'm not sleeping with you again."

"That's a shame," he said back, and I couldn't tell if he was amused or sad. I decided amused. Placing my head on one of my folded arms, I grudgingly allowed the slow rocking of the boat to lull me to sleep.

CHAPTER TWENTY-FOUR

The sound of gulls woke me, and I squinted my eyes against the morning light. My shoulder ached from my position on the floor, but the rest of my body was surprisingly comfortable—and warm.

As soon as the thought registered, I felt the press of Reed against my back. He was molded to me, his knees against the backs of my legs, his arm languid along my chest, right above my injuries. Soft breath was ruffling the hairs at the nape of my neck.

Flint had never slept beside me like this, holding me like I was something precious. He'd only enjoyed my body and then been on his way, pants tied securely, stride confident and quick. What would it have felt like, I wondered, if Flint had clung to me like Reed did now. If he had nuzzled into the nape of my neck, the smell of salt thick on his skin, the same as this half-fae did, causing heat to pool in my stomach. Would I have trusted the feeling more and waited for Flint to come around? Or was I doomed to always give myself to someone only after their own ends? But Reed had also wanted to help me. *I could offer it as some sort of apology,* he'd said. It was almost enough to flatten the sickened feeling ballooning in my chest that whispered how weak I was for affection.

My body was oversensitive, reacting to every press of his chest at my back, every twitch of his fingers.

If Reed had been in that barn instead of Flint, would waking up with him have felt like this? Maybe he would have pulled the strands of hay from my hair and laughed against my lips, his rough hands sliding beneath my skirt to find me wet and wanting. We'd divest each other of clothes...

As if sensing my thoughts, Reed shifted behind me, and I could feel the press of him, hard and insistent, against my backside, though his breath was still steady with sleep.

I almost pushed back in spite of myself, until I remembered Reed was getting more out of this than arousal or comfort. My body heat was a power source. And I wasn't ready to be used by him again, even if I might enjoy it. Bodies were bodies and I could give it as freely as I dared, but not to someone I didn't fully trust. I still couldn't untangle the web of my feelings about him.

Before I could succumb to my weak will, I sat up, letting his arm fall to his side in a *thump* I was sure had woken him. I curled my arms around my legs and looked off into the distance. He had rowed far enough that the dying wind hadn't stopped us from reaching Clarcton's harbor. It lay ahead—a crescent scythe littered with long docks, like the teeth of a comb. It was still early, but already I could make out the specks of men crawling over the wharf, loading ships and stumbling drunk into the morning.

Reed let out a soft groan and I could feel him stretch behind me to sit at my back, his arms still pressed between us for the body heat. What a smug, sly creature he was.

"I told you I wasn't going to sleep with you again," I said into the dawn.

"Apologies, little perch. I couldn't help myself." His voice caressed my shoulder, the sound rough like water over jagged stones, just like it had been when he'd pushed into me, sweat against me, and pleasured me with his touch until I'd shuddered with it. I really needed to stop remembering that right now.

I swallowed. "You could have."

Suddenly, his arms came around my chest, and I realized he was sitting with his knees bent to either side of my hips.

A war raged in me, to lean back and accept the embrace, to feel if he was still hard, or stand and escape into the safety of my own space. But before I could pull away, his hold tightened.

"I cannot lie, remember?" He rested his chin in the cradle of my neck and shoulder, his rough beard scraping pleasantly over my skin.

"You're saying you were physically incapable of avoiding me for one night?" I hated the way my vocal cords strained. I was grasping for anger or betrayal or resentment, but his skin was a balm against my own, sheltering me from the cold morning. It was a blessing he *could* be so warm, after the way he'd practically frozen to death just the day before.

"Apparently. I moved in my sleep."

Oh. So, he didn't even mean to. And yet he was touching me now.

"We should get going," I said, more to myself than him.

In response, he simply placed a soft kiss on my neck. His lips were warm and wet, and the faint jasmine scent of his skin, metered with brine, brushed over me just as gently.

"I would rather stay here, with you."

I froze, not daring to turn my head. If I did, I would kiss him, and then I would touch him, and then I would push his shoulders onto the deck of this creaky vessel and climb atop him.

My stomach growled, loud enough to be heard over the surf. I couldn't remember the last meal I'd eaten—something yesterday morning with Conor and my mother?

Reed released me with a soft sigh, carefully standing to make his way back to the benches and the oars. "I should feed you."

"Am I to eat planks of wood?" I mused, letting the morning air cool my flushed cheeks.

He huffed a laugh, pulling a leather pouch from under the bench seat. It jingled with a bit of coin.

"Not much," he said. "But enough to buy some breakfast. All the vessels have a charmed bag in them, usually with silver pieces or live grubs inside. We're in luck this one isn't full of beetle larvae."

I tilted my head, watching him roll up his sleeves and take down the sail. I hated how my eyes sought his forearms with a hunger that rivaled my stomach, the toned muscles painted gold by the sunrise. "The fae just leave money for whomever needs it? What benefactors."

"You have to replace it." He pulled at the oars, and we jerked forward once more.

"Ah," I replied. More fae magics and trickery. There was always a catch—always a deal to be made. It became clear I still had very little knowledge about his world. There were levels to it still lost to me, even though I'd been within Windstone Court's walls for days and peppered Robin with questions. I wondered if Reed would remain living there when he was freed—that is, if he did not die.

"Reed?" I asked, still sitting on the flat platform at the rear. "Where would you go, if you could go anywhere?"

He didn't answer me for the longest time, and I began to think he hadn't heard me, but then he turned his head to look at me over his shoulder. "Where will you go, when this is over?"

I scowled. "That's not an answer."

"Neither is that," he replied.

I huffed, tired of his cagey replies, and remained quiet.

I still knew so little about him, too.

Mouth clamped tight, I watched the city grow closer as he rowed, and said nothing when he jumped from the vessel to tie us to an empty place at the closest dock, his steps practically springy with energy.

Clarcton was bustling now, the scorching morning sun already burning off the fog from the water and baking the streets. Stone-built businesses crowded the wharf, their wood awnings painted in greens and blues and their windows bedecked with parchment signs.

My legs felt unsteady as Reed helped me from the boat and onto solid ground. We must have looked like runaways, with drying blood on our clothes and no belongings strapped to our backs, and yet no one paid us any mind. Men in rough-hewn pants hustled by, carrying barrels, rope, and metal canisters I'd seen canners use for storing vegetables.

Reed placed a hand on the low part of my back, keeping us together as we navigated the crowd. I would have smacked it away, except that it was best for us to stay close.

"Have you been here before?" I asked as we left the main thoroughfare for a quieter street.

"Not since I was little. Once I was in Jassin's service, he wouldn't allow it. Plus, I couldn't go too far from him. Still can't, really."

I looked up in time to see him grimace, noticing some shallow lines at the corner of his mouth. His eyes were sterner than I'd ever seen them.

"You're in pain," I accused.

He shook his head, then pushed me forward so I had to look ahead or trip over my feet. "I'm...uncomfortable. But it will subside when we return."

I hadn't realized he was so connected to the fae that owned him, but it made a sort of repulsive sense. There had to be a punishment for any escape, even a temporary one.

"Will it get wor—" I started, but he shushed me and then opened a door I hadn't yet noticed on the left. It was a bakery with a simple sign hanging on its plain door that read, "Fresh Breads."

With the pouch of coin, Reed bought us a handful of buns filled with sea buckthorn fruit and drizzled in honey, the sharp citrus tart in my parched mouth as we sat at a stout wooden table inside. He made sure to keep his wheat-colored curls low, hiding his ears, and we ate in silence, each lost in our own thoughts. The reality of our mission settled around my shoulders—time was limited, and Clarcton was a decently-sized city.

I downed some lavender and yarrow tea, watching Reed do the same, and wondered how on earth we were going to find this alchemist, convince them to release the magic or science or whatever it was that blocked the fae from their full powers, and then get back to Windstone all before Reed would be forced to...

No. I wouldn't think about that. One step at a time.

"So, this tavern we're looking for, what's it called?" I asked, finishing up another bun and licking at the jam on my fingers.

"The Leaning Candle." His voice was muffled, but at least some semblance of his usual chipper tone could be heard around the honeyed glue on his tongue.

He looked healthier than he had in days, his cheeks pink with warmth and his lips glistening with sugar as he finished his tea. It made me want to lean close and taste those lips for myself, but instead I crossed my arms and waited for him to take his last sips. Even the lines of strain I'd noticed earlier looked somewhat faded, although I knew he must still be feeling some *discomfort*.

"Then let's get going." Wiping my hands on my filthy pants, I walked back up to the bakery counter and the plump woman behind it. She was eager to give me directions to the tavern; her customers eyeing our dishevelment and bloody filth with concern. But it's not like we had the time or money to go clothes shopping.

"Three blocks west and take a right. Head toward the church steeple," I reported dutifully.

Reed nodded, standing, and gave the baker a deep bow she did not return or appreciate.

I hit him on the shoulder. "People don't bow here," I hissed.

"Oh. Right." With a sheepish expression, he exited the bakery and almost stepped directly into the path of a horse-drawn cart.

I pulled him backward, the beasts' hooves kicking up dust as they stormed past, the noise and commotion startling.

Reed's expression was astonished as he spun in my hold, the momentum carrying him directly into my chest. His torso crashed into me, and I stumbled, my feet tripping over each other so that my back almost hit the bakery's closed door. Thankfully, he caught me as well as I'd caught him, and suddenly his strong arms had encircled me in an embrace.

Both breathing in shallow pants, we gazed at each other with shock. Wrapped up like this, with his ocean eyes pouring into mine, the town of Clarcton seemed to vanish. There was just him—just us—no urgency, no worry, no overwhelming and unmanageable thoughts spiraling through me.

His eyes were so clear and blue—

He kissed me. It was quick and hard and unexpected, but I didn't fight him.

Gripping his torn and dirty shirt in my fists, I pulled him closer, opening my mouth. He tasted even better than the sea buckthorn fruit. Sucking and stroking his tongue with my own, I lost myself to the sensation.

A groan rumbled through his chest and his rough hand cupped my cheek, his hips urging me backward until my back *was* against the door of the bakery. Gods, how I had missed this feeling, even just the past few nights. I craved it like a flavor I couldn't quite recapture. And I could feel his need as well, pressed against me in obvious desire. It was as if a hum of energy encircled us, vibrating along every nerve in my body, leftover from the tension between us this morning, now finally unleashed.

He broke away to press hot kisses on my jaw, then my neck, moving down. It was exactly how that night with him had started. And if we had been in a bed, and not on some public street in view of any passersby, I would have let us go there again.

My eyes opened, a scrap of shrewdness squirming its way between us, and I placed a hand on his chest.

He stopped licking at my collarbone and looked up with a heavy-lidded expression that had me biting my lip, but this was not the time. We had a ticking clock and a mission to complete. And we had lives to save, mainly *his*.

"Let's go find this Leaning Candle place," I said on an uneven breath. "We can revisit this idea…later."

Reed sighed, but straightened, putting space between us. "If promises were eels, little perch." I thought he would be disappointed, or even agitated, but his words were mirthful, his energy buoyant. Hells, had I really just confirmed to him that I'd forgiven him? Or just that I wanted him regardless of his betrayal?

"I have no idea what that means," I replied after a pause, but I couldn't help but return his smile.

He held out his hand, the move oddly formal, and I should have playfully pushed it away, if only to keep my heart safe and this boundary between us—one *he'd* carved when he kept my brother's cure from me—but didn't I understand why he'd done it? And would I have done any differently?

I took the offered hand, his palm hot and a bit sweaty in mine, and we paused to check the road before making our way toward the tavern.

Despite the metaphorical blade hanging over Reed's head, his steps were calm and slow as we made our way west down the crowded thoroughfare. It didn't matter that we were sore and still injured; my full stomach and the warm summer morning gave me a strength that kept my shoulders high and my strides light. It was...*hope*, I realized with a start—hope that the two of us together could somehow get this thing done, that everything would work out.

His fingers tightened on mine, as if in solidarity.

Stores on either side of the road sold fish from open windows and various forms of dress from cluttered outdoor displays. When I caught sight of a small bookstore on my right, my feet stopped before the rest of me. I hadn't bought a new book in years, and never from a store full of them; I'd only had the opportunity to buy books from merchants as they traveled through town. The tomes I had at home were all ancient, with torn casings and wrinkled pages, crispy with salt air. I'd read the plays and poems over and over to Conor, memorizing each of the fables, but how many more existed in the world that I had never heard before?

"Do you want to..." Reed started, but I shook my head, ignoring the pang of disappointment behind my rib cage.

New stories weren't more important than his life.

"I can always come back," I said, though I wasn't sure how true that was. We started moving again.

"It makes sense that you would like to read."

"Oh? Because I am so clever?" I smiled, trying to lighten my own mood.

"Yes."

His response cut my teasing in half, and I found myself at a loss for words.

"Did you always?" he asked, briefly tightening his hold on my hand, as if afraid to lose me.

"I liked poetry, even before I could read it myself," I said, nodding. "I loved the way someone could take scenery I'd stepped through dozens of times and describe it in a new and beautiful way that made me look at it differently. My brother liked plays about princes and knights better, so I scrounged together a collection of dramas for him."

As we turned a corner, I spotted the steeple of a church ahead on the left, its pointed spire missing a few shingles, but painted a fresh, creamy white.

Reed's steps faltered beside me, and I was reminded of his tether to Jassin. I wasn't sure how intensely it was affecting him, or if he even wanted me to know, but I edged closer to him, so our shoulders brushed, and kept my gaze forward as if we were on a lovely stroll. These few blocks didn't seem far enough to make a difference, but maybe time was a factor as well.

"Of course, my mother was angry at me for spending the coin on those stories," I continued, to distract us both. "But, then again, she was always angry at me, or at least...disappointed. I used to help her at her kiln, and when I was little it was all fun and creative, but as I got older and I was expected to make pieces to sell, she was never pleased with my work. When I threw clay, the shape was never quite right, when I painted them with glazes, my strokes were too thick, and when I manned the fires, the heat was never high enough, or it was too high. I burned more than one batch, and that's when she banished me from the shop."

"What did you do after that?" His voice was tight, as if with strain, but I could see the wooden sign hanging over the packed-earth street, a tall candle flickering against a dark background. We were almost there.

"I flitted from thing to thing, helping my friend Maire rear her children, doing farm work when there was need. I took to exercising and training horses for a while, before Conor's..." I struggled to find the word, "incident." My chest tightened, the memory of his slowly petrifying body and his despair sitting heavy in my chest. "I haven't really found my calling yet, beyond enjoying dramas and acting, so at least I know I have a future in fae espionage if I grow desperate."

His smile was wry but affectionate as we reached the door to the tavern. I almost wished his look wasn't so soft as he gazed down at me.

We were still holding hands.

Clearing my throat, I pushed open the door into the dim and dingy bar. My shoes crunched over broken glass and clumps of ale-soaked sand as we made our way to the rear where a long, knife-pecked bar curved along the wall.

There weren't many patrons inside, just a few pairs and solitary drinkers peppered throughout, crouched over their dark tables, which was unsurprising given the early hour. It smelled like sweet wine and morning-after sick, so I breathed through my mouth.

"What'll you be having?" asked the bartender as we reached the counter. He was a slim man with a wide smile, his hand busy at wiping the bar with practiced movements. However, his clothes caught my attention. The fabric was new and unstained, unlike all other tavern keepers I'd met. The stitching was fine and nearly invisible against the rich, expensive cobalt linen—I would have killed to wear it. Either this tavern was the most popular spot in Clarcton, or he had some additional revenue.

It was obvious that money and fine goods were important to him, so with sly fingers I pulled the money pouch from Reed's pocket. Reed must have felt it, but he kept his smile genial as he leaned his forearms on the counter and perused the bottles of liquor behind the man.

"Actually, we're looking for a bit of information," I said, quiet as a breeze. A single silver coin glittered against the hard wood as I pushed it forward.

The bartender took it and reached behind him as if to pour me a glass.

"That'll be two silvers," he said, dropping the glass in front of me and filling it with some sort of thin ale that would be worth coppers at best.

I pressed another forward.

"We're looking for someone who may have a history in alchemy. Someone we could hire for a job." I cleared my throat. "Sound like someone you know?"

I looked to Reed, in case he had any details to add, like initials or some identifying feature from Jassin's letter, but he just waited beside me.

The man deliberated, then took the second silver, nodding behind us just as the sound of a chair screeching across the floor caught my attention.

One of the lonely drinkers by the front window was darting out the door, their steps hurried.

"Reed!" I yelled, but he was already ahead of me, chasing the runner back into the street.

CHAPTER TWENTY-FIVE

As I sprinted behind Reed, I could tell the person we chased was short and covered by a cloak that had more than one patch sewn into it—not someone who took bribes apparently, and definitely someone who didn't want to be questioned. They ran like their life depended on it, darting around sailors and townspeople alike, taking sharp turns down narrow streets I never would have noticed.

Reed was on their tail, but I could tell he wasn't used to running nearly as much as he was swimming or trudging through the marsh. His steps were hard against the ground, his breathing harsh enough I could hear it as I followed in his wake.

But eventually our target had to run out of street.

My lungs burned as I kept pace, my flat shoes sweeping across the dirt and adding to the dust plumes Reed and the runner were kicking up ahead. Sweat beaded on my temples, the sun hot on my head as we made another turn. Gods, I wished they would stop running.

"We don't want to hurt you!" I hollered, my voice breathy and harsh. Merchants' heads turned to watch us, and I realized we were heading in a zig-zagging pattern back toward the docks. Stalls went from jewelry and clothing back to fish and spices the closer to the water we traveled.

Hoping I wasn't about to make a foolish mistake, I took the next right ahead of me, leaving Reed to follow the runner more directly, and I pumped my arms, racing ahead. With my eyes trained on the ground to avoid any rocks or horse droppings in the grime, I only narrowly missed crashing into a woman sweeping her stoop. At the next intersection I spun left, just in time to collide with a girl barreling toward me.

I wouldn't have thought she was our mark, but the patchy cloak slapped me in the face when we crashed. On instinct, I reached out to grab her, and we fell together onto the ground, my shoulder taking the brunt of the fall.

"No! Please!" the girl yelled, twisting as she attempted to escape me. "Let me go!" Her face was round at the cheeks, her eyes a verdant green. I could see a streak of soot at her chin.

"I swear, we mean you no harm," I bit back, my hands scrabbling against her clothes.

Reed skidded to a stop and heaved her up, so she was kneeling.

His grip on her cloak almost choked her, and she reached up trembling hands to unclasp it.

"Reed, careful!"

I put my hands over hers and crouched a bit to meet her eyes. "We're just looking for someone." I explained, panting. "I assume you may be that someone, but please...tell me. It's a matter of life and death. I'm from Harnsey, and we desperately need your help." Gulping in breath after breath, I prayed she would believe me. Now that I was back in the realm of humans, I almost missed the fae's backwards way of assuming everyone spoke the truth.

She stilled, her chest heaving, and I saw the tarnished brass rings along her rounded ears, the freckles on her nose, and the narrow dots of her pupils as she gauged my words.

"Are you the alchemist?" Reed asked, seeming unfazed by her age or sex.

We were at the corner of two streets; there was a seamstress' store to my left and a butcher behind me, if the copper smell was any indication. A few people on the road had stopped to watch the altercation, and I worried they would see the slightly pointed ears Reed *almost* hid with his hair, or simply absorb our rough state of dress, and assume we were scavengers.

"Please let me go!" The girl said again, her voice more angry than scared. "Damn that bartender to all Hells, I can't believe he would give me up so cheaply! That asshole. Ugh! Let me go, you monsters!"

"Reed." I glanced around at the spectators, my blood running hot and cold by turn. "We need to get off the street."

He nodded, then put his hand over the girl's mouth and wrapped his other arm across her waist, lifting her feet off the ground.

Good to know those crab-fishing arms are as strong as they look, I mused, and then felt ashamed for how I could find him *attractive* while he was helping to kidnap a human girl off the street, just like every fae creature I'd ever hated.

He only took her further into the alley, his strength enough to avoid her kicking feet and tolerate the fists she pummeled into his arm and shoulders.

With a grunt he threw her down, and I watched with sympathy as her backside hit the floor, causing her to wince. He bent low, pushing his hair to the side, his ears in full view.

"If you understand what these mean, then you know I cannot lie to you," he said. He was out of breath now, and I worried about the pain that must be coursing through him. The lines around his mouth had grown more pronounced. "I don't seek to hurt you—I just need to find someone. An alchemist, and one I don't intend to hurt either."

"Intention and action are two different things," the girl panted as she glared at him from the ground. "And I know you can spin words to suit your needs. Lies can be hidden in the truth."

So, she wasn't nearly as naïve as I was when I had first entered the courts of the fae.

"You're not wrong," I admitted. "But we've got you, so you might as well answer us." I leveled my gaze on her as shrewdly as I was able. If pleading wasn't the key, it was time to change tactics. "If you're the alchemist we seek, we have a boon for your services."

"And if I'm not?" The girl's green eyes peered up at me with low-tilted fury. She couldn't have been more than sixteen years old.

Reed adjusted his hold on her as I stood, crossing my arms.

"Based on the earrings you wear, and the state of your cloak, I'm guessing fine things don't sway you," I noted. "But we have ways of finding out. We could follow you, tracking your movements and making note of anyone you meet in this bustling little port town. Talk to them about what valuable, enviable skills we suspect you to have—*loudly*. Given how that man at the Leaning Candle sold you out, I'm sure others would like to make some silver off you. Or maybe you'll see a family member and we'll do more than talk to—"

"Gods, enough!" Wriggling away so her back was against the stone wall, she swatted at Reed's hands until he released her. "You damned fae and your threats on my family."

"Is that how Jassin got you to interrupt their power?" I asked.

At that, her expression froze. "You're with Jassin?" Ah, and there was the fear I had expected given the way she'd bolted from the Leaning Candle.

Reed stayed low, as if speaking to the girl at her level would earn her trust. "We are *against* Jassin," he said. "And if you help us, we will have the means to kill him."

There was a delay while we waited to see how she would answer. The smell of blood and roasting meat lingered in the alley, churning my stomach, but I dared not raise a hand over my nose.

"Fine," the girl muttered. "I will talk to you. Just...not here."

Reed offered her a hand up and she reluctantly took it, then dropped it like it was filthy. It was, but that was no reason to be rude about it.

"And *you*," she said, pointing at him, "will speak in terse, decisive sentences. If I think for even one moment that you're tricking me, I'll turn your insides to stone."

I wasn't sure if that was something an alchemist could actually do, but if this girl was behind the fae being stuck without power, then I wasn't going to chance it. Standing a bit in front of Reed, I gestured toward the mouth of the street. "Lovely. After you...?"

"Shia," the girl replied, a little haughtily.

Reed and I kept close to Shia's heels as we made our way back toward the center of town. If she made even the slightest twitch, I was ready to grab her cloak and yank her to the ground, spectators be damned.

The path we ended up on was thin and winding, crowded with tall but narrow buildings that seemed to house multiple families inside. Carpets dangled from the windows, and I could hear babies crying in echoes of each other. The road became dark with damp, and I had a sneaking suspicion it wasn't water blackening the dirt.

We approached a structure that had stairs built at ground level, leading below, with a squat wooden door sitting in the shadows. Shia climbed down and fiddled with a large, shining lock that was completely at odds with the rough-hewn door that peeled at the edges.

"This is my workshop, and anything you touch may kill you—human or fae," she warned.

Reed and I shared a wary look as we climbed down after her.

The room reminded me of the cave where Robin did her perfume work—the ceiling was littered with bunches of herbs hanging from twine, and cabinets along the walls were leaking liquids and plant life from their small drawers. But where Robin's table had been full of vials and flowers and candles, this one was laden with books and giant pewter cauldrons. A cushy wing-backed chair in blue velvet sat off to the side near a cold fireplace.

"So, is alchemy a sort of witchcraft?" I asked, moving to tap at a sprig of lavender dangling low over my head.

"Don't touch!" She smacked my hand down, scowling, and then turned to fiddle at the hearth.

"I can get that going for you." Reed crouched beside her, his eyes crinkling, a friendly smile in place. I recognized the sing-song tone from his work at Windstone, when he was trying to make himself as unthreatening as possible.

Shia seemed suspicious by his offer, but before she could argue, I waved a hand at her. "Oh, just let him. He's good at making fires." He probably needed the heat to recharge after expending so much energy, not that I would tell her that, even to gain her trust.

"Um...alright." Wringing her hands, the young alchemist looked around as if for something to do, then gestured for me to sit in the velvet chair. "Now, what do you want from me, and how can it help you destroy

Jassin? He doesn't know you're here, does he?"

I shook my head, enjoying the comfort of the chair and the sweet smell of the bark catching in the fireplace. "Not that we know—the prince sent us."

"The prince...of the fae?"

I nodded. "The marsh fae, anyway. My town touches their borders."

Shia's face lost any color it once had and she swayed, catching herself against her worktable. "The prince knows about me?" she whispered.

"He doesn't know your name, or where to find you," said Reed. He stood and held his palms against the heat of the building fire, the warmth and light swelling so it carried the tang of lemon balm and thyme into every corner of the dank room. "He only knows an alchemist was involved in Jassin's maneuvers. We have been charged with restoring the loss of power Jassin orchestrated. Is that stated simply enough for you?"

Whereas I would ask it with a biting tone, Reed's was soft and under-standing.

The young girl took a breath and studied him, searching as I would for a hidden meaning buried between his words, but then addressed her answer to me. "Promise me anonymity, and I'll give you the information you need."

"We have no reason to give you up," I told her. "You might just be the most valuable weapon against the fae that exists."

"You travel with a fae," she reminded me. "Though his eyes are..."

"Human." I nodded, leaning forward to rest my arms on my knees, my body throbbing. "He is only a half-fae, but your concern is fair enough. We're currently allied against a greater threat, and Jassin threatens every human in Trasia. Though my town is far from yours, it is not so far a journey he couldn't turn his eyes on you next."

Shia glared. "He told me if I deactivated the crucible without his orders then he would come back here and kill my family, so believe me, I *know* he is a threat."

"The crucible?" I repeated, scanning the bowls on her table as if that would explain whatever she was talking about.

"It's the device that interrupts the fae. Well, what's inside it does." She looked back and forth between Reed and me, her hands shaking a bit as she gestured in the shape of a cylinder. "It's a recipe my uncle and I had been working on for years. So long as it keeps burning, the waves of energy keep emitting, and the fae can't transmute themselves or push that energy into other beings. It's like two magnets pushing at each other."

"Pushing energy..." I started to ask, then realized what she meant. "The glamour."

Shira nodded, her eyes livening as if we now shared some secret.

"How has it been burning all this time?" Reed asked, and I thought I heard a tinge of envy in his voice.

"Another alchemical miracle my uncle invented. A series of tubes convert air into lesser gasses that feed the flames." Her pride was evident as she picked up a strange teardrop-shaped vessel with a long down-pointing neck, fixing it to the top of an iron stand.

"What else can you do?" I asked, both fascinated and aggravated by the wealth of possibilities this could afford humans. "With all these inventions and abilities, you must have thought to stop Jassin instead of aid him."

Shia's hand paused in midair. "Don't accuse me of stupidity. There was no guarantee I could narrow the crucible's energies to him, or that any device or poison I concocted wouldn't be discovered before I could succeed. He gave me gold and threats, and—in exchange—the fae world would be thrown into chaos. Why *wouldn't* I take that deal?"

"You didn't think of how your deal would affect those close to the fae lands." I stood, feeling my cheeks flush with more than just heat from the fire. "It didn't just hurt *fae*; Jassin used the interruption to increase the demand for human labor, growing his slave trade. He's been collecting debts and contracts—"

Reed put a hand on my arm, the caress subtle, but enough for me to begrudgingly close my mouth. Berating the alchemist would probably not garner us any favor.

Reed released me. "Regardless of how this has unfolded and the consequences, we told the prince that *Jassin* was behind the loss of power." He spoke slowly so Shia would catch every word. "And as far as I am concerned, that is still the case. Prince Aeden gave us leave to find you and return things to the way they were before, as a way to prove our claims. Once we do, he will punish Jassin—most likely with a painful death—and Winnie and I will trouble you no longer. We will not tell him who you are or where we found you."

"You will not tell *anyone* who I am or where you found me," she corrected.

Reed nodded. "I swear it."

The girl seemed to ponder this before turning to a sheet of parchment on her table. She scrawled something there with a stick of charcoal, folded it, and carried it to the lit fire, throwing it into the flames.

"If something happens to me, that message will wind up in the hands of another alchemist, and you'll find your town burnt to cinders."

I raised one eyebrow. "And you begrudged *us* for threatening *your* family." My tone was acidic, despite how impressed I was with her boldness. I wasn't sure messages like that were possible, but then again, if a harrier bird could repeat a message after drinking blood…who was I to say what was possible or not?

Shia shrugged, then stood back from the table and grabbed a water skin from the top of a cabinet and offered it to me. "This will put out the fire, that's the easy part. But getting to the crucible is a bit more difficult. It's the core of the energy and therefore needed to be at the center of the fae."

"It's at the castle?" That didn't seem wise, what with the hundreds of creatures slithering through the halls, but maybe it was hidden away in some secret chamber. Still, I took the pouch, feeling some liquid slosh inside.

She scoffed. "No, it's in a cave. South of the castle, but still near the coast—Jassin said something about wanting to encroach on the forest if he could, but I think the energy barely passes their territory. Anyway, if you follow the coast you'll find an inlet in the rocks and a cave beyond…maybe twenty minutes of good sailing from what he said was the main syra tunnel?"

I looked to Reed and he dipped his head. He knew what she was talking about.

"We will go there at once and put out the fire." He took the waterskin from me, as if weighing it. "What is this?"

Shia smirked. "Water."

He laughed, the sound rich and sweet.

I had to admit, I almost liked this girl—this *alchemist*. Peering around her workshop, intricate devices strewn about and strange glass vessels holding powders and molten metals, I was reminded of Conor's inventions back home. How he was always trying to learn something new, always hunting for the idea of his next creation. She may be mistrustful and prone to intimidation, but, as a human dealing with fae, I couldn't fault her for that. Maybe we could even learn from her.

"You aren't taking on an apprentice, are you?" I asked, half as a joke.

"Kill Jassin and ensure my family's safety...and I may just allow one."

I hummed thoughtfully as Reed took my hand and we turned to leave. I wanted to ask her more about what she'd made—if she could show me or Conor how to take power from the fae. Maybe with their knowledge combined, she and Conor could conceive of a more *permanent* solution to our antagonistic relationship with the fae, like maybe force them out of Windstone Court, or simply make them disinterested in humans.

One thing at a time, I reminded myself. If we succeeded, there would be occasion to learn more later.

The light of the noon sun was slashing between the town's buildings in violent streaks, creating a patchwork on the dirt road as Reed and I tried to navigate our way back toward the docks. He kept his fingers tight and warm around mine, his stride long enough that I had to hustle to keep up as we wove through dirty sailors and market crowds. People pressed in on us from all sides.

"So," I started, feeling suddenly nervous, "we're heading back toward the castle? To find this...cave?"

I doubted it would be as easy as finding Shia, but maybe luck was with us. Maybe it was all a matter of information and, now that we had it, our mission would sail on smoother tides.

"One stop first," Reed said, a mischievous tilt to his smile.

I cocked my head in consideration, though I didn't think he could see it with his focus trained on winding us through the thickening crowds. "And where would that be?"

He stopped short, so I nearly ran into his back, then waved a hand to the left. The bookstore.

"You said you'd come back." His hand squeezed mine. "I wanted to make sure you got the chance."

"Reed...no." We didn't have time for this. It had taken hours to get to Clarcton, and who knew if the wind would be with us on the way back or if Reed would have to row the entire way, which would mean an entire day and night gone. And then there was the matter of actually *finding* the cave this crucible was stashed in. It had to be hidden well given no creature had yet come upon it and poked at it with its little webbed fingers.

But before I could say any of that, he was tugging me forward. "*Win...yes.*"

The shop was just one green and black awning, with a window display of stacks of books all matched in color, so they faded from the darkest leather to pale linen. I wanted to reach inside and smell them, flip through their pages like a greedy child searching for candy that had fallen to the ground.

"You don't know when you'll be back, and a few minutes couldn't hurt," he continued, pushing open the door. There was no bell to announce our entry, but a striped tabby by the entrance meowed at us as we passed. I gave him a scratch on the chin, thanking the little doorman.

"A few minutes *could* hurt, and we don't even have any money," I hissed, but already my fingertips were skimming over a shelf of history books, all the same size and shape like identical soldiers. The next shelf was more geometry based, and the next was about languages with embossed letters I didn't recognize glinting with gold foil along their spines.

"We still have a couple silvers." Reed's voice was quiet, and I wondered if he was wary of disturbing the books, or drawing the attention of the shopkeeper who had his nose buried in sheets of parchment at a desk to the right.

"Besides..." He cleared his throat, as if it had tightened. "This is one nice thing I can do for you. One kindness. Let me. Please."

Please. My heart squeezed at the tenderness in his tone, and I almost pouted at how unfair my reactions to him were.

I wasn't sure how the "take some, leave some" policy worked with the fae and their boat docks, but if we were successful, then Reed would be free of his contract and he could flee Windstone Court with all the gold his heart so desired, I supposed. And it seemed like this was really important to him, so I browsed, albeit quickly.

I paged through dramas and comedies, poems and fairy tales, and picked one book of verses by a writer I'd never heard of before, clutching it under my arm.

"Oh, wait. This is one I love." I pulled a small volume down, noting the bent pages and stained cover. *The Tears of the Titan.* "I tried to memorize it once, when a merchant staying overnight let me borrow it for a few coppers, but it was too long. I kept to the smaller poems and stories so I could retell them to Conor at night."

Reed held out his hand and I let him take it, then watched as he thumbed through the book, skimming some of the lines. There were some good ones in there: *Who is whispering near the weeds? She is but a silver eel. The prince dangled toes and beads, and so with bites he learned to feel.* All manner of silly couplets that formed an epic about transforming for the one you love.

"I'd like to read it," he said.

I blinked. "You would? But..."

"If you love it, it must be worth the time." He smiled, and I was hesitant to name the emotion that softened his eyes.

He shouldn't be saying things like this, things that would sweeten me up like plum-stuffed pheasant. As soon as the fae were back to normal and Jassin was dead, I would return to Harnsey and he would...do whatever it was he intended on doing. Not that he would tell me what that was. And that's *if* we made it in time and Reed didn't drop dead on the spot from his broken vow or the distance from his master.

Gods, what were we doing wasting time here? A nice gesture was not worth the risk to his life. Something like terror slashed through me.

"Come on, we should go," I said.

The book was only one silver, so Reed purchased *The Tears of the Titan* along with my new collection, and I said a quiet goodbye to the cat as we rushed back to our boat—and back to the task at hand.

CHAPTER TWENTY-SIX

The docks were emptying as crews left with the warm afternoon tide, their sails as wide as houses and twice as tall. Our tiny boat was just where we'd left it, though half-submerged from the rough waters of everyone's coming and going.

A bucket in the front of the boat where our ropes had been curled was our only tool for emptying it, and we took turns bailing water, tiring our arms before it was seaworthy once again.

The energy between us had shifted at some point, and I felt a strange calm settle over me like a veil. Reed, with his easy smile and his damned rolled up sleeves, rowing and humming as he did, and me, flipping the pages of his new book in reminiscence. When I'd first gotten to read its words, I'd felt peaceful and full of wonder, like the possibilities of my life were only limited by the creative string of words I could twist into some grand embroidery.

My own book rested safely by my hip.

"Will you read it to me?" he asked, after a while. The strong, sure strokes of his arms had us drifting past the harbor's edge and back toward open waters, all the while his gentle grin shone on me like morning light.

The way Reed's request swept over me, like a physical touch, was soft and earnest, so I couldn't help but say yes. It was one of my favorite things—to read aloud to Conor and let the words drip and dazzle off the tongue.

And so, as the sun baked us in our little boat, I stretched out my legs as far as I was able, my feet beneath Reed's bench, and I read to him my favorite stanzas. Ones where the prince despaired into a puddle of bright pickerelweed and another where the eel covered her skin in the petals of a water hyacinth and sang to him about her lonely life in the reeds. My favorite, which I saved for last, was about the moon watching over them with so much suffering that she turned faster and faster in the sky, pushing the winds and the tides to punish the sailors who taunted the prince for his affections.

Reed was a good listener, asking me at the end of each piece what I liked most about it, and telling me his favorite lines. It was a silly thing, so unconnected to destroying the crucible or killing Jassin, that I felt unmoored by the attention. If I was not acting or scheming, protecting someone, or endeavoring to manipulate them, was this me as myself? And was this him? So eager to learn, with his goofy smile and lighthearted thoughts, his energy buoyant and unbridled as he rowed?

When I finished, I realized we had stopped moving and we sat in the middle of the vast sea, the islands and inlets we watched for still a ways off.

"Are you tired?" I put the book down on the bench beside me. "Do you need me to take a turn?"

His eyes were steady on mine, a lighter blue than the sky. "I want to kiss you."

"Oh." I blinked. "Well..." I licked at my lips without meaning to, my gaze darting to the very interesting swirls and knots in the wood at my feet. Why did I feel so shy? I had kissed him before—had his body over mine. *Inside* mine. He wasn't some new trinket, shining with oil, freshly placed on the mantle. He was the man who had lied by omission, had used me, had touched me with shaking hands.

I closed my eyes. "I'm not sure you should."

"And if it's my last chance?"

The boat rocked beneath us as my eyes snapped open. "You are *not* going to die. We still have plenty of time to reach the crucible and return before tomorrow night." The sun was still an hour or so away from touching the horizon. Finding the alchemist had been easy, knowing from Jassin's note where she often idled, and I had confidence Reed could navigate us toward the cave Shia described.

"That's not what I mean." He inched forward, letting his forearms rest against his legs. "If we succeed...you will still be gone, won't you?"

I nodded, unsure how to voice aloud a plan I wasn't even sure I had. Yes, I'd return home after this, to a human village full of human people and...do what? I still didn't know. But what was the alternative?

"So now, before we're back at Windstone, I want one final kiss to remember you by."

I crossed my arms, more to give myself a sense of control than to display any real irritability. "Am I so unmemorable you would forget?"

He chuckled, the sound nearly swallowed by the open space around us. "I suppose remember isn't the right word. I want your kiss...embedded in me." His voice grew lower, serious. "I want to memorize the shape of it and the sounds you make when I lick into your mouth. I want your fresh, soft smell to leach into my hair like woodsmoke and stay with me for days after you've wrapped your arms around my neck. I'm not ready to let you go without it. Please."

My heart fluttered and my breath caught, and yet the rest of me was entirely still, clenched tightly against the rampant *want* coiling within my body. Hells, how did he have such an impact on me with just those words? It was as if a taste of poetry had him unleashing all sorts of vivid, graphic desires, seducing me with the image of his lips on mine, me moaning and draping myself over him. I shouldn't care what he wanted. I should care what *I* wanted.

But damn it, I wanted that kiss, too. Wanted him imprinted on my skin, in just the way he described.

I didn't think over how this would make it harder to leave him. Nor did I think of anything beyond the feet of space between us and how quickly I could breach them.

Rash as ever, I took one bracing breath. "Then kiss me."

I thought he would gently kneel in front of me and take my face with his reverent fingertips. It would be slow and measured, to memorize me, like he said. But instead, he reached out for my hands as if to help me stand, only to pull me roughly into his lap. I had no choice but to tumble forward, my knees lifting to rest beside his hips, his arms clasping me tight.

Surging up, Reed captured my mouth with his, bruising my lips with the force. I gasped into his mouth and his tongue met mine, stroking in time with the concentrated grip he had on my waist, as if all of him was moving with the gestures of the waves. My body rocked against his, hot and flushed and wet and *needy*. I had to get him closer.

Gripping at his blond hair, I tilted him for my access. It was a power I hadn't yet felt in him. Normally I was so eager to be swept away, I let him take control. But now I was on top of him, my knees braced against the wood. I could do whatever I pleased.

He hissed as I used my nails on his scalp, and then he groaned, the sound traveling through his chest. I kissed him again and again, using his mouth for my pleasure with no reservations. Rough hairs on his chin scraped my skin and made me even more sensitive, so when he nipped at my bottom lip, some strange whine escaped me.

As if to bury it, I kissed him back harder, wondering if his half-fae blood would taste the same as my own. I bit, just shy of finding out.

His hips bucked beneath me, his body obvious with its desire.

"Do that again," I whispered, and he did, grinding up into my core over and over until I was a panting, scrambling mess atop him.

His warm hand found my breast beneath my shirt, his thumb caressing my nipple, and I almost cried. Gods, it was all so good. The way he touched me, like he would take everything I had to give and ask for more—like he reveled in me—was almost more than I could take. His eyes met mine, ocean blue to oak brown, and his fingers *squeezed.*

"Reed!"

My head tilted back, and I was nearly blinded by the span of white and gray clouds above us. We were utterly alone, so small compared to the vast emptiness on all sides, but as I looked back down, he consumed my entire vision.

"I want you," he groaned. His thumb and forefinger tweaked me again, his hips still twitching as his body begged to take me. His other hand was tight on my waist, urging me backward and forward to rub against his erection

Black flashed through his eyes. "I want you more than I've ever wanted anything on this earth."

The honesty of that confession would probably scare me later. I'd dissect it for secrets when I could think straight. Until then...

I reached between us to loosen his tight breeches and touched him, feeling the solid heat in my hands throb. Grip tight, I stroked him slowly, teasing.

"Then have me," I whispered.

"Faster," he said on a groan.

I did as he asked, watching as he closed those black eyes and tipped his head back, exposing his throat to me in a way that made me want to bite.

This was a new game between us, it seemed. He would ask and I would give, and I couldn't feel shame for that. There was a ticking clock and a doomed end to us, but in this moment, I struggled to care.

I thrust my hips with the motion of my hand, riding us both just to find the barest pressure of my knuckles and—just when I was about to *beg* him to touch me—he pulled my face back to his, kissing me in time with the motion, fucking into my mouth the way I wanted him between my thighs.

"Shit, Win..." he mumbled against my lips, pulling back, and when I opened my eyes, I saw his arm and the swath of skin visible at the collar of his shirt shift into dark smoke. I wondered if the fingers still tormenting my breasts had become shadow as well, but they didn't feel any different against my flesh. If anything, they felt hotter. Stronger.

He wrestled against something inside himself, trying to reign in his power, but I shook my head, continuing to pump him in my fist. My body was molten and desperate for him; I didn't care what form he took so long as he just kept *touching* me.

"Give me everything," I said.

He pulled his hand from inside my shirt, the skin black with coils of smoke, and used it to hold me as he fell forward, landing on his knees. His mouth was back on mine, rabid with lust, and then I was on my back in the boat, his head haloed as it blocked the sun. He ripped my pants low, doing the same to his as I scrambled free to open my legs for him.

Cool wind rippled between us and Reed's shadows retreated back into golden skin as he settled between my thighs, pushing into my body in one hard, swift thrust.

I cried out, choking on a moan as he took me, his hips pounding as if to hammer the length of him so deep I would never forget the feel of it.

We didn't slow or gentle our caresses. His calloused fingers frayed me raw, and I scratched his back into splintered tributaries. Our kisses were more teeth than tongue, and I screamed and thrashed and writhed while he forced into me every ounce of his passion, my arms wrapped so tightly around him it was a wonder he could breathe. He held my hips so roughly I prayed for bruises. Desire consumed us like an ocean wave, taking us over.

It was the most delectable way to drown.

He lifted one hand to grab my chin, forcing my eyes to his face while he drove into me harder, his pace punishing. "Winnie..."

I nodded, asking for more, and his hand tightened. My legs shook and my core clenched around him just as he pressed one final, dragging kiss to my mouth. I gasped, shaking.

The rumble of his groan in my ear had my body pulsing and I cried out, my pleasure like a war cry, echoing him as he lost all finesse and emptied inside me.

When we were finally sated on each other, the sun was low enough to be blocked by the edge of the boat, the shade covering our bodies like a thin, cool blanket.

It was like the calm after a storm, the petrichor misting from each step in the woods, the sky's shoulders slumped with relief. I caught my breath with my head pillowed on his arm. One of his heavy legs weighed me down, and I felt very much like a tree when a snake curls in spirals up its bark. Gods, my brain was a mess of imagery and feeling and this sensation that I was floating above my body.

Was sex always going to be so...revolutionary with Reed? I felt different after having experienced it, and I could tell from the astonished look on his face while his chest heaved against my arm that Reed was dealing with something similar.

But there was no *always*...this was it. This was our goodbye.

My fingers clenched against his knee like a muscle spasm.

In a different world, maybe, there would be a montage of scenes where we made love in tall grasses and against brick walls, my skirt pushed up in haste with my back to a boulder in the woods, and his hips thrusting up into me from his place on a sandy beach. But those were all fantasies better printed than lived. Maybe that's what I could do with myself, when this was all over. I could chip at the marble of a page until a poem befitting him was revealed.

But as I looked over at his face, smiling as he came down from the high of our hungers, I didn't think I would be able to do him justice; the gradient of his clear-water eyes and the texture of his beard against his cheeks...the way his fae power took him over as he came inside me, eyes like night and his flesh drifting from soft shadow to rough skin.

Hells, I needed to *stop it*.

Pulling my clothes to my chest, I sat up and looked around to make sure there were no fishing vessels anchored nearby to watch us and then started tugging on my tunic. My hips ached deliciously.

"That was incredible," Reed breathed.

"It was," I agreed, not looking at him.

Brushing damp strands of hair away from my cheeks, I attempted to put myself right, adamantly not looking at his muscled, gold-dusted body as he did the same behind me.

"You seem uneasy."

I turned my head and watched the ripple of his abdomen as it disappeared behind his shirt. "I'm fine."

He paused. "And a liar."

"That's what humans do," I reminded him. We lied to protect ourselves, or those we loved. We lied for all manner of reasons.

"I wish you wouldn't."

I tied the strings of my damp, dirty pants, and closed my eyes against the surge of frustration and...*indignity* that flushed my skin, then took a deep breath, smothering any rising tears.

"Did I hurt you?" he asked.

I spun, nearly tripping as the boat dipped with the waves. "No. That's not—I'm fine. Honestly. I'm okay and it was good. It was *amazing*, actually. But we have more important things to worry about right now, don't you think? How far are we from the castle?"

Reed hesitated and then held one hand over his eyes to squint into the horizon. "Another couple of hours, I think. We drifted but I can get us there. Though...I think we should wait."

"Wait until what?" A sweeping gust had bumps racing over my skin, and I waddled carefully back to my spot on the bench I'd claimed, the books of poetry forgotten on the creaking floor. Thankfully they hadn't gotten wet except for one corner of my new book's cover.

Reed dropped to sit at the oars, but didn't touch them. I hated that he was facing me, so that I couldn't escape his gaze.

"If we go in the dark there's no telling what creatures will be active in the area," he said, his tone guarded. "The crucible may be lit, but if that's our only light we'll be at a disadvantage. And it wouldn't surprise me if kelavees and syra, not to mention non-fae creatures like crayfish snakes or cottonmouths, were flooding the inlets in this warm weather, maybe even sharks."

He was careful to make sure what he said were only musings and not outright facts, I noticed, but he did have a point.

There was a pleasantly dull pain in my body as I adjusted in my seat, the soreness a reminder of how intense we'd been with each other just minutes ago, and now I was jittery and trying to find something to do with my hands while the sky blackened around us. I tapped my fingers against my leg.

Reed's eyes caught the movement, and I stopped.

"If it's dangerous at night then we should have stayed on land," I argued. "Maybe slept in a real bed somewhere that's not a dungeon."

"It's not like we have the coin for that, though I suppose I could have threatened or intimidated our way into an inn."

I barked a quick laugh. "Intimidated?"

"You don't think I can be intimidating?" He inflated his chest, as if to make himself seem larger, but his smile crinkled, ruining the effect. "I can be menacing."

"Maybe to the fiddler crabs."

He clutched at his heart, pained. "Now, little perch, that was unkind."

"I am unkind, then," I said with a shrug, my mouth going flat. "And you really should use my name sometime."

"You are not unkind." He lowered his hand, his eyebrows scrunched together. His voice was unerringly gentle. "You can be ruthless and without mercy, but not to those you love or are devoted to. You are too protective for that. Only, sometimes you are so good at pretending, I can't truly decide if you feel that protectiveness toward me. I...wish that you did. Since I feel that way for you. Winnie."

He cannot lie, I tell myself over and over again, but he can choose his words so carefully they might as well be falsehoods. He feels protective toward me? But that could mean anything. I feel protective over my mother's herb garden, in that its destruction would be inconvenient. And if he means more, like how I feel for Conor, or how I once considered Flint, then he could spell it out more clearly. Was he referencing the devotion he wanted, or just that same desire to keep himself alive? Not that it would matter. This was a fun romp, and we'd enjoyed and used each other in a myriad of ways, but that was all this could be.

"Let's save the confessions for the morning, shall we? You're obviously addled by our...well, by me."

"Constantly," he agreed.

I retreated to the flat end of the boat, despite the early hour—it was only just twilight, but I feared what I would say if I kept talking to him. Words spill faster in the dark, and after tomorrow there would be nothing left to spill. I would go home, and Reed would flee to some distant land to enjoy his freedom. I would miss his body, sure, and his easy smile and dragging laughter...the teasing lilt to his words and the strength he uses to push through his mistreatments, the compassion he shows—*Gods, STOP!*

Pulling my shirt tight against me, I rested on my side, in the same exact spot Reed had just taken me apart, and closed my eyes, praying for my mind to be quiet.

But it wasn't. Even hours later when Reed lay beside me, giving me space to avoid him, my thoughts oscillated between hope and despair, naïve dreams and reality.

All I did was twist myself into knots, memorizing his words all the while telling myself to forget them.

CHAPTER TWENTY-SEVEN

I was exhausted when my eyes cracked open the next morning, the salt crusting them shut so I had to rub at them with my knuckles until I saw kaleidoscopes of color.

"Morning, Winnie."

Reed was gently rowing, keeping our speed slow enough I had to assume it was to not disrupt my sleep. Gray streaks of light swept over the ocean, and I knew the sun had risen only minutes before.

"Have you been up long?" I asked.

"What is long?" he replied.

I rolled my eyes as I stretched and took stock of our location. We had definitely moved closer to land—I could make out the hazy towers of the castle, like a faded line of ink smudging a page. We'd be there shortly.

"I guess long is subjective," I grumbled. So was loyalty and protectiveness and devotion. While I readied myself for the day, finger-combing my hair and gingerly doing my business over the side of the boat while Reed turned his head, I wished the night had been longer—or maybe shorter. I hadn't slept much, despite the rhythm of the ocean and the heat of Reed's palm as it had found my waist now and again. I also wished I had my weapons.

I was woefully unprepared to face any creatures in the mangroves once we entered, and though Shia had made it seem like the crucible was without any safeguards, I itched to hold my dagger or a caltrop in my fingers. Unfortunately, I'd have to rely on Reed and my own wits, instead of the shield of iron.

The morning stretched over us as we angled our route past the castle and down the coast, following the young alchemist's directions, and through the hazy morning light, I could see the signs of pain around Reed's mouth. He'd been away from Jassin for long enough that I knew it must be a kind of torture in itself. At least we were moving closer to his captor now, instead of further away.

While Reed navigated the shallows, curving us around mounds of rock and sunken trees, I kept my eyes peeled for a sign of the inlet. Purple coneflowers swayed in the sun, and frogs jumped in loud *plops* onto floating lily pads. The bulrush grasses loomed taller here. I swept the stalks aside with my arm as we passed them, trying to peer through the masses. All I could make out were hordes of flying insects darting about, and the odd splash of some finned creature. If we were wandering aimlessly among the swaying canes for long enough, would Reed's discomfort at being away from Jassin grow into agony? Would I need to forge on ahead on my own?

The thought filled me with more anguish than made sense, and not for the first time I wished for some kind of curtain that I could draw over my emotions, muting them to focus on the task ahead and not the dozens of ways I might be soon devastated.

Reed's sure strokes seemed to slow even more. "What are you thinking?" he asked.

It was like he could spot the most minute change in my posture or my breathing; I imagined it was probably a skill he gleaned watching every move his fae masters made, anticipating a punishment. Still, it rankled me.

"I'm thinking my feelings are more trouble than they're worth, sometimes." And then, as the memory struck me, I added, "But you can calm them, can't you?" He had manipulated my emotions once when I was growing frantic in Jassin's room, caressing my skin with smoky tendrils that somehow buried my fear.

He didn't answer at first, and I turned to look at him over my shoulder. I presented my hand to him, as if he could stroke me with those soft, warm wisps of shadow and wipe my anxiety from my mind.

"I...can't," he said at my questioning gaze.

"But you did before."

"Only a trick." He shook his head. "Something I thought would engage you enough—be strange enough to divert your panic. It was a kind of...seduction."

I lowered my hand and raised one eyebrow. "So, there is no magic to it?"

"Only your own," he replied.

I turned back to the front, simultaneously embarrassed and comforted. It had just been another fae lie, but one that had proved I had my own sort of bravery, I supposed. Or it had shown I was prone to distraction where Reed was concerned. Maybe both were true.

Shielding my eyes from the sun, I resumed my watch. Still, I almost missed the narrow cove.

"There." I pointed, my heart hammering as the path came into view. If you weren't looking for it, it would seem like a dead end of stalks of horsetails and bulrush. But to the left, a strait of water curved away from the ocean, nestled between denser vegetation.

We aimed the boat there—though it was wide enough to crush the flowers on either side—and pushed down the watery path. Marigold pollen littered the water and collected on the bow as we turned left and then right, as if we were passengers on a great snake. The landscape became crowded with low trees and the remnants of some cliffside, so I leaned to the side, trying to make out any shadow that may be hiding Shia's cave. We had to be close.

Reed's hand yanked me back, just as the buzzing of insects around us quieted.

"Don't lean so close to the water," he said quietly. His oars were barely scraping the muddy surface, and he settled back into his seat.

A splash sounded nearby, hidden within the foliage, and something groaned and thrashed. We both stilled, waiting to see if whatever it was would come closer. I imagined all manner of beasts bursting from the stick-like stalks, each worse than the last, but after a moment the sounds of the marsh returned. A frog croaked to my right, startling me.

"Hells!" I hissed, hand to my breastbone.

"I think this is it."

I turned to see Reed aiming for an embankment littered with clods of loose grass, a tall and menacing rockface just beyond with its visage split down the middle.

The cave of our crucible.

It took little effort to ground our boat—the thick mire underfoot sucked it in with ease. I expected it would take much more exertion to free it when we returned.

His ankles disappearing into the mud, Reed helped me off the boat and lifted me up into his arms. The hold was familiar and reassuring, his body radiating heat. I could see sweat trickling down his neck from exertion or maybe pain, so I wriggled and gestured toward the ground. Instinct told me to be quiet here.

Reed only tightened his grasp until we were on the highest part of the bank, where the ground was more solid, before he lowered me to my feet. My body grazed his on the way down and I tried not to remember the feel of his muscles beneath my fingertips, and the way they flashed black in the throes of passion.

"Ready?" I whispered as soon as I was stable.

He held up the pouch of water in response.

Creeping into the cave felt like taking a cold, damp breath after burning in the sun. The wet walls widened into a spacious hallway, with only pointed spires hanging dangerously above our heads for company. At the highest tide, I would imagine at least an inch or so of water to flood inside, but that didn't explain the moisture higher than my shoulders. Ahead was a flickering light, beckoning us closer, and I kept my hands loose at my sides and my feet ready to run. This would be a prime home for some nasty creature, fire or no fire, but as we reached the rounder middle of the cavern, there were no signs of life.

There was only a metal pail with a round lid squatting under a shelter of stretched leather. The fire beneath it was caged like an animal, and the strange tubes circling and rising from it reminded me of a squid's many tentacles.

Reed held out a hand to keep me back as he looked around the room. I could see the spread of shadow across his arms, his body ready for battle as much as mine.

Only, no monsters surged forward, and there were no places to hide in the cavern—it was a jagged dome, empty except for a bit of glowing algae near the ceiling.

"It feels like something crawling over me," Reed muttered. "The closer I get—" he took a step toward the fire, "the more I feel like I'm...buzzing."

"Maybe I should do it." I took the pouch from him and uncorked the water. I was human, at least, and if there was some sort of magical backlash it would most likely leave me unharmed. I hoped.

"Be careful."

As I walked up to the fire, my eyes traced the pipes, memorizing their form to show Conor later. If Shia was unable or unwilling to remake this device in the future, I knew my brother would not hesitate. Towns would pay good money for this kind of protection against the fae.

Light pulsated from above and I turned my eyes up to see the algae along the stalactites shifting, the blue-green mass bunching and retreating, brightening and dimming. Like giant icicles, they sparkled and began to drip. A glowing droplet fell in slow motion, creating a streak of light reminiscent of a shooting star, and then it landed on my forearm.

"What the—" I tucked the pouch under my arm and moved to flick the glob, but then something sharp and *hot* pricked my exposed skin. "Shit!"

Brushing the algae away, I could see a patch of red skin that slowly started to weep blood through each of my pores. Though the spot was only as big as my smallest fingernail, the sensation of burning made me hiss in a breath.

Another streak of light plunged to my right, landing on the ground next to my feet. And then another right in front of my face, almost grazing my nose.

Backing up as quickly as I could manage, I nearly tripped into Reed as he reached for my shoulders, tugging me against his chest. He took my arm and inspected the leaking wound while pulling us away from the crucible.

A veritable sprinkle of algae was peppering the ground near the fire, but as we moved further and further away, they settled, the blue-green light waning into a barely-there glow.

"It released toxins," Reed said in a rough voice as he peered at the bloody hole in my arm, and then he pressed his mouth to the sore and *sucked*.

"What are you doing?" I tried to tug away from his grip, but the day in the sun and the warmth of my body beside him must have restored his strength because he barely moved as I struggled.

He pulled again with his mouth, and I felt the press of his teeth just as the burning sensation began to ebb.

A shiver wracked its way across his shoulders as he hunched over my forearm, and I wondered if the poison was eating away at him from the inside.

"Reed, stop, it's better. Stop!"

Spitting to the side so the red splash of my blood landed on the cave floor, he then checked the wound once more, turning it toward the entrance to study it in whatever light still eked through.

A series of tiny red specks clustered at the site of the algae's touch, but nothing seeped from it. All that was left was a feeling of tight pressure, like the leftover discomfort from burning my finger on a hot pan.

His blue eyes met mine, and I could see his lips were tinted red while his face gleamed pale and gray in the algae's glow. "How is it now?"

"It's fine," I said, finally taking my arm back, "really."

Reed cleared his throat, the sound low and full of gravel. "It would have continued to eat through you. Usually, Cirosa algae is harmless and stays on walls, but someone must have conditioned it to respond to nearby movement."

"So, it's...guarding the device?"

Reed nodded.

I peered at the wound on my arm, thinking about the trickle of falling algae that could have easily become a downpour. "You shouldn't have risked yourself. It could have eaten through your throat if you swallowed."

He lifted one shoulder. "Half-fae remember?" Dark smoke wreathed his collarbones and neck before settling back into his skin. "It's harder to transform here, closer to that...*thing*, but I can still heal in small measures."

The cool air in the cave whistled along the walls, sweeping away the decaying, sulfuric scent of the marsh, and not for the first time I wondered if I could somehow leave this device intact. The waters were so dangerous already, but once we put out the crucible's fire—if we could get to it—the wetlands would go back to being even deadlier. There was no guarantee the fae prince would make allowances for humans in exchange for this favor. The only thing he had truly promised was letting Reed live.

With our backs pressed to the damp cave wall, Reed and I studied the lake of algae writhing on the ceiling. He shifted beside me, and I looked up to see his profile sketched in the blurry light of the far away fire. His blond hair was mussed from the wind and his lips were still stained with my blood. Regardless of my unease, I still had to try. We had saved each other over and over again since I'd come to Windstone Court, and it wasn't in me to leave a story unfinished.

"If I'm fast enough or cover myself with something, I can put out the fire and duck back out," I offered, wishing we'd brought something more substantial to carry water in, like a barrel.

"Not much will stop Cirosa toxin," Reed replied, looking me up and down. "Surely, nothing you have on you."

I crossed my arms, the pouch of water still tucked into my side. "So, what do you—"

"I'll cover you."

Blinking, I watched his body shift like air in the heat, then darken bit by bit until he was almost entirely transformed into smoke. Eyes strained with concentration, he put his arm forward. I could see the struggle it took to maintain the shape; tan skin rippled beneath the shadows now and again.

"Are you sure?" I asked. In response he pulled me against his chest, bending me forward with the blushing familiarity of someone who had maneuvered my body once before, and leaned forward so he covered my shoulders like a cape.

"Just hurry, and we'll be fine."

His voice was different in this form, warmer, like the soft touch of his shadow-coated skin, but I ignored my reaction to it and focused on stepping with him, bent forward, and keeping us close like some silly festival game.

As soon as we were an arms-length from the crucible, the light above us pulsed again, and I hurriedly uncorked the bag of water and began pouring it over the fire as it roared beneath the metal pail.

Reed tensed above me as splashes of glowing algae mixed with the water soaking the ground in front of me.

It took the whole pouch, and just when the flame hissed and died like any cooking hearth, the smoke rising in dark plumes to hover above us, he yanked us backward and released me from his hold.

I turned, only to watch him frantically brush off globs of algae with a smoky hand, his face twisted into a grimace. Patches of red skin mixed with black shadows, and he hissed with pain as he shook the last drops free, careful to avoid spraying any of the hazardous muck my way.

His whole body changed then, growing more solid and defined. *Bigger.* It was like his muscles absorbed the darkness, becoming distinct though they were still made of smoke. They ticked with strength as his torso reformed, seemingly unclothed despite the linen tunic he'd been wearing only seconds before.

A rush of power flowed over him like a full-body shiver, and I saw Reed for the first time as his full fae self, his blond hair now a halo of curling darkness, his eyes glistening black in his shadowy face. My eyes trailed down to his waist, tapered and swirling with the same inky smoke, and below was...

His whole body was smoke and shadow—*naked* smoke and shadow—and he was gorgeous.

"H-how does it feel now?" I asked, darting my gaze back up to his face. "Is the buzzing gone? The fire's out so I take it whatever was suppressing your—" I started to gesture up and down his body and then stopped, annoyed at my own rambling.

A dark chuckle echoed within his chest, and then in one smooth motion he settled back into his human form, including pointed ears, blue eyes, and a full set of clothes. I was almost disappointed by that last bit.

"Everything feels fine," he said, clenching his fist as if relishing the strength there. "Better than I've felt in weeks. And yes, the buzzing's gone. It's...silent."

"So, I guess that's it then." I peered over at the crucible, which didn't seem more sophisticated than a many-limbed kettle now that I could study it without the tall flames in the way. I wondered if there was a way to break it before we left; it would be just our luck for Jassin to restart the fire before we could get back to the prince.

There were no loose rocks that I could find around us, and the stalactites were too high to reach, but Reed must have come to the same conclusion I had, because with speed I hadn't seen from him before, he darted to the crucible and smashed a fist into the pail, denting it and shattering the glass tubes that had been feeding the fire. Algae pulsed and dropped, but he only winced at the pain and then retreated, healing himself with bursts of smoke that seemed darker than before.

I recorked the water pouch, feeling at turns shocked that this was all over, and suspicious that it was not. Dazed, I allowed Reed to take my hand in his as we began the trek from the cave and back into the balmy day. Something about the air felt different now...lighter maybe. As if cloud cover had drifted away from the sun and now the verdant plants along the ground were soaking in the light. The moss was soft and springy under my feet as we passed through the cave mouth.

A screech had us stopping short, and my eyes found our boat just a few yards below.

Three massive spider-like creatures had half-climbed inside it, their many eyes now trained on us. They were green like pond scum, a myriad of tall toadstools sprouting from their backs in blues and whites, glistening with some kind of slime. The biggest one had wrinkled plates of oyster mushrooms climbing up its legs. The pincers jutting from its mouth parted and clicked, and that screech sounded again, the two others wiggling as if with agreement.

I retreated up a step, about to rush back into the darkness, but Reed held tight to my hand.

"Maybe if we leave, they'll just...go away?" I whispered. "They're probably just looking for food in the boat and will move along when they don't find it..." That could happen, right? They were just spiders after all. They were as big as dogs and tinted with fae magic, sure, but they were bugs all the same, so I'd imagine they would see us as predators. But the way the largest monster lengthened its legs, standing a bit taller, said otherwise.

"Leave it to me." Reed sounded almost pleased as he gently nudged me to the side. "I haven't felt this strong in a while, and I would hate to waste an opportunity to show you."

"Show me what?"

His hands darkened into smoke. The transformation smoothly traveled up his arms and down his torso, into his legs until it appeared as if he were being dipped into black tar. Just as before, his clothes vanished, revealing chiseled shadow where before there had been human skin I'd petted and kissed. Wafts of the smoke seemed to stretch and linger away from him only to return, and I wondered if that smoke could *feel*. It seemed even easier for him now, in the sunlight. The morning rays appeared to be swallowed by his heart, while his body rippled and wavered in shapes still grazed by the dappled sun. As he turned from me, I saw the chiseled muscles of his back flex and, despite my fear, I found my gaze dropping to his impressively sculpted ass. I didn't even have time to mentally berate myself before he was off and moving.

He leapt toward the spiders in a way that reminded me of ink being poured—one moment in a vessel, the next—unleashed. The dark shape rushed and surrounded the monsters, their screeching elevating to a scream. While the two others bit and lunged at his form, he strangled the first, his strength vicious, his touch destructive. It thrashed against him, and I lost sight of its eyes and limbs as Reed encircled it. The edge of a mushroom would push through the smoke here and there in the scuffle, only to quickly disappear. Reed then seemed to expand, pulling in the other two as if he'd tired of their antics. It was like smothering a fire, the way he covered them, or maybe it was more accurate to say he was drowning them. Either way, the screeching stopped, and when Reed's shadowed body reformed into solid muscle by the boat, all three spiders were crushed. They lay on their backs, lifeless. One of them was still slightly twitching.

He turned to me, and I watched that black grin turn into the flushed lips I knew so well. He brightened into flesh and bone—scars and clothes and all—and it was somehow both terrifying and also exhilarating to see him shift so easily. He ambled toward me and the move was graceful, and so predatory I wondered if this was how the spiders had felt to watch him approach. But, despite my trembling hands...I was no longer scared. Not really. Or maybe I was, but it was stifled by astonishment.

That mischievous tilt to his lips, like the look of a proud boy when he shows off some new creation, fell at my stunned expression. "Did I frighten you? I thought..."

"You thought what?" My voice was subdued as I tried to untangle my feelings and slow my heart. It pounded from the violence and the strain of the last...however many days of danger and chaos and conflicting desires. Maybe I had just hit some sort of limit. Numbness encroached on my limbs.

"I thought you would appreciate the power," he said, sounding unsure.

I nodded dumbly as something sour churned in my stomach. *You can be ruthless and without mercy*, he'd said. Did he think I was like the fae he had grown up with? Creatures who used violence whenever they could avoid the consequences of it?

"I just wanted you to know that I can defend you now, Winnie. My ability to shift is not just for distraction." He rubbed his hand over his blond curls before turning his back on me to push the spiders over the edge of the boat. They made splashes big enough to have water flooding the muddy bank. "You've done so much for me; I've felt useless in comparison. Forgive me if I got a little...exuberant."

"Oh."

He seemed to give me a moment then, before offering his hand to help me into the boat. His palm felt warm and calloused, and I was reminded of how he'd stroked his fingertips over me the day before—how they had gripped my hips, his eyes flashing black. He had always been part creature and—though seeing it in action had made it all more *real*—he was still the same Reed. As always, he made sure my steps were steady on the swaying boat when I came aboard, and watched me with the same tender, open expression he kept shuttered from everyone at court.

With exaggerated gentleness, he sat in front of me and took the oars, pushing them into the muck to shove us back into the narrow strait.

"So, are you?" Reed asked. The boat inched against the thick silt, jerking me in a nauseating tempo.

"Am I what?"

His blue eyes grew a bit distant. "Are you frightened of me?"

At last the boat was floating freely, and Reed lifted a leg over the edge of the bow to swish his mud-covered shoe in the water, cleaning it, before doing the same with the other. He wrinkled his nose at the cold water on the edges of his pants, but seemed to prefer that to coating the bottom of the boat with dirt. The moment was awkward enough I couldn't help but smile.

"No. I don't think so," I said after a moment. Despite this new energy, I knew he wouldn't use his ability to harm me. And despite the tricks he'd played and the betrayals I'd suffered at his hands, I trusted that he cared for me. He had taken an arrow for me, and sucked toxin from my blood—it was hard to ignore that just because his body was now suddenly...different.

Reed took up the rowing, navigating us through the turns in the tall grasses, and I watched the cave and its alchemical interior fall out of sight over my shoulder.

"I want you to hear me on this, Winnie." Reed waited until he had my full attention, his ocean eyes shining. "I promise I would *never* intentionally hurt you. It makes me happy that you've seen me as I am and have not run screaming. I care about you, deeply. And I hope..." he stopped, as if struggling with what to say next, and I thought my heart might just squeeze out of my chest. "I hope that when you return to your life, you remember me fondly."

I endeavored to keep my expression neutral, though some crack might have echoed behind my ribs. "I will."

He nodded, as if satisfied, and I quickly looked away, focusing on the very first thing that caught my eye so I could school my heart and expression into pleasant indifference. A dragonfly with too many wings, pure white like dandelion fluff, was hovering to my right. I held out my hand to it, but it sped away.

"All the best," said Reed, as I dropped my hand back to my lap, "the gatholflies bite."

"Of course they do," I mumbled.

We spent the rest of the ride in a stilted silence, each unsure how to broach any safe conversation beyond musing on what awaited us back at court—each unsure how to say goodbye.

CHAPTER TWENTY-EIGHT

As the boat glided toward Windstone—the speed making me wish the same vessel would fit through the narrow maze of the mangroves for when I eventually headed home—more and more noise floated to us over the water. The waves crashing on the rocks were no match for the roars and shouts inside the castle, and as we pulled into the same cavern-like dock, no lazy Peleg in sight, the cacophony only grew louder.

Torches flickered against the salty spray as we scrambled from the rough water and tied up the boat. A scream had me stopping in place, until it ended in raucous laughter.

Reed held tightly to my hand, leading me up the now-familiar dank steps and passageways toward the heart of the revelry. The air took on a spiced quality, like I was breathing in ash and heavy perfume mixed together, and I shuddered to wonder what the scent covered.

We turned a corner to find a couple of abyssot writhing against each other along the wall, just as a syra transformed into a stream of water to splash at them, as if in rebuke. Hearty chuckles followed. We watched a crogwyn race down the hallway, a lendani male chasing it, his gorgeous green hair swirling in unseen winds while he blew fire-laced kisses at his prey.

"Keep close," Reed whispered, urging me behind him. I had no problem complying. It was as if the entire court was raging in lavish abandon. Skirts and doublets littered the floor between scorch marks and puddles I hoped were saltwater. We stepped around the messes and finally reached the unguarded entryway to the court's dining hall. There were no guards *anywhere*, I noticed, or there were, but they were joining in the debauchery along with every other fae and monster.

Their abilities had all returned, and they were celebrating as if all their wishes and dreams had come true. Even the creatures who hadn't been much affected were joining in. Snail shells rained from above and I looked up to see an abyssot clinging to the ceiling, their pale, naked body swaying with the discordant music barely audible under the sounds of the party.

It was so crowded I couldn't even tell where the tune was coming from.

"We need to find Prince Aeden!" I yelled, so Reed could hear me. His time was growing short to report back, but the obvious return to normal functions here had to mean he was released from his bargain, wasn't he?

"I'm trying!" He shouted back.

A group of fae danced ahead, their skins a flickering blend of gray and teal and peach, and I gasped as I saw the figure being swept up in the dance, passed from one set of hands to another.

Jassin. His silver hair was bloody, his black eyes were open but dazed, and he was emaciated, as if his body had been sucked dry. A fae man held him in a mockery of formal dance, spinning him around and around. The group laughed hysterically, and though I felt sick at watching the limp, tortured fae, I could not deny I felt the treatment was deserved.

I gripped Reed's fingers tighter and looked up to see him staring at the display with shock.

"They must have taken the return of their powers as proof," I said.

Reed didn't nod or even twitch. I wasn't sure if he hadn't heard me, or if he was simply reeling.

"Come on," I urged, tugging him away. He let me.

"I'm free," he said, as if to himself.

"Yes. Or you will be. But you'll still be dead if we don't return to the prince." At least, I was pretty sure that's how this worked. Better safe than sorry, in this case.

Pushing my way through the crowd was an exercise in daring. Syra hissed at me, and more than one set of claws grazed my skin. Fae looked down their noses at us as we struggled to get to the back of the room, crushed on all sides by the creatures of the court letting loose their inhibitions and yelping in delight.

And there he was, lounging on his throne with a glass of blood-colored wine in hand. Prince Aeden had streaks of red on his chest, beneath a shirt that was more a fisherman's net than cloth, but he was hale enough I knew it must have been Jassin's and not his own. He'd apparently done the torturing himself.

"There you are!" the prince said in greeting, carefree and charming as he waved a magnanimous arm in our direction. His fangs were stained and his voice slurred with drunkenness.

We made our way to the dais where his elaborate chair perched, and Reed lowered into a bow that I attempted to mimic. My eyes caught on splashes of blood on the stone floor.

"Like pretty pale shrimp you curl at my feet," he mused, "and yet, you have the bite of a kelavee, it seems!" His laughter had a cold shiver rushing over my arms as we stood. Were we supposed to thank him for the...compliment?

Reed took a step forward, to be heard over the din. "We dispatched the alchemist's device, and they will not move against the fae so long as they are left in peace," he reported.

"And I suppose now you are looking for your reward? Well, let's at least raise a cheer in your honor—" he flicked his fingers like shooing a fly, and the air in the massive room whistled and churned. The beginnings of a tornado formed above the crowd, pulling at the rags and gemstones of the fae, whipping their hair and even their fins in its power. Every being in the room went silent at the show of might. "We have these two to thank for your return to supremacy, pleasure, and merriment. Let them hear you!"

The sounds unleashed were like the shriek of a thousand birds of prey, echoing along the walls and traveling for what must have been miles, warning every creature in the marsh and the ocean that the fae were back, and more riotous than ever.

"And now—" the prince leaned forward and stroked three bloody fingertips down Reed's forehead, leaving streaks over the bridge of his nose and on either cheek, "you can take your prize."

I wasn't sure what this meant, but the screams grew to a fever pitch.

"What's happening?" I asked, but Reed only blinked and turned toward the group dancing with Jassin between their arms. The fae was more body than soul, flopping between them like ribbon kelp caught in a tide.

One of the lendani, a towering female with green-tinted skin and a dress made entirely of white slipper shells, spun Jassin to hold him beneath his arms. She presented him like a gift for Reed to inspect as the fae's head lolled to the side and his feet dragged across the stone floor.

Jassin's chest moved in sharp, fear-laced breaths, the only indication he was still alive.

I watched as Reed walked away from me, his body darkening and shifting into smoke. The crowd parted for him, so his shadow stretched dark and solitary back to my feet. It seemed to move on its own, or maybe my vision was swaying.

They were offering Reed the killing blow. And he was taking it, though I wasn't sure he even had a choice. Would he be incapacitated after, I wondered, or was the blood the prince offered the key to bypassing whatever magics in the court kept violence at bay?

Once Reed's entire body was wreathed in black smoke, the plumes twitching in peaks along his shoulders, he stopped in front of Jassin and pressed a hand to his master's face, lifting his jaw. At first it seemed like a caress, and then Reed's palm pressed over Jassin's nose and mouth.

I thought the court would grow hushed, or at least lean in with interest, but this last step of whatever vengeance the prince had begun was apparently more trivial than whatever had come before. Instead, they all continued their dancing and shouting, grinding to some thumping sound I thought might be their own stomping.

Jassin didn't seem to fight the touch, only glared at his killer as he suffocated on the smoke of Reed's hand, growing weaker by the second.

I expected to feel disgusted or at least appalled at the murder happening in front of my eyes, but I remembered the slash marks on Reed's back, the years of cruel treatment and cold rooms and degradation he'd suffered, and felt surprisingly little as Jassin's eyes finally fell shut.

Reed stood there a moment longer, as if to make sure the deed was done, and then in one fell swoop he returned to his human form, his blond hair glowing in the sparse lights twinkling throughout the room.

The female fae lifted the body higher, eliciting another awful screech of triumph from the court, and then dropped Jassin's corpse unceremoniously on the ground, startling me.

Reed spun, eyes finding mine, and I could see his body trembling even at this distance. A mix of emotions flitted over his face: shock, bewilderment, hope, and a certain kind of wariness.

Surrounded as I was on all sides, the crowd now reconverged into one mass of twisting, winding bodies. I held out my hand for him to come back to me.

I had killed more than one fae creature during my time here, and I wouldn't begrudge him for taking out the man who had possessed and abused him. This was a different world, with inhabitants who played by different rules, but he was still the same Reed—evasive, yes, and restless, but also caring, and sly in a somehow endearing way. He could be sweet, and generous with his trust and his body. Desperation had pushed him, but some intrinsic innocence had kept him from losing himself.

I could see as much as he shook, taking wooden steps toward me like I was some sort of salvation.

He was about to take my offered hand when arms pulled him away from me. I gasped before I recognized Robin's tall frame. She was healed from whatever magic had punished her for her violent transgressions, and she hugged Reed to her chest with such force I imagined he was breathless with it. Good—I hoped it could keep him together while he processed everything that had just happened.

They lingered against one another, and I looked away from the intimate embrace, feeling the prince's hot gaze on my neck.

I cleared my throat and turned to meet Aeden's once-more languorous gaze. "Reed has met your deal, hasn't he? He's free?"

Leaning forward and spilling some of the wine, he licked his purple lips and sneered. "The fae do not make deals they don't intend to keep."

That was a confirmation as good as any, I supposed.

"And will you...think on my request?" I continued, though my heart was pounding and every instinct told me to take this victory and *run*. "About a relationship with the humans who border your territory? They—I mean, I—would still like to provide you with an envoy. We could help each other."

At that, Reed finally reached my side, Robin close behind him, and his relieved huff of breath meant he'd heard Prince Aeden's declaration.

"I'll consider it, but for now you are ruining my view. Be gone. I'll send word via harrier on my decision."

I almost tripped over my feet to get out of his way, glad I knew now what a harrier was and didn't have to lower myself any further by asking.

He pointedly ignored me as I muttered my thanks, his whole attention centered on the court members kicking and shoving at Jassin's body. I flinched at the sight, but then a woman with bright red hair stepped forward. She was a syra with light blue skin and webbed hands that ended in sharp, black claws, and she hissed at a lendani who had been slapping Jassin with her tail. With tenderness, the syra picked the body off the floor and padded away on bare feet. A lover, maybe?

Before I could ask, Reed surprised me by spinning me around, high in the air, and when he lowered me to the ground his blue eyes were sparkling like sapphires.

"Thank you, Winnie," he said, voice barely audible over the din.

"I didn't really do anything," I argued. He was the one who had found the information on the alchemist, got us to Clarcton, and helped put out the fire. I had just...been along for the ride.

He shook his head, reluctantly releasing me back to my feet just as a small troll-like creature tugged at his pant leg and started speaking in a language that sounded like gargling water. Despite the sounds, the creature's expression was impressed as he gestured to where Jassin's body had landed and started shaking Reed's hand. There was a respect to the way the creature bowed his head, and I noticed the members of court had stopped jeering so much at us—or Reed at least—as if grudgingly accepting him for now as closer to fae than human. I garnered no such treatment, though, and someone elbowed me sideways away from Reed just as another fae grabbed my arm.

I spun, ready to fight, but the hand on me was Robin's, and I allowed her to tug me toward a stretch of wall littered with paintings of deadly blue jellyfish. Reed watched me go with something like melancholy before turning back to the smaller fae. A crogwyn joined their conversation, patting Reed's shoulder in congratulations.

"I believe these are yours," Robin said, capturing my attention. With gloved fingers, she handed over a satchel she had resting on her shoulder, then pulled it open so I could see two of my iron caltrops inside, as well as the dagger I had lost some time ago.

I took it and settled the bag against my chest, realizing how naked I had felt being unarmed in this cesspool of monsters.

"Thank you for keeping my weapons for me. And for...everything else." I was unsure how to verbalize the potion she'd made or the injury she'd taken, but she dipped her head as if she'd heard me.

"I would say it was a pleasure, but I hated having the iron in my home, or anywhere near me. I am glad to be rid of them."

I laughed, the sound surprising even me, and a few long-eared heads turned in my direction, gazes still sharp with disdain.

"You should leave now before someone decides to glamour you," Robin said in a hushed tone at my cheek. Her body bent over mine, creating a shield between me and the party. "You may have done the prince a service, but you are still a human. Take a boat, don't swim. Reed showed you where they are, yes?" *Right, fae have their powers back*, I realized. I could be glamoured and lost to my family forever.

Reed was blocked from my vision, but I nodded, then leaned sideways in an attempt to find him. Was he reveling with the rest of the court now that it seemed they'd partially accepted him? Was he waiting to say one final goodbye to me?

"Yes, but...are they—" I started, and licked my suddenly dry lips. "Will Reed be okay?"

Robin nodded. "This will buy him some respect for now, or at least an approximation of it. Half-fae are a peculiar group, swinging between one extreme and the next depending on how they serve the court. He'll need to hurry to dig himself a place here, lest he be forced out. Now, I am grateful for all that you have done, but you need to go before we can no longer protect you."

She was right, and fae could not lie. I was in more danger than ever with my identity exposed and a raucous group of celebrating monsters on every side.

I saw Reed's blond hair and the craggy, ash-tinted flesh of the crogwyn swaying drunkenly beside him. Reed's animated laugh, a bit too loud to be comfortable, reached me as he patted the creature's shoulder and aimed to steer it back toward the syras' tide pools and the buffet tables.

"But, I..." I started after him, wanting to say *something* before I left this world behind me, but Robin stopped me.

"I will tell him whatever message you wish, but you aren't safe here.

Quickly."

And this was it, I realized. The ticking clock had run out, our story had ended, and this adventure would now be nothing more than memory and scribbled lines.

Nothing is for free, little perch.

You look as beautiful as ever.

I hope that when you return to your life, you remember me fondly.

I wished I had taken the time on our ride back from the crucible to tell Reed my own truths—truths that could not be relayed in an easily regurgitated message. But all I could do was swallow my disappointment and put on a serene face as if leaving was a small thing, barely worth Robin's time. It was a role I struggled to embody.

"Tell him I'll miss him and I..." I hesitated, trying to find something meaningful that wouldn't be a blatant emotional expulsion like *I could almost love you*, or *I wish you wouldn't let me leave.* "I wish his days to always be warm."

Robin said nothing, her black eyes shining in the bouncing firelight, but her smile was tender and somewhat sad as she gently turned me and pushed my shoulders in the direction of the exit.

The castle was a blur as I ducked through the swarm of revelers and fled down hallways and staircases, retracing my steps to the interior docks we'd entered from. After a few wrong turns and doubling back, I corralled my wits and located the cavern. I'd worried Peleg would have returned to his post and I would need to bargain for my freedom, but as if Robin had orchestrated it, the room was empty but for the vessels bobbing and pulling against their lines.

For the familiarity I decided to take the tiny sailboat, its flat deck easy enough for me to clamber onto. The knot Reed had left was loose and simple to undo, and then with jittery arms I was pushing off. As I sat, I noticed my book of poetry beneath the bench, as well as *The Tears of the Titan*; Reed had forgotten to take it. With a quick flick, I tossed the book onto the stone floor beyond the docks, hopeful he would find it, or that it would somehow make its way to him, the same as my message to Robin.

The oars were still wet from our way in as I rowed, and I fought the saltwater threatening to leak from my eyes. I couldn't wait to be home and be blessedly dry. Already, the muscles in my back heaved to get me away from Windstone as fast as humanly possible.

Every inch was a blessing, and yet each push away also felt like some tether around my chest was growing tighter and tighter.

I aimed the boat north, knowing the coast would curve inward and bring me closer to the mangroves, so I could drift around them. In the monotony of my exercise, I practiced what I would say to Conor and my mother when I returned. *Good news, the fae might stop stealing away so many people for slaves, and I might have landed a job as some sort of ambassador to the prince of fae. Either way, we have to stay in Harnsey until I know for sure. That's fine, right?*

Given the surge of people likely fleeing Harnsey, I would hopefully be able to find some sort of money-making venture in the meantime, maybe more farm work taking care of pigs and cleaning fish of their scales. Something to keep me busy. Distracted.

Though it was still light out, I could see the pale and transparent disk of the full moon hanging above me, watching me row. Would the moon feel sorry for my struggle against the tide and spin faster and faster to bring me fair winds? I paused, as if to give her the chance. But no, the air was still and there were no sounds but the calls of gulls and herons, and the splash of the oars as they sliced into petite waves.

By the time I reached the tributaries that would curl around my familiar mangroves, continuing along the coast since the boat couldn't fit within, my arms were shaking and my back and sides burned with fatigue. Hells, what I wouldn't give for Reed to be here in my stead, his bulking arms ticking with power, his blond curls fluttering around his face.

At least drifting by the edge of the trees meant I had to move slowly. Algae floated to my left, and tall stalks of cattails and feathered grasses stood like a fence ahead, so that when I passed them and saw the gnarled, twisting roots stretching up into thick canopy, it was like finally seeing my front door. My shoulders lowered and I let loose a breath. This part I knew, and if I had made it on foot, then I was more than capable of making it in a boat, even with the longer trek around instead of through. The buzzing didn't even bother me much now.

I was halfway past the system of roots and tented trunks when I heard the first splash. Pulling in my oars, I scrabbled to fetch the bag at my feet to get my dagger and one of the caltrops, clenching one in each hand before I scanned from left to right, trying to determine where the noise had come from. I was floating like a lone frog surrounded by gold-ringed snakes and hungry snapping turtles, my tiny boat easy to tip. But whatever thought to hunt me was going to get a face full of iron. If it was a manyda, I could hit them anywhere, but if it were a lendani or syra or even a kelavee I'd have to aim for the face or chest and hope my strike landed true—and fast.

Another splash, this time from behind the towering frame of a tree beside me. My heart was a frantic beat in my chest, but I kept my breathing steady and my eyes trained for any sign of whatever monster slithered toward me.

The creature must have dived beneath the surface because the water had gone quiet once more. A litany of pleas echoed in my head. Maybe they had passed me by. Maybe there was a school of snapper it had decided to chase instead.

A head popped up from the water, only a foot or so from the edge of my boat and I bit back a scream, ready to throw the caltrop, but my arm halted in midair.

"Reed?"

He shook his hair like a dog, a sheepish smile on his tired face. "There you are. You made it farther than I thought." He was out of breath, treading water absentmindedly when I knew his feet would most likely touch the ground.

"I almost threw iron at you, imbecile!" Lowering my arm, I let the weapon fall to the floor of the boat with a muffled clang. My dagger followed. I could feel my heartbeat in my every inch of my body—a wild pattering I struggled to control.

"And yet you didn't." He drifted closer and then put both his hands on the wooden ledge, as if ready to pull himself up. If he did, I was pretty sure his weight would dump both of us in the water.

I put my hand on his, stopping him, and he peered up at me, a playful tilt to his lips.

"What are you *doing* here?" I asked. He should be back at Windstone making alliances and finding work, making a place for himself just as I needed to do back home.

"Finding you," he replied, as simple as stating the weather.

"Alright, yes, you found me. Was it just...did you want to say good-bye?" His hand was chilled beneath mine, his fingers pruned from swimming.

He shook his head. "I wanted to say hello."

I stared down at him, refusing to play this game where I dragged answers from him and prayed they weren't clever manipulations of the truth.

His eyes searched mine in return, in a way that had my hands sweating from something more than the strain of paddling this damn boat. The waves seemed to quiet this close to the mangroves, or maybe that was because my focus had narrowed to his chest above the waterline and the pink glow of exertion on his cheeks. He was still wearing his clothes from before, now soaked and formed tightly to his skin.

"I want to go with you, to your town," he admitted, and my gaze shot back to his face. "I want to stay with you. If you'll have me."

An image of Reed at my mother's kiln, glazing plates unevenly with his thick fingers, crossed my mind. We could build a second bed, to give Conor his space, and my brother could ask him all the questions he harbored about the fae. My mother would like him too, I thought, with his cheerful attitude and his strength...

I closed my eyes on a sigh, annoyed by my own foolish fantasies, and then leaned my elbows on my knees, bending closer. "To do what, exactly? Play at being human for a while? Wouldn't you miss Robin?"

"I could play at being human forever, if needed. And Robin could send me messages whenever she wished. Maybe she'll even send me some perfume as a parting gift." He licked his bottom lip and lowered his eyes, as if suddenly sheepish. "I would vow myself to you, like I did to Jassin. With no contract required."

"What do you—" but before I could even finish forming my question, he raised himself higher, tipping the boat just enough so his face was almost level with mine.

"Winnie, I would swear to follow you, to be yours, to help you and care for you as long as you'd permit me. I know I am not all human, but free of my ties to court...I find no desire to stay there, and every desire to be here. With you. Wherever you land."

My mouth was dry, and I swallowed nervously. That sounded almost like a marriage proposal. But I knew better than to take proposals at their word.

"You really mean it?" I asked, my voice breathy. "You couldn't...people in Harnsey wouldn't accept you, if they knew. You couldn't shift into your fae self, at least not in public, and you'd have to find work."

Reed nodded. "Yes, I mean it. No more omissions, just simple words. I want to be with you." He let those words settle, like ripples fading into my skin. "And as for shifting—" he lifted a hand and I watched as smoke swirled through his fingers before he sifted them through my hair, "I'm fine saving that for when we're alone."

My neck and ears flushed, becoming warm as I remembered the way those dark shadows had touched me. I adjusted in my seat, warmth beginning to pool low in my belly.

He was really ready to do this, I realized, something like joy rising like a buoy within my chest. And it could work.

Reed could catch crabs and learn a trade like forging—where he could always be close to fire—or simply work with me in capturing the fae that tried to encroach on our land, Aeden's blessing or not. His abilities would make my home life much more exciting, that was for certain. As would his affections. Once the matter of Harnsey was decided, Conor could go to Clarcton to learn alchemy, and we could go with him. A new town, a new life...it was all possible.

I imagined reciting to Reed all the poetry I'd collected, my new tome included, and lying beside him at night to keep him strong. We could see plays and musicals, and maybe then I'd find the courage to audition for one. I had narrowly avoided death on multiple occasions now; it wasn't as if acting for a crowd could be more terrifying than playing pretend for a murderous fae.

The anticipation racing through my veins was effervescent.

"I left *The Tears of the Titan* on the docks," I told him, as if this was a sticking point.

"Then I guess I shall have to secure us another copy," he replied.

Feeling a strange sort of power, as if I were fae myself, I tilted up my chin, fighting a smile. "Then swear it, Reedling. Swear yourself to me."

Reed's smile was brighter than a sunrise as he took my hand in his, bringing it to his mouth to place a kiss against my palm.

It was like the promise of a grand new adventure. A new role I was truly elated to play.

"I am yours, little perch," he whispered along my skin. "This, I swear."

And I was also his. Leaning closer, I kissed him softly, and as our lips met and the smoky jasmine scent of him curled around us, the boat tipped further and we broke away, laughing with abandon before I could tumble into the brine.

"Okay," I said, recovering my breath, "let's get you into this boat."

He nodded, eyes full of tenderness. "Yes, let's go home."

The End

THANK YOU FOR READING!

If you enjoyed *Shadow of the Marsh*, please use the QR code below to leave a review – every comment counts and it's an indie author's best bet to finding new readers!

And follow me on social media!

CassandraMortimer.com

and TikTok/Insta @cassandramortimerlit

Acknowledgements

This book was an exercise in playing with my favorite tropes and making my setting as lush and poetic as possible. To that end, I'm pretty happy with the result you've got in your hands, but I owe the polished and printed product to some amazing beta readers—Liz, Joe, Claire, Kelsi, Kelcey, Chad, Danielle, and Kat (perhaps the only person who liked this book's original title, *Foul Water*). I'd also like to thank my rubber duck, Tim, who helped me create some of the gruesome monsters swimming through these pages, and my amazing editors Sarah, Sophie, and Tina, for helping me figure out where em dashes go and how to not dangle some modifiers or some such logistical things...

Thanks so much to my friends and family for spreading the word about my books (i.e. forcing your relatives to buy a copy) or in my mom's case, telling servers at her favorite restaurants to check them out—y'all are keeping me afloat, I love you, and I hope you enjoyed the *Autumn Effect* easter egg—if you found it!

And if you're just picking up this book on a whim or based on someone's recommendation, thank you for taking the chance on an indie author who has dreamed of publishing her books since roughly 2003, it means the world.

Cassandra is a romance-obsessed individual with the memory of a goldfish and the purse of an eighty-year-old-woman. She once tricked her teenage crush into being her boyfriend, and then in true rom-com style, he married her. The two of them now live happily ever after in Boston, MA with their cat Pumpernickel and some very-packed bookshelves.

When she's not busy binging love stories in all their various mediums or working at her day job in media/publishing, you can find her at work on her next novel.

She graduated from Emerson College with a degree in Writing, Literature, and Publishing, and has had short stories published in *The Big Bad: An Anthology of Evil*, *Harvest Time* from Inwood Indiana, "Rotten Leaves Magazine," and *The Emerson Review*. You can check out her debut novel, *The Autumn Effect*, on Amazon/KU, B&N.com, or wherever self-pubbed books are sold.